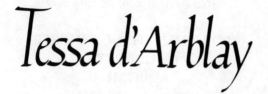

Tessa d'Arblay

Tessa d'Arblay

MALCOLM MACDONALD

St. Martin's Press
New York

Library of Congress Cataloging in Publication Data

Ross-Macdonald, Malcolm.
    Tessa d'Arblay.

    I. Title.
PR6068.0827T47   1985   823'.914   85-2674
ISBN 0-312-79350-2

First published in Great Britain by Hodder & Stoughton Ltd.

First U.S. Edition

10 9 8 7 6 5 4 3 2 1

for John Wood
where it began

Tessa d'Arblay

Chapter One

"Natural Causes," said the jury, and "Natural Causes" was the coroner's verdict. Peter Laird had died of "Natural Causes".

Tessa left the courtroom before the concluding formalities. The whole business was still so hard to grasp – even now, a month later. Poor old Peter had seemed so well right up until the very day of his death. It was frightening. How could we ever tell?

For early May – indeed, for any time of year – it was hot. The street was like a hob. She stood uncertainly at the top of the broad stone steps and felt the heat radiating up at her. In the courthouse, the heavy old stone walls had kept the place somewhat cool; but here it attacked her like a living thing. She could feel glowing worms of it edging inward at her cuffs and ankles; she could sense its pressure on her shoulders. She spread her parasol.

"Be all right going home will you, Miss d'Arblay?" the sergeant asked.

"Yes thank you, Sergeant Keene. I'll take a cab."

Keene had been one of Peter's friends, too. He had known Tessa since her childhood. On her fourth birthday, in 1868, he had called to the vicarage to see her father in connection with some missing church property; and then he had stayed for the party and had performed a comic recitation from Thomas Hood. But he didn't like to be reminded of it these days.

"You shouldn't have come at all," he added. "I'll escort you to the rank at the corner."

"Oh I don't want to put you to any trouble. . ."

"I know you don't, miss. But you already have."

"You're as tactful as ever!" she told him.

"Tact catches no criminals."

They made an odd pair, sauntering along the street, not really knowing what to say to each other; she, tall, angular, lithe in all her movements; he, only slightly taller, powerful as a bear; both restless in each other's company.

5

"There'll be murders done today," he said with a kind of savage glee.

"I don't suppose that surgeon – Dr. Segal was it? I don't suppose he could have made a mistake?"

He ignored her. "People drink too much, see. Because of the heat. They start remembering old wrongs. Then they want to right 'em."

Sparrows were dipping in the Metropolitan Horse & Cattle Association trough halfway along the street, sprinkling water all around. Some fell cool on her muslin sleeves; but the untouched parts of her merely felt all the hotter. She wanted to talk to Keene but instead her mind seized on a ridiculous fantasy in which she ran naked through a crowd of onlookers and jumped into the trough. She grew angry with herself.

That sort of thing happened so often these days. Important thoughts would be pushed out of her mind by some quite ludicrous (and often scandalous) image. Sometimes it made her wonder if she was entirely right in the head.

"Yes!" Keene barked to fill the silence. "Forsooth!"

Peter used to say *Forsooth*.

"You should have stayed at home," Keene went on. "Doing your pretty little paintings."

Tessa contained her annoyance. "Art has nothing to do with prettiness," she said evenly. "Art could make anything beautiful."

"Even murder?" he asked scornfully.

"Of course. What is a crucifixion if it isn't murder? There are beautiful crucifixions all over the world. And just think of the battle scenes and the . . ."

"All right, all right. Sorry I spoke. Even so, I don't know why you came. A coroner's inquest is no place for a pretty young girl."

"Peter was a good friend," she reminded him. "Also I found it so hard to believe – this brain-tumour business."

"Oh?"

"You don't?"

His expression was dubious, watchful, provoking her to talk.

She now wished she hadn't started this particular hare. "What strikes me as being so odd," she tried to explain, "is that Peter was so *well*. There never was a man who seemed more fit. It's

6

frightening, don't you think? I mean – *any* of us might have one of these tumours. You or I, this very minute. And we could go out" – she snapped her fingers – "just like that!" She looked at him for some response. Getting none, she added, "We haven't the first idea about what's really going on inside our heads, have we."

"Are you saying you think his death was odd?" Keene sighed and sucked his teeth. Without pausing for her denial he went on: "Funny thing about detective work – my inspector and I often talk about it. You'd think it'd be an ideal job for a woman. It's nearly all drudgery, nearly all dull routine and pure repetition – all the things women are so good at. And even the exciting bits – you'd think they'd be right up a woman's street."

"But I'm not at all implying there's anything suspicious about his death. It's just that . . ."

Again he ignored her. "The exciting bits are all about people, see? Questions about people – what did he look like . . . what was she wearing . . . were they telling the truth with their eyes but something else with their mouths . . . all things like that. And you also need a head for gossip. You'd think women were born detectives, wouldn't you? You know why they're not? You know the one fatal weakness your lot's got?"

"You're going to tell me, whatever I say."

"This is what the inspector and I have decided. The thing that will always stop you lot being good detectives is the thing you're exhibiting now: *intuition*!"

"You're putting words into my mouth!" Her voice sounded querulous in that somnolent backwater of a street. "I'm not questioning Dr. Segal's competence. In fact, I'd very much like to talk to him – about the mind, you know. Things like that."

"Things like that," he repeated flatly.

"Behaviour – you know. People always said my mother was eccentric when she was alive. And my Aunt Bo . . . well, she is a *bit* odd, isn't she? Wouldn't you say?"

Keene snorted. "The whole of your family's behaved oddly as long as I've known them. And that's an ungallant number of years by now."

She suspected that her question had made him uncomfortable, and that his jocularity was a way of saying he didn't really wish to discuss it with her. She felt snubbed. "The fact that you've

7

known me ever since you dandled me on your knee, Sergeant Keene, and recited *The Drowning Ducks*, doesn't give you the right to . . ." Again she heard how petulant she was beginning to sound. Her complaint shrivelled in the heat.

"Does your father know you're here?" he asked conversationally.

She knew he was only trying to change the subject, but she was annoyed with him now. "Is that a question or a music-hall song?" she asked. "If it's a question, I consider it rather impertinent. I am twenty-four years old, you know."

Keene stopped and stared at her. "I consider it raahther pertinent, Miss d'Arblay," he said at last, mimicking her accent. "If you were to fall down in a swoon, what with this heat and all, and if I wasn't here, no one'd know where to send you home, would they! I call that pertinent, don't you?"

"It may be pertinent to him. But it's very impertinent of you. Anyway, you *are* here. Lord, what a stupid conversation!"

He sniffed. "If you say so, miss."

"I know *you* don't think so."

"I do not."

She could see he was actually half-amused. She smiled at him and the atmosphere at once grew more cordial. Because they both wanted it so. "I'm sorry," she said. "You must forgive me if I'm a little on edge. I certainly don't want to fall out with you. Quite the opposite." She smiled to humour him and then asked swiftly, "What's Dr. Segal's address, d'you know? Is it buried somewhere in that encyclopedic mind of yours? I think I will go and see him."

He grinned and shook his head. "I couldn't divulge that, Miss d'Arblay."

"I expect he's in the register."

"Very likely."

There were three cabs at the rank. The sergeant held open the door of the first. "I wish you luck, miss."

She folded her parasol and deftly prodded his instep with the ferrule. "Humbug, Keene – forsooth! And I'm not getting into that cab. The poor horse is a bag of bones. I'll leave you to take the driver in charge. He really deserves to be prosecuted." She looked at the next cab in the rank, challenging Keene to lead her to it and hold its door open, too.

He turned abruptly on his heel and began walking back the way they had come.

She went alone to the next cab, whose driver had nodded off to sleep in the heat. She rapped her parasol against its side. He came awake, blinked rapidly, and screwed up his eyes against the pain of the light. Then he became aware he was still second in the rank. "Take the cab in front, lady," he said, his voice rasping with phlegm.

"Come down at once and hand me in," she commanded.

"No, you don't understand," he began – but then he stared toward a point somewhere behind her. A moving point. From the look on his face she knew Sergeant Keene was coming back. The man's next words confirmed it: "Where was you wanting, lady?"

She heard the sergeant's bootfall on the paving stones immediately behind her. "Twenty-three Finsbury Close," he commanded. His voice, deep and gravelly, and so near, made her eardrum click.

Without turning around to look at him she said, "The very *pertinent* address! But I shan't go there today, thank you. Dr. Segal can wait until tomorrow. Or some other day." She looked back at the cabby. "Shepherdess Walk, if you please."

"Down Shoreditch?" the cabby asked in disbelief. It was one of the poor areas of London, next door to Whitechapel, the poorest of all; and though elegant females were not unknown in those parts, their elegance was of a rather brassy kind, far removed from the demure and modest appearance of the young lady who now proposed to enter his cab.

"The Old Vicarage," the sergeant added.

"Ah!" Light dawned.

"And anyway," she insisted, "it's not Shoreditch. It's Islington." Strictly speaking, that wasn't true; but the vicarage was in the better end of Shoreditch – the end that *counted* as Islington.

The sergeant opened the little half doors and handed her up. She saw he was troubled. She raised her eyebrows, to prompt him.

"The mind's a funny thing, you know." He shook his head and pulled a face. "Some inquiries are best left alone. I wouldn't worry about your family. Things have a way of sorting themselves out."

9

"We'll see," she answered evasively. But when the cab was bowling along, she said to herself, as if she might otherwise forget it: "Twenty-three Finsbury Close."

Chapter Two

When Tessa arrived home she let herself in quietly by the front door, hoping to go upstairs and change without rousing the house from its usual afternoon slumber. But she almost fell over her father, who was lying full length on the marble-tiled floor of the hall.

"Are you all right?" she asked.

"I've never seen you from this angle," he answered. "You look quite different. And yet you are demonstrably not different. That is to say, the entity which by custom we denote 'Tessa' is. . ."

"I take it you *are* all right."

"I thought the marble might be cooler," he explained. "The month of May has no business to be so hot."

"And is it cooler?"

"Yes." He sat up, dusting off his no-longer-quite-so-white shirt. He frowned. "There's something I ought to ask you something I ought to ask you something I ought to ask you. . ." He went on repeating the phrase while his fingers drummed on the floor. Then he brightened. "Oh yes! I ought to ask you where you've been?"

She helped him up and gave him a quick kiss. "Out! Is Bo at home?"

Aunt Bo (who would never let Tessa call her "Aunt") was the identical-twin sister of Tessa's late mother, whose first name had been Sinney. The twins had been given these unusual names by their father, Haligon Body, the Cornish mine captain who discovered the famous Wheal Jessica tin lode. He had first called it the Bosinney lode in an attempt to flatter his neighbour, Sir William Bosinney, into sinking some capital into a new

10

mine – the mine that was eventually called Wheal Jessica. In that first flush of enthusiasm he had also baptized his newly born twin daughters Bo and Sinney; by the time he discovered that Sir William was in no position to fund even an egg-and-spoon race much less a tin mine, it was too late – the girls were Bo and Sinney Body, and Bo and Sinney Body they remained until they were transmuted into Bo Fletcher and Sinney d'Arblay by, respectively, Captain Arthur Fletcher of the Merchant Navy and the Reverend Gordon d'Arblay of the established church.

Captain Arthur Fletcher of the Merchant Navy had died five years ago, in 1883, in Fiji, in circumstances that, though not mysterious, were extremely complex; nothing that the Body family engaged in was ever simple. Bo had then come for a short visit to the Old Vicarage. What with one postponement and another, it had already lasted five years; and now, with Sinney's recent death, it looked set to consume the rest of her life.

"Is Bo at home?" Tessa repeated.

Her father was still grappling with their previous conversation. "So you've been *out*, eh? Then you were doing Good Work, no doubt. What an example you are." He suppressed a yawn. Then he added with surprising vehemence, "I wish Bo would go out. I wish she'd go away for ever."

"Why?"

"I keep thinking she's Sinney. You remember when your mother was ill – toward the end – and she couldn't find her glasses?"

"Yes?"

"Well, I found them this morning. And Bo came into the room immediately after. And I said to her, 'Here they are, my dearest'." His face crumpled at the memory. "I keep forgetting. I keep forgetting."

Tessa had a sudden fear he would cry. She grasped his arm and hugged it to her. "She shouldn't wear mother's clothes the way she does. At least she could change the trimmings or something. I'll speak to her."

"Bless you, child. Don't say I said anything. But she'll listen to you."

"She *doesn't* listen to me. But of course I won't tell her you said anything. Not that it'll make the slightest difference."

"Like Good Works," he murmured as he wandered back into

11

his study. "Doing *some* good without doing *any* good! Now there's an interesting point. It is possible, you see, to speak of doing some good, and yet truthfully to report that it has not done any good. The mysteries of language! Yet what else have we, eh?" He was not mocking her, but excusing himself. The Rev. Eli Howells, the local Methodist minister, always referred to him as, "My recruiting sergeant".

As she went up the second flight of stairs she had another of those half-glimpsed ideas that hinted at importance and vanished into nonsense. She thought of this house, seen from the outside, so sober and respectable, everyone's idea of a solidly respectable vicarage. That, indeed, was the way it had appeared to her as she stepped out of the cab. Yet the moment she had put her nose inside, what had she found? The owner of the house, a vicar of the established church, lying supine on the marble floor – and for no better reason than that he thought it might be a little cooler there! It occurred to her that people were like that, too – the outside was quite different from the inside. All those people who knew her as a respectable, well-brought-up vicar's daughter. . . what would they think if they could share those fleeting thoughts that ran so often through her mind?

How could anyone ever get at the truth?

She met Bo at the stairhead. When she saw her aunt's dimly backlit silhouette against the great stained-glass window at the end of the landing, Tessa knew what pangs her father felt; that outline was her mother's, and not merely because the clothes were hers, too.

"Well?" Bo asked, as if her patience had already run out.

"Well what?"

"I know where you've been, my dear. What was the verdict?"

"Oh – natural causes."

"Men!" Bo said and, turning angrily on her heel, vanished through one of the doorways.

"That's a splendidly illuminating comment, Bo!" Tessa walked past her aunt's door and into her own room. There she unpinned her hat and took off her gloves. She felt instantly cooler, and ready to go back and face her aunt.

Conversation with Bo was always a wearing experience, not merely for the sudden darts and lurches of her thought, but also because of her strange intonation. With most people you can half-listen to their words and pick up the rest from their tone of voice. But Bo's voice was so light and her intonation so erratic, she seemed to be making it up as she went along; she misdirected you a dozen times in every sentence.

"What d'you mean – *men*?" Tessa asked as she went back into Bo's room.

"It's a sort of game they love to play – inquests . . . rules of evidence . . . judges in wigs. Freemasons. They're not really interested in the truth."

"I think the truth came out all right. Poor old Peter had a tumour. And it . . ."

"You were in love with him, I know," Bo said suddenly. "That's the truth I'm talking about."

"Don't be absurd!"

"You were. The very heat of your denial proves it. Lord – why do we have to depend on men of all things!"

Tessa sighed. "How d'you feel, Bo?"

"Hot."

"Why don't you put on some cooler clothes? You must have brought back dozens of tropical dresses. And, talking of your own wardrobe . . ."

"It's in memory of your mother, dear. Poor Sinney! Besides, there's years of wear left in it and I may not have too long myself."

Tessa gave up – as so often. "What I really meant was, how d'you feel in yourself? Are you well?"

"If you weren't in love with Peter, you ought to find someone else. It's a pity he's gone. You musn't stay a spinster. Above all, you mustn't stay a spinster, my dear. Strange things happen in the minds of spinsters. The mind's a funny thing. I saw some rum goings-on during my travels with dear Captain Fletcher. Did I ever tell you about the time we called at Haiti?"

"Yes, you told me about Haiti."

"Well, the mind's a funny thing. Just try and remember that."

"Are we an ordinary family, Bo," Tessa asked. "Is there any history of madness?"

"People often called Sinney *eccentric*," her aunt admitted. "That's the English way of saying mad-but-rich. But I doubt, in fact, whether Sinney was mad – or truly eccentric. She was undoubtedly strong-minded (like all of us Bodys). And she was

13

also – though she's my own sister I have to say it – she was also disastrously ignorant. And not just of book learning, either. She knew nothing of life and people. She was the instant friend of every idle mendicant and plausible sponger who crossed her path. There never was a stouter champion of all idiotic causes; nor a more confident mine of misinformation on every subject under the sun.''

''But she wasn't mad?'' Tessa insisted.

Bo shook her head cheerfully. ''You may not realize this, darling, but you owe your own superior education entirely to your mother's ignorance. It so shocked your Grandpa d'Arblay that he felt he ought to do something about it.''

''I don't think my education's all that superior.''

Bo snorted. ''That's because you don't know many other young girls of your own class!''

''I have no standard of comparison for so many things. I just have to read books and the papers and make up my own mind.'' She sighed.

But Bo laughed. ''Good thing, too! The girls of your own class are empty-headed ninnies for the most part. Not many of them had a fine scholar like Grandpa d'Arblay to teach them. You may thank Providence he was a long-standing widower with a fair bit of money and more than enough time to undertake your education himself.''

''I just thought he enjoyed it. I certainly did.''

''Oh, and so did he. Too much. He, I may say, was no great believer in education for women. I'm quite sure he intended to impart no more than the usual accomplishments – reading, writing, a smattering of classical tags, and enough arithmetic to oversee the household accounts. But he was a learned man, as you well remember. What's more, he was actually fond of learning. And you were such an apt and challenging pupil. That's why he went much farther than he ever intended – to the point, indeed, where you no longer needed him. That was a terrible day for him, you know – when he saw what he'd done, when he realized you could go to the library and take out books on chemistry, geology, comparative grammar, musical scores, medieval poetry . . . all those things that used to take your fancy.''

''And painting. It wasn't just books.''

14

Bo picked nonexistent lint off her satin bedspread. For Bo, Tessa's interest in painting (which verged on an obsession) did not exist; the very word was unhearable.

"Your father must press for a new curate," Bo said decisively.

"Did you think Peter behaved at all strangely, toward the end, I mean?"

"There was a certain glow in his eyes when he looked at you, of course," Bo began. "I supose you know he was as passionately in love with you as you were with him." Then her mind saw a new path. "But take care – it's not always easy to tell. All men are a bit like that. They get that look in their eye when they see a pretty woman. They're devils. I wish your father . . ." She fell into a brief reverie. Coming out of it, she added, "Will you?"

"Will I what?"

"Talk to him about it, of course. What have I just been saying? I sometimes think you don't hear a word I utter. I don't know where your mind is half the time."

And Bo was so positive that for a moment Tessa even wondered whether it was she, rather than her aunt, who had mentally withdrawn from the conversation.

"I will talk to him about it," she promised.

Bo brightened at once. "Bless you, my dear."

Back in her own room, Tessa wrote it down, in case she might forget it:

23 Finsbury Close.

Then she added: *Soon!*

Chapter Three

The house was grander than she had expected. It proclaimed Dr. Segal as a proprietor of some wealth, a careful man, but not a poor one. The building, indeed, the whole terrace of houses, was almost new; each dwelling was tall and narrow, with four principal floors plus basement and attics. The walls, which faced south onto Finsbury Close, were of deep red brick with carved stonework around the doors and windows. These were houses for doctors, barristers, wholesale merchants, and "people in the City". In fact, the northern boundary of the City of London lay just two streets away.

Dr. Segal's house was different in that it stood at the end of the terrace and so commanded two views – one to the poor east, one to the rich south; it also had a small side garden as well as the back garden enjoyed by each other house in the terrace. From the street all one could see of either garden, back or side, was the disciplined top of a tall, stout hedge of privet. The doctor was obviously something of a private person.

As she mounted by the front steps she noticed that the cast-iron railings were already being attacked by the corrosive air of the city, even through what must be several layers of new paint. The bellpull was a brightly polished brass lever. Beside it the nameplate read: Dr.G.D. SEGAL, M.R.C.P., F.R.C.S. and then, in smaller type below: Surgery in mews at rear.

She went to look at the mews, which were opposite the side-garden. There a two-storey brick building housed the surgery, consulting rooms, and dispensary. She debated whether to call there rather than at the house itself, but in the end decided upon the house; after all, her visit was more private than professional. She pulled the brass lever; deep within the house a bell jangled harshly.

As she waited, she turned to face the street. The houses opposite were smaller, affording a view of the dome of St. Paul's, less than a mile away to the southwest. The day was generally less than a mile away to the southwest. The day was generally oppressive and overcast, but just at that moment the sun came out over the cathedral, warming the grimy black of its stones to a dark grey-green. This fanfare of light lasted a moment only; the window in the clouds passed on and the building was black once more, streaked white where the rain had etched the ancient stone. It looked like an incompetent marble cake.

The door was answered by a maid, a young woman of Tessa's own age and height but blonde in colouring. Her movements were nervy, her face foxy and alert, her eye restless. Tessa gave in her name and her father's card but said merely that she had an important request to make of the doctor. The maid let her into the lobby and asked her please to wait there and she'd see was the doctor at home.

Inner doors of patterned glass barred Tessa's view of the rest of the hall. While she waited, she took careful, nervous stock of the lobby: a dark-brown tiled floor with Roman motifs; a brassbound elephant's-foot umbrella stand with two men's umbrellas and a silver-topped cane, also a broken shooting stick; a locked letter basket, empty; an oak hallstand carved with pussylike lions, peering out among fronds of acanthus – all the gloves in the drawer were men's; the silvering on the looking glass was poisoned with growing circles of damp, but the damp had not come from this house. The walls were papered in a dark pattern of maroon, crimson, and purple. It was all very heavy and masculine. There was nothing to suggest the presence or influence of a Mrs. Segal. Even the perfume on the air of the house was spicy rather than feminine; it was like the exotic aromas that sometimes drifted up from the East India Dock.

Until that moment Tessa had no idea why she was making such a careful note of all these details. Suddenly it struck her that she was trying to crowd out a certain fear – what on earth was she going to *say* to Dr. Segal?

"Do forgive me, doctor, but how do our minds really work?"

"Er, it's just that I was a friend of Peter Laird's and I saw no sign of any abnormality in his behaviour, so. . ."

Impossible phrase after impossible phrase went tumbling through her mind. She had just decided to drop the whole thing and leave when the maid returned and asked "of what nature the request might be"?

"Er. . . it doesn't matter. I was mistaken," Tessa said. "Convey my apologies. I'll go."

A change came over the maid. She looked around, shut the inner doors, and stared intently at Tessa. In some subtle way, she was no longer a maid. Tessa was only half-surprised when the woman said, "It's up to you, of course."

"I beg your pardon?"

"May God strike off my head were I to encourage a body to tangle with that one." She jerked her head toward the interior, presumably toward her master. "But if you really need the doctor" – she winked – "this is the place, all right. I could tell you things you could hold over him. He wouldn't refuse."

Tessa, too innocent to grasp the innuendo at once, stared blankly. "Who are you?" she asked. It even seemed possible that this was, in fact, the mistress of the house, playing the maid as some kind of prank or forfeit.

"Saunders, Miss." She curtseyed, dropping briefly back into her role and her cockney accent. "As I say – it's up to you. He's the devil – but so's the other thing."

The woman's strange manner and incomprehensible words piqued Tessa's curiosity. She simply *had* to meet Dr. Segal. She drew herself up and said, "Please tell your master that my request arises out of the death of Mr. Peter Laird."

The maid's eyes narrowed. She seemed about to say more but then went to do as she had been told, forgetting to close one of the inner doors. Tessa eased it further open with her parasol. The spicy perfume was immediately stronger.

She no longer felt worried. When she met Dr. Segal she'd talk about the tumour – how the news of it had surprised her and so on. If he opened up and showed willing to talk, she could steer the conversation around to the more general question. Calmly she surveyed the newly revealed interior.

The hall was lined with that same dark paper. The tiles, burnt umber in colour, ran uncarpeted to the foot of the stairs and beyond, to a green baize door. The only furnishing she had time to notice was a black oak sideboard, carved in the style of the hallstand. Again the impression was exclusively masculine; this was either a bachelor establishment or the house of a very subdued woman married to an overbearing man. Dr. Segal had not struck her as overbearing when she had seen him in the coroner's court.

He came out at once, as soon as the maid passed on this new information. "My dear Miss d'Arblay – do forgive me for keeping you waiting out here. . ." he began. Then, when he could actually see her in the light of the lobby, he paused. "But weren't you at the inquest yesterday?"

"I didn't think you noticed."

"Oh, I did. Indeed I did. Do come in. Are you alone?" He looked around, though it was quite obvious no one else was there. He led her into his drawing room, leaving the door open. The overwhelming impression here, too, was of darkness – a dark, Turkey-red carpet on polished black floorboards; distempered walls of brown and purple with hand-painted swags and tracery in vermilion and rose madder; solid, chunky, carved furniture of oak – all gothic in its inspiration though not in its actual detail. The chairs and settee were of buttoned leather, stained in a blue so deep as to be almost black.

"How oppressive this heat becomes," he said. "One longs for a good thunderstorm to wash it all away."

"And we'll get it," she said.

"May I offer you some refreshment, Miss d'Arblay?" He opened one of the cupboards and peered inside. "I see some Malvern water here."

"A glass of Malvern water would be most acceptable, thank you, Dr. Segal."

She now saw how groundless her fears had been. Dr. Segal was actually a rather colourless man, more impressive in the witness box than in this domestic setting; perhaps he hoped that something of its rather aggressive masculinity would rub off on him.

The water was stale but he appeared not to notice. He poured a tumbler for himself and settled opposite her. There was so little reflected light in the room that, although the windows were large, she could barely see his features. "Now," he said. "You mentioned Mr. Large?"

"Laird."

"Of course. Stupid of me. Laird – yes. May I ask if he was some relation of yours?"

"Just a friend. Quite a good friend."

For some reason the doctor stared nervously at her. "I'm so

19

sorry," he said at last.

Again Tessa had the strange feeling that some kind of clockwork mechanism was powering all his movements (and even his thoughts if that were possible). Her eyes were growing accustomed to the gloom; she found she could begin to read his expression. His gaze was full of sympathy. His voice, when at last he spoke those two words – "I'm sorry" – was deep and resonant, unlike his everyday tone. Perhaps she had judged him too harshly? Perhaps he was an intensely shy man who chose to hide himself behind that mechanical exterior.

"It was a shock," she said.

"Of course, of course."

"So unexpected."

"It's the way these things are, I'm afraid." He smiled limply, as if apologizing for the design of the human brain. "They come absolutely out of the blue."

"And no one can tell in advance? I mean – there are no warning signs?"

"Not as a rule. Fortunately, the condition itself is a rare one."

"Fortunately for *some*," Tessa said. It sounded more like a correction than she had intended.

He frowned and then nodded. "Oh yes – I see what you mean. Well, Mr. Laird was one of the rare unfortunates, I'm afraid." He stirred awkwardly. "Forgive me, Miss d'Arblay, but did you have something to tell me, ah, in connection with this business? I mean, how, ah, closely did you know the poor gentleman?"

"Have *I* something to tell *you*? How could I? No – I came to ask about it."

His face darkened. "Ask? What can you possibly want to ask? What do I know about it?"

"Well you did the post mortem, Dr. Segal."

"Ah! Yes – of course. You want to ask about *that*!"

She wondered if he'd been drinking. Anyway, it wasn't going to work. She stood up. "I think I've taken quite enough of your valuable time, doctor."

He rose, too, but in agitation. "Not at all. Not at all. But what did you want to ask?"

"You've already answered the question. I wanted to know if these tumours show any symptoms. But – as you say. . ."

"That's a strange thing to want to know, Miss d'Arblay.

20

You're sure Mr. Laird told you nothing?'' There was a curious edge to his voice.

"About what, Dr. Segal? I mean, we discussed lots of things."

"Evil? Did he discuss evil with you?"

Tessa pulled a wry face and edged away from him. "Possibly. . ."

"Ah!" he pounced on the admission. "I knew it!"

"Is that a symptom of one of these tumours?"

He put his index-fingertips together and pressed the point firmly against his lips. He pressed so hard that his fingers and his lips vanished inside his mouth – as if his teeth were on hinges. He retreated from this self-assault and stared at her. "You must tell me all you know," he said at last. It was a command. He seemed about to add more, but before he could speak the maid opened the door and said, "Please Dr. Segal, sorry to disturb you, Dr. Segal, but there's a gentleman with a broken leg over in the surgery, sir." She was now pure cockney again; and she was studiously avoiding Tessa's eye.

The interruption annoyed Segal. He fished a sixpence from his pocket and held it toward the maid. "Take this and give it to some urchin to run to Bart's and get them to send an ambulance. I can't be disturbed now."

St. Bartholomew's Hospital, or "Bart's," was only a few streets away.

Tessa was astonished that the doctor should consider their conversation more important than treating a broken leg. She was about to say as much when the maid went on, "But he's one of your patients, sir."

"Oh confound the fellow! Did he give his name?"

"I forgot, sir. He's in a bad way, sir."

"You're a fool, Saunders." He pocketed the sixpence and turned to Tessa. "Miss d'Arblay, I'm so sorry about this. May I ask you to wait? Would you mind very much? I want you to meet a colleague of mine. A Mis .., ah, Dr. Rosen."

"If you ask it, then of course I'll wait, Dr. Segal. I'm already most grateful to you for giving me your val. . ."

He interrupted her, having turned on the threshold of the hallway. "Did Mr. Laird ever mention any notebooks to you?"

"I don't think so. . ." Tessa was still thinking of the poor gentleman with the broken leg. "I'll try and remember," she

21

said. "But do please attend to your patient."

Still he hesitated.

"I won't leave," she reassured him, thinking that was what had him worried.

Uncertainly he turned from her. His eye fell upon Saunders. "You attend to your duties," he snapped. Tessa saw that he could be overbearing. Perhaps there was a Mrs. Segal, after all.

As soon as he was gone the maid turned to Tessa and, with an excited grin, said, "It's a rum do all round, isn't it!"

Tessa, keen to find out all she could, ignored this cheek and smiled. "Tell me about Dr. Segal," she invited. "Why did you first of all hint that I ought to leave and never come back?"

"There's *things* going on in this house, Miss d'Arblay."

"Things?"

"*Dark* things – black magic and witchcraft!"

"Oh!" Tessa's interest waned. "This is eighteen-eighty-eight, you know. Not fifteen-eighty-eight."

Saunders appeared to come to some internal decision – though she said nothing. She beckoned Tessa and went out into the hall again. She left the polishing rag on the sideboard and walked to the green baize door at the end of the passage. There she paused and, with a dramatic flourish, said, "Beyond this door 'tis six-hundred-and-sixty-six!"

Tessa's interest revived slightly. There was an odd ring of conviction in the maid's words. "What can you mean?" she asked.

"I mean you probably ought never to have come here. But now you are here, you ought to know something of the man you've tangled with."

"Tangled!" Tessa said crossly. "You keep saying that word. It's no such thing."

"*You* may not think so." She shrugged. "Very well, then – I'll be about my ways." She became cockney again. "I'm sorry, I'm sure, if I've. . ."

Tessa made up her mind. "Suppose you're right? Tell me – what's in that room?"

"You'd have to see it with your very own eyes."

Tessa glanced cautiously up the stairway.

"We're alone," the woman promised.

"Isn't there a butler?"

22

"He's doing the wines. He'll be at it another hour. Him and Noakes, the footman." She drained an imaginary glass to the dregs and winked. "I'm the only one above stairs. They sent me up to answer single knocks." Then she added confidentially, "I don't belong upstairs really."

"Is that a fact!" Tessa walked toward the baize door, eager now to be done with it as quickly as possible. She pushed through ahead of the maid.

"No," the maid confided, "I'm not a domestic at all. I'm really an actress. I'm only here between engagements."

Tessa held her peace.

If the rest of the house was dark, this room was positively funereal. It was completely lined by bookcases of ebony. Every book looked ancient; all were bound in leather. The ceiling was black, with golden stars pricked out upon it in zodiacal constellations; dotted lines of silver hinted at the Goat, the Virgin, the Scorpion. . . and others. In the centre of the floor was a table of black limestone with geometric designs of coloured marble let into its surface. The carpet was black and had a five-sided figure woven into it. And there was a number – 666. So that was all it was! The window was curtained with heavy black bombazine, and, although the drapes were open, and although the sun was now shining outside, the effect was claustrophobic; nor was it helped by the reek of that spicy perfume, which here was overpowering.

"There!" Saunders said. "Now tell me it's just his way of collecting butterflies! There's whips and everything in those cupboards."

But at that moment, Tessa saw something which put it all into perspective. She almost laughed, for in her mind's ear she heard Bo's voice complaining about "men" and "dressing up" and "ritual" and "Mumbo-jumbo!" For there upon one of the chairs were three very familiar objects – a ceremonial apron of leather, a silver trowel, and an ornamental mallet. Her father had an almost identical set.

"Haven't you heard of Freemasons?" she asked the maid. "This is just their tomfoolery."

Now that she looked at them more closely, most of the books in the shelves seemed to be about Freemasonry, too.

Saunders was unabashed. "And this?" She pointed to some

prints hanging inside one of the bookcases.

Tessa recognised them all. There were two oleographs of paintings by Rembrandt, *The Anatomy Lesson of Dr. Tulp* and *The Anatomy Lesson of Dr. Deyman*. Both, naturally, showed a partly flayed or disembowelled corpse – as did the third: *The Reward of Cruelty* by Hogarth. It showed a corpse laid out upon a slab; one demonstrator was cutting open its belly and pulling out its tripes while another was dissecting its eyes, while yet another – an apprentice, he seemed – was flaying its feet. They were gruesome scenes, all right; but they were probably a fair picture of what anatomy lessons might have looked like in former times (and probably looked like now, give or take a peruke or a ruff collar).

On closer inspection, however, she noticed one curious feature. In all three reproductions someone – and a skilled artist at that – had overpainted two of the faces. Dr. Tulp and Dr. Deyman and the central figure of the Hogarth trio had been skilfully turned into Dr. Segal. The name "Jubela" had been worked into their costumes, as in a political cartoon. Hogarth's foot-flayer and one spectator in each of the Rembrandts had been given a new face, too – the same face: with a full, dark beard, bushy eyebrows, sensuous lips, and the most compelling eyes. This character was named "Jubelo" in the cartoon fashion.

There were other prints, too – a *Hanging of Judas* by some baroque artist, showing the victim disembowelled, also a cast of a small Hellenistic sculpture, *The Flaying of Marsayas*. . . but she had seen enough.

Just as she turned back to Saunders another print from that same Hogarth series, "The Four Stages of Cruelty," appeared before her mind's eye. It showed the Cruel Man standing at bay above the murdered corpse of his mistress, who was heavily pregnant. It struck her then what Saunders had meant in saying "if you really *need* the doctor. . ." She blushed, pulled in her stomach, and looked intently at the prints again.

"All very unpleasant," she agreed. "But nothing more than that, surely?"

"And what about out there?" Saunders asked. "What about them?" She pointed at the window.

Tessa was still feet away when she gave a start. The garden was filled with naked women.

"You can only see them from here," Saunders said. "He did

them. That Rosen.''

''Doctor Rosen?''

''Doctor!'' the maid sneered. ''The only thing he's doctor of is doctor of evil. He took a drill to some of them – it'd cringe your blood.''

Tessa was too taken up with the strange sight to absorb that comment. By now she realized they were merely painted statues – famous ones, too, like Aphrodite, and the Venus de Milo. But they had all been painted in true flesh tints – even, she noticed, to their body hair. They were so lifelike it seemed prurient to be staring at them.

She glanced away. Her eyes happened to fix on a tall, solid, wooden gate, leading out into the mews. Above it the thick privet hedge grew together again, framing a gap of no more than ten inches between the top of the wood and the ragged bottom of the ingrowing hedge. Through that gap she could see one of the windows on the upper floor of Dr. Segal's surgery opposite. Standing there, staring out – staring at her, it seemed – was a powerfully built man with thick, curly-black hair that joined with a glossy, wavy beard to frame his face and give it a vividness that almost glowed. All those details she acquired in passing. What riveted her were the man's eyes, which were of the palest azure blue. It was the face of the man labelled ''Jubelo'' in the three altered prints. The garden was short, the mews was narrow, the sun was bright. The image of that man seized her; she could not look away.

Saunders, following her gaze, breathed sharply inward. ''That's him!'' she whispered in tones lifted straight out of some melodrama. ''Rosen! Oh I pray to my sweet Christ he can't see us.''

Chapter Four

Saunders ran. Tessa grew angry at the woman's hysteria. She knew the type well. They'd tell you they were scared out of their wits when all they meant was that they had been startled. She was annoyed at herself, too, for allowing the stupid woman to entice her into this room, where she had no right to be.

She walked back into the hall, shutting the baize door behind her. Saunders had picked up her duster and resumed her polishing as if her wages depended on wearing a hole in the wood. Everything about her was so exaggerated – even the vehemence with which she now whispered, "He's coming! You'd best get back in the drawing room, miss."

"You're ridiculous," Tessa said as she swept past, feeling ridiculous herself for engaging in such banter. She went into the drawing room and pretended to examine the picture over the fireplace, *The Building of Solomon's Temple* by . . . she could not make out the signature. But it was a good painting. Anyone could see that. A bit of homage to Whistler – in the colour mainly. And a lot of Blake – the fire and vigour. And that complete assurance, too.

Her ears caught the first sounds of the returning Dr. Segal. Someone was with him – this Mr. Rosen or Dr. Rosen, she presumed.

They paused in the hall. She heard Segal say, "It's your evening off, I believe, Saunders?"

"Yessir."

"Mr. Rosen would like you to go to his place again."

"No!" the maid said quickly. "Never!"

Then Rosen spoke. He had a deep, bass voice, but sharp rather than muffled; it seemed to crack open the air, though he was speaking softly. "I'll pay you well," he told her. "But you already know that."

"I don't care about the money. I'm not going. I'm not going to do that again. Never. It's wickedness, so it is."

If she was really an actress, Tessa thought, she wasn't a bad one – whichever was her true self. Much as she disliked the maid and her hysterical way of exaggerating everything she could not help taking the woman's part in this particular argument, which she was being forced to overhear.

Rosen said, "You pay her too well, Segal." Then, obviously turning to the maid again, he added, "Come now. What harm did it do last time, eh? You enjoy it really – you said so, yourself. What woman doesn't enjoy such admiration!"

"Don't you dare!" the maid answered.

Had one of them tried to caress her? Tessa cleared her throat sharply.

There was a momentary silence, broken when Rosen said, "The money will talk her round to it. This coyness is just to put her price up."

"Go below!" Segal told the maid. Moments later he stood in the doorway. "Ah, Miss d'Arblay, do please forgive us . . ."

"Certainly not," Tessa answered. "Not after *that* disgraceful scene."

"Oh?" Segal's surprise was genuine.

Now Rosen stood in the doorway, looking at her with the same piercing eyes she had seen from the garden-room window. She forgot whatever answer she had been going to make. While he stood there, looking at her with that cool, sardonic smile, she could not take her eyes off him. Her heart began to beat wildly. He was not tall but he radiated a sense of power. "A disgraceful scene?" he prompted. The corners of his mouth twitched in an amused challenge.

"Yes." She recollected vaguely what they were talking about. "What would you call it?" she added apologetically.

Rosen looked away from her as he crossed the threshold. "A confounded nuisance! That's what. When my model turns up all enthusiasm for her first sitting and sits like an angel, and then – having pocketed her fee, mark you – she refuses to come again. You're right, young lady. It *is* disgraceful."

Tessa felt so ashamed. This could be none other than *Dante* Rosen, the famous painter! The picture over the mantelpiece was undoubtedly by him – why had she not seen it at once? She watched him in a kind of paralysed fascination, wondering how even to begin to apologize.

27

But he was not looking at her. His eyes roved around the room. They seemed to take in everything, to note its shape, its colour, its texture, where it stood in the hierarchy of tone. She knew he was able to see things she was missing – things she would always miss. How often she had craved that gift of more-than-mere-sight! Every time she laid down her brushes, after finishing yet another competent little painting, she knew that something essential in the scene had once again evaded her grasp.

At last he looked toward her. He smiled benignly at her discomfiture but his eyes seemed to pierce into the very core of her being. "Young lady – beautiful young lady in blue! – I do believe you thought you were overhearing quite a different conversation!"

She smiled sheepishly, at both the flattery and the impeachment. His eyes twinkled. "Forgive me, but I don't believe we've been introduced?"

Segal leaped in. "My fault! My fault! Miss d'Arblay, may I present Mr. Dante Rosen, the painter."

"How d'you do, Mr. Rosen. I've heard of you, of course. More than that – I've been an admirer of your work for years. I'm delighted we've met at last. But I wasn't aware that you're also a doctor?"

When he frowned in bewilderment she turned to Segal. "I'm sure you said *Doctor* Rosen."

Before Segal could answer, Rosen said, "So many things in life are different once we penetrate below the surface, Miss d'Arblay. Like. . ." He let the rest of his sentence linger while he raised her hand to his lips, kissed it lightly, then – absentmindedly, it seemed – held on to it while he looked into her face. His gaze was frank and admiring.

She suddenly saw what it was about his eyes. From a distance she had taken them to be pale blue; now he'd drawn closer she saw they were, in fact, dark blue, almost violet, with a strength of colour she had seen only in the eyes of young babies. What gave them their distant pallor was the fact that each dark-blue iris was ringed with flecks of greeny-gold. She found the combination fascinating. He knew it, too.

". . . like you, for instance," he completed the sentence. "I too am glad we've met at last."

She gave a little laugh of surprise. "What d'you mean – 'met

28

at last'?''

"What I say."

"But I can't believe you know of me."

"Indeed I do. I'm told you're quite a painter yourself."

She felt the beat of her heart again. Dante Rosen was world-famous. Not fashionable, perhaps; not one of the rich Royal Academy painters. But a celebrated man nonetheless, especially among other painters. His name was mentioned in practically every issue of the avant-garde art journals. "How can you possibly have heard of me?" she asked.

"I met an aged, aged man," he quoted. He was still holding her hand; the contact was electric. His attitude dared her to snatch it away and, at the same time, begged her not to.

"Old Friendly?" she asked. That was the name of one of her favourite sitters and the only "aged, aged man" she knew – an elderly tramp with the head of a biblical prophet.

Rosen let go of her hand at last. "Old Friendly," he confirmed.

She sat down; the two men followed suit. "Has he sat for you, too?" she went on.

He shook his head, still wearing that smile which suggested he knew all her thoughts. "He absolutely refuses to. And I'm afraid it's all your fault, Miss d'Arblay."

"Mine!"

"Indeed. He says no one will ever paint a portrait of him half as good as the one you did."

She laughed in embarrassment and tried to change the subject. "I hope you don't offer him money, Mr. Rosen. You know why he's called Old Friendly, I suppose?"

"No?"

"Because that's his pet name for the vile stuff he drinks whenever he has the cash to buy it – french-polishing spirit usually. He gets blind drunk on it. And I do mean blind. He has a great speech on Freedom when he's drunk. Has he delivered it to you yet?"

"He certainly has!" Rosen's laugh was infectious. She began to like him more than was wise on so short an acquaintance. He went on, "But I'd love a crack at him. He has a head that Rembrandt himself would've paid a fortune to sketch."

A daring idea occurred to her. "Come to my studio," she

suggested. "I'm sure I can get him to sit for me." Her heart was in her mouth in case Rosen refused.

"That's amazingly generous of you," he answered. "How on earth may I repay such kindness?"

"Tuition?" she suggested and hung on his reply. In case he should refuse she added, "I was recently a pupil of Sir Frederic Leighton."

It shook him. Leighton was the President of the Royal Academy (and a friend of Grandpa d'Arblay, who had been an early patron – but she felt it unnecessary to explain all that). His eyes narrowed. She feared she had offended him; the Academy was derided in Rosen's circle. "I take the business of art seriously," he warned.

His tone angered her. But she noted, too, that his patronizing air had gone.

Segal smiled at last. He had not been happy at the way Rosen had monopolized the conversation.

She was on the point of rising to take her leave when the big clock in the hall struck one. Segal took out his pocket watch and checked it. The butler appeared in the doorway and, seeing Tessa, raised an inquiring eyebrow.

Segal turned to her. "Well, Miss d'Arblay, we are now in something of a quandary. Our business is not concluded, but the old tyrant has caught us out. Our luncheon is only a small and simple cold collation, but we should be honoured if you'd consent to join us?"

She shook her head. "Thank you, doctor. I think I really ought to be. . ."

Rosen interrupted. "Stay, Miss d'Arblay," he said, pitching his tone exactly half way between a command and a request. She gazed at him until her silence forced him to add, "Please?"

"Why?" she asked.

"'I think I really ought to be going'?" He quoted her and pulled a face. "Goodness, how conventional! I hope you're not a conventional sort of young woman."

She rose to the challenge, coolly. She knew he was beginning some kind of obscure game but she hid her excitement at it. "Very well." She turned to Segal, making clear it was *he* who chiefly interested her. "I should like to know a little more about. . . the business we were discussing."

Rosen came swiftly between them and offered her his arm. "You fascinate me, Miss d'Arblay. A pupil of Leighton, eh? I want to know all about you. What does a pupil of that august dauber want with such a humble genius as me?"

"Ever so 'umble, Master Copperfield!" Tessa laughed. But his eyes forced her to be serious. "It's all I really want in life, Mr. Rosen."

"No husband? No family – you'd rather paint?"

"Yes."

"That's a great sacrifice for a woman. Tell me this – suppose the Devil were to appear before us now and offer you a genius that would tower over Rembrandt himself. . . what would you yield up in return?"

"Oh ten times *everything!*" She laughed uneasily.

"You grow more interesting by the minute."

Ever since she had dropped Leighton's name, Dante Rosen had become truculent. The tone was mild enough, the banter friendly, yet it did not conceal an overbearing personality underneath it all. She saw that he was a man who'd be quick to take advantage of a weakness.

The dining room was decorated in the same richly sombre colours as the rest of the establishment. She now felt sure the taste was more Rosen's than Segal's; he was the dominant one of the pair.

He certainly dominated that small luncheon table, bringing to it an invigorating sense of London's artistic and literary world, which, of course, he knew intimately. He was a friend of Oscar Wilde, and repeated many of his epigrams. And, as a founder member of the New English Art Club, he was also a devoted admirer of "Jimmy" Whistler, as he called him. Tessa was filled with envy. She longed to know all these people.

She tried to think of just one non-academic name to throw into the conversation; she remembered that another great painter, Walter Sickert, was rumoured to have moved into the East End recently. "I suppose you've heard Mr. Sickert's hired a little studio over in Whitechapel?" she said.

"*Sickert!*" he exploded. "That impostor! You don't mean to say you think *he's* a painter?"

"He's a member of the New English Art Club."

"To our eternal shame. That drooling idiot lives in a fog.

31

Painter, indeed! You've only to look at his daubs to see he's no such thing. He's got no more idea of colour or shape than . . . '' Rosen was speaking so violently that bits of food escaped his lips. Dr. Segal cleared his throat meaningfully and stared at his friend.

Rosen took a grip on himself, wiped his mouth on his napkin, smiled, and said, ''Forgive me. Some subjects quite carry me away – and Sickert is one of them. A drop more wine, Miss d'Arblay?''

''Wine!'' She looked at her glass in dismay.

''What did you imagine it was?''

''Fruit cordial of some kind.''

Rosen laughed. ''Well it's old wine for a new friendship.''

Segal interrupted. ''We ought to get to the matter in hand, Rosen. As I told you, Miss d'Arblay believes her late friend, Mr. Laird, was involved in some strange sort of business.''

''I said no such thing!'' Tessa protested.

''Oh, forgive me. That was what I understood.''

Rosen turned to Tessa. She got the feeling they were acting out some kind of rehearsed conversation – but perhaps that was just the strange effect of the wine. ''You know, Dr. Segal even consulted Sir William Gull.'' Rosen spoke the name with a kind of awe.

But this interjection was surely impromptu, for it seemed to startle Segal. ''Never mind that!'' His tone was sharp.

Rosen laughed uneasily. ''Our new young friend ought to know how thorough and conscientious you were, Segal.''

''But,'' Tessa tried again to insist. ''All this has nothing to do with . . .'' It was useless. Rosen turned to her and added: ''Sir William is a leading savant when it comes to brain tumours, you know. He is, or was, the Keeper of Guy's Hospital Madhouse.''

''Yes yes yes!'' Segal said angrily. ''But he didn't examine Mr. Laird. Not in person. He only saw the photograph. The one I appended to my post-mortem report. But the lesion was quite plain. The diagnosis was never in doubt. Even a first-year student, looking at that photograph, would have reached the same conclusion.''

''We're at complete cross-purposes,'' Tessa managed to say at last. ''I'm not calling your competence into question, Dr. Segal. Good heavens! No – I just came here to, well, ask you a bit more about brain tumours.''

The two men exchanged quick glances. Rosen smiled. "May I ask why?" he said. "Well not just brain tumours. In fact, not really brain tumours at all. Oh dear!"

Rosen was staring at her intently now. "The mind," he said. "You're interested in the mind." He smiled with great assurance. "You've come to the right person."

She knew he meant himself, not Dr. Segal. Also – and to her surprise – she found she was actually no longer interested in the mind. She would much rather get to know Dante Rosen – see his paintings, meet his friends, hear them talking about art. . .

It was a pipe dream, of course. She wasn't anything like good enough. They'd only laugh at her. But anyway, she no longer wanted to talk about the mind, or madness – and certainly not about tumours. She thought the best way to stop that line of conversation was to trot out some childish thoughts she'd had the other day. "I want to know," she said, tapping her forehead, "why is it that, if my thoughts are all going on in here, inside my brain, why don't I feel as if *I'm* in there, too? Why do I feel I'm outside it, out here?"

Rosen roared with laughter and looked at Segal. "Out of the mouths of babes and sucklings – and of beautiful clever young ladies in blue!" he taunted. "Riddle her that you St. Andrew's scholar!"

Segal cleared his throat. "There's no easy answer," he began.

"Humbug!" Rosen said. "There's no answer at all. The Greeks were right. Our minds are in here." He tapped the base of his breastbone. "To say that the mind is in the brain is like saying an army is in its general."

"And to say that your mind is *anywhere* at all would be the grossest flattery," Segal told him.

Rosen smiled. "But it's everywhere, old fellow. Here. . . in Tite Street. . . at the Café Royal. . . the Lyceum. . . the New English. . . and" – he turned to Tessa – "at the moment more than half of it is in your studio, dear young lady, eager to see what a pupil of Leighton's has made of one of the finest heads of the century."

Chapter Five

Late that night the Old Vicarage was disturbed by a hammering at the kitchen door. Spencer, the upstairs maid, Hill, the butler, and Mrs. Carver, the cook, lived out and had long since gone to their homes. Tyker, the groom, lodged over the stables at the far end of the garden. But Hooper, the scullerymaid, slept in the attic. Given time, she'd get out of her bed and answer the door. First she'd wait five minutes to allow the caller a chance to give up and go away; then she'd take another five to shrug on a dressing gown, light a lamp, and crawl downstairs. Tessa could not bear to lie there and listen to the hammering. Especially as it was raining stair-rods. Anyway, Hooper would only answer the door and then come straight to her for instructions.

As Tessa went down the bare wooden treads of the servants' stair she had to shield the candle-flame from a guttering draught. With annoyance she saw the cause of it. A small casement at the half-landing had been left slightly ajar and rain was beating in upon the sill. The strength of that downpour made her think of the wretched creature outside and, wedging the wet and swollen wood almost shut, she hastened on down, almost extinguishing her light in the rush.

The kitchen door onto the yard had two bolts, a chain, and a lock. As she dealt with them she realized how laughable such precautions were, especially when someone had chosen to leave a window open just nine feet above.

The caller rushed indoors without a by-your-leave, almost knocking the light from Tessa's hand. "Just a moment!" she protested.

The stranger turned. Her heart fell. The visitor was Saunders. "I'm sorry, Miss d'Arblay," she said with mechanical insincerity.

Tessa counted down her anger. "I'm surprised we've any door left," she said. "I thought the hounds of hell were at your heels."

"The hounds of hell!" the woman repeated with a curiously

34

toneless relish. Her accent was as middle-class as Tessa's. Her general manner was calm; that is, now she was safely indoors, she moved very little. But her eyes were restless. Several times she glanced at the now-closed door as though, having cursed its solidity all the while she hammered upon it, she now doubted it would stand up even to the drumming of the rain. She was soaked to her very skin; her clothes clung to her in gleaming drabness. Her blonde hair, darkened by the wet, was pasted to the fringes of her face.

"Well? What are you doing here?" Tessa asked impatiently. "Does Dr. Segal know of this?"

"He's the one I've come about. I didn't know the skies were going to open like this."

Her sodden clothing was a moral blackmail. Tessa nodded toward the range. "Stoke some life into that thing," she said. "I'll look out some dry clothes for you. The rain seems set for the night, what's left of it, so you'd better stay, I suppose. Don't for one moment imagine you're *welcome* here, though."

Pausing only to light the gas lamp, she stumped away upstairs and rummaged about in a chaos of old cupboards, finding a petticoat here, a chemise there, and an old dressing gown somewhere else. At one stage Bo poked her head out of her bedroom door and asked if anything was the matter.

"I declare I hope not," Tessa said grimly, which Bo took as answer enough.

And indeed she hoped not. Saunders had the makings of a limpet; do her a kindness and you'd never see the back of her. The search took rather longer than she had expected. By the time she returned to the kitchen, the woman had the fire roaring brightly and the kettle was beginning to moan away on the hob. Cheerful and welcome though it was, she resented the fact that Saunders had made herself so much at home in so short a time.

The maid still had her wet clothes on. They were steaming now in the glow from the fire. Faintly on that steam Tessa caught the tang of the spice which pervaded the doctor's house and which had been so strong in the Freemasonry room. With that power which smell, and smell alone, possesses, it transported her back almost bodily to the doctor's drawing room and luncheon table. To Dante Rosen. Briefly she saw again his strangely coloured eyes, fixed on her; heard his voice, bathing her.

35

"You'd better get out of those things," she said.

The maid unbuttoned the wet bodice and held it awkwardly, not knowing where to put it and not wanting to hand it to Tessa as if to say, "Deal with this."

Tessa liked her for that diffidence. "I'll hang it up," she said. As she carried it into the dark, over to the clothes horse by the scullery door, she raised it near her nostrils so as to catch again that lingering spice.

Saunders stepped out of her dress, which, being a good linen, almost stood, freelance, beside her.

Tessa reached for it, but the maid picked it up again and said, "Here, I can't have you doing that for me. It doesn't look right."

Deftly Tessa relieved her of it. "Time enough for that sort of talk when you're dry," she said. "You stay by the fire. I'd rather devote twenty seconds of my time to carrying your clothes than twenty hours nursing your chill."

The woman grinned. "You're a saint, miss!"

"Don't think you can soft-soap me! All I really want to know is why you've come here at this hour?"

"I came to warn you, Miss d'Arblay."

"Well that's very kind of you, Saunders, but I've a warning for you first – I'm not as soft-hearted as you seem to think. If it wasn't raining, I *would* kick you out. You have the smell of trouble to me. I think you're tired of being in service up there at Dr. Segal's and you imagine you see a softer billet here."

Saunders heard her out calmly. "You'll soon think otherwise, Miss d'Arblay. Would you mind if I closed the shutters?"

"For heaven's sake!" Tessa scolded. "The yard wall is ten feet high. If anyone's climbed over it and is standing out there in that downpour – all for the sake of a peep at your skin and bones – they deserve the chill they'll surely get. And so will you if you don't change out of those things. Goodness, you should have applied for lodgings down at the workhouse – they make short shrift of such modesty there."

"Would you mind turning your back then, please, miss," Saunders asked diffidently but firmly.

Tessa gave an exasperated groan and went to check that she had rebolted the door. Then, for good measure, she checked on the window catch, too. While doing this she caught sight of the woman's reflection in the glass. Saunders had removed her wet

36

shimmy and was carefuly examining her own body, as if for ticks or leeches. Whatever she was seeking she failed to find it – or them. "All right then, Miss d'Arblay," she called out cheerfully. She was standing with her back to the fire. "Sorry about that." She now appeared to have no qualms about standing naked in front of Tessa. "Skin and bones" had not been an apt description; she could understand why Rosen had been so keen to have her as his model. She wouldn't mind painting the woman, herself.

"So," she challenged. "You're a great actress, eh? A grand lady of the theatre."

"I didn't say that. But I've been on the stage four years. That's no lie."

"And why aren't you on it now?"

"Because of a certain misunderstanding with a certain manager who wanted me to provide services not originally speculated."

"D'you mean stipulated?"

"Something like that. Maybe you don't know how it is with men when they have that power?"

"Doesn't it often happen with actresses?" Tessa looked her meaningfully up and down. "Especially with you?"

She could see the woman trying to decide whether or not to lie. An uncomfortable little laugh yielded victory to truth.

"Then what was different on this occasion?" Tessa pressed.

Saunders looked around vaguely. "I don't enjoy talking about it."

"I'll get you a towel." Tessa went over to the corner cupboard. "I don't enjoy asking these questions either, Saunders. But I don't know anything about you – so how else can I decide what value to place on this warning you want to give me? So I repeat: What was different this time?"

As she returned with the towel she saw the woman shrug with a kind of trapped helplessness. "No different, I suppose," she said in a flat tone. "No different from half of them, anyway. With some men its all take. Others – there's a bit of give along with the take. But this one was all take."

It sounded like a line from a play. "So you wouldn't give? Or you took, too? Are you 'on the scarper,' as they say around here?"

37

Saunders looked winded. "You could do a mind-reading act!" She accepted the towel and rubbed disconsolately at those damp patches the fire had not reached. "He won't go to the police, if that's what's worrying you."

In bending over she revealed a part of her back. Tessa saw a number of strange marks; she would have called them bruises except that they were all horseshoe-shaped. Saunders appeared to have been kicked a number of times by a very minute pony. "How much money is involved?" Tessa asked.

"Only what he owed me. A month in *Forsaken Rachel*."

"How much?"

"A fiver. He did owe it to me, though."

Tessa relaxed and stretched her hands toward the flames. She had to admit it – there was something fairly likeable about this strange young woman – maidservant . . . actress – whatever she might be. Infuriating but likeable. She held out the dry chemise, warm from the fire. "Very well, Saunders. I'll believe you're what you say you are. But how did you get from that to the cockney skivvy I met this morning" – she looked at the kitchen clock – "yesterday morning, up in Finsbury Close?"

Saunders, snug in the shift, relaxed too and set about drying her hair. Her answer was muffled by the towel. "A cockney gel is what I was born, Miss d'Arblay. Not quite a skivvy, perhaps, but close enough."

"Where were you born? What does your father do?"

Saunders dropped back into cockney. "Wivvin the sahnd o' Bow Bells. But I can put aitches on oranges when I need to." She laughed and resumed her middle-class accent. "My dad's a post-office clerk. Not a mile from here – in Long Lane. There's a strong desire for improvement in our family."

"Didn't Dr. Segal want references?"

"Well now we're coming to it. It wasn't Dr. Segal who employed me. It was Rosen. The Demon, I call him."

"So I've noticed. You do make rather a point of it, you know. I must say I found him charming."

"Oh he can play the gentleman when there's a lady in it. He can turn on the charm like a gas-tap. But you just wait till he turns it off! That's like the sun going out. You'll do anything for him then – until you're cured." She snorted. "I'm cured! If I told you what he wanted me to do tonight, you wouldn't believe it – mind-

38

reading act and all. You wouldn't believe it."

"More taking without giving?"

For a moment Saunders was nonplussed. Whatever her relationship, past or present, with Rosen, it was too complex to be explained in such shorthand as "taking" and "giving." She shrugged and repeated herself, "You'd not believe it."

"Try." Tessa was now bursting to know.

Two eyes peered out from the cave of the towel. She shook her long, damp-darkened hair back and then began drying the ends of it. She spoke each word separately and distinctly. "He wanted me to lie on a bed with a dead man – a real live dead man – while he did his drawings."

Tessa stared at her, open-mouthed.

Still in that same plodding tone, Saunders went on, "Now ask me which medicinal friend of his supplied the corpse."

There was a chair behind Tessa; she sat down.

Saunders, seeing that she was more than half believed, went on, "There's something. . .I don't know. . .*rotten* – degenerate – about all your artistic folk nowadays. Rosen's not the only one. They're all taken up with this. . .rottenness. Last time he made me pose on the back of a pig. A real live pig! Tied down with ropes. And none of your side-saddle. I had to sit astride it – naked on those bristles! Well, you heard me this morning. That's why I wasn't going back."

Tessa stood and began to pace about. One half of her shared the shock and disgust; but the other half could still hear Dante Rosen saying, "I hope you're not a conventional young woman." In the end she said, "You can't judge art by ordinary standards. If you're any sort of an actress at all, you'll understand that already."

Saunders sniffed. "I see."

"What's that meant to imply?"

"He's already got you, has he?"

"Now you're being absurd again. Anyway, if you're so shocked, why did you go to his studio tonight? Why did you even go back to Finsbury Close after the time with the pig?"

The woman looked away. "I wish I could answer that. Even to myself. I can't say. But when that Demon looks at me – I don't know. He has the Demon's way with him. It's to my own shame, I know, but he can make me do things I don't want to. He can,

like, mesmerize a body. Or he *could*. As I say, I'm cured now."
She spread the towel to let it dry and then began to put on the
remaining clothes.

This response to Dante Rosen, so similar to her own, both
excited Tessa and embarrassed her. She wanted to talk about it
but lacked the right words. Then, noticing that the kettle was
singing just short of the boil, she asked, "Would you like a cup of
tea?"

Saunders glanced at her cannily. "You wouldn't have
anything a mite stronger?"

Tessa hesitated. "Medicinal, I suppose," she allowed at
length. "Or, as you would probably say – *medical*. Cook has some
brandy in the cupboard."

"Lucky old cook!" Saunders chanted.

Tessa poured a small glass, which she handed over reluctantly.

"Won't you have a nip yourself?" the maid asked.

"You're being very kind to me tonight, Saunders, but no
thank you."

The other grinned at the rebuke and downed the glass in one.
She gasped at the relief. "It won't be men, it'll be that stuff will
ruin me. I was drinking in The Ringer's when Rosen found me.
All he needed to do was hook his finger, and out I followed like a
lamb – into service. Me in service! Still, I was good at it, wasn't
I! I mean, I fooled you."

Tessa marvelled at this degree of self-deception. Saunders
failed to notice because she was pointedly emptying the dregs of
the brandy into her upturned mouth. This was followed by a
hope-filled look and an encouraging smile in Tessa's direction.

"No," Tessa told her.

Saunders stared at the empty glass, then through it at the fire.
"You're right," she agreed. "It's my ruin. *The Ruin'd Maid*, eh!
I was a year in that. Happy days!"

"What now?" Tessa asked. "Will you ever get back on the
stage?"

"I shall have to find myself a powerful prospector, so that . . ."

"Protector."

"That's right. So that Davitt wouldn't dare."

"Davitt. Was that his name?"

"'Sudden Death' Davitt." She carried the empty glass over to
the sink. "So you see, Miss d'Arblay, I came here to warn you

about meddling with those two. They're both rotten. They do rotten things.''

"How did they behave after I'd gone?" Tessa asked.

"The usual funny stuff."

"Funny stuff?"

"Well – dressing up, and candles, and opium, and Latin, and . . . other things.''

"Other things?"

Saunders hesitated and then stared defiantly at Tessa. "All right – since you ask – Segal likes hurting women. One of the maids there, he pays her five shillings a cut – with a cane. Ten if there's blood.''

Tessa thought she had never heard anything quite so preposterous. Saunders saw her scepticism and added. "It's the truth!''

"Have they done such things to you?"

"No thanks! A live pig and a dead corpse is quite enough for me,'' Saunders answered, then, seeing that Tessa's doubts were not dispelled, she suddenly pulled back her sleeve and exposed her forearm. "What about that, then?''

It was a bruise, identical to the ones on her back. "How did you come by it?'' Tessa asked.

"Don't you know?'' Saunders looked to see if she were joking. "What d'you *think* caused it?''

"Well, I know what it looks like. Two miniature horseshoes. But that's ridiculous.''

"When the Devil rides! I never thought of that.'' Saunders laughed. "No – it's teeth, love. Bite marks. That's what it is. He bit me.''

"Segal bit you?"

"Not Segal. Him. The Demon.''

Tessa was appalled. "Does Rosen also enjoy hurting women?''

To judge by her expression, Saunders now clearly wished she hadn't started this line at all. "Not exactly. I mean, not in that way. I mean . . . well, he gets you going. You know?''

Tessa didn't know – or not exactly – but she nodded so as not to halt the flow of revelation. Above all, she wanted to know how Dante Rosen's teeth marks could be seen in such abundance on the woman's bare *back*.

"When he's got you going, you don't notice it. 'Love bites', he

41

calls them. Look, I don't want to talk about it. I just wanted to say, keep away from those two. If you get mixed up with them, you'll know *all* about love bites and pain, believe me! You'll be what you might call a connosyer of pain."

"Or what I might call a connoisseuse?"

"Something like that."

Silence fell. A hot cinder dropped from the fire. Saunders flicked it nimbly with her naked toe onto the stone hearth. "Well, and what'm I going to do?" she asked.

"You can come and pose for me," Tessa suggested. "If there's any actress in you at all, it'll make a change from the drab old sacks I've usually had to put up with. I'm no 'powerful protector' but I can offer you a few weeks' employment. And no pigs or corpses."

Saunders nodded gravely. "All right. I'm very grateful, Miss d'Arblay."

"There's just one poser, though. My people don't like to admit that I have anything to do with painting. They pretend I'm out doing Good Works. So you'd better be my companion, or personal maid, or something. Can you manage a character in between skivvy and Great Actress?"

Saunders smiled. "I shall endeavour to give modom every satisfraction." She caught the note of fake-gentility to perfection.

"I'm going to loathe you!" Tessa warned with a laugh. "You'd better sleep in my room for the few remaining hours of this night. There's a daybed up there you can have. So – step back into your boots and go ahead of me up those stairs."

As they left, the fire was already dying. The kettle, which had finally come to the boil, began to sing its way down to its regular, all-night simmer.

At the turn of the stair Tessa tried to finish closing the casement but the wood was too swollen. She gave up. This foul night was no more one for burglars than it was for the rest of humanity.

The daybed was by the window. Tessa handed the candle to Saunders while she took an eiderdown from the cupboard and one of the pillows from her own set. Throwing them on the daybed she said, "There you are."

Saunders did not move.

Tessa looked at her more closely and saw that she had put the candle down on a chest of drawers, immediately in front (as it happened) of the photo of a group taken at her twenty-first birthday party.

Saunders was staring at the picture. Tessa went to her side. "What is it?" she asked.

For a moment she thought the maid had not heard, but then she pointed at Peter Laird, who was standing in the back row. "That man there."

"Yes?"

Saunders looked again at the photograph.

"You've seen him before?" Tessa asked.

"I'd almost swear it. I'd almost swear I've seen him before. I'd almost swear he called on Dr. Segal. Three or four times, he came. For all those stupid games."

Chapter Six

Peter was buried in Highgate Cemetery. Tessa represented the d'Arblays. The ground was sodden from the overnight downpour but the heavy rainclouds had passed, leaving the day bright and sunny; there was even the hint of a return to the high-summer conditions of the earlier part of the week.

The mourners around the graveside numbered no more than twenty, of whom most were professional colleagues of Peter's. He had been a pharmacist. His parents, who farmed somewhere up in the Lake District, had travelled down yesterday. They were staying in a guest house near the vicarage. Sergeant Keene, who had consulted Peter upon forensic matters from time to time, was also there. He had been at the church service, too, where he had bowed stiffly toward Tessa but avoided coming close enough to speak.

There came that terrible moment when the coffin was seen for the last time as it vanished into the maw of the grave and the parson began the ritual of "earth-to-earth, ashes-to-ashes, dust-to-dust." Peter's mother, a large-boned countrywoman with a face honed sharp by the Cumbrian winds, broke down and turned inward to her husband for support. Tessa, who had been holding her other arm, also succumbed briefly to tears.

The group of mourners began to break apart. They came up to the Lairds to offer their condolences, speaking with mumbled reticence, brandishing the frailty of language in awe of our common mortality. When Sergeant Keene began walking away downhill toward the main gate, Tessa joined him.

"I'm going to ask you a great favour," she said.

She walked deliberately slowly, knowing it might take some time.

He grunted. "I thought as much. You've had that look ever since the church."

"Did you know Peter very well, Sergeant Keene? I don't mean just to talk to. But d'you know what he did in his idle hours? Did you know any of his other friends?"

The sergeant stopped and stared at her – a trick of his that was by now familiar. She could imagine how it might unnerve a wrongdoer, though it had no such effect on her. "Suppose you tell me what's behind all this," he suggested.

"If you promise not to give me another lecture on intuition."

He grinned. "You're the one who's asking the favour, Miss d'Arblay. So I'll promise nothing."

"Very well. D'you know any group of people who go in for devil worship and black magic and rituals and things like that?"

He looked at her again, not quite able to believe she was being serious. When he saw she was, he exclaimed, "Bless us!"

"But do you?"

"I've heard tales, of course. But in forty years of service I've never actually come across it. Why?"

"Is it against the law?"

He shrugged. "If it is, it's the kind of law that also prohibits archery on feast days in the Strand. Why d'you want to know, anyway?"

She paused before answering. "I called on Dr. Segal yesterday. I think he's involved in that sort of thing."

Keene sucked in his breath sharply. "Segal's highly respected among us. He's a first-class police surgeon, I know that much."

"I don't doubt it," she answered – wondering how on earth she was going to work around to the big item of news without making it all sound absurdly dramatic.

44

"Hard to imagine him as a devil worshipper," Keene added.

"What about Peter, then?" She tossed it in casually and held her breath.

He stared at her and then at the grave.

"Yes – that Peter," she confirmed. "I know it's hardly the day to be asking it . . ."

"Impossible!"

"That's what I thought. And yet one of the maids at Segal's house showed me the room where they keep all their equipment. She told me they go in for witchcraft and whipping and . . ."

"Witchcraft and what?" Sergeant Keene asked quickly.

"Whipping. They whip one of the other maids there. They pay her five shillings a cut. Double if there's blood."

The sergeant swallowed audibly, then took off his hat and mopped his forehead. "D'you know what you're saying, Miss d'Arblay?" he asked.

"I know, I didn't believe it either." She wondered whether or not to tell him about the "love bites", too.

He cleared his throat. "Look – I wouldn't try and understand that sort of thing if I were you, miss."

"What d'you mean – that sort of thing? You're talking now as if it's commonplace. But first of all you said you'd never come across it in forty years."

"That was witchcraft, Miss d'Arblay. I've never come across a case of witchcraft, as I said. We're living, after all, in eighteen-eighty-eight. But this other business is different. Howsomever – it's not a fit subject for a respectable young lady. So a word to the wise: drop it."

"'This other business' . . . I don't understand."

He sucked a tooth and said, "Last time I was here I saw a fox, you know. Cheeky little thing!"

"You mean you're not going to talk to me about it?"

"I told you – it's not a fit subject. Go back to something nice – like tumours." Then, with studied casualness, he added, "And this maid of Segal's – she identified Peter as a member of the witchcraft circle, did she?"

"Yes. That's what I find so . . ."

"And what might her name be?"

"Connie Saunders. But she doesn't work there any more."

"Got a grudge, has she?"

"Not at all. She found a better position."

"Between yesterday and today?"

"As a matter of fact, she works for me."

The sergeant laughed. "You take the blooming biscuit, you do," he told her.

"I just find it so extraordinary. Don't you? I mean, there was Peter, a man I thought I knew quite well. A gentleman, and a truly gentle man – kind, considerate . . . he had every good quality. And then last night, when Connie Saunders saw Peter's photo, standing in that group at my twenty-first, when she saw him and said he used to come to Dr. Segal's and take part in all that black magic and whipping that poor girl – well . . . it's shattering, that's all."

Hesitantly Sergeant Keene took her arm. "Don't upset yourself, my dear," he said, with a gentleness that surprised her. He and she had been on bluff-joking terms for so long that this change was almost embarrassing. "I don't want to open up the whole subject, but I will tell you this: Whipping, or flagellation, to give it the usual name, *is* commonplace."

"Flagellation!" She laughed. "You mean it's like monks doing penances? Scourging one another. Oh I know all about that."

He stared at her again. "Monks, is it?" he said. "That's a new one on me. A fact a day. Anyway (so help me – I never thought I'd hear myself telling this to a lady!), this flagellation business goes on every night in dozens of places all over London. Don't ask me why – I can't see it myself."

"But . . . Peter!"

"Let me tell you – the most vicious murderer I ever knew was as mild, as inoffensive a little chap as you'd ever hope to meet. A pork butcher, he was. Within six weeks of selling up the shop, he killed his wife, her sister, and two of his nieces! I'll spare you the details but he was a master of his trade. You see? You can never tell with people. You've no idea what goes on behind all those respectable façades when the lamps are lit and the blinds pulled down. We're a funny lot – people."

They had reached the cemetery gate by now. The horses, between the shafts of the waiting cortege, stirred comfortlessly in the warm breeze and dreamed of summer fallows; they could smell the new-mown grass in the cemetery and hear the susurration of the leaves.

46

Tessa and Keene went out and stood, waiting for the others, on the foot-pavement between the railings and the carriages.

"You spoke of a favour?" Keene prompted.

"Oh yes. Segal mentioned a photograph he attached to his post-mortem report on Peter. I suppose . . ." she fished ". . . I suppose it's just lying somewhere now, gathering dust? Out of sight, out of mind?"

Keene grinned. "Go on."

"I'd like to borrow it for a week or two – if no one would miss it." She faced him and opened her mouth wide, saving him the trouble of miming horror and shock.

He laughed. "Pardon me if I said you take the biscuit. You take the whole bag of 'em." His eyes narrowed. "What would you do – I'm not saying it's possible – but what would you do if you did have the loan of it for a week?"

"One of Segal's colleagues, who was also there when I called – he mentioned that Segal had shown the photograph to some eminent surgeon called Sir William Gull, and . . ."

"Physician, not surgeon. He's the queen's physician. Sir William Gull."

"Oh!" Tessa was crestfallen. "Oh well in that case I suppose I'd better forget it."

"Forget what? What were you proposing to do?"

"Well, if he hadn't been quite so eminent as all that, I was going to make up some near-true story, and go and show him the photograph, and . . . well, just use it as a way of getting him to talk about . . . the mind and things like that." She put her hand to her mouth and laughed. "I'm beginning to sound a bit cracked myself, aren't I." But she was soon serious again. "However, if he's the queen's physician . . . that's that. He'd never agree to see me. Anyway, it's not important."

Keene stared at her shrewdly and appeared to be giving her suggestion quite some thought. But all he said was, "Hmm."

He straightened himself and became more brisk. "Must be moving on, I suppose," he told her. "My regards to your father."

She smiled with relief at not having provoked another lecture on intuition or meddlesomeness.

Keene saluted and walked away.

She turned to look through the cemetery railings, up the hill toward the little knot of mourners, including the Lairds, who were still a good furlong away. She began to think of the especial pain of surviving one's own children. She had lately finished a book on the Brontes, all of whom had died before their father, so the subject had been on her mind even before the Lairds had arrived.

Suddenly her attention was caught by a movement among the graves between her and the approaching party. She saw a man, dressed in full mourning. There was, of course, nothing odd in that – given the nature of the place. The oddity lay in his behaviour. He was standing where a statue of an angel, flanked by living cypresses, would conceal him from the funeral party (though not quite from the entrance, where Tessa stood); and from this semi-concealment he was watching the party through a pair of binoculars.

His arms grew weary. He lowered them. He turned, bringing himself to face the gate. Once again he began to raise his glasses, but halfway up he paused.

Tessa could not mistake that dark, full-bearded face. It was Dante Rosen. And he had seen her looking at him.

He raised his hat and bowed stiffly.

She made no response. Rosen, doubtless believing he had not, after all, been observed and that her apparent staring at him was mere chance, once again raised the glasses to his eyes – this time looking directly at her.

She was furious. Staring straight back at him she mouthed the word *wait* and began a brisk walk back into the cemetery and up the path. On the way she passed the Lairds, who looked questioningly at her, for she was sharing their carriage back to Islington.

"I've just noticed the custodian of the grounds," she explained, nodding vaguely in Rosen's direction. "I wish to have a particular word with him. I shan't be long."

As she drew near the angel and the cypresses, Rosen stepped out onto the path.

"Well, Mr. Rosen!" she challenged. "This is surely strange behaviour?"

Remembering all that Saunders had told her last night she approached him with a mingled loathing and fascination. He lifted up his cloak and from its folds produced an artist's sketching block, which he held out for her inspection. He smiled confidently. Those teeth had bitten Saunders' naked skin. She had a sudden, sharp picture of him doing it; she wondered what it felt like.

But when she saw the sketches he had made, her anger dwindled. Nothing else could have melted it so swiftly. His work was brilliant; his mastery of line and character was absolute. Every member of the little party who had so recently stood around the grave was there, immortalized. Mrs. Laird, gaunt and haggard with grief. Her husband, weatherbeaten and reserved. The others – all were unmistakably individuals.

She turned the pages. . . turned them back again. He was smiling at her. "Is something wrong, Miss d'Arblay?"

"No," she said hastily. But she could hear her own disappointment.

"Something missing, perhaps?"

"No."

He took the book from her and flipped through it to the final page – all the while his eyes never left hers. "Were you looking for these?" he asked. "I kept them especially apart. Such beauty is not to be mixed with common clay."

They were sketches of her. And, of course, they were exactly what she had been seeking. She caught her breath to see how sympathetically he had drawn her.

"To stand closer," he explained in that deep dark voice, "would have been an intrusion. Hence. . ." He patted his binoculars, now packed back in their case. "Corot actually used to paint landscapes with the help of binoculars."

She nodded. Looking at him, she knew exactly what Saunders meant when she said he needed only to crook his finger and she had followed. Tessa determined not to fall into the same trap. "I would have believed you without the authority of M. Corot," she told him sharply. "In any case, you still haven't explained why you came here *today*?"

"I'm often here."

"But why?"

He smiled at the sky, marshalling his thoughts. "We no longer live in a classical age, Miss d'Arblay. Art must move to the human extremities. Grief is one of them." He smiled, trying to provoke an answering smile from her. "In my work I explore them all. I should love to show them to you – all of them. One. . . by one.''

She ignored the hint. "But – today of all days, Mr. Rosen. You knew I'd be here. You knew Peter Laird was a friend of mine.''

"But of course I knew you'd be here.'' He laughed. "That's the whole point.''

She was not ready to face any of the potential conversations that might follow. "Very well,'' she said as she moved away.

"Miss d'Arblay?'' he called after her.

She turned the barest minimum necessary to show she was listening.

"I want to take up your offer.''

"What offer?''

"To come to your studio. To paint Old Friendly.''

"I've changed my mind about that. I don't think I want to see you again, Mr. Rosen.'' She walked away briskly enough, but even she could hear how hollow rang her tone.

Chapter Seven

The morning after the funeral Tessa took Saunders to her studio, which was in the least derelict corner of an ancient church property down a small back alley called Bleeding Heart Lane. The lane, which also contained the vicarage mews, lay just outside the back garden gate. Though Saunders had grown up only a mile or so away, she had never strayed into this part of Shoreditch and had no idea such a venerable building had survived.

"It goes right back to the fourteenth century, you know,'' Tessa said. "It used to be the church's tithe barn. But when the area got built up, they had to find other uses for it. The timbers of the original barn are still there, though. You'll see them. They form the gallery of the inner courtyard. The roof was taken off but the uprights were left. It's like a building turned inside-out.''

"Oh, I think I've heard about it. Is that the place that used to be a pub?"

Tessa pioneered a path among some half-weeded sweet peas. "Yes – or a coaching inn, anyway. But that was quite recently – in the seventeenth and eighteenth centuries. Before that it was" – she lowered her voice – "a disorderly house! Ben Jonson called it The Wenching Barn. Then it was a charnel house for suicides, because it's not on consecrated ground. The Boney Barn, they called it. After that it became The Old Thatched Barn. That's when it was a coaching inn – when they built the courtyard. Then for the last forty years or so it was a depot for the London and Blackwall Railway – the Barn Depot, they called it."

"It's always been barn-something or something-barn," Saunders pointed out. "What's it now? The Studio Barn?"

"Let's call it that! I don't often talk about it to anyone. My family pretends it doesn't exist."

"I wish I had a family like yours. Mine's so . . . *normal*."

Tessa laughed. "I'm sure you mean that as a compliment."

"Except Pol," Saunders added.

"What about Pol?" Tessa asked.

"She's what *we* pretend doesn't exist."

They stepped out by the back gate into Bleeding Heart Lane. Tyker, the groom, was washing the dogcart in the sun. "Morning, Miss d'Arblay," he called out. "You got a visitor." He nodded toward the studio.

Rosen! Tessa thought. But then she heard the voice: "Freedom!" it roared. "Freedom, lads! To live free men under God's free sky!"

"Old Friendly," she said.

There was a mighty crash. The two women exchanged glances and then, Tessa leading, ran toward the entrance. It was supposed to be blocked off but urchins and vagrants had forced holes in the hoardings. The old archway leading into the inner courtyard sagged dangerously, forcing them to creep in against the walls, where there was some illusion of safety.

The centuries-old dust still flew about the yard, pinpointing the site of this particular collapse. It was almost directly opposite the entrance arch; a section of the upper gallery had fallen in. When they arrived, coughing and out of breath, they saw that Old Friendly must have been standing just beside it; a single, small timber had felled him. He lay, unconscious and peaceful-looking, on a pile of old rubble at one edge of the new fall.

"We're in as much danger here as he is." Tessa checked superficially for broken bones but found none.

"Shall I go out and send your groom for an ambulance?" Saunders asked.

"Better still, ask him to bring the handcart in here – Tyker's his name. He'll have to break down the hoarding a bit. We'll take the old man round to the nuns' hospice in Cole Place. He's known there. If they find anything seriously wrong, they can send him on to the hospital at Mile End."

Saunders, glad to be leaving the ricketty old place, ran back the way they had just come. Tessa straightened out the old fellow and made him as comfortable as the heap of rubble allowed. His breathing was becoming irregular, she noticed. He reeked of spirits.

Saunders was soon back with Tyker and the handcart. The undernourished body was surprisingly light. The old man groaned and then settled again on his new bed of horse blankets. Tessa thought of the death carts in the Great Plague, over two centuries ago; perhaps they had trundled into this very courtyard: "Bring out your dead!" And perhaps at that time someone else had stood here and wondered whether the same ritual had not been enacted among these very timbers at that even earlier holocaust, the Black Death – now more than half a millenium ago. She often tried to imagine all the lives that had been encompassed by these now-crumbling walls, lives that still had some tenuous claim upon her and upon this age as long as brick stood upon brick or mortise clasped with tenon. But the span of those years was inconceivable to her. Even to try to think of it would bring on a frightening sense of hugeness and an imagined roaring, like the beat of colossal wings.

"Come on!" Saunders shouted, waking her from her reverie.

The hospice in Cole Place was run by the nuns of St. Ethelburga's. Tessa knew them moderately well. Her father's constant reference to Good Works (as a euphemism for her painting) had pricked her conscience from time to time and driven her down there to lend a hand. To test her resolve the nuns often gave her the worst tasks, but she didn't mind. There was satisfaction in hard physical work; it was almost a pleasure after a day at her easel, especially those days of mounting frustration and anger, which seemed to grow more, not less, frequent as she developed her skill and saw her shortcomings more clearly.

Sister Magda received them. Tessa liked her; she exuded the sort of calm all nuns were supposed to feel – half-solemn, half-joyful, all serene. Tessa had been surprised at its rarity. The amount of sniping and backbiting that went on among the sisterhood was dispiriting.

The nun looked over the old man and said, "He's not long for this world. Put him in Little Hospice. It's empty at the moment. You can get those rags off him and give him a lick and a promise. I'll bring a nightshirt."

When the nun had gone, Saunders said resentfully, "Who's she when the cat's at home?"

"One of the best," Tessa answered.

She was by now used to stripping the stinking rags off elderly and diseased bodies and washing them (or, if they were dying, giving them "a lick and a promise"). But she could feel that Saunders, though she held her silence, was uneasy. Tessa smiled to herself to think that she, who had never experienced anything more daring than a few chaste kisses, and could still count their total, was, in fact, less prudish at this work than Saunders, who had almost certainly done It. She wondered if women ever talked about It.

Sister Magda brought the nightshirt, which the three of them eased around the dying man. His breathing was now rapid and shallow.

"What about a doctor?" Tessa asked.

"There's not much point," the sister said. "I should think he's got a liver like a thundercloud. Old Friendly has downed his last gulp of Old Friendly, anyway."

"Drank himself to death," Saunders said.

"We'll stay by him," Tessa offered. "I owe him that. I wish I had my sketchbook. No! That's selfish."

They sat in the quiet of the dying, one each side of the bed, and spoke, for some reason, of childhood. Old Friendly had once, in a lucid moment, told Tessa of his first memory – seeing the Duke of Wellington ride in triumph through London after Waterloo. He had been taken to the parade by an old man who remembered the first time people sang *Rule, Britannia,* which was almost a century and a half ago, now. Tessa repeated these memories for Saunders and added, "If I live into my eighties, it'll be nineteen-forty, and I can tell my grandchildren I once met a man who once met a man who sang *Rule, Britannia* at its birth, two centuries ago!"

And that was what started them talking of childhood.

Tessa, an only child, remembered hers as a time of innocence, when ferocious play and eager learning and solemn duty had flowed together in one headlong, passionate progress.

Saunders, respectably poor, but living closer to outright depravity, could never have called her young girlhood "innocent". She had walked a narrow path on the edge of the abyss; daily she had been able to peer into its depths and see the damned at their pleasures. Whatever virtues she had – she chose them. And yet, for all that worldly wisdom there was still an irreducible innocence at the heart of her, which made her capable now of asking, "D'you still wonder what you're going to be when you grow up? I do. Even though I know all I ever want is to be an actress."

"Don't you want a home?" Tessa asked. "And a husband and children?"

"No." Saunders sniffed. "Which doesn't mean I won't get lumbered with them, I suppose."

"Yes," Tessa said, matching her tone to that of Saunders. "All I really want to do is paint. But I'll probably end up a vicar's wife."

Saunders looked at her askance. Tessa asked why.

"Well – when I said lumbered, I meant *having* to. But I didn't think vicars. . . you know. Not vicars. Non-commissioned preachers, yes, maybe. . ."

"You mean nonconformist preachers?"

"Something like that. They're devils, those lads. They know what they're at! Give a hellfire sermon and get the girls all worked up. Oh – they *know*! There's one can't keep himself out of Pol's house. But I wouldn't have thought it of your regular right-down vicars."

Tessa laughed. She was about to seize her chance and ask Saunders about It when Sister Magda came in and handed Tessa a card.

Her heart began to race. She read:

Dante Rosen
The Garrick Club
The New English Art Club

"He's here?" she asked with studied casualness.

"In the lobby."

"I'd better see him, I suppose. Do you mind?"

Sister Magda said no.

"D'you want to stay?" Tessa passed the card over to Saunders, who disguised her fear in melodrama; she looked at the sister. "Can I turn nun for about three minutes? Or is there a back door?"

Sister Magda smiled. "There are three back doors."

"Good, I'll take all of them." At the threshold she turned back and said to Tessa, "If you can keep the Demon here for an hour, I'll get my brother-in-law to go up to Segal's and collect my box."

Tessa promised to do what she could.

Rosen strode in like a lord of creation. His elegance could not have stood in stronger contrast to the austerity of the hospice. Tessa knew that, no matter what Saunders said against him, no matter what the truth about him might turn out to be, he was the only man who excited her – the only man who could stir her passions in this complex way, which included both fascination *and* dislike, wanting *and* fear.

He looked down at Old Friendly. "They told me," he said. "I came to see you in your studio. That groom of yours told me."

"Did you come to apologize?" she asked.

But he seemed not to hear her; he was staring down at the old man still. "Death," he murmured. "Dying. . . what is it? Night's black messenger."

She felt this high-flown image trivialized something that were better dignified by silence, or even by the inconsequential chatter of everyday life. She saw him suddenly as a visitor from an alien circle, from a literary-artistic London that had little meaning here.

He pulled out his sketchbook and, throwing aside his cloak and hat, sat himself down at the foot of the bed and began sketching intently. "Last chance," he said in quite a different – more honest – tone.

Silence reigned for several minutes.

"What are you thinking?" he asked.

55

"I'm thinking you're pretty ruthless."

He laughed. "Don't you suppose an artist has to be?" When she didn't answer he added, "There are thousands of very talented people about, you know. One big difference between the best of them and genius is . . . 'ruthlessness', to give it your name."

"Is there anything you wouldn't paint or draw?" she asked.

He smiled at the simplicity of the question. "Well now. If you were to come rushing in to wake me up at two in the morning to say there was the most gorgeous sunset and a cheeky little wirehaired terrier with a red rose between its jaws – I might just not spring to my easel with . . ."

"No!" Tessa laughed. "You know what I mean. Is there anything too horrible?"

He looked up and held her with his eye. A shiver ran through her. "I'm not sure I understand," he said. "Tell me your idea of what's horrible."

She shook her head.

"Drowning kittens?" he suggested sarcastically. "Pulling wings off dear little butterflies?"

His teasing stung her. "You know Saunders has left Dr. Segal," she told him.

A fleeting anger passed across his face; then he smiled again. "In point of fact, it's we who've left Saunders. She had no more to offer us."

"Is there a sudden abundance of unbruised skin up at that house then?" she asked sharply.

His eyebrows shot up. He looked at her with a new respect. "I see. What a box of surprises you are! I imagine there's no need to ask where she's employed now?"

"Did you draw all those goings on?" she asked.

"Don't confuse relentlessness with ruthlessness," he said.

"But did you?"

"Goings on?" He snorted a single laugh. "What has Saunders told you? D'you think you got the truth out of her? D'you imagine she's capable of recognizing truth even if she saw it? Her mind is a crowded rabble of half-resolved characters, all aspiring to be middle class."

Tessa bit her lip, trying not to laugh, despite her anger.

"What's worse," Rosen went on, "she hasn't bothered to

56

introduce them to each other, so, like all true bourgeois, lacking an introduction, they cannot possibly talk among themselves. If they could, they might combine into a trade union and force some kind of discipline upon their creator.''

Tessa could no longer contain her laughter; it was all so true. "What really happened then?" she asked. "What was all that about a pig?"

For reply he flipped through the pages of his sketchbook and held it open at a quick study of a nude woman – unmistakably Saunders – sitting joyfully astride a large, amused-looking pig, drawn as if trotting; one of her arms was raised in a salutation of triumph.

"It's brilliant," she agreed. "But why?"

"That's the one question you can't ask about Art. Art is its own sufficient reason. The whyness of things is for Science. The whatness is Art's demesne."

"Did she have to sit *on* the pig, though? It hurt her, you know."

"Hurt? Go on – it made her uncomfortable."

"Was it necessary, though?"

He looked at her speculatively. "I take it," he said, "you're going to get her to pose for you?"

Tessa nodded.

"But she hasn't yet done so?"

"She's agreed to. We were going to begin this morning, but. . ." She pointed toward Old Friendly.

"Well, when you start you'll soon discover that if you don't give her something to keep her mind on her work, that rabble inside her begins to creep out of its hiding places and then it takes her over."

"It all seems so reasonable when you say it. Her version is so different."

He resumed his sketching of Old Friendly. "Her version? You've only heard *one* of her versions."

A bar of sunlight had stolen slowly up the bed. Flies chased among its dust motes in darts of lightning blue and shimmering black. In that spotlight the old man did not merely resemble, he *became*, a prophet of old. His wrinkled flesh clung to his bones as if a vacuum plucked at it from within.

She was glancing sideways over Rosen's shoulder, peeking at

his sketch and almost dying of envy. What a facility he had – to capture so much of life in so few lines! There was something magical, something almost frightening, about it.

"How?" she asked.

"Genius," he told her.

She looked sharply at him but he wasn't joking. He glanced at her. His right eyebrow went down, the other shot up. Deep folds marked the resulting crush of skin. She had an image of herself running her lips over those corrugations, but she suppressed it.

"What about all the magic and mumbo-jumbo?" she asked.

"It amuses Segal. He needs it, too. Some people need a drink before they can relax and talk. He needs his little rituals. We all need something."

"And mesmerism?"

He glanced sharply at her. "You have been talking a lot! Or someone has. Yes – mesmerism, too. Segal needs it. I don't. For me it's a parlour game."

"You don't deny it then."

"Why should I? A mere parlour game, as I say. People think it's some kind of divine gift. Perhaps it is. But tell me this – suppose every time you wanted to paint you only had to make a few passes over the canvas and abracadabra! – there was a finished masterpiece. Would you still be interested in painting?"

She shook her head.

"You see. Even if you had the gift, you wouldn't use it. You need to do it the hard way. As I was saying – people have their needs. They're tied to them – obsessed by them. But the secret of life, or so it seems to me, is to find which of our needs we can safely shed."

"You talk as if you're above it all!" she sneered.

He gazed at her solemnly. "Not at all, Miss d'Arblay. I, too, have my needs."

She blushed. He smiled to see it. "A clean sheet of paper and a good drawing pencil, for instance," he said. Then his attitude suddenly changed. "I'm a fool," he confessed. "You ask serious questions, important questions, and I play games with you. Forgive me."

"You haven't honestly explained your obsession with . . . rottenness, as Saunders calls it. I don't think it's enough to say

58

that Art justifies itself. If it really is so completely neutral, you couldn't sneer at sunsets and roses, could you."

He nodded at the truth of it. "You constantly surprise me, Miss d'Arblay. I don't imagine your experience of life. . . people. . . the world, in all its infuriating variety – your experience of these things is not all that great, would you say?"

"Of course it isn't. How could it be?"

He smiled. "That's quite another question. It could very easily be enlarged, you know. But the fact remains that at the moment your worldly experience could be crammed into a thimble. And yet your thinking about it is really quite profound. You have a gift for seeing things almost *without* experience. I wonder what sort of painter you are?"

"Heavens! Very ordinary – quite the amateur."

He shook his head, as if to say he'd no longer take her word for it. Then, remembering the thread, he said, "You want to know why Saunders-with-pig is preferable to roses-at-sunset."

"I want to understand why you and so many others share this obsession with sickness, death. . . rottenness!"

"Hmmm. I wonder if you could shed your obvious need for middle-class moral scruples?" His tone did not invite comment. Then, it seemed, a memory struck him. "It's like something Oscar once told me. I asked him the same question, you see, in my days of youth and innocence – oh yes, I also had them!"

"What did he say?"

"He said, 'It's like feasting with panthers, Rosen.'" He turned to her. "D'you understand that, Miss d'Arblay? Feasting with panthers!"

The image was so vivid and yet so precise that, for a moment, she more than understood. Its meaning actually possessed her. For that flash of time she and the image were one, and to feast with panthers was the only purpose in life. Its passing was like a new weaning; it left her immediate world more drab.

"Have you read *A Rebours* by Huysmans?" he asked. "That'd explain a great deal to you."

"'Against the Grain'," she translated.

"Not bad! Though in this case 'Against Nature' would be better. Yes – 'Against Nature'. Shall I lend it to you or are you one of those tiresome people who only has to have a book recommended and you know you'll never read it in your life?"

59

"What's it about?"

He smiled at her directness. "The last frail descendant of an ancient aristocratic family turns his back on the world and devotes all his time to the cultivation of his senses. Not coarsely, you understand. Quite the reverse. He seeks the perfection of refinement in sensations that are ever-more exquisite and obscure. There are some marvellous chapters on perfumes, for instance."

He was drawing again, now. Avidly. His pencil flew across the page. To Tessa each new line seemed to make it perfectly complete – until the next was added and she realized she had been mistaken. It was like a rising note that went on rising in power and beauty, yet never became a scream or passed beyond audibility. She wondered if he would ever reach that stroke which would finally overburden the drawing – was there a limit to this special magic of his fingers?

"Well?" he asked.

"I don't know when I'll get time to read it."

Chapter Eight

When Rosen had gone Tessa helped lay out Old Friendly and then, late in the afternoon, went home. Spencer, the above-stairs maid at the vicarage, told her that Saunders was unpacking her boxes, which her brother-in-law had brought over from Finsbury Close. Tessa went up to change and to wash away the smell of poverty, but Bo waylaid her before she reached her room. "Who is that extraordinarily pleasant young lady one meets here and there about the house?" she asked.

"D'you mean Saunders?" Tessa replied in unbelief.

"Oh do I? She was most courteous to me. And so well spoken, too."

It didn't sound much like Saunders, but it couldn't be anybody else. "Old Friendly's dead," she told her aunt. "I've been helping the nuns to lay him out."

"Old what? Do I know this person?"

"Old Friendly. Yes. I showed you some drawings once."

Fleeting distaste shot across the older woman's face. "If only you could try your hand at some pretty little water colours!" she said in a rare moment of bluntness. "Husbands don't object to that sort of talent, you know." She sighed and looked around for some distraction. Finding none, she said, "Your father's getting worse. If he doesn't press for a curate soon, I shall talk to the bishop myself. I had to go into his study and tear up his sermon for Sunday. It was quite impossible."

Tessa said wearily, "I am not going to intervene any more in this cat-and-dog business between you two. You go around dressing like mother simply to provoke him – don't try to deny it, I know you do, and it's most heartless of you. And the only way he can see to get his own back is to give those sermons, just to embarrass you. But you're the one who starts it. If only you'd wear your own things, and do your hair the way you used . . ."

"If this pleasant young lady is going to be staying for a while, I hope you'll take lessons in courtesy from her."

"I hope she'll teach me a great deal more than that!"

The front doorbell rang.

"She is a model of gentility. Have you prepared a room for her?"

"She's sharing my room. It's more than big enough."

"Oh." Bo frowned. "No midnight feasting, mind!"

Tessa gave up. She was about to go to her room when Spencer came upstairs to say that Sergeant Keene was waiting below and wished to see her. She followed the maid down. The sergeant was standing in the hall, taking a mental inventory of everything – though he must have seen it all dozens of times before.

"Have they offered you some refreshment, Sergeant Keene?" she asked. "A glass of beer, perhaps?"

"That'd be most acceptable, Miss d'Arblay. I hope I don't intrude?"

"Not at all. That must mean you're not on duty. Come into the drawing room."

He followed her in. She pulled the bell cord. "I said this means you're not on duty?"

His eyes narrowed. "I don't know, miss."

The maid came in. Tessa asked her to fetch a glass of beer for the sergeant.

"I've been thinking about our conversation in the cemetery yesterday." He rearranged his cuffs several times as he spoke. "I'm uneasy, I don't mind admitting it. I don't like to hear that Dr. Segal and Peter Laird were known to each other."

Tessa smiled. "Don't say you have some *intuition* about it, Sergeant Keene? Forsooth!"

He rolled about awkwardly in his chair. "I knew you'd bring up that! Well let me tell you, my clever young lass, the intuition of a detective sergeant who's seen as many years service as me is quite a different kettle of fish from mere *feminine* intuition!"

Tessa, enjoying his discomfiture, closed her eyes and shuddered with distaste: "Even so – intuition is intuition!"

The maid came with the beer – in an earthenware cup on a silver tray. It brought Tessa down a peg or ten.

"You see how often *we* entertain!" she told him.

Keene sipped at the cup and nodded, as at a friend glimpsed across the bar. "I've tasted worse in cut crystal," he complimented her.

"To be serious, though," Tessa went on, "isn't it a bit like opening up an old wound? I mean, suppose poor old Peter was involved in some kind of witchcraft or flagellation business – there's no point in raking it all up now, is there? And if Segal's involved, too, that would give him every reason to say nothing. It's a sleeping dog, don't you think?"

"Very likely." He nodded. "Yes – very likely. And yet I can't just leave it there."

"So what are you proposing to do?"

"That's the rub, Miss d'Arblay." Again he fidgeted uncomfortably. "I think there's Freemasonry in it. Which makes it difficult for me, if you see what I mean."

"Not quite."

"Most of the senior members of the Force are Masons. I could end up getting my knuckles rapped."

"For cowardice?" she taunted.

"Yes – the same kind of cowardice as stops you trying to fly out of your bedroom window. So I've been thinking. And what I've been thinking, Miss d'Arblay, is that it wasn't a bad wheeze of yours – going to see Sir William Gull."

She stared a him suspiciously but held her peace.

"Yes," he went on, "not half a bad wheeze. You could, ah, show him the photo and see what sort of response you get."

Tessa fell into the trap. "*If* I had the photo," she answered – thinking that was the objection.

But he drew forth a small manilla envelope and, leaning forward with a smile, laid it on the table at her side.

"Also if I had any intention of doing it," she added lamely.

"I'd be very grateful." There was a twinkling assurance in his eye; he knew she'd agree.

"But I can't just knock on his door. What can I say to him?"

Keene grinned. "The number of criminals I've seen come to grief because they had to back up someone else's lies! No – much better you invent your own tale, miss. You won't come unstuck so fast."

When the sergeant had gone, Tessa went upstairs, the envelope in her hand and half a dozen unlikely stories running through her head.

If she had not expected to find Saunders in her room, she would never have recognized the quietly elegant young woman who sat demurely in the window seat, reading the poems of Emily Bronte. She was wearing a prim little pair of spectacles; her hair was quite different; the sit of her shoulders – the whole cut of her – was so utterly un-Saunders-like that Tessa could only stand there with her mouth open, the photograph and all else forgotten.

"'Ello, ducks!" Saunders said in broad cockney and laughed.

Tessa made her stand up and turn about and face the light – and still she could hardly credit the transformation.

"Which of you is the real Saunders?" she asked.

"I don't know. Is there an *r* in the month? What's in the embalope, then?"

Tessa sighed and told her what sort of problem Keene had just dumped in her lap.

Saunders pulled a face. Tessa asked why. "I don't think you ought to mess around in Rosen's affairs. What did he want, anyway – at the nunnery?"

"Nothing really."

"What did he say to you?"

"Nothing of importance."

"But charming with it – yes, I know. You won't listen to me, will you! That man is evil. You should just stay clear of him."

Tessa smiled and brandished the envelope. "But this is Segal, not Rosen."

Saunders shook her head. "If it's Segal then it *is* Rosen. You tell your sergeant friend no thanks."

"I tried. Honestly, I tried. But it's just because he is a friend you see. Anyway, it seems such a little thing to do. I don't imagine I'm going to learn anything from Sir William, even if he does agree to see me. And suppose I do? I'll just pass it on to Sergeant Keene and then we can forget it."

Saunders gave a trapped sort of sigh. "I could talk myself blue. Well – someone's got to protect you." She grinned with sudden relish at the role. "Here – shall I find out if there's anything known against Sir William, to his discredit? Something we could threaten him with? Pol could find out easily enough."

"Your mind always turns first to the very fringe of what's legal, doesn't it!"

"All right, then – chivalry. That's always the second-best way with those who fancy themselves gentlemen. We shall demise some appeal to his chivalry."

"Devise."

"Something like that. Have you got *Kelly's Handbook to the Upper Ten Thousand*? Let's see what sort of gentleman we're dealing with."

A few minutes later she said, "Crimes! Look at that! You read it, Miss d'Arblay. It's all jawbreakers to me."

Tessa paraphrased: "He lives at number seventy-four Upper Brook Street, Mayfair. He's retired from general practice but he remains the personal physician of the Prince of Wales, the Physician-in-Ordinary to the Queen, the Fullerian Professor of Physiology at the Royal Institution, a gold medallist of the University of London, and the Resident Physician of Guy's Hospital. He's also on the London University Senate. I expect he knows *everyone*!"

"Except you. Still, you can't find a needle without a haystack, as they say. So pick up that pen."

Together they concocted a letter to Sir William explaining that Tessa was a relative of a man who had died recently. The family doctor had certified death as being due to a cerebral tumour. There had been a post-mortem to confirm it. She herself quite accepted the finding but her mother refused to believe it; indeed, she was so distressed by it all that Tessa feared for her sanity. It would make *such* a difference if she could tell her mother she'd visited the greatest physician in London, who had taken one look at a photograph of the tumour and had said without hesitation ("as I'm quite sure you *will* say, Sir William") that the family doctor and all the other doctors involved had been right. Would Sir William, she concluded, consider coming out of retirement for just thirty seconds to perform this great act of mercy and set at rest the mind of a dear old lady whose declining years might otherwise . . . and so on.

They posted it at once, before second thoughts and wiser counsels could dissuade them.

The following evening the fifth and last delivery of the day brought a brief reply in Sir William's own hand: "Please be so good as to call upon me tomorrow at three p.m. when I shall endeavour to set your mother's mind at rest. But do not bring her – in case I am unable to provide the assurances you seek. Perhaps an aunt, or some other relative, might accompany you?"

"It's a good thing he wrote 'p.m.'," Saunders said, reading the letter over Tessa's shoulder, "else we just might have gone there in the small hours."

"We?" Tessa asked.

"Well – are you going to take your Aunt Bo?"

Tessa thought it over. "I know I'm tempting the gods, Saunders, but I suppose it'll have to be you."

"I won't let you down, Miss d'Arblay. It'll be the performance of my life."

"Oh no! Oh no! Oh no! Anything but that. You're my married sister-in-law – with a . . . sore throat or something. Just sit tight and croak occasionally. You understand?"

"Look – don't worry."

"It's an order now, Saunders. You try any grand-dame nonsense and you're out on your ear."

The following afternoon, Tyker drove them in the dogcart through the West End, up Bond Street, and into Brook Street. It was so long since Tessa had been in this part of London she'd forgotten how fine the houses looked and how rich people were. The smallness of Islington and the general down-at-heel grime of the East End had come to seem normal.

Tessa herself was far from poor. In fact, thanks to a legacy from her Great-Aunt Jessica Body (for whom the Wheal Jessica tin mine once earmarked for Bosinney had eventually been named), she enjoyed an income of about three thousand pounds a year; but she spent very little of it. No one outside the family knew she had money, and she wanted to keep it so. She couldn't understand how people could flaunt their money the way they did ''up West,'' as East Enders called it.

At precisely three they rang the bell at number seventy-four, Sir William's London home.

Chapter Nine

They were admitted almost at once and shown straight into the drawing room, which overlooked the street. The lace-curtained windows framed the drooping head of Dresden, their horse. Tyker was fixing his nosebag.

Tessa approved of the room; it betrayed a simple taste. There were no more than two dozen ornaments, most of them in a Chinese Chippendale cabinet facing the door. The rest of the furniture was antique, too, and of the same period as the cabinet. From ''Great Men of Our Times'' she knew that Sir William had begun life in humble circumstances, the son of a poor widow at Thorpe-le-Soken in Essex. Had it not been for a kindly local rector, who taught the boy free, he would never have entered medical school. From there he had gone on to become, after nearly fifty years in practice, the richest doctor in London. Some said he was the richest doctor in history. Yet the house was more like the house of, say, a younger son of an old aristocratic family sent out to make his own way in the world with the gift of a house in Mayfair and some old, unfashionable furniture from the family home. Perhaps it was more important to Sir William to aspire to what he lacked – an ancient lineage – than to parade what all the world knew he possessed – money.

She decided that if ever she lived in a ''grand house,'' it should be no grander than this.

"Well well well!" Saunders said. She had made a beeline for the bureau and was avidly reading the letters scattered upon it. Tessa had no time to scold her, for Sir William could be heard approaching. Saunders must have had the ears of a bat for, by the time he entered, she was already six feet from the bureau and admiring a dull little portrait.

"Miss d'Arblay, I hope I've not kept you waiting long?" Sir William was a powerfully built man of medium height. Though he was in his seventy-second year, he did not look it. He walked across the room with a slight limp, but his movements were still agile.

He was every inch the sort of man you'd expect to be the queen's physician – courteous, grave, and exuding a massive confidence. Tessa felt doomed; what had seemed so easy in her imagination was now revealed as impossible. Full of misgiving she introduced him to "her cousin, Mrs. Saunders, from the country".

Saunders said, "I'm from your part of the world, I believe, Sir William – Thorpe-le-Soken?"

Tessa stared at her in astonishment. Hastily she began to fish in her bag for the photograph.

But she wasn't fast enough. Sir William picked up the name with delight. "Thorpe-le-Soken, eh! You know I grew up there? Were you born there, Mrs. Saunders?"

Tessa stared at her "sister-in-law," trying to project the shriek that rang through her head: "Shut up! Shut up – you idiotic creature!"

"Oh no, Sir William, I'm from London. But we live in that part of Essex now – and I wasn't in Thorpe half an hour before I'd been told of you. You're *the* Essex hero!"

He basked in it, of course. Then he began to ply her with questions about the local families. Tessa, heart-in-mouth, listened as Saunders neatly side-stepped: She and "hubby" didn't actually live in Thorpe but in St. Osyth, several miles away. . . their circle of friends lay more in Frinton and Bridlington – and, anyway, they didn't move in Sir William's salted circles.

"Exalted circles!" Sir William echoed, hearing the expected word rather than the actual one. He seemed about to say more – perhaps to tell them something of his childhood there – but his hesitation gave Tessa the chance she had been

67

awaiting. She leaped in: "We don't wish to trespass upon your valuable time, Sir William . . ." She held the envelope containing the photograph tentatively toward him.

But his thoughts were a hundred miles away. "Thorpe-le-Soken!" he said quietly. "I think my next visit there will be my final one." He smiled at them. "I mean, I think I'll be carried there."

Tessa began to see that Saunders's intervention might not, after all, have been so disastrous. It had certainly broken the ice. Sir William was no longer the grave royal physician. "Surely that's many, many years away!" she protested, thrusting the envelope a little nearer.

He sighed. "I think not, Miss d'Arblay. I had a minor stroke last year, you know. You may have noticed that I still limp from it?"

She assured him she had not.

"And one or two little incidents since. These are the signs, you know. These are the signs."

His frankness struck her as only slightly odd. After all, with a family like hers, her yardstick of other people's behaviour was a mile long. And anyway, seventy-one-year-old retired gentlemen were entitled to their eccentricities.

"Talking of signs, Sir William," she said. "I wonder if you would mind telling us the signs of a cerebral tumour – in a person's behaviour, I mean?"

He threw up his hands. "My dear young lady, they are so varied. One of my patients would keep hearing an express train. Yes! Roaring into his head on this side and out through the other. The only effect it had on his behaviour was that he couldn't help ducking every time he heard it." He laughed loudly. "Another man developed morbid fears of being attacked. Carried a looking glass to see around every corner. Others behave erratically – solemn as judges one minute, skittish as schoolgirls the next – and quite unaware of any change. Extraordinary. So, you see, you can't be dogmatic. Suppose you describe your unfortunate relative's behaviour in the weeks before his death – and I'll tell you if it sounds like the work of a tumour."

"He died completely unaware he had any such affliction."

"Are you sure, Miss d'Arblay? Perhaps he concealed it from you?"

"I doubt it, Sir William. He was not the sort of man to do that, believe me!"

"Well, that is most unusual, I must say. Show me the photograph. You mentioned a photograph in your letter."

His fingers reached out for the envelope, took it, and delved within.

When he pulled out the photograph his whole manner changed. He froze. He frowned. He darted an accusing glance at the two women. He looked at the photograph once more, looked at the back of it, shook his head, then stared at Tessa with an expression poised between bewilderment and anger. "Is this a prank of some kind?" he asked.

"Why, no." Tessa felt her mouth going dry. "I assure you, Sir William. Why? Is that not a brain tumour?"

"You didn't tell me the name of the doctor?" he said, making a question of it.

"Dr. Crawford," Tessa gave the name of their own family doctor. But just half a second behind her Saunders said, "It was Dr. Segal!"

Tessa felt her fingernails digging into her palms through the kid of her gloves.

"Well – which?" Sir William looked from one to the other; all his charm had vanished.

"Connie, dear. You weren't there," Tessa said with steely firmness.

Saunders came back with: "It was Dr. Segal who did the actual post mortal. He took that photograph, Tessa my sweet."

"Segal?" Sir William said agrily. "Did you say Segal? I didn't properly catch you the first time. Is that Dr. Gwyllam Segal of Finsbury Close?"

"The self and very same," Saunders said dramatically.

He looked back at the picture. "And Dr. Segal claims this is his photograph, taken during the course of your late relative's post-mortem examination? I find that hard indeed to believe."

"Is something wrong with it, Sir William?" Tessa asked, quite certain now that their imposture was in shreds.

To her surprise he smiled at her – a smile of commiseration. "Something is very wrong with it, Miss d'Arblay. It could not be more wrong. I suspect you are the victims of . . . well, of *what* I hardly know."

He pushed the photograph back into its envelope and gazed pensively out of the window. Suddenly he started from his reverie. "I say, is that your horse out there?"

"Yes."

"Oh. I thought you'd come by omnibus."

"By omnibus?" Tessa had never travelled on a bus in her life.

He smiled at her surprise. "I go everywhere I can by omnibus," he told her. "They've improved so much of late – you really ought to try them, you know. Why pay a cabman a shilling for a twopenny journey, eh? And the view from the upper deck – why, it's a new London if you've only ever seen it from a carriage. In fact," – he pulled out a fob watch and snapped open its lid – "at this hour I usually take the 'Bayswater' to Elgin Crescent and walk back home through the park. The good old dark-green 'Bayswater'." He rubbed his hands together. "May I be so bold as to suggest that we take your carriage and go for a short drive now – as far as Kensington Gardens, perhaps? It's such a fine day."

Here was another change. He was now a jolly uncle. But there was something forced about it. His jollity was masking a worry; his eyes were not smiling at all.

Saunders rose happily to her feet. "What a glorious notion!" she said.

Tessa reminded her that theirs was no "carriage" – just an ordinary dogcart. But Sir William was not so easily put off. He said a dogcart was a step up from a humble omnibus, and in any case the fashionable hour in the park was over; it wouldn't matter if they went on a beer dray.

At this point Tessa learned that Saunders's amazing gift of mimicry did not extend to laughing in a middle-class accent; the kind of laughter she now emitted could be heard every day, braying through any alehouse window east of St. Paul's.

Sir William recognized it, too. It produced a subtle change in his manner. Toward Tessa he continued to behave with the reserve and correctness of a gentleman. But toward Connie Saunders he began to relax. His jollity became more natural. Of the queen's physician not a trace remained.

"In any case," he was saying as he stood up to usher them back into the hall, "the police may move your coachman on. The street's rather narrow just at this point, you see."

70

"It's my belief narrow streets should be closed to thorough-traffic," Saunders said grandly. "Narrow streets should be kept for Presbyterians."

Tessa held her breath, but Sir William, after an initial grunt of surprise, produced a burst of laughter. "I say, Mrs. Saunders – *narrow* streets for Presbyterians! That's very good, you know. And *broad* streets for Church of England, eh?"

When he had on his hat and gloves and they were seated in the dogcart (not to say squashed, when it came to him and Saunders), he said, "One good joke deserves another. I heard a splendid little tale at dinner last night. This'll amuse you. The peas they served with the duck had lost their colour and George Grossmith said they should be sent down to Acton. Of course, none of us could see any point in it. But then he explained – Acton's the best way to Turnham Green!" He chuckled again at the joke. "Turn 'em green, you see? Turn the peas green!"

By the time they were in the park – in public view, that is – he was serious again. They went in by the Stanhope Gate and cut straight across to The Ring. The park was bright in its newly washed greenery. The fashionable crowd had gone home to tea and Rotten Row was now occupied by the demimonde, so the dogcart stayed on the respectable Ladies' Mile. There were plenty of ordinary people about, enjoying the sun.

A cooling breeze came off the waters of the Serpentine, where a half-dozen or so hackney rowing boats were milling around in the usual incompetent way. Sir William watched them scornfully for a moment and then cried out to Tyker, "Stop!" His manner became crisp. He smiled at the two women and said, "Twenty minutes in a little rowing boat, eh? Once round the Serpentine. Show those nincompoops how to do it?" It was not really a question; he was already getting out.

"What a romp this is!" Saunders said in a half-whisper to Tessa while Sir William made the arrangements with the boatman. Tessa, worried at what the exertion of rowing might do to an elderly gentleman who had already suffered one stroke, not to mention several "little incidents," hissed, "I'll give you romp when this is done!"

Tessa offered to row but Sir William was adamant. "What Essex mudlark would yield an oar to a lady, eh, Mrs. Saunders?" he cried jovially as he handed them into the unsteady little craft.

"Even so, Sir William," she answered, "I expect you'd sooner it was on The Naze than here on the Serpentine. Especially on such an egregious day."

He seemed not to notice her quaint and variant usages. A faraway look came into his eyes. "The Naze!" he sighed. "I was destined for the navy, you know – as a boy."

"You'd have been Admiral-of-the-Fleet by now," Saunders said.

Goaded by the compliment he plied the oars with a strength that surprised the women; the little boat nudged them both hard through the crush of their bustles. But he soon settled to a gentler pace; after all, they had nowhere to go but there and back.

He eased oar when they were half-way out – about fifty yards from the boat stage. That sharp, businesslike manner returned as he delved into an inside pocket and produced the photograph. "And now there's no possibility of our being overheard," he said, "will you kindly explain the meaning of all this?"

He was looking straight at Tessa. She felt she had no choice but to tell the entire truth – leaving out only Sergeant Keene's name.

"So you've lied to me," he said. "And no little lie, either."

Tessa answered, "I told you as near to the truth as I felt I could. There are others to protect."

"You gave me a reason that would flatter my vanity."

"I gave you a reason that would keep you out of any further inquiry – unless you yourself chose to take part."

He thought awhile and nodded. "Yes, I see that." Enigmatically, he added, "You weren't to know."

"Is Dr. Segal an acquaintance of yours, Sir William?" she asked. "Or even, perhaps, a friend – since you know his address, I mean. In any case, am I to assume his diagnosis is correct?"

He shrugged. "As to that, young lady, I'm afraid I cannot say. You see, this photograph is not Dr. Segal's at all. Nor has it the slightest connection with your late friend's post-mortem."

"Are you sure?" The question was out before she realized she might have phrased it better.

He smiled. "As sure as I am of anything in this world. I can even tell you – that photograph is of the brain of an old man who died in the Guy's asylum about ten years ago. His name was John Jepson." Sir William saw Tessa frown and he smiled. "You wonder how I can be so sure? I'll tell you – the photograph, you

72

see, is mine.''

"Yours!''

"Mine. A month ago – six weeks perhaps – Dr. Segal came to see me about . . . on another matter. And – quite in passing – he asked me if I had a good, clear photograph of a particular type of brain tumour. He wanted it, he said, to assist in an identification. I gave him a stereoscopic pair.'' Sir William held up the photo. "This print is one of that pair.''

Tessa absorbed this news in silence – a silence that Saunders, mercifully, did nothing to shatter. In fact, she was staring at Sir William in something like awe.

"I imagine,'' Tessa went on, "that Dr. Segal made a simple mistake. He must have attached the wrong photograph to his report. Isn't that the most likely explanation?''

Sir William shook his head. "Of all explanations, young lady, that is the least likely, I'm afraid. Our physical individuality is not just in our faces, you know. It runs throughout our frames. I was no surgeon but I've conducted hundreds of post mortems in my time and I can tell you, I never saw any two innards that were more alike than any two faces.''

Tessa sighed. She had been hoping to go back to Keene with a simple little tale. Now it turned out that not only had Segal lied to her about tumours having no symptoms, he had told a far worse lie to the court.

"May I ask what you intend to do about it, my dear?'' Sir William's voice was gentle, but his eyes, which never left her face, were unreadable.

"Nothing, Sir William. I don't want anything more to do with it. In any case, the photograph was stolen from *you*.''

He cleared his throat delicately. "So you will leave it to me to deal with Dr. Segal?''

"Gladly!''

He smiled broadly. "That is most satisfactory. He shall live to regret it – that I can promise you. Now, I'll be obliged to both of you if you'll refrain from mentioning this anywhere we might be overheard.''

All the way back to Brook Street he was the jovial uncle once again. He was even able to convey an invitation to Mrs. Saunders: On her next visit to London she was to be sure to look him up and bring him all the news of Thorpe-le-Soken. He did

73

not, however, invite them back indoors. They had to go to Claridge's, farther along Brook Street, for tea and the calls of nature. That, in turn, meant Tessa had to postpone the blistering row she had stoked up for Saunders.

Chapter Ten

"He knows George Grossmith!" Saunders was filled with awe. "I expected the queen's physician would be someone important, but I never thought he'd be quite so important as that."

Tessa coldly selected a Vienna pastry and asked, "Who's George Grossmith?" Even the Claridge's waiter, trained as he was, raised an eyebrow.

"Who's George Grossmith!" Saunders echoed. "Who created the part of Robin Oakapple in *Ruddigore* last year? That's all! And Ko-Ko in *The Mikado*? And the Lord Chancellor in *Iolanthe*?"

"And Bunthorne in *Patience*," the waiter chipped in. "And Stanley in *The Pirates*."

"Now you're before my time," Saunders told him. She turned to Tessa. "See? Everyone knows George Grossmith. Haven't you read *A Society Clown* yet? His memoirs. Everyone's talking about them. And what about his brother, Weedon? Sir Henry Irving's just engaged him to play Jack Strop in *Robert Macaire* at the Lyceum when the new season starts."

Tessa shook her head. So did the waiter as he moved away to another table.

But as soon as they were alone, Tessa said, "Never mind George Grossmith. Perhaps you'll explain yourself? A quiet-as-a-mouse little country cousin was all I asked for. I don't know what you think you're supposed to be."

Saunders was crushed.

"Well?" Tessa insisted.

Saunders nodded tightly without looking up.

"You won't escape just by keeping silent."

A large tear welled out of Saunders's left eye and rolled

down her cheek. Tessa's heart sank. She looked around in embarrassment. "Oh, for heaven's sake, Saunders! Don't be such a baby – I didn't mean. . . all I said was. . ."

Saunders gave a little twitch of a smile and looked up. "I can do that any time I want," she said. Then she laughed. "But only with the left eye. Isn't that funny? I could never do it with my right."

"How very clever," Tessa said crossly. "But I still want an explanation. You risked the ruin of everything, the way you behaved."

Saunders dabbed away the tear; her sniff was pure, genteel craftsmanship. "I had him eating out the palm of my hand."

"But you weren't to know that. For all you knew, he might have shown us the door as soon as you mentioned Thorpe-le-Soken."

A superior smile twitched Saunders's mouth. "When it comes to the art of bending gentlemen around the little finger, Miss d'Arblay, I hope you're not going to claim your experience is superior to mine?"

In her annoyance Tessa oversugared her tea.

"Anyway," Saunders went on, "talking of actors – our Sir William's in a class on his own, don't you think?"

Tessa did not take her meaning.

Saunders was surprised. "Don't say you believed him? What he said back there?"

"Of course I did. He's a gentleman."

Saunders dropped her chocolate cake.

"Here, that's my dress you're wearing!" Tessa cried. "D'you mean you think he wasn't telling the truth?"

"Some of it. I believe him when he says it wasn't a photo of Mr. Laird's post-mortal. But. . ."

"Post. . . oh – never mind. Go on."

"I also believe it'd be worth finding out if there ever was a porter called Jepson at Guy's Hospital. And did he die in the madhouse there? And did Sir Wily do a post-mortal, and did. . ."

"Mortem! Post-mortem!"

"Yes – did he do one of those? I think you'll find the answer to all those questions will be *no*."

"But you must be wrong! What possible reason could he have

for lying?''

"You don't see it?''

"I'm afraid I don't.''

"It's what they call in the theatre 'the back-door clause'.
Look – what'll happen when you tell Sergeant Keene and he
starts digging? First, he'll go to Sir W. for corobbery – and
he. . .''

"Corroboration!''

"If you say so. And he denies it all. He says he certainly can't
remember any porter called Jepson at Guy's. And old Keene will
check and he'll find there wasn't. And that's Sir William's way of
saying *keep out!*''

Tessa was appalled. "You mean he thought all that up on the
spur of the moment?''

"Well, it's second nature with people like that. He didn't need
to think at all.''

"What d'you mean – people like that?''

"He didn't get to be England's top doctor just by staying up
late and reading books, did he!''

"My goodness, Saunders. You have a jaundiced view of . . .''

"The way things are,'' she answered. "I told you – you're too
innocent to be let loose.'' Then, in the tones of an ultra-genteel
lady, she added, "D'you suppose I dare have another cake?''

Against her will, Tessa laughed. "Oh, Saunders, you really are
. . . I don't know! I fully intended to part company with you.''

"But I haven't told you the half of it yet! It's my belief Sir
Wily's going to keep the Law out of it because he wants to handle
it his own way.''

"What makes you say that?''

"The letter I was reading, on his bureau. I wish he hadn't
come in so soon. I recognized the writing straight off. It was the
Demon's Disciple's.''

"Dr. Segal?''

"The self and very same! I quote!'' She closed her eyes to
dramatize her recall. "'My dear Sir William, I cannot begin to
tell you how grateful I am for your generous support of my
candidacy for a degree beyond the Royal Arch. The title of Grand
Inquisitor sounds imposing enough, but . . .'''

"Go on,'' Tessa urged.

"That's as far as I got. But isn't it enough? Now d'you see why

I brought Segal's name in when you mentioned that other doctor.''

"It sounds like something to do with Freemasonry.''

"Of course it is. That's the 'other little business' Sir Wily was talking about. I think he's going to deal with the Disciple through the Masons, not the Law. That's why he lied about Jepson – so if the Law tried to interfere, he could confuse them.''

Tessa felt cheated. She was used to dealing with duplicity at the simple domestic level of servants and their rivalries – not this urbane deception that masked itself behind the code of a gentleman. "I just want to turn my back on the whole thing,'' she said.

"Also,'' Saunders went on, "I subspect Sir Wily hasn't long to live – and I think he knows it. Being a doctor himself, I think he knows he's ailing with something that's going to do for him, soon. All that business about being carried back to Essex. And . . .''

"Talking of Essex – what was all that? How did you seem to know the area so well?''

Saunders smiled. "I've an aunt at St. Osyth – my dad's sister. We always went there every summer. I know all that part of the world. So, when we found out he was born at Thorpe-le-Soken. . .''

"My goodness, Saunders, you took a risk.''

"Broke the ice, though, didn't it! You wouldn't have got half as much out of the queen's doctor as I got out of the grown-up Essex mudlark.'' She grinned. "Here! He wouldn't mind meeting *me* again for a bit of mudlarking, did you notice? If I could be sure he'd introduce me to George Grossmith, I would, too. If I could only be sure of that! Grossmith's what I'd class as a powerful'' – she paused before the word to get it right – "pro-tec-tor.''

Tessa looked around at the potted palms and aspidistras. The room was almost empty; the little trio was playing an energetic if cut-down Mozart quartet; they could not be overheard. "You mean you'd . . .?'' she asked.

"Yes. I mean I'd oblige him.'' She stared back calmly.

Tessa looked about them once more before leaning forward and asking, "Does it just happen? I mean, what'd you say to him?''

Saunders shrugged awkwardly. "Don't need to say anything.

Just don't say no. Think about something nice.''

"Isn't It nice?''

"It's like comforting a crying baby. At least you know it'll bring you peace and leave you free to get on with things.''

"What d'you think about?''

A faraway contentment came into her eyes. "Curtain-up on a full house! A theatre . . . an audience . . . it's like a huge embrace. It's like hundreds of arms all around you. Yes!'' She was decisive. "That beats the devil!''

"Tell me why your family pretends your sister Pol doesn't exist.''

Saunders laughed. "Pol! Sometimes I really envy her. She's got the power. She knows how to say yes-*and*-no. That takes a bit of explaining, don't you think? There she is in that place full of women who get paid never to say no, and full of the men who do the paying. But who is it they really want? Whose honeypot do the wasps all want to get drowned in? Our Pol's! And she says yes once in a year of Sundays; and she picks her time and man with about as much feeling as a snake!''

"All because of saying no!'' Tessa said.

"Yes-and-no. Any old prune of a spinster can say no. Any old street cruiser can say yes. It's how to say both and neither. That's a woman's weapon.''

"Well, if you know that, why don't you do it? If you envy your sister the power so much.''

"It's not knowing, Tess. It's being. Knowing doesn't help, unless you're born with it. Pol was born with it, but she didn't know until one young man – a cavalry officer, he was, equerry to one of the princes and all – he went and shot himself because of her. That's when she knew. D'you know what she said? All she said was – 'Give a man enough hope and he'll hang himself.' There!'' She gurgled with laughter. "Think of having power like that, eh? I'd give anything. But I'm too soft, see?''

Tessa stared at her. "I simply can't fathom you, Saunders. Is this really you talking now? Or is it just like trying on another hat? Do even you know who you really are?''

To her surprise, the woman had no ready answer. She thought about it quite a while before she said, "Sometimes I'd frighten myself. I mean I can be so devilish good at it, I'd make my own hair stand on end. I tell myself the wind might change and I'll be

78

like that forever. When I was up at Finsbury Close, I'd even begin to wonder if that skivvy wasn't really me. You know, sometimes it'd make me shiver.''

"It makes me shiver now. What am I to believe? What am I to trust?''

Saunders shook her head sadly. ''I don't know any answer to that. I mean, if you trusted your own ideas about Sir Wily, you'd be in dead trouble now.''

"Instead I trust you – and you're what? A hall of mirrors!''

"Oh no! This is the truth, now. I'm an actress looking for a stage. And I'm not willing to go back to being Wife of Second Citizen. It's the top or nothing. I told you – there's a strong will to better ourselves in our family.''

"Well, you must make up your own mind – whether you oblige Sir William and get your introduction to Mr. Grossmith, or stay with me until you feel it's safe to face Mr. Sudden Death Davitt.''

Saunders sniffed and said uneasily, ''Don't you think there's one or two loose ends about this afternoon still?''

"No – I say forget the whole thing. I just want to go back and paint.''

"I don't think it's that easy, me old duck. I think you must ask Sergeant Keene to find out whether I'm right about Mr. Jepson and the Guy's madhouse. If I am, we could be in trouble.''

"I don't follow?''

"What's Sir Wily going to do now? Somehow, through the Freemasons, he's going to put the knife into Segal, isn't he? And the chances are he's going to tell him why. And what's the first name old Segal's going to think of when he hears it's all about Peter Laird?''

Tessa absorbed this in silence. ''Perhaps it just won't happen,'' she said at last.

"And perhaps it will.''

"Let's cross that bridge when we come to it. I mean – it's absurd to think Segal would do anything to hurt me.''

"Why not? That's his pet hobby – hurting women.''

Tessa had a sudden image not of Segal but of Dante Rosen. Surely he'd protect her? Saunders couldn't be right about everything.

Chapter Eleven

There never was a John Jepson who had been a porter at Guy's Hospital. Nor had any person by that name or anything similar died in the asylum within the previous thirty years (and that took the inquiry back beyond the days of glass-plate photography and stereoscopic pairs). Keene established these facts for the modest outlay of a shilling in oyster pie and beer at The Goat and Compasses in London Bridge Street, just around the corner from Guy's itself; his informant was the present head porter.

"And seeing as the Masons are in it," Keene said, "I'm not!"

"Rank cowardice!" Tessa told him.

He grinned sourly. "Rank's the word right enough."

"What now?" Saunders asked when he'd gone.

"We forget the whole silly business. It's nothing to do with us anyway. The only good thing that's come out of it is that we met each other. So let's go down to the studio, where you can pose and I can get on with some painting."

"And what if the Demon turns up? He was coming to your studio the day Old Friendly died. Don't expect me to . . ."

"If Dante Rosen turns up, I shall be flattered. He's a great painter."

Saunders took her arm. "Listen, Tess. I know we joke a lot, and things like that, but I'm dead serious when I say you ought to stay away from that one. He really is . . ."

"You listen," Tessa interrupted, "did it never strike you that he almost certainly knows George Grossmith?"

Saunders fell silent.

"He certainly knows Mr. Oscar Wilde," Tessa added. "I expect he knows dozens of theatre people."

Saunders sighed defeat. "Very well. But I'll only go on conjunction you promise – no pigs, no corpses."

Tessa laughed. "O happy conjunction! I've already promised you."

"But you don't know that Rosen yet. He can twist anyone.

What if he wants to set up his easy beside yours?''

"Easel. I don't think you should worry. He'll do you justice when it comes to line and colour. And when he exhibits the picture, someone connected with the theatre is bound to see it. And that might just be your chance. You may have been knocking on the wrong doors all this time. After all, what's one more pretty young waif at the stage door – however *obliging* she may be? But an unattainable young beauty in glowing colours in an art gallery? It may be your best way of saying yes-and-no!''

"My only way! You know me – I'm soft as a squirrel.''

Soft she may have been, but Saunders had the most wonderful sense of theatre. Whatever position Tessa asked her to adopt, she gave it a verve and an energy that was startling. The penalty was that she could not hold them for long. But Tessa, making the best of it, spent a happy morning on her drawing donkey, doing brief sketches that borrowed her model's vitality and lifted her work to an exciting level. After lunch she set the most recumbent pose possible, in the hope that Saunders could hold it – even to the extent of actually falling asleep. Then she clamped a new white canvas on her painting easel.

This was always the most exciting moment – putting the palette on the table and squeezing out the prussian blue, the chrome green . . . indian red . . . flake white, rose madder, alizarin crimson, cobalt blue . . . one by one the virgin squiggles took their places around the margin. She poured fresh turpentine and raw linseed oil into the little boats clipped to the edge of the palette; the smell, especially of the turps, was an intoxication. Then she picked up her favourite number-three hog, soaked it in turps, and mashed it with a dollop of prussian blue – the only colour she ever drew with for her underpainting. Then she stabbed at the canvas. No hesitation. No artistic agonizing. Pure joy.

The underpainting was the part she loved best always. She knew that no one but she would ever see it, so it became a kind of secret dialogue with herself. She could forget the outside world and its ideas about painting and indulge herself instead with a childlike orgy of line and colour – knowing it would all soon be overlaid by more orthodox workmanship. Her bold prussian-blue outlines soon contained bright shadows of chrome green or indian red; and the highlights were singing washes of subtle yellows and pinks, worked into each other with most careless cunning.

When she had finished, it was such a dazzling riot of colour (and yet, to her eyes, so well controlled and balanced) that she could not bear to begin covering it with fatter pigments in more natural hues. She decided to let it breathe overnight; in the morning it would be all but dry.

"Rest," she told Saunders. "I don't want to do any more today. You get dressed and let's go up to Victoria Park and walk around the lakes, eh?"

But Saunders was asleep. What woke her was the knock on the door – or rather the voice that accompanied it: Rosen's. "Anyone at home?" he called. His voice floated up through the open window.

Tessa's stomach turned over with that strange excitement she always felt when he was near. "Wait!" she shouted, and she threw Saunders her dressing gown. When her nakedness was covered, Tessa called out, "It's not locked."

He ran up the stairs and entered jauntily, cock-o'-the-walk, looking very summery. "Lovely evening!" Then he saw Saunders and added a piggy *oink-oink*!

Saunders stuck out her tongue and vanished behind the screen to change.

"Mind if I look?" he asked Tessa. "This is a grand place you've got, isn't it. I wouldn't mind moving in here myself."

"What's wrong with Chelsea?" Tessa asked.

"It's five miles away from you."

His eye twinkled. She was sure he knew what a turmoil he was causing inside her. But then he saw her painting, and he suddenly frowned. His jaw dropped.

She burned with embarrassment. "It's only the underpainting," she told him.

He didn't answer. He stood as though carved. He seemed not even to breathe.

"I do all my underpaintings like that," she added haltingly. "But I cover them up. I mean, I can paint better than that."

One part of him was untouched by this paralysis – his eyes. They never ceased their audit. They quartered her canvas like an eagle. At last, at long, long last, he breathed out. "That," he whispered, "is a revelation."

"What?" She was sure he was about to tease her.

He turned to her. "Just once in a lifetime," he said, "this sort of epiphany happens to every artist. I thought I had mine when I first saw Jimmy Whistler's painting. But that wasn't even a rehearsal for this."

"Don't play games," she warned.

"Games! My God, woman – that is the most powerful – the most exciting beginning I've ever seen."

He was serious. Cock-o'-the-walk had gone. So had that old I'm-a-genius bearing, which placed her far down some list of well-intentioned amateurs. In their place was something like. . . adoration? Homage, anyway.

He frowned. "Are you even aware how good it is?" He turned from her and began rummaging around among the canvasses leaning here and there against the walls – her finished or abandoned works. "No," he said. "You aren't." He straightened and looked at her. "They're not bad, you understand. They're competent enough. Better than anything poor old Leighton's ever done, anyway. But that!" He turned back to her underpainting. "That's a masterpiece. You're a master, and I don't think you know it, do you?"

From behind her screen Saunders let out a great snort. "Mistress!" she said, managing to convey both a correction and a warning.

Rosen ignored her. "You've obviously been to Paris," he said. "Why didn't you tell me?"

She shook her head.

"You haven't? You mean you've never seen Cézanne? Gauguin? Lautrec?"

"I've never even heard of them. Are they painters?" She found her voice again.

He buried his face in his hands. "I can't bear it! Don't tell me you discovered it all alone!"

"Discovered what?"

"*This!*" He sounded angry. "The secret of it all! Light! Colour! Passion! You hold it in your hands – don't you realize that? D'you mean to tell me that other paintings like this, paintings with this same primal colour, this same elemental, blessed urgency – that such paintings lie buried forever" – he gestured dismissively at the rest of her oeuvre – "under all that rather timid, conventional scumbling and glazing? I shall weep if you say yes. I shall positively weep."

83

Saunders, clothed again, emerged at that moment. She held forth a clean handkerchief. "If you 'ave tears," she said, "prepare to shed 'em nah."

Rosen brushed the offer angrily aside.

Saunders looked at the painting over which Rosen was making so much ado. "Blimey!" she said. "Jaundice *and* scarlet fever!" Then she turned to Tessa and, with a jerk of her head toward Rosen, added, "You ain't swallowing none o' this is yer, miss?"

"Be quiet," Tessa told her.

"You know nothing about painting," Rosen added.

Stepping out of his field of view, Saunders pointed at him and held her nose. Then she answered, "'E's not talking about painting, miss. This is the old come-all-youse-young-maidens. 'E's doing the one-armed flute player on you – hold this for me while I play a condenser on yer buttons."

"Cadenza!" Tessa said crossly. "Anyway, Mr. Rosen's right. You know as much about painting as you do about music. Condenser!" She turned back to him. "Are you being really serious?"

"More serious, I think, than you." His eyes stared deep into hers, searching for something he seemed unable to find there. She wanted to run her hands over his face; she had to bunch her fists to prevent herself.

He turned to her painting. "Could you ask the model to get back into the pose?"

Tessa turned to Saunders, who merely snorted.

"Please?" Tessa said.

Angrily, Saunders went back behind the screen and undressed once more. When she resumed the pose, Rosen spent several minutes looking from her to the painting and back again. "It's amazing," he said at last. "It's almost all there. You teach me to look at the world in a new way. I think you could even knock Jimmy Whistler off course." He faced her. "What I *don't* understand, though, is how you can paint like this and then go and cover it up with something so ordinary." He gestured once again at her old canvasses. "What's in your mind when you do something that sings like this?"

"I do it because I'm only doing it for me. I mean, I know I'm going to overpaint it."

"Oh God! That is so unfair!"

"Well I envy you your gift for drawing. I'd give my right hand – or half of it – to be able to draw like you."

"And I'd give it all to you if only I could have your grasp of shape and colour! Did we each get the wrong Good Fairy?"

The air was pregnant with impending arrangements.

"Oi!" came from the couch. "D'yer still need me?"

Tessa questioned him with her eyebrows. "Would you think it impertinent," he asked, "if I made one or two minor points?"

She shook her head. For the next five minutes he spoke about the relationship between her painting and the actual scene. She was not representing it, he said, but translating it into a language that was more extreme. She was discovering a power, a violence, a beauty that ordinary people would never realize was there; by painting it she was teaching them to see it, too – and to make similar discoveries for themselves. She was creating a new language and a new grammar – but because she hadn't fully understood what a momentous achievement it was, she wasn't taking it seriously enough. Her use of her own language was slipshod . . . here . . . here . . . and here. He pointed out the inconsistencies and suggested ways to overcome them, ways that might build on her achievement and extend it into realms she hadn't even begun to explore.

She was trembling with excitement when he had finished. All Saunders's warnings were forgotten. Anyway, even if they were all true, even if he brought her nothing but misery in the end, nothing could undo this evening's discovery. In five minutes Dante had mapped out her whole creative life.

He took up her hands and stared into her palms, as if he might find the secret there. His touch thrilled her. She yearned to pull him against her, to lean on him. The very violence of her feeling startled her into pulling her hands away, as from an electric shock. He raised his eyes to her face then and smiled – not arrogantly, indeed, with a curious begging quality. "I want to sit at your feet," he said. "I want to learn your language."

Chapter Twelve

Rosen was there the following morning, sitting on a handcart outside the locked studio door, sketching Tyker, who was grooming Dresden. It had been raining earlier but now the skies were clearing and the day promised to be fine and warm, if a little humid.

"You're a man of your word," Tessa called out as soon as she and Saunders stepped out of the back gate into Bleeding Heart Lane.

He nodded, smiled briefly at them, and went on sketching.

"Wipe those blushes off your cheeks," Saunders warned her in a near-whisper. "If you once let him see he's got you – that's you done for."

"Don't be ridiculous," Tessa replied.

"Well, there's none so blind as those who will not hear."

Tessa was astonished to see how much Rosen had brought with him, not just painting materials but a rolled-up mattress, books, a trunk, two suitcases . . . "It looks as if you're moving in," she said.

"That's right." He peered sidelong at his sketch, as if he might consider it finished – licking and pursing his lips. Again she felt that desire to touch them with her fingers. She was about to tell him he couldn't possibly move in when he looked up at her and said, "You don't mind, I hope? I've been in such a turmoil since yesterday. I've sworn off all salons, all soirées, until. . ."

"Until you've stolen her painting tricks," Saunders interrupted. "Tell him no, Tess. Those tricks are yours. You've got a right to them. Let him go and find tricks of his own."

For a fraction of a second Tessa hesitated. Conventional wisdom plucked at her weakly. But another voice, more plausible, more recognizably her own, told her Rosen was behaving with the ruthlessness of a true artist. . . that she *needed* something of that same capacity for singleminded self-development, or all the talent in the world would not help her.

She smiled. "Of course I don't mind." She took out her key and handed it to him. "You'd better hold on to it while you're here."

He went to unlock the door.

Saunders put her lips close to Tessa's ear and, in a sententious whisper, misquoted: "'A penny-dreadful prison with a lifelong lock'."

Tessa sighed. "You only ever get half of anything right."

"But the important half. Anyway, right or wrong, it's the truth."

Upstairs, she undressed grumpily and took up yesterday's pose again. For a few minutes she was sullen, so that although the outward aspect of the scene was unchanged, its mood was entirely altered; but then her professionalism broke through and she became everything Tessa and Rosen could want.

He unpacked a folding easel, put up a newly primed canvas, and went through the same enjoyable ritual of setting out a palette – except that he kept checking with hers and asking if he could have a squeeze of this tube and that, where the colour wasn't among his own set. The indian red worried him particularly. "It creeps into everything," he said. "How d'you keep it out?"

"Genius," she explained airily.

They painted happily all morning, letting Saunders stretch herself every half hour or so. Most models use such breaks for physical jerks, shaking up stiff muscles and getting the blood going again; Saunders went further, turning each exercise into a miniature play, strutting around in her swirling dressing gown. . . marching like a stage soldier. . . running an on-the-spot marathon. . . shadow boxing. Toward noon one of these random dramas led her to a corner of the studio where the floor was rotten. Tessa had put a box over the hole, and, since by their very nature all empty boxes demand to be filled, this one had slowly accumulated a number of costumes for her models to wear. Saunders's discovery of them was marked by a shriek of delight. "Oh, Tess!" she called out, a child again, "can I rumble about in this box, please?"

"Five minutes," Tessa told her.

Saunders dragged the Chinese screen over to the corner so that Rosen should not watch her dressing and undressing. She needn't have bothered. He had eyes only for the paintings, his own and Tessa's. Encouraged by his praise she had refrained from covering yesterday's work with more orthodox colours; instead she had built upon her first statements. It was a liberation as great as anything she had ever known.

He looked at what she had achieved and smiled somewhat ruefully as he said, "You just can't help getting it right, can you!"

She basked in it. "I'm still so overwhelmed."

"Painting's a window into the mind."

"What d'you see in mine?"

"Happiness. Sunshine. Strength."

She had watched his painting grow all morning, out of the corner of her eye, fascinated to see her own influence appearing there so strongly – and yet overlaid with the stamp of his personality. For he was not slavishly copying her. He was already a master in the New English Art Club tradition. He had the skill and the assurance to take what he needed from her and graft it, still living, onto his own vision – a window into *his* mind.

One could feel his anger with Saunders. The emotion he lent the scene was harsh; his forms were more jagged. Where she had made the colour sing, his almost screamed. Yet his vision was powerful. He had seen in her work something that, in her timidity and isolation from other painters, she might never have grasped; and his genius had taken it and immediately branded it his own. Would the very power of his work, she wondered, shatter the serenity of hers and flood it with that same violence? There was no turning back now. Her scalp tingled. She laughed, not understanding why.

The expression in his eyes stopped her. "Dear God, but you're so beautiful when you laugh," he said.

She wanted to make a joke of it, to ask him if he meant the "beauty of ugliness," which he was so fond of talking about. But again his seriousness held her. He went on, "I'd like to paint your portrait. Laughing, in this sun. You should always be like that."

"There's been little enough to laugh about lately," she said.

"It's about time!" he answered – but ambiguously, so that she couldn't tell whether he was continuing their conversation or preparing to call Saunders back to her pose.

In any case, Saunders chose that moment to leap out from

behind the screen, emitting a fearful roar, and shouting, "I be Robert the Devil, I be!" She had on a pirate hat and black eyepatch, a toreador jacket, and ill-fitting Columbine pantaloons.

Her glee turned to surprise when Rosen shouted, "Right, my gel!" and sprang toward her. The surprise became alarm when he swept her up in his arms and carried her, kicking and shrieking, down the stairs. Tessa ran after them to the stairhead, reaching it just as the street door slammed shut. It was the back door, not the one they had come in by. A great hammering began at once, mingled with oaths and cries of, "Lemme in!"

Rosen ran back upstairs, laughing all the way. "That'll teach her!" he said. "Now let's watch the fun."

The studio was one of the former assembly rooms of the old coaching inn, with windows down both sides; one side overlooked the vicarage mews, the other gave out upon a mean street of poor houses. It was into this narrow street that Rosen had ejected the shrieking Saunders. He hoisted one of the sashes wide open and leaned casually on the sill. Saunders heard the screeching of the pulley above her own contribution. She looked up, just in time to see Tessa join Rosen. "You gob!" she shouted. "You bleedin' Demon!"

No longer Robert the Devil, she had acquired the protective Cockney coloration of the street into which she had been ejected. The fancy dress, which must have seemed such fun up in the studio, was ridiculous out there. Dogs began to gather, barking excitedly; children were not far behind; then came their mothers. Soon she was surrounded by laughing people, shouting joke encouragement and asking where the circus was. She rounded on the front row of children and screamed, "Fuck orf, yer lit'le bleeders!"

It only redoubled their laughter.

The upstairs window was narrow. Tessa had to squeeze tightly against Rosen to see out. His body was strong and still. He yielded not an inch to let her in. She thrilled at the tightness of their contact. The tension in his muscles told of his enjoyment, too.

Saunders dashed to the kerb and picked up a loose cobble. She turned around and looked up at them. "Are you gonna lemme in?" she shouted.

"We're thinking about it," Rosen said calmly. "We've had a

89

glut of Columbines just recently, but you never know your luck. We'll take a vote in about ten minutes.''

"Miss d'Arblay?'' she asked.

Tessa grinned. "Calm down. Just be patient.''

"Right!'' Saunders hurled the cobble through one of the windows. Unfortunately her geography had gone awry for it was, in fact, the window of the neighbouring house. One of the women in the crowd stopped laughing and came forward and thumped Saunders in the back, pushing her down on her knees. Instinctively the crowd formed a circle. Saunders, who already had another cobble in her hand, made short work of the woman, who retired cut and bleeding.

"This has gone too far,'' Tessa said.

"Oh, I don't know,'' he answered. "It may be only just beginning.''

Saunders looked up at them and waved the cobblestone. "You get aht the way, miss,'' she shouted. "Rosen, you black devil, this one's fer you.''

"Just calm down,'' Tessa repeated. Then, to Rosen, "It's no longer funny. Go down and let her in.''

He didn't budge. "She's a free agent,'' he said. "She didn't have to put on those ridiculous clothes. She doesn't have to behave in that ridiculous way.''

Tessa eased herself out of the opening. "Very well, then. I shall do it.''

He let her reach the stairhead before he told her, "I have the key to that door, too.''

"Then *I'll* break a window,'' Tessa flared back.

She had no need. The window opened easily and, despite the encumbrance of those dreadful pantaloons, Saunders climbed in nimbly enough. "Demon!'' she said.

"The Demon and the Fool,'' Tessa told her. "You're as bad as each other. Why give him the satisfaction of behaving like that?''

"Ere! What about my window?'' the injured woman shouted.

Tessa found a sixpence and passed it to her through the opening. The woman seemed about to argue, saw the determined glint in Tessa's eye, and went off in grumpy silence.

"Now come back and get on with your pose,'' Tessa told Saunders.

"I'm not going up there – not after that!'' She glared sullenly at Tessa. "And you – you're a bit of a Judas's Chariot, don't you think?"

"You didn't see what you looked like. No one forced you to put on those clothes, my girl! You're a free agent."

"Free!" Saunders raked the ceiling with her eyes.

"Well – you're free *not* to go upstairs. You're free to stay in those ridiculous clothes all day . . ."

Angrily Saunders ran up to the studio. Tessa followed, smiling. She was less happy when she entered the room and saw Saunders already behind the screen, changing back into her everyday clothes. "Here! You've not finished your pose, young miss!"

"Free agent!" Saunders said sweetly.

"Let the silly creature go," Rosen chimed in. "I'll start that portrait of you. Pity to waste this sun."

Tessa's stomach fell. "Oh no! I couldn't – I mean it's out of the question for me to remain here alone with you."

"Free agent!" Saunders taunted from behind the screen.

"Out of the mouths of babes and sucklings – and even of imbeciles!" Rosen said with an I-rest-my-case wave of his hand toward Saunders.

And why not? Tessa suddenly thought.

Rosen said, "Inside that drab, conventional soul of yours, Miss d'Arblay, I sense the despair of a new, mature, intelligent woman fighting for her very existence. Did you ever meet her?"

"I don't know anything about that," Tessa laughed. "But I fail to see why I should let a stupid creature like Saunders dictate my comings and goings."

Rosen grinned. "Quite right. Put the boot on the other foot. What is she? Nothing but a skivvy. Send her out for some bread and cheese and a bottle of good, light German wine. We'll have a bit of lunch before we start, eh?"

Tessa joined Saunders behind the screen. The woman shook her head violently. "What?" Tessa asked with transparent innocence.

"You can't stay here with him, not alone." She took no care to lower her voice.

"I don't see why not," Tessa whispered truculently.

Saunders gave a cynical little shrug. She whispered, "You're digging your own grave, gel. All I can say is watch out for his eyes. While he's pretending to paint your picture he's really

91

putting the influence on you. I know. Just watch out for his eyes – that's all.''

''Don't worry about me. I know what I'm doing.'' She gave her half-a-crown for the victuals.

When Saunders had gone, she said, ''I'll let you paint my portrait if I can model your head in clay.''

''At the same time?''

''Why not? Let's try.''

He shrugged, not as pleased as she might have expected. It was a strange feeling, to be left entirely alone with a man. She had never experienced it before – except with Old Friendly. But that hardly counted. ''How would you like me?'' she asked.

''Not just yet,'' he said. ''I've not thought of you as a portrait until now. I can't just dump you there like a still life – a cauliflower or something. I want to watch your face, how it moves. . . how it soaks up the light. I want to know more about you. Let's just talk until after lunch?''

She went to one of the sunny windows, overlooking the mews, and brushed the dust and debris off its broad sill. Fortunately she was in her painting clothes – a loose, sensible, pre-Raphaelite sort of dress without a bustle and without stiff-hooped petticoats. She swept her skirts under her and lifted her feet onto the sill, hugging her knees close to her cheek. She turned to him. ''Talk to me,'' she said. ''Say the first thing that comes into your head.''

''If you will, too.''

''All right.''

He pulled up the donkey and sat near her, slightly below, gazing up into her face. If she hadn't the palisades of her knees and skirts in front of her, she'd have felt much less at ease.

''It amazes me,'' he said. ''How can you have had this genius for painting and yet be completely unaware of it? I wonder if. . .''

''I'm aware of it now!'' she interrupted.

He smiled. There was a short silence and then he asked, ''What're you thinking? Remember – we're going to be absolutely honest with each other.''

''I like to hear you talking about me.''

''Why?''

''Because you understand. There's no one else in my world who even remotely understands about art – how all-important it

92

can be. You understand even more than I do.''

''I wonder are you aware of all the other things about yourself – things that are so obvious to me?''

''Such as?''

''D'you know you're extremely beautiful?''

She scoffed but her heart somersaulted.

''You'll see,'' he told her. ''When I've painted my portrait of you – you'll see. You know that nun, the one who showed me in to the room where Old Friendly died?''

''Sister Magda?''

''Is that her name? She's beautiful, too. But I suppose she'll go to her grave without ever knowing it. I don't imagine they have looking glasses there, and I doubt the others will tell her. Don't you think that's a tragedy?''

''Not for her, perhaps. She chose it that way.''

''And what about you, Miss d'Arblay? Suppose you discovered only on your deathbed that you had really been such a great painter – that you had been such a beautiful woman – all your life? Would that be a tragedy for you?''

She shrugged and smiled awkwardly.

''Honesty!'' he reminded her.

''Honesty may be unspoken, too,'' she told him.

''That's too feminine for me, I'm afraid. It's a funny thing about women. I believe you could live quite happily in a world without men. Not just nuns but all of you. And if you could just find some trick for begetting the next generation without us, most of you would probably die thinking your lives had been quite complete.''

Her heartbeat, swelling in her neck, tapped away at her knees.

''So have I enriched your life in any way, Miss d'Arblay, by putting you and your genius on speaking terms?''

''Today has been the best day of my life.'' She nodded toward her painting.

''As it has been of mine.'' He gazed at her through half-closed eyes, as painters often do. When he opened them fully she was overwhelmed again by their astonishing colour. He asked, ''Is there anybody in all the world with whom you can talk in absolute freedom? With absolute honesty?''

She shook her head.

''Nor me,'' he told her. ''Yet I have a feeling about us. I think

93

you and I might be able to achieve such a rapport. In time. It could be something new in the world. A new, better, more honest partnership between a man and a woman. We could explore our natures in ways that no one else has ever managed. Because we're artists we could see things the world would pass by. The gates of perception would fall at our knock!'' He looked at her. ''You know what I mean?''

She nodded.

''I mean all of our natures. The dark side, too. Our Dark Selves. Have you that courage?''

His begging eyes forced her to nod again. She hardly breathed.

''Say it,'' he prompted.

''I hope I have it. I hope I have that courage.''

''I want to talk to you as openly as I would to my twin self. Don't you share something of that feeling already – about me, I mean?'' His next words astonished her: ''Oh, if only we can manage not to fall in love!''

''Why do you rule out love?''

''Love would spoil it. Love reduces our humanity. Love stirs our blood too much. Love fills our bodies with strange juices. Love disorders our sleep and begets exotic dreams. Love goads us with impossible longings, until we cease to understand the truth. And truth without understanding is worse than a knowing lie. Love divides man and woman because it seeks to unite her spirit with his flesh, and his spirit with her flesh – fusing them in one passion. 'Impossible!' our reason protests. But love whispers, 'Not so! I can sanctify all. I can render the flesh sacred and the spirit carnal.' So, Miss d'Arblay, I pray it doesn't happen to us. We'd grow so desperate to become as one, you and I, we'd have no *self* left to express, no privacy to share. Love would diminish us. We must find something far grander.''

His rich, resonant voice melted the words into one flow, in whose depths she heard only random ideas – ''juices. . . impossible longings. . .sanctified flesh. . .fusing. . .passion. . . carnal. . . desperate.'' It drained every ounce of her will – or, rather, it left her with nothing for her will to work upon. There was literally nothing she wanted to do except to go on sitting there, listening, bathing herself in the great sonorities of his voice.

He gazed at her for a long time. She stared back, knowing she was in love with him, wondering now if she would ever be able to tell him of it.

He stood and held out his hands. Like so much else about him the gesture was ambiguous. Did he expect her to fall into his arms? Did he want her simply to put her hands in his?

His hands were palm up, she placed hers upon them, palm down, not gripping. The touch of him was vibrant; she had to force herself to be calm. He slid his hands forward until he could grasp her lightly around the wrist; she did the same to him.

He made no move that might bring them closer – or not physically closer; but there was no need. His eyes already held her in a surer embrace. "To do all the things that lovers do," he said, "but to do them with clear eye and a free spirit! Free of the enslavements of love. Oh! We could make such discoveries, you and I!"

Chapter Thirteen

For two weeks they worked every daylight hour, he on his portrait of her, she on a clay bust of him. Saunders "kept house" – that is, she swept and tidied, made fanciful cold lunches, explored the safer parts of the old building, whitewashed one wall in a desultory fashion. . . but chiefly she read aloud to them from Dicks's Standard Plays – passionate dramas with titles like *A Woman will be a Woman*. . . *A Marriage Noose*. . . *All Fair in Love*. Curiously, she never got a word wrong when she was "in character" – only when she was herself.

For Tessa those were wonderful days. Sunny days. Days beyond the reach of time. Saunders had been so wrong about Dante. Or, if not wrong, she had misunderstood him. An artist cannot be judged as one would judge other people; they had licence to inquire where others were rightly barred; they needed to understand and experience things that ordinary people would, if they were wise, forbid themselves to know; for artists are the advance guard, the avant garde, of moral and spiritual progress. That's what Shelley had meant when he called them the

95

unacknowledged legislators of the world. All her past life, she now realized, had been a preparation for these discoveries.

What would her life have been like, she wondered, if she had never met Dante, if he had been somewhere else that day she had called on Dr. Segal? It didn't bear thinking about. She'd have lived and died without understanding, without knowledge. She wouldn't even have known herself.

And as for getting to know *him*, there was no better way, she thought, than the one on which she was now embarked: to recreate his likeness between her own fingertips. The bravura of her painting somehow carried over into her modelling. The image of him grew in conviction with every passing day; it was instinct with such life that at times she felt a dislocation in space as she looked from clay to flesh.

What sort of a job he was making of her portrait, she didn't know. She told him she didn't want to see it until it was finished. Was he aware by now that she loved him? She thought he must be. He was so sensitive to all her changes of mood. He knew just when she wanted to rest or break off, when she wanted to talk, when she preferred silence. Sometimes it seemed to her that they were, indeed, becoming ''twin selves'' to each other, the male and female halves of one person.

At other times an inexplicable tension would grow up between them, and they'd have to stop work and go out for a walk. If it was evening and the pubs were open, they'd take Saunders in tow and slide into the private bar and talk about life and art over a slow succession of beers until closing time. These episodes helped to mellow Saunders a little in her attitude to Rosen; the horror of pigs and corpses dwindled until she was prepared to allow that *some* might see it as no more than eccentricity. Rosen, for his part, found that Saunders wasn't such bad company after all.

Neither realized how much Saunders' dramatic readings did to ease the general atmosphere until the day came when she had to stay in bed with a summer chill. The silence in the studio, which should have been as creative as it had been in those first few days, was now oppressive. Rosen fretted more than she. ''I've never in my life worked in such a long, sustained burst as these past weeks,'' he said. ''Don't you think I've deserved a day off?''

''Go up West,'' she told him. ''Go and see Mr. Wilde and all your old friends. Ask them if they'll write a part for Saunders.''

He laughed but went on painting – or trying to. She moved as little as possible, knowing it would make his work easier; but the strain on her muscles was beginning to tell.

At length he put it to her directly: "Feel like stopping early for lunch, Miss d'Arblay?"

"Never more willing, Mr. Rosen." She relaxed and stretched. Relief was a warm liquid spilling through her muscles. "I know what. It's not going to rain – let's put everything in a basket and go up to Victoria Park."

"The Garden of Eden. Don't forget the apples." He went behind the screen to change into his fashionable clothes. She decided to stay as she was.

Half an hour later the cab put them down in Approach Road, by the outcast children's home. They made an elegant though not-quite-matched pair – Rosen in a tightly tailored pale grey suit and a neat straw trilby; a painting of him could only have been titled, "Bonjour, Monsieur Rosen!" Tessa felt absurdly happy and proud to be walking beside him. She, in a wide, flowing, floral-patterned dress, her lustrous hair let down and tied casually back, was more of a late Burne-Jones – with a title like, "Summer Joys" or "Halcyon Days!" They walked a careful six inches apart, over Bishop Bonner's Bridge and into the park. Despite the familiarity that had grown between them these past weeks, the nearness of him was still electrifying.

The "thin red line" style of gardening that had recently become fashionable in the parks "up West" was not in favour here. Vast beds of flowers were massed like the armies of old in mighty swathes of colour. For the most part they were in tightly disciplined oblongs and ovals – the product of the head gardener's long winter nights with ruler and compass. But here and there on the long slopes Tessa could make out more ambitious creations. Down near the boating lake were scrolls of purple verbena enclosed in borders of snow-in-summer, like amethysts in a filigree of silver. Near the top of the hill, the design was reversed to give a silver heart surrounded by blue lobelias, scarlet geraniums, bright dahlias, and the dark evergreen of dwarfed laurels. One huge patch of crimson resolved itself into a butterfly, made up of the same varieties of flowers and a sprinkling of calceolarias, prince's feather, and love-lies-bleeding. Beyond the lake was a great bank of recently planted india-rubber trees.

"Let's come back in a century or so," he suggested. "It should look at its best about then."

"It could hardly look worse. I hope they've learned how to garden naturally by then. I hate these geometrical displays."

He was amused at her vehemence. "Harmless fun?" he suggested.

"I don't agree. They pretend you can tidy anything up – life. . . the whole world. They create a false ideal." A memory came to her. "I was lying awake last night, thinking, funnily enough, about Oscar Wilde, how he's the enfant terrible of literature now but one day he's obviously going to be a Grand Old Man. What will his memoirs be like? How will he treat his friendship with you, for instance? I'll bet it'll be like these flower beds. All tidied up. I wonder what Eden was really like?"

He grinned mischievously. "What if it was like Victoria Park! What if this is some ancestral memory, dimly realized?"

She looked at a plant label and burst out laughing. "Yucca gloriosa," she read. "Adam's needle!" She waved her hand over the whole bed. "Mankind's first haberdashery."

"D'you think there was love in Eden?" he asked her, more seriously.

She turned to him. "I'm beginning to think you're afraid of it, Mr. Rosen."

"And you would be right! They were clear-sighted, those first parents of ours. The fruit they ate was of the tree of *knowledge* – not of passion, as the church would like us to believe. They *knew* what they were doing. They taught God to be jealous. Love is a kind of jealousy. Love is an acid in the eyes."

She did not want to pursue these thoughts.

The meandering pathway had brought them to the edge of the lake. For a while they watched the people milling around in the boats. "East Enders can row a great deal better than West Enders," she said.

"How d'you know? When did you last see West Enders rowing?"

"Let's take a boat," she suggested eagerly. "I'll row you this time."

She ran ahead of him to the boat stage. Jogging in her wake he said, "What d'you mean *this* time?"

She paid the hire, just as she usually paid for their rounds of drinks. He appeared not to notice. To him it was just one more way they could show their contempt for convention. She rowed them out to the middle and then, for a lark, she began pulling with only one oar, making them spin in a dizzy circle – "just to give you an appetite," she said.

He repeated his question, "Why did you say 'this time'? We never went rowing before."

She rested the oar and the boat ceased its spinning almost at once. The light southerly breeze began to carry it toward the far bank on a course that would graze one of the islands. She told him she'd been on the Serpentine recently, in just such a boat as this.

"Who was your lucky partner on that occasion?" he asked.

"Sir William Gull."

He went on staring into the placid green of the water. Only then did he appear to register what she had said. He frowned and turned to look at her. "The queen's physician?"

"Yes. *That* Sir William Gull."

"How extraordinary! You know he's a friend of Segal's?"

"Peter Laird was a friend of Segal's, too, wasn't he?" she asked.

He nodded. "And of mine." He smiled at her suddenly. "A doctor and a pharmacist – two useful people to know if you want to liberate the mind from its usual fetters and enter its forbidden regions. Have you ever taken opium?"

"Is that what Peter did – provided opium?"

Rosen nodded. "He could get it much purer than the stuff you buy over the counter. If you haven't tried it, that's quite an experience waiting for you." But then he pulled a face. "It isn't the answer, mind. It can help. Like water wings. But it isn't true swimming. Segal thinks its the only way – drugs and rituals."

"And flagellation," Tessa said, watching him closely.

"You know about that, then. Yes – drugs and rituals and pain. Other people use drink. . . fasting. . . playing the hermit in the desert. . . sensual excess – oh, there are so many ways. And all of them wrong!"

"Ways to what? I don't understand what you're talking about."

"To self-discovery, of course. To finding the answer to the question that plagues us all – what am I really like? Not 'how close can I get to some Greco-Roman ideal, or Christian ideal?'

But 'what am I really like?'"

"And what's the right way?"

"I don't know. I hope we're on it, you and I. The path of fearless honesty? I don't know. But I do know what's wrong with all those other ways: they pretend to be short cuts. In fact, they're a fraud. Just as the swindler never knows the true happiness of wealth, which is to earn every penny of it . . . just as the rapist seizes love's crown yet cheats himself of its kingdom – so do all those who seek short cuts. They cheat themselves of knowledge, even as they possess its outline. They cut the top four foot off the world's highest mountain, then they sit on it in their drawing rooms and say they've conquered it."

"Did you know that Dr. Segal falsified his report of Peter Laird's death?" she asked.

"It wouldn't surprise me. Segal's got some obsession with the idea of dying twice. He promised old Laird once that he'd die twice – and by his own greatest act."

"What does that mean?"

Rosen shrugged and pulled a face to imply he thought it idiotic, too. "Some Freemasonry mumbo-jumbo. The only way to study our silent selves is slowly. I'm convinced of . . ."

"*Silent* selves?" she asked.

He looked at her calmly. A delicious shiver ran through her. "You know very well," he answered. "The dreams we never confess. The thoughts that would burn our tongues. The desires we express only in the silence between our eyes."

The boat nudged a gravel bar running out from the island. "D'you want to hop ashore and eat?" he asked in a suddenly more workaday tone.

She nodded. Her heart was racing with excitement, stirred by his words. He handed her ashore. She held fast to his fingers, even after she was on firm ground. Then she pulled him ashore, still not releasing him. She gazed up into those astonishing, astonished eyes and saw her reflection there. She saw how the sunlight stole through the canopy of the leaves and dappled her cheeks.

She saw that, in his eyes at least, she was beautiful. The space between them dwindled. Their lips met.

Chapter Fourteen

Deep in the uncut grass, Tessa lay on her stomach and peered through the half-empty wine bottle at the lake and the bank of india-rubber trees beyond. The pale green of its glass tinted the afternoon heat. "Dante?" she asked. "Did you ever see the inside of an eye? What's it made of?"

"Something like jellied water." He stretched himself on his back beside her to gaze up into her face. "Why?"

"We look out at things and they're so clear we can't believe there's anything between us and them. I mean I can see every railing in that fence and it must be nearly half a mile away. Yet the light has to get through all that jelly, which must distort it. What's the world *really* like, I wonder?"

"But the distortions *are* the world. Haven't you realized that yet? Otherwise there's no point in being an artist."

She returned her eye to the wine bottle. "Maybe the jelly in our eyes distorts things just as much as this bottle glass? Only we don't notice because we've grown up with it. What about the distortions we don't notice – the ones we've all grown up with?"

He plucked a trembling stalk of grass, the kind called "shivery shaker," and touched it gently beneath her chin. "Here's a few grass seeds touching your neck. Tell me how your senses distort that simple event."

She nudged the grass away. "Stick to the point!"

"I am."

"*My* point. What about the distortions we've lived with from birth – which are now so familiar we no longer notice them?"

"That's what artists are for. Not to see *more* than everyone else, but to see less. To hack a broad and brutal pathway through each age's new undergrowth of prejudice and falsehood."

"Our ideas about morality," she said, "they're like the jelly in our eyes. They produce distortions we aren't aware of. They get in the way of our search for truth."

"Not for an artist. That's why you're one of the most

101

important people in the world, Tess.''

She lay beside him, an inch or so apart. ''I love it when you talk about me. Saunders says you only . . .''

He made a tube of his hands, bridging the space to her ear, and said, ''Shut up about Saunders.''

She giggled and shifted her position until she lay against him. ''Was I right, Dante? *Are* you afraid of love?''

He began to run his fingers through her hair. ''Only of its destructive side. We're beyond love, you and I.''

''How?''

''We can taste all its delights and yet remain free. There's nothing we couldn't do if we had a mind to it.'' His fingers went on soothing her skin. She luxuriated in the sensation, and the silence. ''Tell me what you're feeling,'' he said.

''I could paint it.''

''But can you say it?''

Without opening her eyes she shook her head.

He asked, ''Don't you feel as if we're already lovers? As if we've been lovers for a long time?''

She opened her eyes at that, lazily – to see into his. She nodded. He touched the tip of her nose. ''D'you want that?''

She closed her eyes again, amazed that she felt it so absolutely unnecessary to answer him.

After a long, easeful silence, she returned to the subject. ''Why do we kiss – if we are not to be in love?''

''You tell me,'' he replied. ''Your answers to these conundrums are as worthy as mine. We're making this voyage of discovery together.''

''But what's your answer?''

''When your lover kisses you he binds you down with threads of gold. Each kiss is one new thread – and it gives a little tweak of possession to each old thread, as well. Such kisses say no to life, no to freedom.''

''I want to know more about this freedom before I say yes to it.'' She opened her eyes and raised herself above him on the props of her elbows. ''Wouldn't you like to have me absolutely in your power?''

''Are you talking about mesmerism again? But mesmerism delivers only the shell of a person. And anyway, it would be a short cut. Don't you see? I want you to *freely behave* as if you're in my power. I want me to freely behave as if I'm in yours. But we have to pioneer our way there. No one's ever done it before – love in perfect freedom. Truly Free Love – not the mere sexual licentiousness that passes for it in the gutter press."

She sighed. He plucked another grass stalk and, gossamer-light, caned her face with it. "Will you ever understand it all up there?" he asked. "You're such an intuitive little artist."

"If you did get me in your power – never mind how – never mind all that philosophy for now – just for once – just play a game with me – if you did get me in your power – what would you do?"

He laughed. "Are you trying to seduce me, Tessa?"

"Answer *my* question first."

"Because – just to make it easy for you – let me tell you in advance that I fully intend to yield."

When he saw the frustration pass across her face he became serious again. He dropped the grass stalk and raised his hand to her chin. "If I had you in my power," he said, "I'd do this." With the outer edge of his thumb he began slowly to stroke her throat.

She closed her eyes and breathed out a long "Mmmmmmm!" His touch sent a thrill right down her body; though it was *in* her it seemed to have no location. It was in her scalp; it was in the soles of her feet; it was in neither place.

"And this," he whispered. His fingers touched the pit of her neck and ran delicately up to her ear, then on into her hair. They were never still.

The tips of his fingers strayed beneath the collar of her dress, raking the soft flesh of her shoulders. Then down to the more ample softness below her collarbone. "And this," he said.

A convulsion seized her, making her feel empty and then congested. Its power both thrilled and frightened her. She fought herself weakly to disengage. When she failed, and her mounting panic made her open her eyes, the first thing she saw was the wine bottle, which he must have moved aside earlier. Without thinking she raised herself still further, to reach for it. The movement brought her breast almost within his grasp. The sweet terror of that knowledge came too late to change anything.

Go on then! she thought, though something – a strange, trembling curiosity – prevented her from making any part of the move for him. He held back, too. His hand lingered at the edge of one-man's-land awhile – long enough for the beginnings of familiarity to still her heartbeat; then it moved away, up again to her neck.

Relief overwhelmed her. Its very strength was a kind of homage to the surrender he had not challenged her to make. Safe again, she lowered her lips to his and kissed him with what felt like gratitude. Soon she lay upon his arm while his fingers lightly combed her hair; there she fell into a brief and shallow sleep.

So shallow, indeed, that when he eased his arm away and replaced it with his rolled-up jacket, she awoke. Without opening her eyes she knew he was taking out his sketchbook and pencil, so she lay there in the aroma of him, rising from the sunwarmed jacket, and pretended to go on sleeping. A great feeling of luxury came over her, lying there on the damp, warm earth, with gentle zephyrs of a breeze winnowing her hair and fine hotspots of sunlight dancing over her skin, and knowing he was looking at her . . . and looking at her . . . and looking at her, in the young and easy warmth of that endless afternoon.

Chapter Fifteen

"Who is Simon Liddington?" Tessa asked, bringing the morning's post to the breakfast table.

"I'm sure I told you, dear," Bo said. "He's your father's new curate."

Tessa nudged her father with the envelope. "I didn't know you were getting a new curate. Here's a letter for him."

"Ten letters," he murmured. Then he looked up from the acrostic in the *Gazette* and asked, "Schliemann?"

"No – Liddington."

"Liddington." He looked back at his paper. "Well-known in archaeological circles."

"Is he!" Tessa was pleased. "Well, that'll make a change from knitting. Poor Mr. Sweetman."

"Who are you talking about?" he asked.

"Your new curate – this Reverend Simon Liddington who is so well-known in archaeological circles."

"Good heavens!" Her father stared at her. "What an astonishing coincidence! 'Well-known in archaeological circles' also happens to be today's acrostic in the *Gazette*. Ten letters. D'you think that's an omen? Funny – he never mentioned archaeology to me."

Tessa gave up and returned to her place.

D'Arblay stared at the envelope. "Liddington. Archaeology, eh? I shan't know what to talk to the fellow about. Why on earth have they sent him here, I wonder? You'd better take him under your wing, Tessa my child. Show him around – the way your mother used to."

"Bo and I will manage," she reassured him.

"Archaeology!" he repeated sadly. "Well, we've had worse. We've had worse. Still . . . if he's as well-known as you say, I'll try him. I was so sure it was Schliemann, too." He pencilled L,i,d,d,i,n,g,t,o,n down the acrostic, but very faintly.

Bo saw Tessa drawing breath to attempt an explanation; she laid a hand on her niece's arm to restrain her. "Remember what your mother always used to say – if they can survive here, they'll survive anywhere else, too. If it wasn't archaeology, it'd be some other misunderstanding. Like poor Mr. Sweetman and his knitting."

Tessa nodded in resignation. She picked up her teaspoon and dashed the tip of it against the crown of her boiled egg, neatly scalping it. The white was hard, the yolk nice and runny, just the way she liked it. She sprinkled salt onto her toast and cut it into fingers, or "soldiers." Then, with a quick glance at her father, who believed she ought to have left such ways in the nursery, she plunged the first soldier deep into the runny yolk, twirled it, and then lifted it, dripping gorgeously, to her mouth. Bo watched in fascinated disgust. "You'll have to stop eating like that if Mr. Liddington is a hearty-breakfast man," she said.

"When's he coming?" Tessa dipped and devoured the next soldier. "How old is he? Maybe he's still trainable. I managed to train Mr. Sweetman to eat soldiers."

"Only because he was infatuated with you."

"Then I'll have to infatuate Mr. Liddington, too."

"One day God'll punish you if you go on talking like that," Bo warned. "He'll make you fall in love with a man who won't even look at you – and serve you right if you ask me."

"What I actually asked you, Bo, was when he's due to arrive? Has his room been prepared?"

"This afternoon. I'm sure I told you."

"Oh."

Bo said with heavy sarcasm: "I hope that's quite convenient to you, Tessa dear. Greet him. Show him around. The way your mother used to. I know you lead such a busy life these days."

"Careful, Bo!" Tessa warned. "You're in danger of mentioning the Forbidden Subject – what I actually devote my life to doing."

"Lord alone knows what that might be."

"What's that supposed to mean?"

"Lord alone knows," Bo repeated. Then with equal fervour, as if it were just as much a part of her niece's moral instruction, she added, "If you turn that egg upside down in the cup, you can pretend it's whole again. We always used to do that, your poor dear mother and I."

"It isn't at all convenient, as it happens," Tessa said. "Someone else will just have to do it." She stared hard at her aunt and added, "It's a case of if the cap fits! Not to mention the corset, the bustle, the dress, gloves, stockings, and shoes. If you haven't the time, either, he must just cool his heels until tomorrow. The fact is, I've finished my bust of Mr. Rosen and Mr. Rosen thinks he'll finish his portrait of me this afternoon. And then, by way of celebration, we're going to the theatre."

"Indeed!" To Tessa it seemed that only her aunt's tight collar, by trapping her skin at her throat, prevented her eyebrows from travelling right over her scalp and down the back of her neck.

She added in a tired-conciliatory tone: "Not à deux, if that's what's worrying you. Mr. Rosen, Connie Saunders, and I – and no doubt others – will all be of the party."

Bo sighed with resignation. "Well, you are of age. And thanks to that scandalous legacy from cousin Jessica, you have independent means. You suffer absolutely no parental control" – this last with a venomous glance at the preoccupied figure of her brother-in-law. "You don't move in Society, so you have no reputation to guard. And in any case, you're twenty-four

106

and well past marrying age. What possible objection can there be to your cavorting around with Mr. Rosen or anyone else – chaperoned or not? Day or night?''

Tessa laughed – in a tone more teasing than harsh. "Really Bo! This can't be jealousy?''

Her aunt's chin shot up three inches. "Don't you worry on my account, miss!''

"Well, just so that you won't think me a creature quite abandoned to the wild and sudden impulse, let me tell you now, in good time, that next week, on Midsummer's Day, I shall be going away with a party of friends (yes – Mr. Rosen among them) to Amesbury, on Salisbury Plain. And there we shall make corn dollies and a mile of daisy chains and watch the dawn of the summer solstice over Stonehenge and do other dreadful pagan things. I give you due warning.''

"Stonehenge!'' her father cried. "That's it! Ten letters. Well known in archaeological circles! That's clever!'' He pencilled it in rapidly, as if he were afraid of forgetting it. Then he added with a smile, "I can see you'll have no difficulty getting on with this Liddington fellow. He's a keen archaeologist, I hear. By the way, Bo my dear, have we any idea when he's coming?''

Early that afternoon Dante Rosen finished her portrait.

Two days ago her clay bust of him had been carted gingerly down to the Whitechapel Foundry for casting in bronze. Since then she had stood by an empty modelling easel, wondering why muscles and joints that would go uncomplainingly through a day of work could not abide one minute of idleness. So when Dante said, "There!'' and laid down his palette, she wanted to jump and turn cartwheels of relief, or at least to strut around like Saunders (who had recovered from her chill and could at that moment be faintly heard reciting a dramatic monologue down in the courtyard).

"Are you ever going to look at it?'' Dante asked.

She walked toward him, still avoiding the picture, and put her arms around his neck. "I want you to know, Dante,'' she said solemnly, "that whatever mess you've made of it, I'm still quite fond of you.''

Intense annoyance passed across his face. He unpeeled her arms brusquely and flung them to her side. "Look at the bloody thing!'' he told her.

107

She turned around – and caught her breath. What she saw before her was beyond all doubt a masterpiece. The violence that had come out in his unfinished painting of Saunders was here held under his full control – contained within the painting to give it a monumental power and life. Every brushstroke said (to her) an unmistakable *I love you*!

"Well?" he prompted. She could hear his shivering.

"I'm privileged," she said quietly. "Not just that you chose me but also that I'm the first to see it. There's something about great art. . . .." She was unable to complete the thought. "To look at it one way, it's just a patch of colour in a coloured world; but in another way I can already feel it belongs to all mankind. It's already part of history. I can imagine it on a wall in the Louvre or the National Gallery, a century from now. People going especially out of their way to see 'the Rosen' and wondering who was 'Tessa' – just as we wonder. . ."

"No they won't," he interrupted. "The d'Arblays will hang beside mine. In fact, it'll be called The d'Arblay Room."

She smiled fondly but insisted, ". . . just as we wonder who was Hélène Fourment or Saskia or the Maja?"

"The Nude Maja," he told her. "That's what I want next. I want to paint you nude." His hands gently enclosed her hips from behind and eased her toward him. She offered no resistance – so much so that he almost toppled backward. To steady himself he put his arms around her, one on her stomach, the other where her breast actually rested on his outstretched hand. *So it's now*, she thought.

His breathing broke into a shiver. "God – how I want you, Tess!" he murmured. "I've been dreading finishing this painting because I knew it would become intolerable."

"Oh Dante!" she said; but her tone was flat. It surprised even her. She wanted to become his lover, she wanted to know what it was like, and yet there was no great rush of feeling from her body to make that moment of yielding easy. On any other day it would have been there; she was absolutely sure of that. Dante was now the single greatest thing in her life – the only man she would ever want. So why did she not now yield herself to him, when she had spent the past few weeks thinking of little else, preparing herself for it? Why did her flat little voice pop out now and surprise her like that?

He heard her tone. Desperation made him bold. His hand rose to enclose her breast. The pressure on her stomach intensified. She felt herself melting. *Now?* But her flesh cried out, too soon, too soon!

She turned and tried to bury her vulnerability against him, to rekindle there in the shelter, away from those brusque hands, that melting passion which had come to her so often. But he was not quite tall enough to offer that escape; when his lips sought hers, she could not hide them beneath his chin nor sink her head upon his chest. And when, lower down, he pressed himself to her, he did not – as a taller man might have – waste the gesture among the gathered folds of her dress; his hardness found the flesh and bone of her. She felt his stiffness there, understood it, was calmly curious about it – but nothing more than that.

Nor, she discovered, was her back less vulnerable than her front. His urgent hands on the thin summer cloth turned muscle into lemonade; their touch was a fizz, their pressure a branding. The yielding softness began to envelop her stubborn and surprising resistance. It was going to happen after all. A vortex was rising around her. "No," she said in tones that surely meant *yes*.

But he mistook her and stopped. "Don't say no. Don't say no. Don't say no!"

It was a fatal pause. His passion, and the break in their rhythm, frightened her virginity and froze her longed-for yielding. A brief anger took its place and then, in turn, vanished, leaving only a space. In that fraction of a second, control passed to something within her, below the level of her senses. Mind and flesh still whispered *now!* and struggled to regain the lost narcotic of his thrusting rhythm. But a deeper urge, the essential female, deaf and formless, knew it did not have to be now. It dismantled her craving, throb by throb, until she could step outside herself and watch the still-feeling shell of her. That was the extraordinary thing – up there on her skin the dizziness still raged; but it was a pale fire on an ocean of cool regard.

She kissed him, and took pleasure in the kissing; yet the watching half of her was awestruck at the way her longing had simply curled up and vanished.

He sensed it. His urgency grew desperate. "You monster! Look at yourself!" He spun her to face the portrait; his one trump

109

card. But he had already played it. Her hands gauged precisely where his would plummet; her fingers, already there to meet him, adroitly absorbed the impact, then opened and closed in a swift scissor to entrap him. He said, "I've given you immortality and you deny me one small death of the soul!"

"We will!" she said to placate him, thinking her bright certainty was but a small mortgage of tomorrow's Tessa, and one she could redeem as easily as this. "We will, my love! But not here. Not now."

His clutch on her imprisoning hands strengthened. She felt the power of his arms and knew how quickly he would win any contest of brute strength. He shuddered. "You!" He made the word a bestial growl; it stirred something bestial within her, too, so that she was no longer quite so certain of her refusal. Her heartbeat fought the pressure of his arms. The powerful crush of them, against her chest, against her stomach, stilled her blood. A voice within, idiotically calm, told her she was losing consciousness. And then it wouldn't matter.

"We will," she repeated, but that thin soprano promise was a crumb to an elephant. The twin titans of his anger – thwarted lust and wounded self-esteem – raged on.

In a swimming world she ceased to struggle. Her hands went limp. He cast them off like gloves.

Free to stray, they strayed. Over her dress, into the folds of her dress, into the openings of her dress, into the openings of her flesh, into the hot and secret places. The calm dolt within her, rooted in the flying blackness at the margin of knowing, watched it all . . . took note of its novelty . . . felt no wonder.

In the end it was her sheer lack of response that defeated him. His movement ran down like clockwork on a small spring. Weak once more, he slumped upon her strength, a chastened fool, becalmed in the wreckage of his vanished lust. His hands, marooned where no man's hands had ever been, were like revellers sobered by disaster in a sudden dawn. He could not even bid them move – had to wait for her to unpeel them.

But no thunderstorm can pass without its last diminuendo. "I'd better not come here again," he said flatly.

She assessed him: He was angry still, but his anger was cold. Did that make it the more dangerous? She had not experience enough to tell. It occurred to her that he was a man of too-easy conquests; past success had cost him present judgement.

"My God!" he said; and now his voice was bitter. "You know what you're doing! You and civilization! If I wanted you before, I'm half-insane with it now." But the emotion was too intense – and in a curious way too fragile – to survive its passage through so many words. By the time he had finished speaking, his tone fell like a verdict, denying bail to his lust – which, after her cooperation was withheld, was all it had become.

What could she say? All the obvious things would ring too smug. She touched his face. Her gesture breathed hope rather than commitment. He managed a rueful smile in return. And so, by the strange alchemy that sometimes transmutes lust to love, they saved tomorrow as another fixture in their lives.

He held wide his arms; his smile withdrew all menace from their gesture. She slipped into his embrace and felt safe once more.

"What happened?" he asked. "There were feelings back there I've never had before."

"Before?" she echoed. She caught the smell of herself upon his fingers. "Too many befores!"

He said nothing. His tongue slipped onto the lobe of her ear; he was learning. "When?" he whispered.

She tried to think of some reason why he should not seek to know.

His tongue trembled. He knew what effect it was having on her.

"In a desert," she said. "On a wave. In caverns measureless to man. Come as a raging bull, as a shower of gold."

He withdrew and stood free, conceding the day to her. As a free woman she smiled at him and added, "And where time itself is infinite."

He nodded tightly, as if to say she had already constrained the business far enough. He ran his fingers through his hair, through his beard, his moustache. She knew it was an empty gesture; his true purpose was to sniff at the honey-salt of her. There was now an awkwardness between them. They no longer knew who to be. Their former selves still cowered in shock, refusing to emerge.

"Well!" Her brightness was painful to her. "Time certainly isn't infinite today."

"Oh?"

They were creating a new and unreal kind of normality; she knew she must leave, and quickly; "if the wind changed" (as Saunders would say), they might be stranded forever in this limbo.

"You are coming to the theatre tonight?" he asked.

"Good heavens, yes." Her laughter was brittle. "I wouldn't miss it for worlds. But this afternoon is for duty. I have to show father's new curate around the parish – Lord help him!"

"You have to?"

"I absolutely promised my aunt Bo."

Chapter Sixteen

As soon as she was away from Dante, beyond the touch and feel of him, she began to regret what had happened – or, rather, what had *not*. Why had things gone wrong, especially when she had spent so many hours daydreaming how wonderful it was going to be? Her body had still wanted him. Her mind had not wavered in its desire for experience and for the understanding that must surely follow. So what within her was capable of such contrary judgement? Where was the power so profound it could set aside both her physical craving and her moral will and leave her marooned in that strange limbo, devoid of feeling, empty of thought?

Unhappy and bewildered she wandered out into Bleeding Heart Lane. What now? She couldn't go home; this Simon Liddington might be there. She couldn't return to the studio; Dante, understandably angry, had put his painting of Saunders back on his easel and was attacking it with relish.

Saunders herself appeared in the archway leading from the courtyard. "'Ello, ducks," she said. "Where are you sneaking off to?"

"The hospice." She answered on the spur of the moment. "I've neglected them shamefully."

"I'll come too. My soul could do with a bit of a wash."

They set off for the main road. "Painting finished?" Saunders asked.

"It's wonderful. You've watched it growing. You have to agree – it's wonderful."

Saunders nodded reluctantly. "I wish he'd do one of me like that."

"Don't you admit you misjudged him, Saunders?"

"Maybe. There's certainly more to him than I thought. But I still can't help wondering how he'd be if you hadn't had those painting tricks he wanted to steal off you. He plays with people, you know. He definitely does. I've seen him. He plays with Segal – sort of eggs him on to things he'd never do on his own. All right – Segal wants to do them anyway. I grant you that. But there's things he'd never have dared without Rosen egging him on."

"What?"

"Just things. You'd have to have been there. You've got to see it for yourself – the way he works on people."

Tessa sighed at the uncertainty of everything. "Really you're saying you haven't misjudged him."

"He's different with you. Sometimes I almost get the feeling he's a bit afraid of you. I hope that's what it is."

"You *hope*. Why hope?"

"Because, d'Arblay me old duck, if it's not fear then he's just laying back a while and wondering what grand bit of devilment he can egg *you* on to. Saving you up, see?"

"Oh you're wrong you're wrong you're wrong."

"He's not finished with Segal yet. And a blacksmith can only have so many bellows in the fire." Saunders spoke with great finality.

Tessa toyed with the idea of telling her what had just not-happened. Perhaps she'd be able to explain it.

But she let too long a pause elapse. The silence would give her words too much weight.

"Penny for your thoughts?" she asked.

"It doesn't feel like a Thursday," Saunders told her.

"Very funny!"

Saunders at last heard the tension in Tessa's voice. She glanced at her in anxious bewilderment – but was also at a loss for anything to say.

Their roundabout approach brought them to Cole Place by way of Distillery Row, where, in a room set apart from the hospice, a room that opened directly onto the street, the nuns had set aside a refuge for the streetwalkers of Hoxton and Whitechapel – an alternative to the pubs, which provided their only other shelter. Tessa and Saunders were just passing the open door of this room when a loud laugh came from within. Saunders stopped. "I know that voice," she said. "D'you mind if I go in there for a moment?"

"Don't be too long."

Rather than wait, Tessa went round the corner to the convent to see what they might want in the way of help this time. To her chagrin, no one remarked upon her absence; the routine of the place had closed over her withdrawal, leaving not a ripple. It took some while to find the appropriate nun – who could then devise nothing better on so short a notice than that Tessa should go through two cupboards full of laundered sheets and sort out those that needed further bleaching or other attention. She handed over the key to the linen store. Tessa, who in her restlessness had looked forward to some more heroic task, accepted this surrogate with calm resignation – or so she fondly imagined, until the sister called after her, "They also serve . . . you know!"

When she regained the street she was annoyed to discover that Saunders was still in the refuge. She poked her head inside. Silence fell. She walked in. It took her eyes a moment or so to adapt to the gloom. The first person she saw was Saunders, squatting on her haunches and holding out her arms toward a young child – a solemn, dignified, observant little three-year-old girl. "Come on!" she called. "Come to auntie, then!"

There were three or four other women there, mostly young ones who could afford to show their skin in daylight. One of them was older, in her forties, but still with a passable complexion; she appeared to be the mother of the child.

"We wasn't doin no 'arm, miss," Saunders said in her skivvy's whine.

"Come on," Tessa told her. "We've work to do." These young prostitutes always made her feel uncomfortable. They were women yet they were not women; a third gender.

Saunders grinned and turned again to the child. "Drop a little curtsey then to the fine lady," she commanded.

114

The child obeyed, giving a most stately plunge. "What a little courtier you are!" Tessa said. "Can you tell me your name?"

"She's a right-down reg'lar queen!" Saunders laughed.

In the corner of her eye Tessa saw the mother glaring furiously at Saunders.

"My name's Alice," the child said.

"Well, you're a pretty little girl, Alice," Tessa stooped and told her. "Alice what, may I ask?" She glanced up at the mother. "Is she yours?"

The woman hastily shook her head. "I'm looking after her for a friend. Crook's her name. Alice Crook. Mother was Annie Crook."

"Was?"

The woman made an isn't-life-awful grimace. "She got an abscess on her brain, poor thing. She's been in the orspital since April. They say she won't never come out again." A repeat of the grimace bracketed this news.

Tessa looked the child over. She seemed well cared for and happy. "You can manage, can you?" she asked the woman. "You know that if the mother goes . . . (she glanced heavenward) and you look after . . . (a barely perceptible nod toward the little girl) the Board of Guardians may grant you a certain sum each week – one and sixpence, I think?"

"One and fourpence, miss. Yes, I do know that, thank you. But there's four of us take turns, like, to look after her. We manage all right – and we don't want no Board of Guardians poking their noses in."

It was an extraordinary response from the sort of woman who never had two pennies to rub together and who was always "on the scrounging lay." There was something furtively triumphant about her manner, too – as if Tessa's suggestion had been a bit of a private joke.

Tessa turned to Saunders. "Come on."

Saunders stood and dusted her hands on her apron. She followed Tessa into the cobbled street. As soon as they were out of easy earshot of the refuge she said, "You'd have to laugh to hear it, Tess."

"What?"

"Well, that Polly Nicholls – she was the one you spoke to – always knew she lacked a bit of furniture up in her attic floor, her and that Annie Siffey, but you'll never believe what they've corncocted this time. Little Alice there – she's only third in line for the throne of England!''

Tessa laughed.

"It's the truth!'' Saunders grinned. "One gin and she'll swear it. Her real name's Sickert, see. Alice Sickert . . .''

"Sickert? There's a painter by that name,'' Tessa said. Her voice petered out when she saw the other's smile and wagging finger.

"That's the fella! You've not heard the half of it!'' Saunders was enjoying the tale and its telling.

They went into the hospice and along the corridor to a dark little inner courtyard. The sheet store lay on the far side. As soon as they were out in the narrow well of light, Saunders continued: "That Sickert taught young Prince Eddy all about painting. Did you know that?''

"No.''

"And he did more than teach him. This was in his studio up West. These painters – they're all like The Demon, you know. He introduced the little prince to the artistic way of life, as you might say. Physically he introduced him to poor Annie Crook, who was behind the counter in the little tobacconist shop opposite, and . . .''

"You mean specifically, not physically.''

"Something like that. Bit of both, actually. Anyway, what they're saying – Nicholls and Siffey and a couple of others – they all knew Annie, see – because Annie went on the game from time to time, like the rest of them – what they're saying is it soon got out of hand and into Annie, as the saying goes. And the little prince, who can't make friends with anyone without also falling in love with them, too – as soon as he saw he'd sprained poor Annie's ankle – well, he only goes and marries her! Borrows Sickert's name and marries her! And that's the royal offspring who just did a right-royal curtsey to you.'' She laughed again. "Honestly! Did you ever hear anything like it!''

"Never mind that,'' Tessa answered. "It's dangerous talk – you'd better tell this Nicholls woman. There are laws against talking about the royal family like that. Tell her they'll chop her head off in the Tower.'' She began walking toward the linen store. "Go and tell her now, in fact.''

116

Saunders laughed, but Tessa made it clear she was serious.

Alone again she felt in her pocket for the linen-store key. The door behind her opened again. She turned, thinking it was Saunders having forgotten something. But it was a young clergyman.

"Miss d'Arblay?" He advanced toward her.

"Dr. Liddington, I presume?"

He laughed. He was quite good-looking – tall, with fair, curly hair, a strong jaw and determined mouth. His pale-green, deep-set eyes looked down at her coolly. He was in his mid-twenties, too old for a first parish. She wondered if he'd been sent here as some kind of punishment.

"How d'you do," he said, holding out his hand.

It annoyed her, for it was her place, not his, to make that first move. But she shook it nonetheless.

"What's all this about archaeology?" he asked.

She laughed. "I'm afraid that's something you're stuck with from now until you move on, Mr. Liddington. Even if I explained how it came about, you wouldn't believe it. Be thankful it's archaeology. Poor Mr. Sweetman had to live down a quite undeserved reputation as a secret knitter – and all because of a sermon he gave on the casting of pearls before swine, which he pronounced 'swain' – and my father, who even at his best only listens to half of anything, heard 'plain' – and what with all this business of 'purl and plain' and 'casting off', he assumed it was a sermon about knitting and . . . well . . ."

"Poor Mr. Sweetman, as you say. Then I am glad it's to be archaeology."

She unlocked the storeroom door before she turned to him and said, "I have to look over some sheets for the nuns, Mr. Liddington. Are you in a helpful mood?"

"I'd be delighted. Shall we wait for Miss Saunders to return, perhaps?"

"Oh, you know about her?"

"Your aunt told me. She said I'd find you both down here, doing Good Works."

She heard Bo's intonation in his repeat of the words. "Indeed," she said grimly. "Well, I don't feel like waiting for Miss Saunders, I'm afraid."

"Oh . . ." He was at a loss.

She looked him in the eyes and said, "I hope you're not an utterly conventional young man, Mr. Liddington."

He didn't like it but was too courteous to say so outright. He clasped his hands together – in a curious way it suggested handcuffs – and nodded toward the door. She led the way inside. "Where were you before here?" she asked.

"This is my first parish, Miss d'Arblay."

"Oh?" She decided upon the pile of sheets she wanted to inspect and turned to get a low stool; but he reached over her and lifted them down; it was a large pile but he managed it effortlessly. He was, she felt, proud of his strength.

"I know what you're thinking," he said. "I'm a bit long in the tooth for a first parish. The fact is, I took a medical diploma first – so with your 'Doctor Liddington' you presumed correctly. However, during that time I decided to become a missionary. So I studied for Holy Orders after I qualified. Better late than never."

She picked up the first sheet and took it nearer the window. He grasped one end and helped her, turning each side to the light. "And here you are," she said, "a missionary in the darkest East End!"

"Many a true word! Indeed, it was while studying for Holy Orders that I began to read Engels and Booth, who opened my eyes to the fact that we have our own Dark Continent here at home."

Tessa wondered how the young man was going to get on with her father, who believed Church of England Christianity was a gentleman's faith, quite wasted on the lower classes.

"That sheet has a bit of rust," she said. "Put it for bleaching." While they were unfurling the next, she watched the curate and decided there was something just a little smug about him. He knew how handsome he was. He knew how competently he was moving. He knew precisely how right he was in his opinions. These qualities vaguely threatened her. She felt the need to put some distance between them.

While she was wondering how, they did a silent gavotte, gathering and passing the corners of the next sheet. Their eyes met. He said, "I'd better confess to you, Miss d'Arblay, before you hear it from some other quarter, that I've already been living in the parish for a month. I took a casual labouring job and I've

118

been living rough – 'skippering it', if you know the term – and also sleeping in common lodging houses and the casual wards of workhouses. So you see I do know this parish, and its people, rather better than you might expect.''

Tessa digested this in silence. ''Show me your hands,'' she commanded.

He complied. Their skin was tough, with hardened callouses at the bases of his fingers. ''It doesn't look like your first time, either,'' she said.

He shook his head, agreeing with her. ''So – we surprise each other. You certainly surprise me.''

''Do I?''

''Yes, when one hears of a vicar's daughter who spends all her time doing Good Works one thinks. . .''

''Oh dear!'' she interrupted him. ''Before you go on – let me take away my own quite undeserved reputation. I do not Do Good Works. The fact is. . .''

''But your aunt. . .''

''Neither she nor my father can face the truth of what I really do. The fact is I am a painter. Not a pretty little water colourist, you understand. An artist. I spend almost every hour of every day selfishly locked away in my studio, painting. They cannot accept the truth of that – so. . .''

''And yet I find you here? Exactly as your aunt said I would.''

She smiled inwardly, thinking of the precise chain of events that had brought about the coincidence. ''For the first time in. . .in far too long,'' she answered. ''It's true I do lend a hand here from time to time, but not nearly often enough to qualify me as a Doer of Good Works.''

He laughed. ''Well, I'm sure you *paint* good works, Miss d'Arblay.''

''I do.'' She set aside another sheet for turning sides-to-middle.

''Actually,'' he went on, ''I'm none too sure of the morality of Good Works. The social order – by which I mean Money and Property – they damage people. And we philanthropists, what do we do? We patch 'em up and send 'em back for those same forces to damage and exploit all over again.''

''Is that so very different from patching up their souls on Sunday for the Devil to exploit all week?'' she asked.

He pursed his lips and nodded, conceding the point.

There was a silence and then he said, "You're extraordinarily easy to talk to, you know. I expect you have a lot of friends?"

"No. In fact, I've lived quite a solitary life. I didn't go to a school. I mean, I was taught at home."

"Were you solitary from choice?"

"I've made one or two good friends recently. I suppose I've regretted not making more – earlier, I mean. I never thought about being solitary before that." She wondered why she was unfolding to him in this way.

He seemed to understand her bewilderment. "Do box my ears if you think I'm trespassing," he said jovially. "My curiosity's insatiable, I'm afraid. It always gets me into trouble. What sort of painting do you do?" He quoted Ruskin's famous libel on Whistler: "D'you 'fling a pot of paint in the public's face'?"

"That sort of thing," she laughed. "But I earn nothing by it, not even a farthing. What about you? Have you got any brothers and sisters?"

He shook his head. "Another solitary child. Perhaps painting is your form of insatiable curiosity. Did you always know you were going to be a painter? Was it destiny, I mean? Or did it take you by surprise?"

She had to think. "I suppose it took me by surprise," she said at last. "But then it was as if I'd always known it – though not in so many words."

He nodded. Was it just a mannerism or did he actually understand?

"What about you?" she asked.

He smiled self-deprecatingly. "Always knew I was going to be a *reformer* of some kind. Reform souls. Reform bodies . . ." He spoke as if it were all past.

"But now?" she prompted.

His eyes twinkled. "Got the marching orders a bit wrong, I fear. Most reformers do. Just look at them! Up early and late, buttonholing the world, strutting around like animated pincushions, plaguing the ears of the populace with good advice . . . when all the time the real reforms" – he tapped his own breastbone – "get overlooked."

He had an extraordinary gift for conveying his ideas by gesture as much as by his actual words. For, though he spoke in such a clouded shorthand, she had no doubt of his meaning. "If you were a monk," she said half-jokingly, "you'd have begun in a healing order, then hopped over into a teaching order, and now I suppose you'd be looking around for a contemplative order."

She turned from him as she spoke, to hold her corner of the sheet to the fading light. She became aware that he'd dropped his end. She turned to see him staring at her, open-mouthed. "What?" she asked.

"What you just said. It's quite extraordinary. In one brief sentence you've managed to clear away months of confusion in my mind. Fffft! Like that!"

"I was only joking really."

He shook his head, as if still somewhat dazed. "The Church is right – and you do right to remind me of it. In her ancient wisdom she is right. No single order can perform all three tasks. How much less, then, can a single man hope to do? I'm sorry. I've let this sheet trail in the dirt now."

"Just put it with the others. So which of the three will you choose?"

"Oh, I've already chosen. What you've just said, though, has made it easier to lay the other two aside for a season. We must first know ourselves. But more than that. We must understand . . . so many difficult things. Why is there so much suffering in the world? Why does an allegedly perfect God allow so much that is evil to go on – and on? How can we be made in His image and yet be so corrupt?"

"And why does the Devil have all the best tunes!" she added.

"That too, yes." He laughed. "But at least one question has already been answered."

"Which is?"

"Of all the parishes in the world why was I directed to this particular one? And why, on this afternoon, were my feet guided here?"

121

Chapter Seventeen

On the morning of Midsummer's Eve, the day they were to set out for Salisbury Plain, Tessa idly asked her father how one could really *know* anything. As soon as she saw the glint in his eye she knew what a mistake she had made; she hardly needed Bo's venomous glances to underline the fact.

Bo vainly tried to head him off. "Of course we know things," she said scornfully. "What an idiotic question! I know this tea's getting a bit stewed. I know I like soft-boiled eggs. I know it's not raining outside. I know what day it is – or I did when I got up."

"Thursday," Tessa said.

"And," Bo looked sternly at her brother-in-law, "I also know, Gordon dear, that I shall have a raging headache if you start with your epistemologies and eschatologies . . ."

"No no, my lamb. It's really quite simple." The bit was already between his teeth. "Though incidentally, talking of epistemology, you listed five quite different types of knowing just now. But you, my dear," he turned to his daughter, "are more interested, I think, in the knowing of knowing itself."

"Actually," Tessa began . . .

"Yes yes. Quite. A fascinating question. I was drawing some geometrical shapes the other day and I was forced to ask myself: If I saw a perfect circle, would I recognize it? And I concluded that I should. But how could that be, I hear you object – since I most assuredly have never seen a perfect circle? And I answer you that I have seen so many imperfect ones during the course of my life that I should be able to infer a perfect circle despite those imperfections – for they are all imperfect in *different* ways, you see! I should be able to infer from them a *tendency* towards perfection."

He beamed around at them. "Ah, the power of inference! It is surely the basis of all knowledge. I then asked myself: Suppose I had no compass, should I still be able to infer a perfect circle? Again I was forced to conclude that I should. For, with no more than a pencil and a straightedge, I should yet be able to construct a many-sided figure – one with so many sides, indeed, that it would approximate to an imperfect circle. And from there, as I have already shown, it is but a short step to the inference of a perfect circle. A Neanderthaler sitting in his cave, scribbling on the wall with a piece of burned charcoal could have done it.''

''What I actually meant,'' Tessa tried again . . .

''I know, I know. What has this to do with knowing – with the knowing of knowing? Why, this! If my Neanderthal forebear sitting in his cave and staring at a few scribbles on its wall can from it infer the existence of a perfect circle – and I think I have shown conclusively that he can – well, cannot we, staring at the moral scribble of this most imperfect world which is all around us, cannot we in the same way infer the existence of a Perfect Being? Too many people, you see, look at the moral imperfections of the world and from them infer an indifferent geometer. But it is not so!''

He rose and, in passing, kissed Tessa on the head. ''Thank you my child. I must go and write that down before it eludes me. You have given me my sermon for next Sunday.''

''Yes – thank you!'' Bo added heavily.

''What I actually wanted to ask was how we know about people? How can we know whether they're good or bad?''

Her father paused briefly in the door and shook his head. ''Philosophically speaking,'' he answered, ''the question is almost barren of interest. It begs too much of itself. It is built around a tautology.'' He went.

''Thank heavens for little mercies,'' Bo muttered.

Simon, who had sat quietly throughout the exchange, at first amused then spellbound, said, ''Quite fascinating. Your father's absolutely right, you know.''

''Now we're feeding two of them!'' Bo snorted. She turned to Tessa. ''You'd better hurry if you're to get to the station in time.''

Half an hour later the two young women set off in the dogcart for Waterloo. Saunders was posing for this weekend as Mrs. Sanderson, a fitting chaperone for Miss d'Arblay. ''Does your father ever talk about ordinary things?'' she asked.

''Vegetables,'' Tessa answered defensively. ''He knows quite a bit about them. And chess.''

''Vegetables and chess,'' Saunders echoed, as if committing

the fact to memory.

They arrived in good time for their train. Dante, who had spent the night back in his own studio in Chelsea, was waiting for them at the barrier.

"There's been a very slight change of plan," he said, just as the train began to pull away from the platform.

"Oh?" both women looked up in disappointment.

"Nothing to be alarmed about," he added. "It's just that we're not going to be staying at the White Hart, after all. Instead, well. . . you don't know Mars Gloab, by any chance?"

"Marcus Gloab?" Mrs. Sanderson asked in great excitement. "*The* Marcus Gloab?"

"He's Marcus in London, but Mars on Olympus. Naturally – if one may use that particular word in connection with Marcus."

"But that still doesn't say who he is," Tessa insisted.

"He's the owner of *six* theatres in London – that's who," Mrs. Sanderson said. "The Pearl in Hackney, The Vortex in Hoxton, The Alhambra in Kensal Green, The Palace of Fun in Bow, the. . ."

Dante interrupted with a laugh. "My goodness, Mrs. Sanderson, you seem to know more than the bailiff."

"Are we really going to stay at Olympus!" Mrs. Sanderson went on excitedly. She turned to Tessa. "That's his country house, you know. In Wilkshire."

Tessa laughed. "Is it close to Stonehenge?"

"Close enough," Dante said. "It's in one of those surprising little hidden valleys you almost fall into wherever there's a dip on Salisbury Plain. But to call it a 'country house' is a bit misleading. If you imagine our studio, or the whole of the Old Thatched Barn, in all its original glory, transported into the middle of a tight little wooded Wiltshire valley, a real, rambling Jacobean sort of place, full of secret passages and priest's hiding holes, you'll have some sort of an idea. . ."

Mrs. Sanderson cut in with a much more important question: "Who else will be there? Theatrical people, I expect."

"One never knows at Olympus. It may be a large gathering, or it may be quite intimate. Also – something else you ought to be warned about – no one has a proper name there. Especially at Midsummer. So if a certain Sebastian Melmoth happens to be

124

among the company, don't call him Oscar. And if a Baron Renfrew engages you in conversation – or in anything else – try not to call him Your Highness.''

''Will George Grossmith be there?'' Mrs. Sanderson hacked a broad swath through Dante's elegant maze.

''Look for his deputy – Mr. Porter . . . or is it Pewter?''

''Are you making all this up?'' Tessa asked. ''Why are you being so mysterious?''

''Midsummer! Mystery's heytime.''

Talk of ''Your Highness'' reminded her of that recent encounter with Annie Crooks's little girl in the nuns' refuge. Tessa wiled away several miles of their journey by telling Dante how four East End prostitutes were taking turns to rear one of the heirs to the throne. As their laughter died, Dante added, ''Oh yes – I almost forgot. One man who'll certainly be there is Barbazur; he'll bear an astonishing resemblance to Dr. Segal.''

The train steamed on through the southwestern suburbs and, after brief flashes of doomed countryside, through Kew and Esher. At every station crowds of people got on and off. Tessa wondered where they all came from – and where they were going. It hardly seemed possible that so many people could have necessary errands, all on this one day. What would they have done before there were railways? They couldn't all have gone by coach. Did the very existence of railways *tempt* people to make journeys?

She tried to settle to the book Dante had lent her – *A Rebours* by Huysmans – but found herself uncomfortably stirred by the hero's obsession with the pleasures of the senses. Dante, lounging opposite her, was trying to make sketches.

''How d'you like the book?'' he asked when he saw her lapse into a daydream.

She shook her head and shivered.

The line was in open country by now, heading for Woking; real country, with big farmhouses and large herds of cows, not the uneasy mixture of smallholdings and villas on the fringes of the city. In one field, full of tall grasses mingled with poppies and marigolds, they were cutting hay. Three men with scythes were just clearing the last of the headlands. She could see the farmer hitching a great carthorse to the haymower. In the neighbouring field a gang of men, women, and children were turning hay that

125

must have been cut some days ago. The farmer's wife and three servant girls were coming down the lane carrying baskets of bread all covered with white cloths, and enamelled canisters of tea, no doubt sweetly sugared. No doubt, too, stoneware jars of beer and cider lay deep in the cool of the hedgerow, under patched and fading jackets that had been the gentry's Sunday best half a century ago.

The scene was spread before her like a toy. Suddenly she wanted more than anything to be down there among them, innocent again, stripped to her bodice, with the sweat running down her and the haydust prickling her and her muscles aching and her ears straining for the creak of the gate as that blessed relief party arrived with its bounty of fresh, warm bread, all rich and yeasty, and the hot, sweet tea.

The train sped on; the fields dwindled, leaving her marooned in her own sense of loss, which was formless but acute. It surrounded her like an ice shell. She could sit still no longer. She snapped shut the book, startling Mrs. Sanderson momentarily out of her magazine, and went out into the corridor; Dante soon joined her.

"What an innocent life!" She pointed generally at the fleeting countryside. "Did you see those haymakers?"

At that moment a steep cutting plunged them into a green gloom. Its sides were dank with weeping, sootdark stones. "Innocent?" he asked. "Idyllic, perhaps, but hardly innocent. What d'you know of rural life?"

"I went haymaking when I was a child."

"You remember only your own innocence."

"Yes. Often."

Ever since what had not-happened in the studio he had been distant with her. She wanted some way to tell him everything would be all right now – they could become lovers this weekend if he wanted. She had tried conveying the idea in so many ways – standing close to him, touching him gently as she passed, taking his hand when they walked to the pub or park together. . . But his geniality was gone. His charm was gone. She didn't feel he was withholding them – or not deliberately, as Saunders had warned he would; it was more as if he couldn't help it now.

Unfortunately, whether or not it was deliberate, this withholding of his charm was having all the effect Saunders had predicted.

Tessa felt ready to do anything to turn on the tap of his good grace and humour once more. If she had unwittingly humiliated him, she would humiliate herself ten times more deeply, just to show how much she cared. If he wished to punish her, she would punish herself far more severely on his behalf. He needed only to ask it of her – whatever it might be. There was nothing she would not endure.

"What's really going to happen this weekend?" she asked.

He grunted a single sour laugh. "Actions sad. Actions comical. Actions compulsive. Actions sad-compulsive. Actions comical-sad. Actions sad-comical. . ."

"No – really! Is it to be a big party? It's not fair. You've been there before, I'll bet."

He went on staring into the dark, dank cutting. "Truly I don't know," he said. "The only people Mars Gloab mentioned in his letter were Segal and some theatrical associate of his – he didn't say who. Theatrical associates and women are like coins to him – they pass anonymously through his pockets in a steady stream."

"Women?" she said.

The sides of the cutting grew less steep, a ragged burnishing of blue began to top it out, first in patches then in streaks.

He turned to face her; his eyes still lacked the lustre of his former delight. She felt desolate. "Of course there'll be women," he said. "Mars Gloab is a short-cut merchant. So's Segal. They're all short-cut merchants."

There was a tetchiness in his words. She touched his hand. "I don't mind, Dante. I mean, I'm ready now. But not for anyone else. There's no one else but you. I just. . . I mean, I don't want to. . ." She could not reduce the beauty of the thought to the crudity of the only words that fitted. "Kiss me," she said. "Hold me. Tell me it's going to be all right."

Chapter Eighteen

Mars Gloab himself came to meet them at Amesbury station, the terminus of the branch line. Or, rather, he came to meet Rosen. His face lit up when he saw his friend but darkened when he noticed the two women beside. He waited for no introductions but grasped Rosen by the arm and led him away up the platform.

"Well, I never thought he looked like that," Mrs. Sanderson said.

He was a tall, restless, lean-built man in his mid-thirties. His face seemed carved, with a proudly Roman nose, curving lips, and deepset eyes. His long curly hair was even blacker than Rosen's. He had about him the air of a convalescent; he clutched his clothing – a rich toga-like gown – to him and seemed to shrivel from contact with the warmth of the day. The discussion between the two men was plainly of some warmth, too.

"We may be staying at the White Hart after all," Tessa said, preparing herself for that disappointment.

"You were going it a bit with Rosen, weren't you?"

"Oh, I didn't think you noticed."

As the men's conference proceeded, Mars Gloab glanced several times at the two women – first with distaste, then with reserve, then with interest, and finally with a kind of conditional pleasure. When he came striding back toward them, leaving Rosen to trail several paces behind, it was as if he were just arriving and his smile were for old friends.

"Mrs. Sanderson? Miss d'Arblay? My darlings – you're so very welcome!" He had a vibrant, light voice – much lighter than his appearance had led Tessa to expect. His smile was jovial but his eyes were hard and restless; they undressed the two women on the spot. Curiously enough, Tessa felt, there was nothing personal or lascivious in his action; it was more of a professional habit. It was thorough, for all that.

"This year we have utterly forsworn our usual midsummer frolics," he said. "So you must consign to sweet perchance all you may have heard from our dear friend Rosen. Another year, mayhap, another year. Instead, we propose a most" – his eyes lingered in a further audit while he chose his words – "intimate and novel affair. That much at least one may safely promise."

Mrs. Sanderson gave a nervous giggle and said, "Is George Grossmith of the party?"

He gave no sign of hearing the question. Instead he bowed with mocking dignity as he ushered them through the wicket gate to the station forecourt. The porter carried their luggage to a dogcart, which set out at once for Olympus. They followed at a more stately pace in a rather showy black and gold phaeton, four-in-hand, the master himself driving. Halfway there, as if by magic, a lighted half-corona appeared between his fingers. He pulled out a silver case full of the same brand of cigar and was on the point of offering one to Rosen when he said, "Forgive me, my angels!" and offered them instead to the ladies. Mrs. Sanderson accepted one with delight and stuck it in her fichou.

Mars Gloab smiled. "No need for that, my sweet. You'll find boxes of them all around the house."

They drove in silence. The blue cigar smoke, which smelled curiously bonfiry, hung in milky wreaths against the dark treeshadows. They had gone about two miles along a winding, wood-girt lane when he said, "My children – prepare! We approach our country cottage. As Oscar so brilliantly puts it: 'Where every prospect teases, and Man is doubly vile!'" He slowed to a walk as they approached the bend. The ladies leaned forward, eager for their first glimpse. Tessa, sitting beside Dante, gave his hand a secret squeeze, hoping to convey her feeling that this house was destined to have some special meaning for both of them. He smiled back, but not as he had smiled of old. She felt she had become some experiment; he was watching not so much her as her progress. Very well, she thought, if this was to be a kind of initiation test, she'd show him how well she could take it. She wouldn't let him down. He'd be as proud of her as she was of him.

The name Olympus conjures up white marble and cloud-capp'd heights, all in Elysian sunshine. Mars Gloab's Olympus was quite the opposite. Rosen's earlier description: "the Old Thatched Barn, in all its original glory, transported to a tight little wooded Wiltshire valley," was accurate enough in a general sort of way. Even so, the actual sight of it came as a surprise. But thinking about it later, trying to explain to herself the events of that extraordinary visit, Tessa could not say why.

Was it merely the fact that, as they came around the bend, the house happened to sit in the shadow of a small cloud, so that, though the land all around lay bathed in warm sunshine, the actual building was dark and gloomy? Or perhaps it was the very theatricality of the place – the Old Thatched Barn rebuilt on a vast stage and stretched upward by the scene painter. . . the Old Thatched Barn drowning in the dark of the valley, aspiring desperately toward a light it would never reach.

Or did she have a genuine premonition of what lay in store?

As they drew closer she realized that its appearance of decay was entirely contrived; the creepers that hung about it had been carefully draped there by skilled gardeners; the ruined towers were mere follies whose apparently crumbling stonework was held fast by good cement and straps of wrought iron – frozen, as it were, in the act of tumbling.

The pace dwindled to a slow walk as they passed in by the portcullissed gate. She had time to notice that the cracks in the walls had been deliberately scored to a depth of about two inches, then filled with sound mortar and limned in black paint.

Mars Gloab gave a soft chuckle. ''Would one ever believe it is but six years old?'' he asked.

Tessa pointed to what looked like fourteenth-century brickwork and some even more ancient stone incorporated into one of the walls. ''But I see you built it on the ruins of an older house.''

Another satisfied chuckle. ''No, my angel. You see there the foible of the present owner, your own, your very own, yours truly. And you may well believe the troubles I experienced in persuading my masons to carry out my design. Oh never tangle with your masons, my precious!''

''You mean to say that *nothing* was here seven years ago?''

''None but the feather'd maidens of the wood.'' He let loose the reins and took off his gloves. ''And the scaly females of the peopl'd flood. . .'' With the fingertips of one hand he delicately sampled the smooth skin on the back of the other, alternately. ''. . . who, when lust or hunger calls. . .,'' he continued, but Mrs. Sanderson had already cut across: ''The ivy and the creeper looks so old.''

130

"The power of filthy lucre, my pet. Do not its force resist! It will command all – even life and death, as you shall see. As you shall see!" He gave a stage-villain's laugh, suggesting that their entry to Olympus had been the signal for some masque to begin. "Always keep it by you – or hold fast to that which, by pandering to lust, covetousness, envy, or greed, may procure it! We're all in that trade – all of us here. What – eh Rosen? Panders? Eh? Procurers?"

Rosen laughed. His eyes met Tessa's and again she had the feeling she was on trial.

Mars Gloab braked the phaeton in front of the newly ancient portico; they all got out. But instead of taking them through the house he led them around to the lawns on the south side, where a long arcaded cloister nestled beneath leaning bays and beetling towers, all carefully built out of plumb.

Peacocks in pride strutted about the fastidiously unkempt garden. Weeds and flowers, cheek by jowl, packed every bed and corner. There was nowhere for the eye to rest; every lawn was just too short, each pathway made an awkward bend, every young tree had been placed just slightly wrong – and was now being trained out of its natural habit. Colours that could have blended, if differently disposed, fought one another instead – pale green with white, silver with grey, gold with yellow – and always the darkest of them lowered in the sunniest places. Not one of these deliberately arranged defects was so blatant as to leap out and assault the eye; rather the effect was one of subtle unease. The visitor looked around and saw, first a neglected garden that was carefully tended – then a colourful garden that was oddly drab – then a richly variegated foliage brought together to produce a mystifying uniformity . . .

"It's a nice place, all right," Mrs. Sanderson said. "We never had a garden. I once planted a whole packet of seeds but not a single one of them regurgitated."

No one responded to this news.

"Carrot seeds," she added.

At that moment, Mars Gloab caught sight of Tessa's book, whose spine had slipped out through the opening of her bag. "Oh delights!" he cried. "You angel! Rosen – you didn't mention this. She is one of *us*!" He turned to her again. "And for that, you, my darling one, shall be at the head of the feast tonight."

131

She glowed with his approval and glanced at Dante, whose smile was now encouraging.

Gloab gave a wild, naughty-boy grin. "Yes – head of the feast! Won't Barbazur be furious! *A Rebours* indeed!"

"Barbazur?" Rosen asked. "Is he here already?"

"He came yesterday." Gloab's eyes flagged a peck of gossip. "He's out of sorts today. Most of last night he attempted to rouse JaBaalOs. Of course, my dear, it was quite useless, as one could have told him had one not been rather busy elsewhere. The fool ignored the moon, you see. He was furious. But – tonight's the night!" He turned again to Tessa. "And now, my own, my wonderful Mademoiselle des Esseintes" – that being the surname of the effete young hero of the Huysmans book – "do please praise our little garden extravagantly!"

Tessa understood his affectation, thanks to her reading of the novel. "It is," she said, "quintessentially decadent!" She checked with Dante, expecting to see him smile in approval at her answer. But Dante looked only at Gloab.

The master's mood had switched abruptly. Instead of being pleased he smiled at her with a contemptuous kind of pity, and said in a manner quite different from his previous pose, "You think that's all, do you? Then let me show you more. Let me show you all!" He raised his hand pointing the way toward a Moorish gate, but at that moment another cloud scudded quickly over the face of the sun. Simultaneously a wind-devil came down off the hot grasslands on the plain above and roared through the garden. The peacocks screamed like the damned. A moment earlier their world had been bathed in tranquil summer; now, mere seconds later, it cowered in twilight before the onslaught of a full autumn gale. Whatever Mars Gloab had been about to say, or to show them beyond the Moorish gate, he now thought better of it and, with the miniature storm at its height, he turned toward the house – content to leave upon the unquiet air a hint that some dark force might also wander here, abroad. And that he had the power of it.

As quickly as it had started, the disturbance passed away. Once again the place sweltered in full summer's radiance. The peacocks strutted vainly, stately. The bees looped from bloom to bloom to bloom. In the majestic, airy elms the doves once more began to moan.

"Come," Mars Gloab commanded. "Let the revels commence! We must find your costumes."

Great oak-framed doors set with leaded lights were ranged along the back of the cloister, all wide open to the summer day. He led them through the one at the end, farthest from the point of their arrival. They found themselves in some kind of great hall that reached the full height of the building. It was unnaturally dark. Mars Gloab's sandals rang a train of slaps on the polished floor, and so deep was the gloom that Tessa found herself following the sound rather than the pale ghostshape of his toga. Thus she failed to notice until they had almost gained the farther door that a bed had been placed in the centre of the hall. That it stood at the heart of a five-sided figure painted on the floor. That a young girl lay in it, as still as death.

Tessa hesitated. She turned. A nun was seated at the bedside. In her hands she held a bowl. It was half-full of blood. Tessa drew closer. She saw that the cross about the nun's neck hung upside down, but the significance of that did not strike her at the time.

The blood in the bowl was sputum. Its red stain lingered on the girl's lips; they and she were milk-pale. Her breathing was shallow and laboured. It could only be a galloping consumption.

Mars Gloab answered her silence. "She's dying," he said mournfully – or, rather, with a kind of mournful glee. "We were married but this morning."

"Oh – I'm so sorry . . ." she began.

He roared with laughter and then, seeing the girl begin to stir, put his finger to his lips, as stage drunkards do. He giggled "Ssshhh!" at himself and the company. Rosen patted him on the back, but whether in admiration or to humour him and also propel him toward the door, Tessa could not tell. As they went he murmured, only half to them, "Ah! A dying girl . . . a beautiful, young, dying girl . . .The pity of it! The waste! It is surely the loveliest thing in all creation." He paused and stared back at the poor little creature in a kind of ecstasy. "The waste!" he repeated in whispered reverence.

When they reached the passageway beyond, he added, "And tonight shall see our single honeymoon."

"Has she been ill for long?" Tessa asked. "Have you tried. . ."

"Couldn't say." He became quite matter-of-fact as he slit-opened a door and half-squeezed himself into the room beyond it. At the same time he wafted them toward the stairway, where a woman in a floral costume, vaguely Greek in style, was waiting to show them up to their chambers. "In fact" – he was almost into the room by now – "I only bought her yesterday." Through the last crack of the opening he added, "We had to scour the county for one as good as that."

The main stair was a broad fantasy of carved oak. It groaned beneath them but the structure was so massive that Tessa felt sure the creaking woodwork had been part of the carpenter's original brief. Halfway up, she spoke: "Surely he said 'brought' not 'bought'?"

Nobody answered her.

When they reached the first landing Rosen told their guide, "You take these two ladies. I know where my room is."

The woman nodded and led the other two straight along the passage.

"Are you a maid here?" Tessa asked. "What's your name? I'm Miss d'Arblay and this is Mrs. Sanderson."

"I'm called Thais here, Miss d'Arblay. And I do maid's work – among other things"

"What *other* things?" Mrs. Sanderson asked (thinking she already knew the answer).

"Entrails," the woman said – in precisely the same matter-of-fact tones as a maid in some other house might have said, "flowers."

She paused before a varnished, comb-grained door; the graining suggested a miasma rather than wood. "This'll be your room, Miss d'Arblay. And Mrs. Sanderson's next to you. There's connecting doors between them if you wish."

"We wish!" Tessa affirmed.

As she was about to enter she glanced back along the passage. Rosen still lingered at the foot of the stairway up to the next floor. On impulse she turned and ran back to him. "Come to my room tonight?" she said.

He looked calmly at her. "I'm not sure," he answered. "There are too many unknowns here. You among them."

"Me? But I told you – I'm sure of myself now."

"See whether you still feel the same by midnight."

134

Chapter Nineteen

"I'm Inphignea!" Mrs. Sanderson came excitedly into Tessa's room. She was already dressed in the Greek(ish) costume that Thais had brought up a few minutes after she had shown them into their rooms. "Aren't they heavenly cool! Why can't we always dress like this? Who are you?"

"Iphiginea," Tessa corrected her.

"Oh – you're almost the same as me, then. Are we twins? The Terrible Twins! Why aren't you changed yet? Who were they? Greeks, I suppose. Or Sabbins."

"No. *You're* Iphiginea – that's how you say it. Not Inphignia."

"Oh well – something like that. Anyway, who are you?"

Tessa stared out of the window.

"What's up, love?" Saunders asked.

"I'm just a little bit frightened."

"Go on! It's only a lark."

"Dante's behaving so oddly, though. Don't you feel it?" Tessa turned from the window to find Saunders staring pointedly at the ceiling.

"All right!" Tessa said. "I know you think you warned me, but it's not like that."

"It never is, love. Anyway, who cares about him? Show him you don't give a hoot. Start making eyes at the other men. Haven't you ever done things like that?"

"It's more complicated than you think, Saunders."

"You're not going to leave, are you? It hasn't started yet."

"Exactly."

"And we don't know who else is here. Let's . . ."

"We know Segal's here."

"Well – you're not afraid of him, are you? Let's wait at least until we know who else . . . I mean, suppose we heard next week George Grossmith was here – or Pewter, or whatever he calls himself at midsummer? I'd die of renovation."

Tessa looked at her uncertainly. "I don't see how you think it's

135

going to be fun.''

"All right, it's *not* going to be fun, then. But that's no excuse for leaving. We've all got to do lots of things in life we don't like, d'Arblay me old duck.''

"You'd say anything, wouldn't you! First you say it's fun, then when that won't wash you turn round and say it's a kind of duty, instead. Truth to you is like dialogue in a play – you think you can keep on changing the patter until you get something the audience likes.''

Saunders punched her playfully. "Come on, d'Arblay! You don't know what's in it for you until you try.''

"I keep thinking of that poor girl. . .''

Saunders stared at her and then burst into laughter. "It's all *acting*, love. None of it's real. You didn't think it was real, did you?'' She pointed at the floor. "I'll tell you another thing – that's not Marcus Gloab down there – not the one you'd meet in London. What? Runs six theatres – knows what's happening every minute of the day in each one – can tell you all the acts – and the profits off the bars every week for the past year. He's come down here to play the giddy goat, that's what. It's all charades. Little boys dressing up. Enjoy. . .''

"Little boys in grownup bodies and grownup minds with grownup thoughts!''

". . . Enjoy it, I say. All right – it's not the sort of charades you or I would play. But change is as good as a rest – and it's better than an IOU, as the bishop says. And talking of changing. . .''

Tessa, still undecided, said, "But suppose it's a kind of double charades? Suppose they're playing charades with a real, dying consumptive girl?''

Saunders smiled. "But they're all *gentlemen*, my dear!''

Tessa was trapped in the silence between conscience and self-will. Also there was the knowledge that if she left now, she'd probably be saying goodbye to Dante forever. Dante must have said something to Gloab at the railway station; he must have guaranteed the impresario some kind of response or performance from her and Saunders. Now she had to fulfil that guarantee – even though she had no idea what it might be. Indeed, the very fact of her ignorance was somehow the essential part of it all. She was being secretly challenged to *do* something tonight and no one was going to tell her what.

Saunders went over to the neglected costume, which still lay upon the bed. "Oh, yours isn't Greek. Mine is – as if you couldn't guess! It's from one of his shows, which I saw. The Sabbin Women."

"Sabine."

"Something like that."

"You know what happened to them – the Sabine women?"

"It all took place off-stage though. Very decorable, I do assure you. Half the house wanted their money back. What's yours supposed to be, then? Nellie Gwynne? You know what happened to her!"

Tessa gave up. "No, not Nell Gwynne. I think it's someone's idea of what an eighteenth-century French shepherdess might have worn."

Saunders held it up to herself and whistled. "While keeping flocks by night? It's more than flocks you'll be keeping with this. Especially by night! Très décolleté!"

"D'you speak French, Saunders?" Tessa asked.

"Not good French. There was a Huge No woman in the next court from us. I don't know why they all called her that. But I used to help her. She taught me quite a bit, but I expect it's all very peasant, you know. 'I-a Marrrie!'" – she supplied a sample – "'Tu va prrrennez la vache au marrrche'!' Still, it brought in one or two small parts."

It reminded Tessa of a peasant woman she had met on a holiday in Normandy once. "With your ear for accents," she said, "you'd soon speak properly."

Saunders was trying to decipher the nickname pinned to the costume. "Millie. . . Desperation or something."

"Let me see." Tessa came over, read the label, and snorted. "Mademoiselle! M,l,l,e is short for mademoiselle. And 'desperation' happens to be des Esseintes! Here am I asking if you can speak French and you can't even read!"

Saunders tossed her head. "Some can read easily and some can't." She grinned her forgiveness. "Go on – put it on. You can always change back again if you don't like it."

Tessa had to allow that Saunders in the Greek costume looked even more fetching than usual. She began to unbutton her own bodice.

When the precarious fancy dress was more or less around her

she said, "Oh no – I'm not having that! I shall have to put my camisole back on. Look – I'm almost naked here. These things'll fall out at the first chance."

Saunders laughed. "You can't wear a camisole, love. It'd be like a top hat in Ancient Rome. No – we'll fix that. Just be calm a minute, now." She pulled the bell cord.

When Thais appeared she asked her to fetch a bottle of collodion gum, with the help of which she soon had the dress so well (and yet so invisibly) fixed that Tessa could have danced a hundred fetes-champetres and embarked for a thousand Cytheras without granting one of the revelations for which her costume was otherwise designed.

"Won't you drive them mad!" Saunders clapped her hands and put them to her lips.

Tessa fell into the spirit of the thing. She longed for just one glass of wine to steady herself and appease her hunger.

Saunders, now back at the window, cried out, "Ohmigawd! Look who it is, I'll swear!"

There were half a dozen people down on the lawn: Mars Gloab, Rosen, Segal, an unknown man, and two women. The women were in the same Greek-ish costumes as Saunders; the men were all in druidic sort of gowns.

"Him," Saunders said.

Tessa studied the unknown fourth man, a short fellow with a round face. "You know him?"

"I should say so – that's 'Sudden Death' Davitt. Maybe you were right, d'Arblay. This is no party for respectable women. We ought to go back to London – or is Southampton nearer, with the boats for France?"

"You need some *moral* collodion, Mrs. Sanderson," Tessa told her. "When did Mrs. Sanderson ever meet Mr. Davitt? And what, pray, can Mrs. Sanderson possibly have to fear from a chubby little tenth-rate theatrical manager? Or are you saying your acting ability isn't quite up to Mrs. Sanderson any longer?"

Mrs. Sanderson (as she once again became) stared haughtily at her looking-glass image. "Let us," she said grandly, "repair us below and put an end to their subspence."

"I'm ravenous," Tessa said. "We can always leave straight after dinner if things start getting out of hand."

"Anyway," Saunders slipped the final bit of steel into her own

138

backbone, "faint heart never won fair play."

Tessa laughed as they went out and made for the stairhead. "You and words! It's like throwing stones in a pitch-black room."

The consumptive girl – or consummate actress? – had been removed from the great hall. Saunders scored the double when she swept out through one of the doors and cried, "What a magniloquent evening!"

Their laughter was such as one might hear in church – mindful of God.

Here they were mindful of Mars Gloab, the bell-wether to the group. The latecomers were introduced as Iphiginea and Mademoiselle des Esseintes, the virgin one. Tessa gathered that her strange soubriquet was a badge of high honour among them. The other two women were Demeter and Persephone. Dante was Jubelo. He smiled encouragingly at her. Segal – no longer Barbazur, it seemed – was Jubela; his gaze was cold; he seemed not to recognize Iphiginea. Davitt was Jubelum. He glanced at Iphiginea also without apparent recognition. Mars remained Mars Gloab.

Their host's behaviour, coupled with the fancy dress and the even fancier names, had led Tessa and Iphiginea to expect a jolly if rather decadent sort of dinner party. But now Tessa realized she should have taken a stronger hint from Dante. Something big oppressed the air. They were all a little frightened.

A ghost of hopeful dread seemed to move among them. It had a subtle effect on Tessa, who was now quite determined Dante should be proud of her. That spirit began to weld her to the group. Mars Gloab said, "Our little circle is now complete."

The magic that had earlier produced a lighted cigar now apparently created a smouldering censer from the folds of his toga. But the incense was not that of her father's church during Corpus Christi; it had the spicy tang she had noticed in Segal's house, and again on Saunders's wet clothes that night at the vicarage. She glanced at Iphiginea and saw her nostrils catch it, too. Not with any pleasure.

Mars Gloab swung the censer around to fan up the burning resin. The others sought its fragrance, blinding their eyes and raising high their faces to broach the thickest wreaths. The air was now calm again. It was early evening still; the sun had many hours of sky to fall.

He barked a sudden command: "*Baal!*" The three men moved to his right. "*Osiris.*" The women were wafted gracefully to his left – except Tessa, who was beckoned to stand before him, where the fumes were strongest – so strong, indeed, as to render her dizzy. How easy, how pleasant, it was, simply to obey. No need to decide anything. Just do as others did. Already she half-yearned for whatever they were seeking.

Mars Gloab turned. They began a stately walk toward the Moorish gate, singing a dirgelike song. A beautiful song, Tessa thought. Everything now seemed beautiful and somehow. . . happy. Why had she ever thought this garden strange? With difficulty she made out the words – *Favilla in saeclum solvet.* . . Not until they reached *Illa dies, irae dies*, did she recognize it as Peter Abelard's great pilgrim hymn, Day of Wrath, sung backward. Its blasphemous beauty touched her even more deeply than the primal, uncomprehended simplicity of the music. Lulled by that powerful fragrance, she began to hum the tune and to slip in the odd word from her memory of the hymn in its sacred form. Mars Gloab turned and smiled. Iphiginea raised an uncertain eyebrow.

The land fell between two long mounds, like ancient tumuli, meeting in a vee. Down that narrowing chasm they processed toward the dark, elongated mouth of a subterranean grotto. The sides of the entrance were of a pink-veined marble, carved in folds and curves to resemble some kind of violent natural upwelling. From beneath the encircling tufts of cottongrass and maidenhair fern a seepage of hidden springs kept the stonework gleaming, cold and pure.

Iphiginea leaned toward Tessa and stage-whispered, "Recognize it? The mucky devils!"

Gloab silenced them with one glance. Tessa stared angrily at Iphiginea – hoping Gloab noticed it.

Each man as he entered stretched wide his arms and touched both walls; caressing them with a ritual lingering, each murmured three times the word, "Give!"

Mars Gloab, standing in the vestibule, turned upon the women and commanded, "Yield!"

At once Demeter and Persephone went down on all fours and, subjugating themselves to an unseen yoke, crawled through the tall entrance and on between the straddle of his legs. Iphiginea pulled a dramatically dubious face at Tessa and, with a stage-whisper of "Hold onto yer hats!" followed them. Tessa was about to drop to her knees when Mars Gloab, wreathed in incense, held out his hands. She joined him in that cloud.

"Do what thou wilt," he said. "That is the law."

It was the prompt for another song, this time a roundelay of the three words, "Here come we!" in all possible permutations – "here we come. . . come we here. . ." and so on. A short, sinuous tunnel with dank walls rippled back the sound. The incense was now so strong Tessa thought she would pass out. She imagined herself falling; yet felt no threat of it. The rock was hard; it was also soft and yielding. And though solid, it also seemed to pulsate beneath her.

She could no longer even imagine what danger might be. She looked for Jubelo but he had vanished into the dark.

The tunnel emerged into a large, echoing grotto whose walls were visible only in random patches, where the guttering light of ancient candles held at bay the underworld night. At its heart lay a mighty shape whose crisp outline contrasted severely with the swirl of rocks around it. Tessa suddenly realized it was, in fact, a coffin – but a coffin vast as a room. It occurred to her that the thing had always been here, coeval with this maw of earth and conferring upon it a certain meaning – which merely hinted itself at her and then fled.

A stab of light rent one flank of the shape. Demeter and Persephone had pulled aside black drapes to reveal an entrance; the coffin was, indeed, a shrine within a shrine. Mars Gloab alone went in. The others ranged themselves along the outside of the nearer wall, facing it, bracing their feet and hands apart to touch it and their neighbours. Tessa quickly copied them. Jubelo was Tessa's right neighbour; the door was to her left. She placed her cheek against the coffin; hard and cool and smooth. There in the dark with Jubelo at her side, the touch conferred a sense of peace. Moments later Mars Gloab drew apart an interior curtain and she found her face was pressed against a windowpane, little larger than her head. Each of them had such a window, but little Jubelum (or Davitt) who was at one end, next to Iphiginea, had to strain on tiptoe to see inside.

The light was dim. It was some moments before Tessa made out the bier. A body lay upon it covered with white satin.

141

Unmistakably a body, unmistakably female and miserably wasted, it was the body of the consumptive young bride.

Mars Gloab walked slowly around it, filling the air with incense.

"Baal!" the three men broke out in sudden unison, a jab of exertion on the syllable. The coffin wall swayed.

"Osiris!" the two women answered softly, with a fainting tremolo.

"Baal!" Again the coffin wall recoiled.

"Osiris!" As the women drew out the word they sagged at the knees and fell as far as the elasticity of their pressed flesh would allow.

"Baal!"

"Osiris!"

The chants merged. The sharp, commanding monosyllable of the men and the sibilant, yielding triplet of the women filled her with a pleasurable drowsiness. Jubelo's hand slipped over hers and in some curious way they became especially united by the ritual. His cry pierced her; her yielding was to him.

The atmosphere was briefly broken by a giggle and a scuffle in the dark down at Iphiginea's end; but the shock and fear of the others triumphed.

A languorous yearning filled her. All the tension and conflict in her life had drained away; in its place a contentment, divinely granted. "Do what thou wilt!" It was so profound and yet so simple. Blessed simplicity! "Do what thou wilt!" Why had she never understood it before?

Time stopped.

Time stops.

The hunger within her is cosmic. She craves. . . everything. She is a shell of sentient flesh, crying, "Feed my emptiness!" She is a whirlpool that would suck in all the world's sensation, all its knowing, all mankind's experience. She feels it is all *here* in this womb of time, patient for its rebirth now, in her. Yet she has dwindled to one vibrant nerve, impatient for that graft of understanding, and sick because she cannot comprehend it.

Craving for she knows not what, fevered with that craving, blissful in the certainty of *soon*, calm in that bliss, she yields her virgin Word to him, merging herself with the wall, whose very fibres now have come to life. Their voices ring out, battling their own muted echoes. The pace quickens, the action grows more violent. That cosmic hunger is no longer hers. It belongs to all. Or perhaps it is she herself who is no longer separate. The do-not-touch-me of her outer skin has gone. It is merely a layer in a self that flows beyond, through more and yet more layers – invisible auras of herself that now reach outward, melting into the auras of others and uniting them in one magical longing.

At the peak of their chanting, in the very nick of denying its climax, Mars Gloab takes hold of the cloth where it covers his young bride's head. Silence falls, broken only by Iphiginea, who giggles.

. Tessa presses her face tight against the glass. All the meaning in the world is now inside. It will be revealed – she knows it – when the girl's face is laid bare.

Mars Gloab begins to lift the cloth.

Chapter Twenty

Her face is pale as watered milk; all trace of blood has gone. Tessa at last sees the beauty in such a death. Its revelation draws the circle inward, between the parted curtains, chanting, "Do what thou wilt – in death is new birth," as they process widdershins around the girl.

Mars Gloab yields ground ahead of them until he stands in an ecstasy at her feet. He motions Tessa to stay by the head; Iphiginea he places behind him; the others know unbidden where to go – the Three Juwes beside her torso, Jubelo and little Jubelum to her right, Jubela to her left; Demeter and Persephone stand one each side, level with her thighs. When each is justly placed, they take up the white cloth and stretch it horizontal. They sing:

Would any feather'd maiden of the wood

The Juwes roll the sheet down to just below her collarbone. The wasted flesh models every protrusion.

Or scaly female of the peopl'd flood

The two women furl back the material over the dead girl's feet, all scrawny bone and tendon.

When lust and hunger called, its force resist?

The men roll down the sheet to show her tiny breasts, two vulnerable jellies veined anoxia-blue.

In Abstinence or Chastity persist?

The women fold their edge upward; the space between her knees is a dark nothing.

And cry, "If Heaven's intent were understood.

The men roll their end, more slowly now, until it rests upon the dimple of her navel. Her shrunken flesh is concave from her lowest ribs.

These tastes were giv'n but to be withstood."

The women fold their dwindling edge until her starling thighs lie bare to the evening warmth.

Or would they wisely both these gifts improve—

The men spin their almost-vanished portion down until their roll lies upon the women's fold. Pubic hair, black as a raven, startles the gleaming white of the cloth.

And Eat when hungry, and when am'rous – Love?

On *Love* they all turn to Mars Gloab as for a signal. Three times he swings the censer back and forth, first over her right thigh, then over her left. With each swing he intones "Hiram. . . Abiff. . . Hiram. . . Abiff. . ." In those confines the heady fumes are overpowering. Tessa must lean upon the bier. In her dizzy euphoria she sees but does not comprehend. They fold the sheet ends inward to a compact bundle. Demeter and Persephone raise the girl's knees and place that bundle beneath them. Her knees fall outward, spreading wide her thighs. Into that vee of revealed bed Mars Gloab places the censer, careful not to touch or mar the perfection of her samite flesh; its pallor seems to suck heat from the very air.

From the folds of his gown Mars Gloab draws a Mason's trowel. Jubela gives out a sigh. Gloab holds it high above his head. Its bright silver is a flourish in the mellow candlelight. He passes it to Jubela with a ritual grace, saying "Do what thou will – oh my brother in evil."

Jubela bows and takes the implement. He turns to face the girl. For a moment – as he tightens his grip upon its enormous handle – Segal the surgeon shows through the ritual personality.

144

Meanwhile, Jubelo takes the girl's jaw in one hand and pushes hard, stretching her neck – so slender it seems to the watchers that he must surely break it. Jubelum fishes a golden bowl from beneath the bier and holds it beside her left ear.

Jubela places the gleaming point of the trowel carefully beneath her right ear. "In the sacred name of Jahweh," he says, "in the twice-sacred name of Baal, in the thrice-sacred name of Osiris, we the Three Juwes resurrect our most heinous sin. JaBaalOs be with us in our darkness, else we perish in the inner light."

"So be it!" the rest intone – all except Tessa, now a single, observing point at the head of this grisly feast.

With a skilled flick of his wrist, Jubela tears the point of the trowel through the dead girl's flesh, right around her throat and up to her left ear. A deep blue-red gash opens at once and beads of dark blood start all along the cut. Jubelo is swift to staunch it with a piece of cable tow. Jubela holds the trowel tight in the gash on her left side, above the bowl, keeping open the severed vessels. Sluggish gouts of blood slither down its silver face and fall into the gold. Tessa's mind records only these facts. No voice tells her what to feel.

Jubela intones: "We sanctify this our butchery with the two most sacred marks." Deftly he cuts two sides of a triangle into her right cheek, saying, "Holy Royal Arch." He then repeats the performance on her left cheek, saying, "Arch Royal Holy."

He places her left hand upon her breast and nods at Jubelum, who once again bends down to fish for something beneath the bier. It is obviously heavy. As he lifts it he has the misfortune to break wind. He says, an octave above that nether note: "Oh Christ!"

Iphiginea, still in the dark beyond Mars Gloab, collapsed in helpless laughter. "Oh come on, Tess," she said. "This is barmy. Let's go and find something to eat."

Demeter and Persephone, solemn as tricoteuses, left their places, grabbed their offending sister, and bundled her out by the door. But she struggled free and came back. She plucked at Tessa's sleeve. "Come on," she urged. "I've seen better than this on amateur nights."

Tessa stared at her; no comprehension showed.

Iphiginea grew alarmed. "Tess!"

The women grabbed her and this time carried her out toward

145

the day, or what remained of it. A door slammed. There was a hammering. When the women returned one of them was bleeding from a scratch, the other had a swollen eye.

Tessa turns her attention back to the bier; the men have vanished beneath a large black cloth emblazoned with cabbalistic designs in golden thread. Demeter and Persephone dive beneath it also, leaving her alone.

Her scattered senses make no tale of what they hear and feel. Incantations. Slithering, sucking noises. From Mars Gloab, hunched beneath the cloth, ejaculations of ecstasy.

He rises again. The two women also. They are all three naked. He is sexually roused. He punches himself toward the open vee before him. The two women press their naked bodies to him, rising and falling in his time.

There is a stir beneath the cloth. "Now!" The Three Juwes cry. It billows up toward Tessa. Its blackness engulfs her and then vanishes, revealing a carnage. The girl's feet skinned red raw. Her torso opened, heart glistening on her chest, intestines over her left shoulder.

JaBaalOs raises the reeking censer and swings it over the charnel. "Oh my beautiful, my most beautiful bride! Cleft for me! Cleave for me! Cleave unto me!"

Assisted by the two women, he climbs upon the cadaver. They part the corpse's sex for his easing. Lust lodged, they climb also upon the bier and lie beside him.

The three Juwes cover the celebrants' heads with the black cloth, leaving the writhing white bodies at their games. They weigh the cloth down with two prepared stones, tapping each with the silver trowel and saying, "The Rough Ashlar. . . the Perfect Ashlar."

Pale buttocks rise and fall, rise and fall.

Far off a door splintered inward. Saunders was there. Her hands plucked at Tessa once again. "Gawd, what a stink! Come on, love. I thought you said you were hungry?"

Tessa at last cried out, "No!" She clutched at Dante's arm. He stood at the far end of the universe, not hearing her. He fished a sketchbook from inside his toga, held his pencil against the light, squinted at the tip, and then began to draw.

She was aware of moving. Hands guiding. The floor and walls melting together. Dampness. Daylight. Grass again.

146

The Moorish gates. The house. Oak doors. Oak floor. Saunders said, "We need something to wash the taste away." A dark wooden cupboard with leaded lights. Saunders' foot smashing the glazing. Her hand. Her slim fingers retrieving a half-corked winebottle. "It says Naughty St. George or something. Quite appropriative. Want a gulp?"

Tessa stared at it. Somehow they were on the lawns again. Rooks squawking at the fading sky; the lowering sun gilded Saunders's hair. "What's up, love?" she asked.

Tessa stared. What were words?

"It was that incense stuff. I should have warned you. Gawd, when little Davitt shot himself I almost perished!"

"They. . ." Tessa began-and-ended.

Saunders put an arm around her. "It's all over. I told you it was just a lark."

Tessa shook her head. She touched the wine bottle. Saunders held it to her lips. She took several deep gulps but did not feel them.

From beyond the gate came the sound of someone relieving himself of an explosive pint of wind. A voice said, "Enter the Fairy Queen." Moments later, "Sudden Death" Davitt (he was certainly no longer Jubelum) came bouncing jauntily onto the lawn. "Thank Gawd that's over for another year," he said to himself.

His face fell a mile at seeing them. "Oops, ladies! Sorry pardon!" he said. "I've got it something chronic tonight." Social duty done, he clapped and rubbed his hands. "Well – anyone feel like a bit of dinner? We're in good time and they do a grand spread down at the White Hart, I can promise you." He looked from one to the other. "No? No takers?"

Mrs. Sanderson, as she had quickly become again, looked down at her costume.

"Oh – we'll change out of this daft clobber," he said, scornful that it needed saying. Then he laughed. "Here! Didn't that trowel work well, with the blood in the handle and all! It even scared me – and I'm the one who had it made for them!"

He looked at Tessa, noticing her state for the first time. His face crumpled. He took her hand. His was warm; hers, cool. She liked the touch of it.

"You thought it was real?" he asked.

147

She nodded.

He uttered the opening consonants of several unspeakable words and shook his head. "They should of told you. It's all games, love," he said earnestly. "Stupid, upper-class kids. That's all."

"But all the. . ." Tessa waved her hands vaguely over her torso.

"Sheep's guts, love. Old Segal got up to some caper last night and killed it. Sacrificed it, he calls it. Butchery's more like. But that's all it was – the guts of some poor old sheep. It didn't half stink under that cloth, I can tell you. Never mind your incense. Still, it was a pig's guts last year, and that was worse."

"I'm starving," Saunders said.

Tessa began to laugh. They both watched her. The laughter grew more wild. Nervously Davitt raised his arm to strike her, but Saunders stayed it and, taking Tessa by the hand, began to lead her toward the house. The laughter exhausted itself before they reached the doors. "We'll join you in about half an hour, Mr. Davitt."

Chapter Twenty-One

"But the girl. . .," Tessa said. "She looked dead."

"What? The little ratbag?" Sudden Death Davitt helped her up into the dogcart. "That's her trade. Hilda Benson's her name. She's been dying onstage for years."

"Yet she wasn't breathing, Mr. Davitt."

He helped Mrs. Sanderson up, too. They both sat on the driver's bench. "That's that Rosen," Davitt explained. "He knows how to put the fluence on her, see. It's some special kind of trance. What did he call it? Cata. . .something."

"Catapault," Mrs. Sanderson said with great conviction.

"No!" Davitt's face creased as if in pain. He was wearing the loudest check suit Tessa had ever seen, topped with a bowler hat as round as his face and body, and made of the same raucous check. ''No!'' he repeated scornfully, rolling himself up and into the seat between them. ''Gee up! It was cata. . . oh, it's on the tip of my tongue.''

''Catalogue,'' Mrs. Sanderson offered with identical certainty.

Davitt peered closely at her and burst into a sudden grin. ''Gotcha!'' he cried. ''Connie Saunders! Or I'm a Dutchman. Well, Connie my old darling!''

A white-faced Mrs. Sanderson stared back at him. ''I *beg* your pardon?''

''Come off it. You're Connie Saunders. There can't be two of you,'' he cackled. Tessa watched in fascination. This jovial reaction was not at all what Saunders had led her to expect. He went on: ''It's been nagging me ever since you two came out on the lawn. 'What a magniloquent evening!' I knew that rang a bell. I said to meself, 'SD – this rings a bell!''' He turned to Tessa. ''But you I don't know, Miss d'Arblay. Are you on the stage, too? It's a good name, whoever thought of it. Tessa d'Arblay. Worth a good ten bob a week extra that name is.''

''I'm afraid I haven't the faintest idea what you're talking about, Mr. Davitt. The word you were looking for, by the way, was catalepsy.''

''That's right,'' Mrs. Sanderson confirmed. ''I told you it was something like that.''

He piloted them carefully through the narrow exit of fake-crumbling stone. ''What a shocking great pity,'' he sighed when they were out upon the highway. ''If you tell me, Mrs. Sanderson, you're not dear old Connie, then, of course, as a gentleman, I have to believe you. But I could have sworn you were Connie Saunders.'' He shook his head and sucked at his teeth. ''A great pity.''

In the end, of course, Mrs. Sanderson had to ask why.

''Well, I had a part for dear old Connie,'' he said in a don't-let-me-bore-you tone. He glanced at the sky and shook his head at the unfairness of everything. ''Good part, too.'' Another little tooth-suck. ''*Damn* good part.''

Mrs. Sanderson's toes squirmed inside the thin cloth of her shoes. ''Er – what sort of a part?'' she asked.

Davitt clucked at the horses – a matched pair of grey cobs – and shook them to a stiff trot. ''One of the best ever,'' he said sadly. ''For *her* especially. *Made* for her.''

The twitch rose to Mrs. Sanderson's calves; her legs were on the freedom road. "Yes, but . . . what exactly – I mean . . ."

Davitt still managed the most lugubrious tone. "Why – it would be the making of her, Mrs. Sanderson. Are you at all acquainted with our squalid little profession, by any chance? Because if you are, you may know that once in every actress's lifetime a part comes along that *makes* her career. She can have been around for years – like this Connie Saunders I was telling you about. Now Connie's been around for years, all right – years and years and *years*! Well, it can happen, like I said, to any actress – just by chance she'll get this one special part and suddenly the whole of London's talking about her. And then it's a European tour . . . and America." His euphoria died swiftly. "Very sad!" he concluded. "I've scoured London looking for her, too."

If Mrs. Sanderson's legs could somehow have been connected by rods and levers to the wheels, the horses could now have been turned loose to graze, and the party would still reach the White Hart sooner.

"As you say," Tessa picked up his tone, "it is an enormous pity. Do tell us something about this most interesting actress, Mr. Davitt. Connie Saunders, did you say? Why would this role be so especially suited to her."

"'Role', eh?" He looked at her admiringly. "Miss d'Arblay – I believe you *are* connected with the theatre. But you'll be up at the high-class end. That's my guess. I wouldn't be surprised if you weren't quite the actress. 'Role'! Why it's years since I've heard that word."

"But – about Connie Saunders?"

He patted her knee affectionately and let his hand stray up her thigh; but he was so blatantly cheerful she felt more amused than outraged. Her fingers made a toasting fork and prodded him. "Forsooth, Mr. Davitt!"

He chuckled. "Yes – definitely not my end of the trade. But Connie Saunders – well, now!" He became conspiratorial. "Strictly between ourselves, and don't breathe a word of this to another living soul, I wouldn't want it to get back to the lady in question, but I've a great deal of liking for dear old Connie Saunders. I'd even go so far as to say respect." His voice changed mood suddenly. "Course, I wouldn't deny she's also a lunatic. Oh, I've seen red, I may tell you! She's about the stupidest, most

150

featherbrained, the vainest, the most arrogant, pigheaded, inconsiderate, unreliable. . ." He sighed another moodchange. "But name me one great trouper who wasn't all of those things, eh? All and more? It's the cross we humble brokers to theatrical genius have to bear."

"All and more?" Tessa prompted, wide-eyed. "Can there possibly be *more*?"

Davitt winked at her.

"I've heard quite enough of this ridiculous Connie Sanderson," Mrs. Sanderson said.

"Saunders!" They both shouted the correction.

She tossed her head angrily. "Let's talk of more pleasant tropics."

"No, I'm fascinated." Tessa turned again to Davitt. "You said 'more' – surely there can't be more?"

"You'd never believe it, Miss D."

"Try."

Mrs. Sanderson began to whistle but her lips kept drying in the balmy summer air.

"She gets bees in her bonnet. I'll give you an example, now. I took a concert party down to Brighton to work the pier for the summer season. D'you know Brighton at all? Full of retired colonels who've got it all worked out that England's the Lost Tribe of Israel. Loonies like that. You'd think it was real Connie Saunders country, wouldn't you? Well, you would if you knew her. I mean – she could have made her fortune there. . ."

Mrs. Sanderson left off her wheezling (whistling it was not) and gave a single shout: "In Brighton? Hah!"

"All right." Davitt was still ostensibly talking to Tessa. "Maybe the old spondulicks wasn't coming in as fast as we hoped. Maybe I hadn't been dishing out the oof as thick as the promises. But she's been in and out of theatres all her life. She knows which side to spread the dripping. She didn't have to. . ."

"Climb down, Davitt!" Saunders finally cast the Sanderson skin. "You owed her that five pounds. And she could have taken fifty out of that box. So!"

Davitt's eyes had a faraway look. He spoke to the air in front of him, dreamily, as men misremember days at school. "Five quid? Was that all?" He shook his head. "I'd forgotten." He darted a sudden glance at her. "D'you know – I really had forgotten."

151

Tessa watched them, locked solemnly, eye to eye – two terriers digging for the smallest bone of insincerity.

Saunders came to a resolution first. "Soddit, Davitt, you perishing nark," she said.

"Oh, Connie!" he murmured softly. "Connie! Another week – two weeks at the most – and you could have had the fifty. Never mind your five."

"Grope off, will you!"

"And I tell you straight, gel – if you knew what part I've got for you now, you'd be off this cart in a jiff, you'd be down there on your knees – *on your knees*, gel – and you'd be begging me for it. From here to London, so you would."

Saunders became aggressively cockney. "Yeah – well don't put no candles in the winders, little turkey. Cos I just might be elsewise engaged."

Draping the reins over his forearm, he fished a huge wad of banknotes from an inside pocket and peeled off nine fivers, counting them with slow emphasis. Saunders was gape-mouthed and saucer-eyed. "'Ere – where'd you get all that ready?" she whispered.

"Never you mind – it's all for the new show. Here now – will this convince you?" He handed her the forty-five pounds.

She took it as if it might vanish as swiftly as it had appeared. She counted it – twice – and, still shaking her head in disbelief, absentmindedly stuffed it down between her bosoms.

That intimate contact seemed to authenticate the money, for she suddenly burst into laughter and flung her arms around him. He threw the reins to Tessa and hugged back with equal gusto – and a fair freedom, Tessa noticed. Then he seemed to recollect himself. "Arf a mo, arf a mo," he said, pushing her slightly away from him. "I've not decided between you two yet – which shall be tonight's lucky little lady?" He nodded clandestinely toward Tessa and asked Saunders with jocular conspiracy, "She got money, has she?" He danced a dangerous little buttock-jig on the seat and fluttered his hand in front of him like a pinioned bird, sing-songing: "Anything there worth our while, eh?"

He abandoned the charade before the sentence was complete. They both roared with laughter. The White Hart hove into view.

"Steady the Buffs," he said. "Being slung out I don't mind,

152

but to be refused admission don't bear thinking about, eh?''

"What part?" Saunders asked.

"The Queen of Sheba," he said.

"Straight up and down?"

"Straight up and down. The play's called *Solomon's Temple*. It's made for you."

They took a private room and enjoyed an excellent dinner. Davitt's high spirits lasted through the meal and he kept them entertained with theatrical stories. At one point Tessa felt she now knew him well enough to ask how he had got mixed up in all this play-acting down here at Olympus.

"Don't spoil it, gel," he said. But then he immediately went on, "Marcus Gloab can do me a lot of good, see? So I help him out where I can. I mean, he couldn't go to any of his own managers to supply a consumptive-looking Athanasian wench, clean and willing, and a pair of slave-girls, ditto. Lose face, wouldn't he. So I'm the one. I mark his card – he marks mine. That's how it goes." He winked reassuringly.

"What's an Athanasian wench?" Tessa asked.

Davitt put his head on one side and tut-tutted. "And you a clergyman's daughter!" he said. "What's your Athanasian Creed, eh?"

"Quicunque vult. . ." she began; then, seeing the point, she laughed.

Saunders pulled a dubious face. "That doesn't sound too churchy!" She drew breath. "Qui. . ."

"Don't try to repeat it!" Tessa said hastily. "Quicunque vult means, *Whosoever wishes*. . ." She turned back to Davitt and asked the real question: "Why were Segal and Dante Rosen there?"

"Segal's a loonie, that's why," he told her. "You should have seen him under the cloth, pretending to cut up poor little Benson! It gave me the shivers, I don't mind telling you. He wasn't pretending. He'd have done it if I hadn't been there to count the breakages."

"And Dante Rosen?"

"Rosen's like the rest of us, my love." He rubbed thumb and forefingers together. "The old spondulicks."

"Oh?" The judgement surprised her. "I didn't think he was short of money."

Davitt laughed. "Everyone in the world's short of money, my

153

pet. Did you think he was rich? He's one of those rich people that's in it up to here." He mimed a surface about a foot above his head. "That's your Mr. Dante Rosen."

"You mean Marcus Gloab has paid him to come down here?"

"In a manner of speaking. I mean, Rosen'll get a commission or two – or three – out of it, I shouldn't wonder. He's doing the backdrops for *Solomon's Temple*, I know that much already."

"D'you think he's still in the grotto?" Tessa asked.

Davitt gave a beery laugh. "That worries you, does it?" He nudged Saunders. "Look at her, eh? Are those eyes going green or are they green already?"

"Tell her," Saunders urged, and smiled at Tessa to pay no attention.

His face cracked an avuncular smile. "Well, you may set your mind at rest. All three Athanasian wenches are for his nibs alone. No, but you've got to feel sorry for him, haven't you? I mean, he can't. . . I mean, it's the only way he can. . . I mean. . ." Floundering helplessly, he turned to Saunders. "You tell her, gel."

Saunders nodded. "It'll keep," she told Tessa.

He gave a dirty laugh. "It bleedin' has to, don't it! Keep until midsummer and other high festivals, what!" He leaned his head against her neck and grinned broadly. Tessa noticed for the first time that one of his molars was of gold. He gave a satanic little chuckle to go with it. "Good thing I don't have that trouble, eh?"

Saunders pushed him away, crossly. "The evening is degenuating fast. Go and find one of your euthanasians."

Tessa at last saw her chance to ask a question that had been on the tip of her tongue a dozen times since Mrs. Sanderson had been packed away. "Saunders? Is this honestly the man who put you in such dread that you hid yourself away and became that ill-paid little skivvy up in Finsbury Close?"

"Did what?" Davitt asked.

"When I first ran across this woman," Tessa told him, "she was, or so she now claims, hiding away from you and playing the real-life part of a little cockney skivvy."

Davitt turned to Saunders. "Straight?"

She grinned. "I can't play any part straight, SD. You know that."

He shook his head. "You're your own worst enemy," he told

her. "And you know that!"

She looked down. He put a gentle finger under her chin and raised it. "You need someone to look after you. Didn't I always tell you?"

"To lock me up, you mean." She looked him steadily in the eye. It suddenly occurred to Tessa that Saunders was in love with Davitt – not in a girlish or romantic sort of way but. . . complicatedly, with a mixing-in of dislike, fear, petulance, selfishness. . . perhaps even hatred. Did Saunders herself realize it? Probably not. She was so complicated. As Dante had said, she was like a maze-full of women who had never been introduced to one another; the Saunders who loved little Davitt couldn't possibly tell the good news to all the others wandering around inside her.

On their way out of the White Hart, Davitt poked his head around the saloon-bar door on the offchance. "Hullo hullo hullo," he said, turning back to the women. "A most unjubilant surgeon, my dears. I think we'd better offer him a lift back home."

"Certainly not!" Tessa protested.

Davitt's face fell. "I already half-did." He smiled encouragingly. "Ah go on! Someone's got to take pity on the poor bloke."

Tessa saw how impossible it would be to explain.

"That's the spirit," Davitt said. "He's harmless, really."

Davitt got up front, no doubt thinking the two women would go with Segal in the back. But to Tessa's annoyance Saunders got up on the driver's seat, saying, "Here, give me the reins. You're too drunk." It left her to get in beside Segal.

Saunders and Davitt began a querulous, nonstop duet of reminiscence, argument, blame, and laughter, which, together with the steady grind of the iron tyres on the gravel highway, left Tessa stranded in half-deafening privacy with the doctor.

It was gone eleven and the midsummer night had grown about as dark as it was going to – a kind of late twilight. Blackbirds and thrushes were still in full song, startling the warm air; at this hour their chatter seemed more of a complaint than a gladness. Segal leaned toward her, his face like some night blossom. "So much has happened since last we met," he said.

"I'd be obliged if you kept silent," she told him. "I'm

surprised you dare show your face after this evening's work.''

"Where's Mr. Rosen?" he asked.

"I neither know nor care."

After a while she found the silence oppressive. "Why did you lie to me, Dr. Segal?" she asked.

He snorted. "That's hardly of importance now – considering all *you've* done!"

His effrontery took her breath away. "The fact that you lied to me and were caught out, the fact that you still cannot explain to me what really happened, can only mean that the truth is at least as bad as one's worst fears."

"Fears!" He laid an unnatural emphasis on the word. "So it's fears now, eh? Tell me your fears, Miss d'Arblay."

"My fear is that grown men like you unfortunately play an important part in running the world. What on earth would your patients and colleagues think if they caught you at such tomfoolery as this evening's."

"No," he said insistently. "Tell me your fears."

She shivered. His voice was cold and humid. "I've just told you."

"Your *real* fears."

She said nothing.

"Shall I tell you what they ought to be?" he said.

Chapter Twenty-Two

But Segal did not tell her. Instead he flung himself into the seat opposite and stared at her in a moody silence that lasted the rest of their short journey back to Olympus. She was angry at this sullen capping to what, after her escape from the grotto, had turned into a most pleasant evening. As they went into the house she let the other two scamper ahead and then told Segal, "Just leave me alone. And leave Dante alone, too. He despises the sort of tawdry games we took part in this evening just as thoroughly as I do."

156

"You think you can hurt me as much as you have, and expect that to be the end of it?" he asked.

"I don't see how I've hurt you."

"I think you do, Miss d'Arblay. You know very well what you've done."

"I'm sorry to insist, Dr. Segal, but it's hardly my. . ."

"Sorry isn't enough, my dear. Sorry isn't nearly enough!" He left her standing in the entrance porch.

Back in her own room she undressed and lifted her pillow, expecting to find her nightdress where she was certain she had seen Thais put it. But no nightdress was there. Annoyed, thinking that Saunders must be playing her some trick, she went to the connecting door and opened it, only to find a second door immediately beyond. She was about to open that one, too, when she heard Saunders giggling; the sound was overlaid by a chuckle in the unmistakable tones of Sudden Death Davitt. Tessa turned back. What did it matter, anyway? The night was hot. She hardly needed her nightdress, especially if Dante came to her.

She lay naked under a single sheet, wondering exactly what Saunders and Davitt were doing at that moment. And what would it be like to let a man touch her. . . *here* – caress her. . . *like this*? Not just any man – Dante? She pulled the spare pillow on top of her, hugged it tight, and threw her thighs up around it, rocking herself gently. When it grew warm she eased her grip and began caressing herself as she imagined Dante might, until it produced the most delicious sensations all through her body.

In the silent small hours she came suddenly awake. There was a scratching noise in the wainscot panelling. She strained her ears and located it – behind and a little to her left.

A rat? Her stomach turned; she choked an impulse to cry out. It sounded alarmingly like some small animal scratching away at the mortar. But then came a sound that could only have been made by a human – a grunt, a male grunt, followed by the noise of a brick being dropped.

She remembered Dante talking about secret passageways. Was he trying to take her by surprise? Virgin fear and excitement fought within her as she stood there, picturing her secret lover beyond the wainscot.

She put her mouth an inch from it and called softly, "Dante?"

The noise stopped for a moment and then began again in

157

earnest – as if there were no point now in silence.

"Dante?" Louder this time.

Still no reply. A gnawing doubt hardened into certainty. Dante would surely have answered. If not Dante, then who? Segal – or Gloab? Her blood froze. She remembered the look on Segal's face: "Sorry isn't nearly enough. . ."

She wasted precious seconds in one more futile search for her nightdress; then in desperation she seized up her sheet and wrapped it loosely about her nakedness. As softly as she could she went over to the connecting door, pausing briefly to lay her ear against the one on Saunders's side. She heard gasping; a franker version of her own with the Dante of her dreams.

Had she been asleep for only a couple of minutes, then? Or did It always last so long? Or was this their second bout of It? Half-fearful she pushed open the door and peered into the room. The bed was beside the door but its sheets were empty. By the moonlight she saw them – lying in a wasteland of clothing on the floor, Saunders rolling her head wildly from side to side, making those ecstatic noises, while little Davitt's two white buttocks rose and fell, rose and fell, punching himself into her with a vigour that must surely hurt?

Tessa hadn't the courage to shout. Her fascination squandered more precious time before she tore herself away. The last thing she saw, on a gilded chair beside the bed, was Saunders's corsets, gorgeous things, all purple and red stripes with deep pink lace frills and crimson suspenders. Pressed neatly into the bosom swelling lay the nine crisp five-pound notes Davitt had given her.

The scratching behind the wainscot had been replaced by a metallic noise – a screwdriver working on slightly rusty screws. Suddenly she noticed a hair-crack of light all around one section of panelling. She ran to her window but faced an impossible twenty-foot drop onto a flagstone pathway. Her clothing lay close by the window seat, but she had no time now for struggling with all those buttons, hooks, and drawstrings. There remained only her shepherdess costume. She dropped the sheet and dived into its scanty protection; her hands now had to do what what the collodion-gum had done earlier. She looked around for her slippers but the unmistakable sounds of the panelling being removed drove her barefoot into the passageway.

She took the stairs four at a time. The creaks rang out like

158

pistol shots. She hammered on Mars Gloab's door – or, at least, the door to the room he had entered that afternoon.

Sounds of stirring from within. "What. . . who ..?" a sleepy voice demanded.

"Let me in! Let me in!"

A bed creaked. Someone came padding barefoot over the floor. She gasped with relief and prepared to rush it the moment he opened it a crack.

But he didn't open it at all. "Who's there?" he asked.

"Miss d'Arblay. Please open up. I'm being chased."

He laughed. "Then you're breaking the law, Mlle. des Esseintes! No one is chaste here! *C'est défendu!* Do what thou wilt – that is the law!"

"Oh *please*!"

He laughed again and padded away. Despite all her entreaties he made no further sound or movement. She stopped and listened. The whole house was silent. If Segal had tried to follow her down that staircase, she would certainly have heard him. Therefore he was still upstairs. Therefore she had to go on – on and out. Perhaps she could find some gatekeeper or groundsman's cottage where they'd take her in? Or had they instructions to ignore all such goings on?

She tiptoed along the passage until she came to the door into the great hall – where she had first seen the consumptive girl and the nun. She pushed it open, half expecting to find them back there now, in the white pentangle. The creaking of the hinge rang up into the rafters. Great moonbeams fell slanting inward, planting gothic tracery on the uneven floor.

She had not the courage to walk out into that huge stillness; instead she began to work her way around to one of the garden entrances, hugging the wall as she went. Halfway there she saw a figure – a man – watching her from one of the niches. At first she thought it might be a statue, but then he moved. He stepped out, not quite into the light but into a lesser gloom. There was a triumph in the gesture, as if he could safely risk this revelation.

"Dante?" she asked.

Mockingly he shook his head. Gloab? The niche was close to the wall of his room. Or Segal? The place must be riddled with secret ways. She stood her ground, uncertain now whether she'd be safer inside or out – even if she could reach one of the doors.

He moved again. It was Segal – now she was certain of it. She turned and ran out of the great hall, along the passageway past Gloab's door, and up the vast, creaking stairway to the bedrooms. But this time she ran on, up to the bachelors' floor and Dante's room – wherever it was.

If Segal was down there in the hall, he could not be up here, too. If only she could find Dante, she'd be safe. "Dante?" she cried. She paused to listen, wishing she wasn't so breathless.

Try all the doors.

The first was locked.

"Dante!" she cried more desperately as she realized she'd burned her boats in coming up here.

"Dante!"

She was still so breathless she almost missed it.

"What?" he cried sulkily.

She almost collapsed with relief. His voice came from behind that first locked door. "Open it! Hurry! Oh be quick!" she went on shouting, even when she heard the key turning in the lock. He opened the door a bare fraction but she hurled herself against it and forced her way in. After the almost pitch-black of the corridor the moonlight was painfully bright. She shielded her eyes with an arm. "Oh darling!" she said. One breast fell out of her dress.

"You hot-tailed little harlot!" he answered angrily.

Her mouth went dry, the floor queasy beneath her. She drew breath to scream.

But the scream never came. Segal said, "Make one sound, you ignorant, stupid little whore, and I'll cut your throat from ear to ear." Sharpness against her neck. "Just get your breath back." Menacing, not kindly. His hand on her naked breast, unlecherous, trying to push it back. "You don't tempt me."

The flesh fell out again. "I'll prove it." He tore the flimsy garment to her waist. It sank, leaving only a thin muslin petticoat. That, too, began to slide.

He held aloft a gleaming lozenge – a silver Masonic trowel, smaller, more menacing than the other – and aimed its flash-of-moonlight blade at her. "This can draw *real* blood. Feel it."

"I believe you."

"Feel it!"

A sudden jab pricked her hesitant fingertip, but she was too frightened to cry out. He smiled. "You will please go over and lie on the bed.'' The tone was oddly clipped, compulsive, like that first meeting in Finsbury Close.

He locked the door, then took off all his clothes. Unaroused, he saw her eyes make that discovery. ''Didn't I tell you?'' He sat beside her on the bed.

Sharp silver point beneath her petticoat, where the ungentle tip ran cool metal up her leg and thigh, dragging the clothing.

Make no move. Utter no sound. But him no but. She fixed her gaze where his excited flesh must rise – if excitement was in it at all.

His angry hiss: ''Oh? Willing are you?''

Get him furious enough to start shouting? Would Dante hear?

His lunatic anger boiled over. With vehemence in bare control, he caught tight her petticoat and ripped it off.

Soothing, she sought to stroke his thickly hairy arm. ''Please don't hurt me.'' Surprised not to tremble more. ''I'll do whatever you want, only I beg you don't hurt me.'' She caressed his thigh, Esau-hairy too, parted her own a suggestive inch and more.

His hand fell like a retribution on her arm. The tip of the trowel into her armpit. ''Cry out, and I'll take off half your shoulder. Understand?''

She nodded violently.

''You believe me?''

''Yes!''

He relaxed – but naught to her relief. ''So you'll do anything to please me, eh, little fuckbag? You're all the same with your carnal lusts. Well, clever Miss Friend-of-Sir-William-Gull, no splitarsed sow will ever again have *that* power over me.'' His grip tightening. ''Yet there *are* pleasures we may explore – you and I. Yes indeed! But you won't simply *give*. No high and mighty Lady Bountiful. I'm going to *take* them. Show you what a man is for. And you dare squirm! You dare give the least cry of pain! You'll spoil my pleasure and I'll have to begin again. Have you ever considered the beauty of pain, Miss Friends-in-high-places?''

He relaxes when he speaks. Encourage him. ''Surely pain cannot be beautiful, Dr. Segal?''

''What do you know, filth? Carrion! Night-soil! Pain is woman's true beauty. Her sole claim to rank with man. You only rise out of the slime of your carnal self-obsession when you're in pain. I'm a doctor. I know. You'll see.'' He relaxes again. ''With

161

so little effort I'll produce in you the greatest pain you'll ever know. Oh – God so exquisitely designed the female body as a receptacle for pain! You shall see. *And* you shall let me take my pleasure uncomplainingly. I shall train you.'' He stands up. ''Ready?''

She lies rock-still. How to deflect this madness?

He puts one knee on the bed. Hope! His words have been a trick. He's simply going to rape me! All those threats to make me accept with gratitude. I'm a virgin still. Aren't men supposed to want that? Tell him.

He points his bent-tooth smile at me. ''Don't imagine this has anything to do with sexual lust. Look!'' Slack pendulum of his manhood swings too close, a cheesy odour warmth. ''Not the least aroused you see. Sorry if I disappoint you but that's why I took my clothing off – to reveal my absolute superiority over you. I know you're just lying there, longing for the feel of it.''

He straddles me, a jockey gripping with his knees my thighs. Is this it? It hurts enough. ''Think you can tempt me, temptress?'' He clamps me tighter. ''With your soft, hot, slimy little hell hole?'' Tighter still. ''There's no woman living. . .'' Foul erratic breath. Foul errant words: ''Hot. . . stinking. . . suppurent. . . think I'm a dog?''

He takes rein on himself. ''Here's your first little lesson.'' Absurdly, the trowel goes down where my modesty would put it. Handle toward him by his filthy dangling thing. His gentle fingertips feel upward where my thighs begin; doctor's hands finding bone. Halt. Press. Press. Sweet Christ such pain! I catch my breath. Perhaps whimper at it. He stops and the relief is exquisite.

''You spoiled it,'' he chides me cheerfully. ''Now I must start again. Notice how quickly the pain ebbed? Ah, the sympathetic nervous system – and the genius who named it! All my gift of pain lies in the sympathetic nervous system. When the torment becomes unbearable – as it soon will – just remember that fact, my dear: The moment I stop my wonderful work, it'll all go away. No bruise. No swelling. My trade is in pure pain. My essence. It flows from me to you. . .'' He flexes his fingers and sinks them to my thighs again.

Being ready doesn't help. I think only of my breathing. The pain grows worse, and worse, and still worse. There seems no end to the pressure he can add. I feel me shivering and beg him with my eyes not to count it a complaint. Sweat all over me. My own voice unbidden escapes, ''Oh please!''

His hopes ambushed my lips for it. ''Oh dear!'' he relaxes, but the relief is almost worth it. ''Oh dear oh dear – and you were beginning to be so good. I want to train you to cooperate. Be my faithful little bitch. Here let's throw in some enlightenment. More light, less heat.'' He takes away the trowel, and himself, to seek a candle.

Is it worth a dash to the window? A leap at one of the shrubberies below? Surely even death would be preferable to whatever. . .? No! Well! Whence this sudden strength? I begin to believe I shall survive this nightmare. I begin to hope I shall revenge myself on him. I feel almost warm.

Candlelight settles on the bedside table as he says genially: ''I need to see your face. Please feel quite free to contort your features – if it helps – I shan't mind a scrap. But I can't bear your moving or making a sound. That's the 'true beauty of pain' I was talking about – to see the contortions on a woman's face while she lies so still and silent. Pleading and yet so exquisitely unresisting. Woman is an earth goddess. Like the Earth herself, patient beneath the battering of the elements as they doom her to fruitfulness. Try and feel the poetry in what we're doing – share with me its wider, symbolic majesty!''

His madness wreaks a mad conspiracy of will in me. Am I to lie here and connive at my own descent into *his* inferno?

Again the trowel just so; a ritual. He leans over me for a new purchase. His still as gentle as a lover's touch evokes a dangerous yearning. How can I end my complaisance?

''I've discovered seventeen such places, my darling. And we shall try them all. By the time dawn breaks you shall be such a connoisseur of pain!''

Help me hate him! Oh dear Lord Jesus, I begin to share his lust; I suffocate in his mind. Bring me back my distance!

Ecstatic pain sears from the pit of my neck to the tremble of my knees. Not in me! It is in her – she who responds to him. Her! Her! Concentrate on her. Invigilate her body. Her arms – how free of pain they are. Hide there. Leave the pain to her. But my thoughts open a door to the agony, it pursues me there also; and she exults, the bitch. Cold sweat thrills flush her up and down in waves. Tears of passion in her eyes; delicious great hot salt slugs roll back into her ears.

A whispered stream of filthy language bathes her, me. Against all womankind – or womanhood. Mingled medical jargon. Farrago's religious quotations. Childish sneers.

The words fight the seduction of the pain. The words begin to efface that evil in her joy; they unite me with herself.

By breathing through miasmas of pain I fake the simulacrum of a cry. His triumph. His crocodile tears. His beginning again. But pain's duration is its own strange death. This time she – I thrive all the way into unconsciousness.

It cannot have lasted long, for when she came to again he straddled her still and the sky was no lighter. The trowel was in his hand. He was talking to himself.

"You hurt me so badly, Cynthia. And I could have been so loving. So loving." He was weeping.

He took the trowel and pricked the point of it low on her abdomen. She forced her own amazingly biddable body not to wince.

"I'll show them! Who do they think. . .! Masons. Women. His Mighty Highness! Harlots. All. And they won't dare! The vilest crime and they won't dare!" He dragged the pointed tip upward across her skin. "So! Yes – I'll do so."

Tears-lips-teeth mimed in sound a disembowelment. In the silent interstices, the dribble of odd and singleton words: "Whores. . . Masons. . . for a hundred years. . . die twice. . ." and more that made no sense.

The trowel at her neck traced slow re-enactment of that right-to-left slash. His tears were copious by now. Halfway through he saw her watching him. He dropped the trowel and fell upon her, weeping, weeping. "Cynthia! Oh Cynthia, oh Cynthia."

Automatically she raised her hands to comfort him, stroking his baby's back. "Oh no!" he shouted. "You lewd fucking harlot!"

He was scrabbling wildly for the trowel which had fallen on the floor. This time no mime. Her backward plunge raised her knee. His shriek split her ear. The quickest lesson of her life. Exultant, she did it again. And then again.

And then again.

Two jellied lumps in there skittered around beneath the hammer blows of her thigh like soap in flannel in a washtub in the dark.

His turn to pass out. One heave of all four limbs hurled his male bones to the floor.

She sprang from the bed, trampling him in her haste. She unlocked the door. She had the presence of mind to gather up his clothing and shoes and toss them from the window. Then she wrapped one of his stinking sheets around her and fled. Her well-being astounded her.

Back below in safety there came a gentle knocking at the connecting door.

"Yes?" Her voice was bright.

"All's well?" Saunders asked.

"Of course. Come on in."

The door opened. Saunders, her dressing gown plucked to her, ungirdled, stepped hesitantly in. The first thing she noticed was the still-open section of panelling and the narrow staircase beyond.

"Mice." Tessa told her.

Saunders grinned. "Name of Rosen?"

"I'm sure I've no idea."

"Well, sooner you than me. Here – what was that din?" She gazed vaguely at the ceiling.

"Yes, I heard it, too."

"Why're you getting all togged up at this hour? You going somewhere?"

"Of course I am."

"Where?"

"To watch the sun rise over Stonehenge, of course. Isn't that what we came down here for?"

Chapter Twenty-Three

A machine might feel like this, if machines might feel at all. Her heart was numb, her muscles pugnaciously alive. The last thing she desired was to crawl away and hide. Before she dressed she had filled a basin with water and splashed it mightily over herself from head to foot, uncaring of the carpet or the ceilings below. Now, wandering guideless through the near-dawn up the little chalkstream valley, she desired to do the same with the whole awakening world – seize it in a giant's embrace and dash it invigoratingly against herself. She was ready for it all.

Nothing could hurt her now. The hurtable parts were cauterized. Even physical pain had lost its edge of terror. She remembered her response to it and steered her thoughts elsewhere. Toward Stonehenge. Toward the coming dawn.

She left the valley bottom by an ingrown bridle-path that promised a release onto the broad rides of Salisbury Plain. Darkling, it twisted upward through coppiced beeches, among unnatural gulleys as ancient as mankind's tread upon this chalk – their purpose long forgotten, their very form impregnable to all but the wildest guesswork. They helped her to locate herself, though – as a vanishing particularity in the human scheme of things; their cosmic endurance mocked her two-score-years-and-four as, indeed, it would mock Methuselah.

Emerging from the wood the path broadened among banks of foxglove and brambles, drooping in the heat of night, dusty from a rainless week. In the muffled, mighty twilight she wandered through a world more painted than real. The folds of the plain sprang up in vanishing succession as the pathway rose toward the dawn, until at last the view was halted on the final skyline, not a mile distant; there the world's rim was pricked with those wasted megaliths whose meaning seems always to hover near yet never quite to settle.

Heedless of the path, she set her face toward them and stepped out eagerly over the sheep turf, afraid now to be cheated of the rising sun. The crisp green band upon the horizon was already yielding to its blear pink corona. She began to run, across the metalled Winterbourne turnpike and onward over the plain. Flustered and breathless she failed to notice the solitary male figure until she was almost upon him.

"I wondered whether you'd come," Dante said. He was sitting on the rim of a small depression, knees up, arms loosely linked around them. His casual greeting closed off, for the moment, a score of potential conversations.

"Oh, hello," she said, still out of breath, but taking her tone from his.

"You haven't missed it." He began to stand – wearily, as if he had been sitting there a long time.

"Oh good." When she had recovered a little she asked, "Have you been here long?"

He nodded, yawned, and rubbed his eyes hard. "Ooh!" He hopped tenderly. "Pins and needles!" He took her elbow and steered her toward the western end. "This is where we'll see it best."

Together they walked through the outer circle to stand at the base of the inner horseshoe.

"Why didn't you come to me last night?" she asked.

"I didn't make the conditions, remember? They weren't right."

"Will they ever be?"

He shrugged. "I expect so."

"You're going to punish me for that – I can see."

"That's a childish way of looking at things." He was far from angry. Indeed, he was being quite pleasant. He pointed away to the east, across the Devizes road, where the sky was growing perceptibly brighter by the minute. "See that stone, just before the highway there? The one sticking up?"

"The biggest one?"

"The tallest, anyway. That's the heel stone, they call it. This is the only day in the year when the sun rises directly over it from this position."

"Did they build it that way?"

"They must have."

The flat normality he kept imposing on their conversation was like a shrinking room. She had to break out. "You could have

167

warned me, Dante," she said. "About that stupid ritual."

He stared like a castaway at the burgeoning dawn.

"Why didn't you?" she pressed.

"I did in a way. I told you they're short-cutters."

"You let me walk into it."

They could not look at each other. They both spoke to the sky as to an arbitrator. He said, "It should help you to see the futility of it. Also I knew you'd be safe. But suppose it had all been real! Didn't you feel a certain majesty in it? Imagine it had been real?"

"It *was* real, Dante. In my dreams I know I'm going to forget it was all a charade . . ."

"Then I envy you."

"It was real to me until I got back outside and Davitt told me. Thank God for Davitt."

"Then you miss the whole point," he snorted. "You get the worst of both worlds. Poor you."

"But not you, of course! Oh no!"

"No – not me. I'm an artist. So are you. You *could* learn, if only you didn't get so caught up. Let that be last night's lesson: Don't get caught up. I take what I need from them, and I yield nothing. It's what you should learn to do." He looked back at the dawn skyline, now bright enough to hurt.

She said, "Some burglars broke into our house once. I must have been about six, but I can still remember my mother telling Bo about it. She said it wasn't as if they took anything of real value – the worst thing was just knowing they'd *been* there, walking round our home, touching all our most private things. She said it made her feel unclean. And it's true."

Her tone made him take her arm; she had to steel herself not to flinch. He felt it, too. "What's happened?" he asked.

"Segal came to my room."

He looked her up and down and shook his head in disbelief. "No – I've seen women after . . ."

"Did you know he was going to come to my room?"

"What difference would it make?"

"Dante! You did know!"

"Not so, as it happens. If I had known, I'd have stopped him. I hope you believe that. But it's beside the point, anyway. The point is – what did you . . ."

"God how I loathe you!"

168

He coughed a single, mild laugh and puckered his lips. "What a stupid comment! All right – he *did* come to your room. He did hurt you. What now? Are you just going to wallow in self-pity? Boo hoo – look at me everybody, I've been hurt! You make me sick. You're surrendering the battle to the philistine at the first clash. Why don't you look for the meaning instead? You're an artist – you can *make* it mean something. Catch your shrieks in cups of gold. Segal's life had no meaning until he read de Sade. But Segal's no artist. He won't achieve anything. You could achieve everything that eludes him. Not by doing but by observing. Experiencing. Why d'you think I brought you here?"

"It was so sordid."

"Nothing wrong in that. Oscar says Art is at its peak when it takes the sordid and transmutes it into the sublime."

She said, "There's someone out there." Whether it was true or not she didn't know. She had caught the faintest intimation of a movement in the blinding black between the dawn and the earth. She didn't want to listen to his lecturing any more. But her dislike of him, so strong only moments ago, was now quite mild. She seemed to have lost the capacity for sustained feeling. Nothing mattered permanently now – especially here, where permanence had a different scale.

She gazed at the dancing-bright horizon; surely the first thumbnail of the sun could not be long delayed?

There *was* someone out there!

She said. "If you'd come to my room last night, it wouldn't have happened."

He touched her hair, then her cheek. "When we go to bed, Tess, it won't be the consolation at the butt-end of a bad day. It'll be the only thing in our lives – the only thing we ever wanted to do. It'll be a feast. We won't surface for days."

"A feast with panthers."

After a silence he asked, "Did Segal really come to your room?"

"Go and see for yourself. Ask him. He's probably come round by now."

He frowned askance.

An old memory surfaced. Something her Irish riding teacher had said to her almost fifteen years ago: "Hit the fella where you won't blind him!" She laughed at that memory, not at what she had done to Segal – but that was how it sounded to Dante when she said, "I put my knee where it wouldn't blind him."

At that precise moment the sun broke the skyline. Its light was a livid kiss, on stone, on grass, on flesh. She smiled exultant at its touch – the more so because she knew that he, having waited here all night for this moment of sunrise, was forced to squander it. He could not take his eyes off her. His rooted silence told her exactly how she must appear to him in that crimson fire. Thus Diana with the blood of wild beasts on her lips and breasts. Thus the maenad fresh from her *orgia*. Thus the exultant Amazon.

The approaching stranger, a man, climbed upon the heelstone and stretched wide his arms – crucifying himself upon Apollo rising; he christened this most pagan moment of the year. "Hello!" he cried.

She knew the voice. "Simon!" she shouted – forgetting they were not upon such terms.

"Tess!" he called back, gracing her forgetfulness.

Straight as a dart out of the strengthening sun he ran toward them, slowing to a diffident saunter only when he reached the sungilt edge of the inner horseshoe, mere yards away. "I thought I'd be alone here." He was only slightly out of breath. "They told me you'd cancelled your rooms at the White Hart."

"Come and stand by us," she told him. "It's not quite finished. You'll just see it."

She stood at peace between them, arms linked with each. They stared at the sun.

"Marvellous!" he said with a philistine gusto that caused Dante to cringe – and she could feel it. "Makes one hungry, eh?" he added with the same vulgar heartiness.

She stepped back, pulling them face to face, two gilded silhouettes upon the bloodred heavens. "Dante Rosen, painter, meet Simon Liddington, curate."

Since she would not let go of Simon's right arm, the two men could only bow to each other. She burst into laughter. They looked at her. "Were ever two descriptions less apt?" she asked. "Painter and curate!"

"Try again," Dante challenged. "I give you demon and saint!"

"I say!" Simon protested.

Tessa stepped between them, re-forming the straight line. She

170

marched them toward the heelstone – and to their breakfast, three miles away in the White Hart. "Your chance to do better, Simon," she challenged.

"Seers of a new heaven and a new earth."

"Bravo!" Dante said in a surprised tone.

"But which is which?" Tessa asked.

"What a shame!" Simon told her. "The oracle allows only one direct question. But I'll give you an oracular clue: Liver and loafer!"

Dante's single laugh was more constrained this time. Suddenly he jerked his arm out of her grasp. "Actually," he said sharply, "it's lover and leaver. (Or did he say, "love her and leave her?") I'd better go and see how Segal is." He strode swiftly away without a farewell or a backward glance. She watched him go and felt nothing. Why could she laugh and joke and understand profound things – and yet feel nothing? How could she still want to lie in his arms, feasting with panthers – and yet feel nothing?

Simon drew breath to call him back but she said quietly, "Let him go."

"Funny chap."

She laughed and hugged his arm again, to renew the understanding that he could leave it linked in hers. "Oh Simon – you're so *normal*!"

"Dull, you mean."

"No – normal."

They resumed their walk to the road. Simon, she decided, would make a good brother – strong, kind, decent, understanding, etcetera, etcetera.

"You know why he left so abruptly?" she asked him, and then answered herself: "Because he suddenly realized you were a match for him. I mean, 'demon and saint' wasn't exactly inspired, was it! He only said it because he thought you were as crass as your comment on the sunrise made you seem. That was clever of you. You slipped beneath his guard."

"Crass? Me? What comment?"

"You said 'magnificent'."

"But it was magnificent."

"Of course it was. But do you look at the ocean and say, 'wet!'?"

"Oh."

171

The monosyllable was so woebegone that she laughed again. "Never mind, my dear. You more than made up for it – and that's why he scuttled away."

He caught the contempt in her voice. "Is Mr. Rosen your lover?" he asked.

"Simon!" The sun was bright enough to hurt now. She was glad they had reached the road and could turn more southerly, leaving its brilliance to their left.

"You don't have to answer," he told her magnanimously. She couldn't decide whether he was just crashingly naive – or so utterly suave that he imagined he could ask such a question with impunity – and then top it with such permission.

"You didn't have to ask," she answered.

"Oh – I see!"

"I don't suppose you do, really. How did you get here, anyway?"

"By train."

"I don't mean that. I mean, does my father know?"

"Oh yes, that was quite easy – especially as I seem to be rather well-known in archaeological circles. He told me they even used my name for an acrostic in the *Gazette*. Quite an honour."

She could no longer be cross with him. She hugged his arm again and then let go in order to move around to his left, out of his shadow and into the sun. "You're a nice man, Simon. I'm glad you came." She looked up at him slyly, glad the sun was on his face, not hers. "Why d'you want to know if Dante Rosen and I are lovers? Should you mind if we were?"

He grinned down at her and shook his head in mock-sadness. "Once again, Tess, you've already used up the direct question."

"Give me an oracle then."

He thought awhile. At length he spoke. "For this night? This night now passed? There can surely be but one oracle: 'Naught shall be ill. Jack shall have his Jill.' "

Chapter Twenty-Four

"The condemned man ate a White Harty Breakfast," Simon said, apropos nothing – if you could call porridge, kidneys, coddled eggs, kedgeree, and gorgeous fresh bread hot from the bakehouse and running with butter and honey, *nothing*.

"Condemned?" she queried.

"Aren't we all? In one way or another." He smiled. "This Rosen chap's quite famous, isn't he? I've heard his name."

Tessa couldn't resist saying, "He claims I've influenced him. His whole style has changed since he first visited my studio, you know."

"I say! I had no idea. But you sound as if you don't entirely believe him?"

"Would you, if you were me?"

"I'd like to see your work myself. Would you care for a second opinion?"

"Not really."

He winced. "You're pretty ruthless."

She smiled as if he had paid her a compliment. "I don't think I am. You should watch Dante Rosen when it comes to ruthlessness. As soon as he saw my work, he just moved into my studio, lock stock and barrel – took it over."

"And you, too?" He gazed at her evenly. The mood changed.

"Listen," she said, "can I talk to you seriously about Dante Rosen?"

He gave a guarded nod. "As long as you don't ask *me* the difference between a good man and a bad one."

She frowned at the memory. "What a waste of breath that was!"

"We're born in the wrong age, you know. Philosophy *used* to be about good and bad ideas. Then it became more to do with right and wrong actions. And now it's getting to be exclusively about proper and improper questions. If they go on like this, they'll end up talking only about permissible and impermissible

173

words."

"About Dante Rosen . . ." she reminded him.

"Yes, I'm sorry. About Dante Rosen?"

"He's . . . I don't think I'd quite call it an obsession, but it's close. He's almost obsessed by the notion of evil."

"The *notion* of evil?"

"All right. By evil itself. Oh dear, I'm afraid I'm going to represent his ideas very unfairly. You see, I half-share them and I'm half-repelled by them. But is it the future half of me that shares them, and is it the past half, the childhood half, that feels repelled?"

"Tell me about them."

"It's really to do with growing up, isn't it. No one tells us how to grow up. We sort of vaguely absorb the idea that it's about handling money and suffering fools gladly taking an intelligent interest in the newspapers and so on. But underneath all that there's an assumption of social and moral certainties. No one speaks about them, but everyone publicly assumes them. And the fact is – they just *aren't* certainties."

"In what particular way?" he asked.

"I've met people this weekend who are the absolute opposite of . . . of . . ." She sighed. She could no longer remember what they were the absolute opposite of. "I mean there are so many different people – and I think they're all slightly *mad*! Not enough to show in everyday life. But if you could really take the covers off their minds – d'you know?" She laughed at her own earnestness. "D'you think *I'm* mad?"

"No, no." His eyes encouraged her. "It makes sense."

"Can I ask you a very frank question, Simon?"

"If it cuts both ways."

Their eyes met. She tried to tell him what was in her mind but all she finally said was, "You're going to hate me. I know."

He stood. "Let's walk back to Olympus and collect your things. And Miss Saunders if she wants to come? We can talk as we go."

They each paid for their breakfast – Tessa insisted on it – and then, after the calls of nature, they set out. It was another bright, sunny day. Little fleecy clouds had blown up from the south, dappling the way with fugitive shade. The road to Olympus went nowhere, save to a few farms, before it rose onto the plain and joined the old packhorse trail to Winchester. The two of them had the whole world to themselves once they were out of Amesbury.

He let his silence prompt her.

She said, "D'you think there are things . . . going on in our minds, in the Archbishop of Canterbury's mind, in the Queen's mind, in Lord Salisbury's mind, in my father's . . . yours . . . mine – are there things going on that we'd never confess?"

"We'd confess them to God. Even to think them is to confess them to God."

"All right. But to each other? Aren't we all in a conspiracy to pretend we're quite different from the way we really are?"

"D'you think that's hypocritical? Couldn't it be like people on a life raft, clinging together for support and saying, 'Afraid? Me? Never!' – when really they're petrified?"

She stopped and looked hard at him – Sergeant Keene's gesture. Simon backed away from his own suggestion. "I'm only putting it to you as a possibility."

She grinned. "Suppose the *life raft* itself is our mistake! What if the sea actually holds no threats? What if it's actually as much our element as the air? What if our Dark Self isn't dark after all?" She skipped and took his arm impulsively. "Oh Simon, haven't you ever longed for someone who knows absolutely everything you're thinking? So that you could talk about it with them?"

He pulled her arm through his, to make their linkage equal. "D'you cast me in that role? Or are we talking about Dante Rosen again?"

"I'm talking about me. You can choose anyone you wish to talk about."

He was silent awhile. "I don't think people could ever do it," he said at length. "It's the fable Aesop never told – the lion and the wolf who decided to tell each other every single thought that passed through their minds, and ended up so ashamed of their lionishness and their wolfishness they starved to death."

"You have a bleak view of human nature, young man."

"All right – the sheep and the rabbit, who ended up so ashamed of their sheepishness and rabbitishness etcetera."

She laughed. "I'm not sure that's any improvement."

"What I'm saying is it's hard enough to face our own self-knowledge, without passing out hostages." He patted her arm. "Poor Tess. I'm being no help to you, am I." He drew a deep

175

breath and plunged. "Yes. Of course I sometimes long for such a person. I also long to fly. Do I gather from all this that you're trying to say evil may not be as bad as it's painted?"

"Not quite. But certain things that we call evil may in fact be good. Or neutral. Or evil only if we use them for evil ends. Is the starving child who steals an apple from the rich man's orchard every bit as guilty of theft as the rich man who steals the widow's mite?"

He laughed. "Now you'll see where *I'm* just a little bit mad – because I'd say both were equally innocent." He felt the surprise in her muscles and said, "Yes! I'm one of those utterly impractical dreamers, you see, who think that property is the real evil. If we had no property no one could steal. There could be no rich and no poor. Adam would delve and Eve would spin. Ridiculous, of course. Quite mad. Next question."

"But greed and acquisitiveness are in us, Simon. They aren't just put there by our society. Look at how babies . . ."

"They're in us, all right. They're a raging fire in us. The best way to fight a fire is to cut off its fuel."

They were approaching a break in the woodland that girded the road. Here it led down to a stretch of open meadow flanking a purling little chalkstream, a tributary of the one near Olympus. As they emerged into the full sunlight, he grabbed at the emptiness in front of him. "Look at this bit of air," he told her. "Who owns it?"

"No one, of course."

"Then try to imagine a world in which everything was like that!"

She snorted. "But the only reason no one owns it is that greedy and resourceful men haven't yet found a way of establishing their claim on something so fluid and invisible. They *have* found a way of claiming ownership of water, you'll notice. You just try and fish in this little stream here!"

"And you think *I* have a jaundiced view of man!" His face hung moodily against the green of the water meadow beyond him.

"I want to cool my feet," she said suddenly. "D'you mind?"

"I'll join you. I haven't walked so much for months."

They left the road just before the bridge and went down a long, shallow bank amid a profusion of buttercups, marigolds, irises, and wild orchids. The bank opposite had been poached into the water by generations of cattle from that pastureland. The diverted stream had undermined the bank on this side so that it was now a good eighteen inches above the water – the perfect height for laving heated feet. Simon retreated to the shade of a couple of sallies a dozen yards upstream. She thought he was being discreet, to let her take off her stockings unobserved, but was surprised to see him throw himself on his stomach a yard or so from the bank and then begin to creep toward the water margin like a cat stalking a bird. With infinite slowness he let his hand slide ahead of him, over the edge and into the stream. She had her stockings around her neck and was sitting paddling happily long before he had inched near enough to the brink to be able to see into the depths.

"What's the game?" she called.

He held up a single finger of his dry hand. The tension in his body told her this was no mere game.

She sat there, dousing her feet, luxuriating in the cool of the water, listening to its merry gurgle where it dashed against the stone piers of the bridge, watching chalkhill blues and fritillaries lurching in their silent dance from blossom to blossom, noting how the cows stood shimmering in the sun, each rooted in her own purple lake of shade. . . the entire scene was so flattened by the heat and midsummer light it was already halfway to being an oil on canvas. Far above, tethered on gossamer kitestrings, skylarks were auctioning their manic claims to air and territory. Segal and all pain were in some other universe.

"Ho!" Simon's cry of triumph was pure animal spirit. She turned in time to see a shimmering arc of silver curl in rise and fall behind him – startled silver of trout in a protesting flotilla of sun-silvered droplets, all in a perfect parabola. "Gotcha!" He rose excitedly to his feet and pounced on the wriggling creature. He raised it by the tail and prepared to bring its head down on his upturned bootcap.

"Simon!" she called.

He looked at her.

"Is that fish's life your property now?" she asked – meaning it as a joke.

But he took it seriously. He rose, came quickly to her, and offered up the fish. "Your prerogative," he said, nodding toward the stream.

She took the creature. Its dark button-eye could not beg her; yet she sensed in the flutter of its muscles all the panic she herself would feel if their elements were reversed. "Back you go," she said and raised it to her lips for one brief kiss. It felt cold and clean. Its slime, being living, was somehow cleanly – quite different from that of a dead fish. She put her ankles together, making a runnel of her shins and feet. She placed the fish within it and lowered it gently toward the water. As soon as it touched its native haunt it darted away, green-mottle-glazed again, upstream.

She looked up at him and smiled for happiness.

But he in his guilt mistook the gesture. "All right," he said testily. "You made your point. I know we don't live in a perfect world. I keep my purse as tight as the next man."

She patted the grass beside her. "I hope there's no law against owning a sense of humour," she chided.

He sat down and hugged his knees. He had a healthy, sweaty smell that pleased her. It emphasized his otherness yet enticed her. She realized that if she had not met Dante first she could quite easily have started getting interested in Simon.

Or could she? There had been other young men close to her – or men who would have loved to be close to her – and she had taken no interest in them. No romantic interest, anyway. She had thought she was going to live only to paint. Until Dante. Had he unlocked something within her? Was she now going to endure all those wild and childish passions she should have grown out of long ago – passions made worse, not better, by her years?

"In your heaven-on-earth, Simon . . . ."

"Yes?"

"Will people be able to say '*my* child . . . *my* poem . . . *my* finger'? Will we even have property in our own bodies?"

He pulled off his boots and dangled his feet in the water. They were town-pale; she saw dark woolballs clinging momentarily to his perspiring skin before the cool water plucked them away. He answered her: "When you say 'my poem' you put it perfectly. A poem by Shakespeare *is* undeniably Shakespeare's; and yet, equally undeniably, it belongs to all mankind. Now in my heaven-on-earth all property will be like that. Whenever I try and explain this to people they always think only of what they'd have to give up. But I think of what they'd gain, what we'd all gain. Property creates such fear you know.'' He picked a buttercup. ''And fear is such an enemy of human happiness. That's what Jesus meant when he said consider the liles of the field, how they toil not, etcetera. He meant we could be as liberated from fear as they are. What does this buttercup own? Everything it needs – earth, air, sunlight, the gentle rain.'' He turned to her. ''They say it's a very young man's philosophy – and they're probably right. D'you like butter?'' He held the flower under her chin.

She laughed and lay back in the grass, closing her eyes against the sun and thinking she wouldn't make a great fuss if he tried to kiss her.

''I suppose Rosen's already told you how lovely you are,'' he said.

Her heart leaped, but she answered, ''That's a very young man's question.''

''Crass,'' he chuckled.

''I suppose you couldn't forget Dante Rosen?''

''You took the words out of my mouth, Tess.''

''That's why I asked if we'd have property in our own persons. The lilies of the field don't pine away with jealousy either, do they?''

She felt him struggling for an answer. The buttercup touched her chin. She plucked it, bringing his fingers into contact with hers. She took his hand and brushed it with her lips before she put it against her head. His nails raked into her hair. She encouraged him with a purr. His other hand came up, sandwiching her head between them; his shadow cooled her face.

But no kiss came.

She opened her eyes and looked straight into his, inches away and bluer than the sky. ''This moment will never return,'' he said. ''I can hardly believe it. I've known you little over a week.''

''I knew Mr. Sweetman for a year. Yes Miss d'Arblay. No Miss d'Arblay. Indeed Miss d'Arblay. Dear God – I knew you better inside five minutes.'' She put her hand behind his head and pulled his lips to hers.

His kiss was chastely adoring – quite different from Dante's. If ever she did love Simon, it would be in an utterly different way. The thought occurred to her that she might be able to love both simultaneously – because it would be so different.

"I'm not sure that even *we* ought to approve of this," he said, half-seriously.

She sensed the beginnings of a retreat into convention. No conscious plan to block it entered her mind, yet she heard herself saying, "When you kiss me, Simon, I get feelings about you that girls aren't supposed to have. The curious thing is, though, I honestly can't feel they're so very shameful." His head was beside hers; he had stopped breathing; she felt the tension in him. "In fact, Simon. . . in fact. . . they feel beautiful." When he still said nothing, she added, "Fear is such a destroyer of human happiness, you know."

He hugged her, still at a loss for words. He kissed her ear. She thrilled at the touch of his lips there, turned her face to him and bit his lobe in response. How easy it would be – but for fear.

"Does the young man's philosophy have its limits?" she asked.

He withdrew then and lay on one elbow beside her, looking down into her eyes. "I've never talked about it before. I mean. . ."

"You mean with a woman."

He nodded.

"We're a different species, aren't we," she said. "That's how you think of us." She surprised herself, never having consciously entertained the thought before.

"Are you meaning me, or all men?"

"Is it true of you?"

He gave it a moment's thought and then nodded. "I suppose so."

"You're afraid of us. You don't understand us."

"And what about you?"

She smiled at the chance to say, "Me – or all women?"

He shook his head. "There aren't any other women."

"We're taught how to wheedle you, how to give as little as possible to get as much as possible. You're taught to flatter us. We're encouraged to believe it. We're angels. We're divine. Is all this the sort of thing you want, Simon?"

"Of course not."

"Because silence is a vacuum. And these are the things that will rush in to fill it."

He blinked. "My goodness – it's all happening so fast."

"You planned it to be slower, did you?" She tickled his hand. "I'll bet you did plan something."

"I hoped against hope. That isn't a plan." He grasped her hand. "It's all very well complaining about being idolized, but you are special, you know. You always will be special, to me. Oh God, Tess, I do love you. I think you're the most astonishing, wonderful, beautiful woman I've ever known."

"I don't mind a *little* flattery," she told him. "From time to time."

He took his cue from her and lay on his back at her side. "I wouldn't mind a little wheedling," he agreed. "From time to time, you know."

Their laughter went up into the skies.

Chapter Twenty-Five

"Rosen's still, ah, here then?" Simon asked. "Or hereabouts." He tried to make it sound light and neutral.

"Hereabouts," Tessa agreed.

"He's sponging on you. I suppose you realize that? He's up to his neck in debt. His credit's almost exhausted. You came along just in time."

She shrugged. It might even be true. She added the final ten hymn-books to the pile already counted. They were making an inventory of moveable church property for the insurance. She said nothing.

"And this new painting style of his," Simon continued. "It may be all very exciting to him – and to you, I'm sure. But nobody's going to buy it. He'll be a millstone around your neck." His voice faded on sermony echoes among the old vaulting, swamped at last among the chirping of sparrows from the belfry.

To avoid an answer, she went up to the altar and opened the plate cupboard in the stone wall behind it. She began listing the contents.

"Still," he said airily as he followed her, "it's all in the sacred

181

cause of Art, so we mustn't complain."

She looked up at the Perpetual Lamp. "Talking of sacred art, d'you think that monstrosity counts as moveable? I suppose it does." She added it to the list. "Five pounds would you say? Four, perhaps."

"No, we mustn't complain. We laymen. We *incognoscenti.*"

"As a matter of fact, he's gone up west to sell some paintings."

She moved away to the lady chapel, where an ancient oak press was set into the wall. She found the key and handed it to him. "You open it," she said.

"Why? Is it stiff?"

"No." She stared at the door in uneasy fascination.

"Why then?" he asked. "Some trick?"

"No. But after Cromwell, when they defaced all the paintings and statues, after they reopened the church, they found a man's skeleton in there. The story goes that the verger killed one of Cromwell's army and to cover the crime they hid the body in there. I hate opening it."

He smiled at her and unlocked the door. An eddy of inrushing wind swirled up the translucent pink skeleton of a little spider; otherwise it was empty. "They must have had very small soldiers in those days," Simon said. He picked up the spider husk. "Probably it was no more than this they found."

"Oh!" she said. "So you do know?"

He frowned. "Know what?"

"How easy it is to take something so utterly trivial and enlarge it beyond all reason or proportion."

He tried not to see her point, but then he smiled and, bunching up his fist, gave her a featherlight punch. "I'm sorry," he said. "Don't imagine I don't realize how dreadfully I'm behaving." He opened his hand and stroked her arm. "And you're being wonderful – especially not to turn it into a quarrel."

She laid her hand on his and smiled.

"I'm ashamed of myself," he went on. "I know just how ugly jealousy is. But I can't seem to help it. I've never behaved like this before in my life. But then I've never been in such a turmoil either. I'm so beset by thoughts of you."

"I know, Simon." She kissed him. There was a longing for him in it but she had given up comparisons. And *was* it so wonderful of her not to be turning his jealousy into a quarrel? If

182

their situations were reversed, she'd be more worried than grateful.

"It's true for you, too, isn't it?" he asked. "This overwhelming feeling we have for each other – you feel it, too?"

She sighed. "Honestly Simon, in your brave new world you're going to end up with everything free except people."

"I couldn't bear it if I thought – I mean, I could bear anything but your indifference."

They finished the inventory and went out into the churchyard. The day was overcast and humid. The city air gave it no relief.

"I wish we were by the sea," she said, fanning out her hair in her fingers. "An onshore breeze now!"

"Where are you thinking of?"

"A little beach near Holkness on the east coast. We went there when I was about eight."

"Good Lord," he laughed. "I know Holkness. D'you remember the river behind it, where it opens out into a great lagoon?"

"Yes! Father took me rowing there. He kept saying he was 'catching crabs,' and I couldn't see them! I was terrified."

"Talking of terror. Did you go in as far as the old galleon that was beached in midstream? The one they used as a prison hulk until about thirty years ago?"

"Yes. We rowed around it. I always think of Magwitch in *Great Expectations* being there."

"I spent a night on that old ship," he told her. "For a dare. They put me there at sunset and rowed away. I was fifteen. I've never been so terrified in my life. I heard chains clanking and people groaning and blood dripped down on me and bats crawled all over me." He laughed at the memory.

"Why didn't you just swim ashore?"

"Sharks. Monster squids. Giant turtles with razor teeth. Walruses . . . you know – the usual things you find up any sleepy English backwater estuary."

She hugged his arm and laughed. "Oh, I want to know all about your life, Simon. All the things like that. I wish you'd been my brother. Then we wouldn't have to tell each other. We could just say d'you remember this . . . d'you remember old so-and-so? That's how I want to share you."

"Share me with who?"

"With yourself, of course. Don't be so bristly! I want to know what it was like to start off a helpless little man-baby, kicking your feet in the air and saying mamama, and to end up here, a doctor and a priest and . . . and special. What was that journey like?"

"Well," he began. "After mamama came dadada. And then . . ."

"No!" She punched him. "Tell me in bits. The way you remembered Holkness. I'll always want to listen."

"I'm rather glad we're not brother and sister, all the same."

"We could be step-brother and sister. Are they allowed to be in love?"

"They hardly ever do, though. Perhaps they know each other too well. There's a warning."

After a restless silence she said, "Come on! There's something you've been dying to say all morning. I can feel it."

"I wish I hadn't got so idiotically jealous just now. It wasn't the sort of thing I wanted to say at all."

"Yes, we've been through all that. What *did* you want to say?"

"I wanted to say Dante Rosen is right."

"Oh?"

"In part, anyway."

"Ah!"

"He's right to say we all have a secret self, and he's also right about our being afraid to face it. Also about the dangers of trying to ignore it, keep it locked away, denying it any place in our lives. He's right about all that. But if he thinks the answer is to go to the other extreme – deny our public selves and make a sort of cult of the other, then he's not only wrong, he's dangerously wrong. That's what I wanted to tell you, Tess. That's all. There is another way."

She said nothing. She understood his words but could not relate them to Dante. Simon just did not understand the nature of art; it didn't fit into his neat categories.

"You're not angry?" he asked.

"Of course not, darling. But you ought to understand one thing about me. If you think that painting's just a pastime for me, something to fill the days until I settle down to my proper business as a wife and mother, then you don't understand me at all. I'd put painting before either you or Dante – just as you, I suppose, would put God before either wife or family."

"It's not an actual choice, Tess."

"Of course not. Nor in my case either, thank heavens! I'm just saying if it came to it, that's the way the sword would fall, and I think it's important for you to understand it."

He inclined his head and made the sort of gesture priests make when they want to show how magnanimous and forgiving God is. She saw he accepted the words but had no grasp of their meaning.

"I'm saying," she felt she had to add, "that what I do is very personal. Also difficult. Also unpredictable. Creation's a wild impulse. You never tame it, just as you can never tame a tiger. Every act of creation is like going into the arena with tigers. You just hope you come back singing. And in between times you don't turn aside from anything that may help you. You don't refuse experience. You say yes to life – *all* of life."

He nodded enthusiastically but she could see he did not really know what she was saying.

That afternoon she went alone to her studio. Dante was still up West; Saunders was at the first read-through of *Solomon's Temple* now renamed *Solomon and Sheba* at her request.

To be alone with her work was like an elixir. Ever since Dante placed her, so to speak, in a European context, her assurance had blossomed wonderfully. He needed only to say something like, "You can't help getting it right, can you!" and it became the truth.

She had just begun a new painting. She called it, half-jokingly, a Hymn to Love – figures in a woodland verge, glimpsed through a screen of leaves, with open fields of wildflowers beyond them. But if it ever saw a gallery wall, it would probably be under a more sober, value-for-money title like "Nudes in a Landscape." Dante was firmly against emotive-sounding titles for paintings. "The only heroes we want," he said, "are light, colour, shape, line, and form. Leave the verbal tricks to the porters who carry in the canvasses."

"Hymn to Love" or "Nudes in a Landscape," this new picture excited her. Another milestone – the first painting that spoke directly to her, the first that taught her new things. Until now she had always needed to visit the galleries and refer to the work of other painters; more recently she had let Dante talk to her about whatever she was doing – in a sense, he had to interpret her own work to her before she could understand it. But no longer.

This painting needed no midwife.

That afternoon was one of the happiest of her life. The painting grew in strength and assurance with every brushstroke; she just "couldn't help getting it right." So why, when the light grew too mellow, when she relaxed and soaped up her brushes – why did a sense of hollow unworthiness fill her? Ever since Olympus it had lurked there at the back of her mind, ready to claim her whenever her guard was dropped.

She had tried to argue it with herself. The two experiences – in the grotto and in Segal's room – had been awful beyond description. If she hadn't met Simon so soon after, she didn't like to think what might have happened to her. Yet Dante was right, too. She *was* an artist. She should have found some means to "catch her shrieks in cups of gold," if not at once, then certainly by now. She ought not to need the anodyne of colour, the talk and laughter of quick minds, and the caress of friendly hands – physical pleasures all – to obliterate the shame of her memory. Tessa the painter was a haven into whom the wounded woman could climb and hide for a season; she felt an intimation that other narcotic selves were gathering to tempt her into their sanctuaries, too.

Before she locked up the studio Dante returned, highly pleased with himself.

"You sold them?" she asked.

He grinned. "Guess again!"

"You wouldn't be anything like so pleased if you hadn't sold them."

"Oh, I've sold them. I've also as good as sold everything else I can do in the new style. I never saw such excitement. But it's even better than that. I've sold you too! What would you say to a two-man exhibition at. . ."

"I'd say who's the other man?"

He pulled a face. "Oh come, come! Man embraces woman in such cases. Though in this case, I think it's the woman who should embrace the man. It isn't every female Sunday painter who gets launched with almost a one-woman show in *Grosvenor* Street. Jimmy Whistler saw them – he's keen to meet you." He put his head on one side and acted the melodrama villain. "Isn't that worthy of one little embrace, my dear?"

She put her arms around him and gave him a kiss. "There!"

"That was nice," he told her.

"Mmmm." It was nice, too. Comforting. Undemanding.

She leaned back and held his hands in hers. "What did you get for them?"

He laughed at her earnestness. "Oh, you're turning into a *real* professional!" His eye prepared her for astonishment. "A hundred for the nude and two for the portrait." He winced as he spoke, as if he still could not quite believe it himself.

"Three hundred pounds?"

"Guineas, please. Guineas! What say we strip some of the shillings off them and go out on the town tonight?"

"Oh yes! Are you sure you can afford it?"

"I haven't bothered to count, but I sincerely hope I can't. There'd be no pleasure in it if I could."

She laughed. "What shall we do?"

"We could take a private supper room at the Café Royal? Oscar might turn up. *Anyone* might turn up. It's about time people began to know Tessa d'Arblay."

"And after?"

"We'll find a cavern measureless to man somewhere."

She hugged him again. "Oh Dante – you made your sale in the nick of time, you know. There's nothing I long for more, just at this moment, than *not* to get any sleep. Sleep and I aren't the best of friends just lately."

Chapter Twenty-Six

"There are so many indiscretions, Miss d'Arblay, which this man" – he pointed toward Rosen – "has begged me *not* to reveal to you! I could fill your ear all night. Do pray send him out upon some errand so that we may begin at once!"

"In that case, Mr. Wilde," Tessa answered, "I know precisely where to direct him. He shall go to the zoo."

"An excellent choice. It is where the rest of his friends have longed to send him for the last ten years. You'll earn our

187

unswerving gratitude, I assure you. We'll ask the keeper to house him next to the wombat, I think, don't you? Two hairy, cuddlesome creatures, each of uncertain ancestry, and both of volatile temperament?''

"Oh no. I shan't be sending him as an inmate. He shall go upon an errand. And he'll not return without at least a brace of panthers – for he promised me that tonight we should feast with them.''

Wilde frowned at Rosen with mock severity. "Pillow talk, dear boy? Feasting with panthers, indeed!''

Dante smiled, unabashed. "I wish I'd said that!''

Wilde laughed. "You have, Rosen! You have!'' He turned again to Tessa. "Are panthers to your taste then, Miss d'Arblay?''

"Well, Mr. Wilde'' – she held him with her eye – "here's my dilemma: I'm sure that if the waiter offered them, he'd ask if I liked my panthers rare or well done. And my only honest answer would be *both*! So tell me, pray, in what form are you offering them?''

He roared with laughter. "Oh Rosen! What a find!''

"But you don't answer me,'' Tessa insisted.

He turned back to her. "How? Answer you? I think I must give you best, for I fear my extreme is but your middle ground.'' He examined her critically. "You say you want your panthers both rare and well done? Rosen must go better. He must offer them *bleu* and incandescent!''

She was delighted to see that Wilde, who had plainly intended to do no more than stop by and cast a few pearls, now proposed to join them for their dessert – a flamboyant concoction of water ices and fruit.

His wit was already a legend, of course, but little was ever said about his charm – which she found overwhelming. He had a gift for turning from the inconsequential to the serious, between one word to the next. The philistine press portrayed him as a gilded fop; the avant garde distrusted him as a shallow adventurer in territory they would prefer to keep holy and solemn. Within very few minutes she realized he was larger than them all.

Then it dawned on her that his wit was a mask, for it slipped aside now and then to reveal a very different man, a poet who perhaps feared he might one day comprehend all the great

188

mysteries of life. He must know, she thought, what terrors such comprehension would bring – terrors he now appeased with a paradox or bon mot. She was saddened by these glimpses, even as she drank his champagne and laughed at his brilliance.

In those thirty minutes he evoked in her a profound sense of friendship. Yet she doubted he had a corresponding affection for her – not because he was too mean-spirited. Quite the contrary. It was as if some intuition warned him that each such tie to a fellow human being would hasten on the day of revelation, when the last absurdity would wither before the first truth. . . when the panthers, having feasted the table bare, would turn their rage upon him. The very power of his insight had destined him to stand forever on the outside of that life of which he was, nonetheless, the centre! He *lived* that paradox. Was the same, she wondered, true of herself on a lesser scale? Was that why she understood so well the fleeting sadness she alone seemed to sense behind his gaiety?

Before he left he spoke part of his poem *Panthea*. . .

And thus without life's conscious torturing pain

In some sweet flower we will feel the sun. . . . . . making it rich with his Irish drawl. A couple of fragments only lodged in her memory – one an image of herself and Dante reborn as "two gorgeous-mailéd snakes," slithering over their own graves; the other, two lines intact:

O think of it! We shall inform ourselves

Into all sensuous life, the goat-foot Faun. . .

What the goat-foot Faun achieved she had forgotten; but those two lines, she felt, made a talisman to wear at her throat until the coming of dawn.

When he had gone, Rosen said, "Well, you made your mark there!"

"We're two of a kind," she answered. He pressed her to explain but she would not.

He shrugged away her silence. "And now what is madam's desire?" he asked.

She took one of his hands in hers, his cotton glove in her lace, and said, "In a way, Dante, you've created me. Did you bring me here as your Coppelia?"

"Oh no," he said. "I'm not having that." He spread her hand out before her face and made her look at it. "Your art was all

189

here – it was all in these fingers – before ever you met me.''

"But I didn't realize it.''

He saw she was determined to pin this medal on him. "Very well. Have it your own way. If you think you owe yourself to me, I certainly shan't refuse you!'' His eyes danced.

He was looking splendid tonight, she thought. A gentleman's evening dress is such a dull uniform, yet he managed to wear it with a panache that made her proud. She wanted everyone to notice him – and to notice that he was with her. For her part she was wearing a completely new outfit, ordered before midsummer and delivered only last week: a gorgeous negligee of white silk with pale frills all down the front, a chemise of fine white cotton, and all new underwear and stockings.

"That was a beautiful poem,'' she said. "But I can't imagine Oscar Wilde in love, can you?''

"But he is. He loves Bosie Douglas.''

"Who's she?''

"He. One of the Marquess of Queensbury's sons.''

"Oh.'' Did that explain the distance she had sensed? "What about you?'' she asked. "Can other people imagine you in love, I wonder. Don't you want to be? Don't you want me to be in love with you? Not even tonight?''

Impatience showed in his eyes. "I told you – we Pygmalion-gods are indifferent to it. Anyway, it only betrays us. We're going to discover something much better, you and I.''

"You and I and the goat-foot Faun.'' After a silence she asked, "*Did* you know about Segal that night?''

He shook his head. She wished he would be more positive. She wanted to tell him how, during Segal's torture, part of her had begun to respond to him – not to enjoy, but to share. "Have you seen him since?'' she asked.

"He comes out of hospital tomorrow. Kicked by a horse is the story – where it wouldn't blind him.''

"I don't want to talk about him.''

"It's going to be all right,'' he said. "Let's go now.''

It was a relief to leave decisions to him.

They took a cab but drove only a short distance. The humid day had yielded to a fine, clear night. When they stopped, he squeezed her arm and said, "Shan't be two shakes.''

She noticed everything as it happened – and forgot it at once.

190

The passing carriages, the hints of life at some of the windows – a hand rearranging an oil lamp, a curtain momentarily parting, a shadow passing across a blind, a singer in one house competing with a piano in another. . . a dog barking. Everything was sharp – almost poignantly so, as if it ought to have some especial meaning.

The horse, deep in its nosebag, stirred continuously, flicking its tail; the cab was never still.

Dante returned, paid off the driver, and helped her down to the pavement. ''Where is this?'' she asked.

''Golden Square.''

It wasn't what she meant, but it would do.

The house had the air of a small, private hotel, except that there was no sign outside and no obvious reception area within. Dante led her straight upstairs and along the landing to a room at the very back. A bedroom. The most sumptuous bedroom she had ever seen.

A maid brought two pitchers of hot water and four towels. He gave her five shillings and told her to fetch a bottle of their best brandy. The woman's eyes lingered for a moment in Tessa's and she gave a light, incurious smile, conveying nothing.

Dante took off her hat and cloak, then his own. The unclouded summer night – or early morning as it now was – had a chill edge to it; but a fire burned brightly in the grate. The maid had put some of the water into a copper kettle, which now stood moaning on a trivet near the coals. Tessa turned down the two lamps. The fire sprang up, brighter than before; it glinted balefully on the ivory teeth and brown glass eyes of a bear, whose skin lay stretched before the hearth. Beside the bearskin, facing the fire, was a low, silken divan. She sat upon its edge and began to unpin her hair. But he came up and stood behind her. He put his hand on hers to make her stop. Their fingers entwined. His other hand began lightly, almost absentmindedly, to massage her shoulder. They stayed thus, staring into the flames, until after the maid had brought their brandy and left again. Tessa followed her as far as the door, where she quietly eased the bolt into its housing. Then she plucked off her gloves.

Dante was cupping two glass balloons in his hands, a small tot of brandy in each. With a smile he handed them to her. While she continued to warm them, he took some incense cones from his waistcoat pocket, lit two of them at a glowing coal, and set them to smoulder on the mantelpiece. They had not the spiced fragrance she associated with him; they were more blossomy, more like mimosa. He kicked off his shoes, took off his jacket, and they sat beside each other on the divan.

The firelight on his skin was gentle. She took a sip of brandy and then, setting down her glass, lifted her hand to his face and stroked it with her fingertips. He did the same to her.

She closed her eyes and leaned back. His touch became hypnotic. His fingers never rested as they caressed her brow, her cheeks, her neck. . . and made lingering forays up into her hair. She pulled his head close to hers. Their lips met again, again, again – brushing and breaking. She pressed more violently but he withdrew an inch or so – cooling her excitement.

His hand strayed around behind her neck, to the topmost button of her negligee. The silence grew oppressive. "Wombat!" she murmured, opening her eyes directly into his.

He answered, "Panther!"

She turned her back on him and swept up her hair to let him use both hands. "Of uncertain ancestry," she added.

"And volatile temperament." He went on to unhook her corselette and untie the ribbon of her chemise. His fingers found those places where eyelet and whalebone had marked her flesh; in their new liberty they massaged every itch. "You're a beautiful woman, Tess," he told her. His caressing hands said the same as they strayed up and down her spine. . . around the sides of her ribs to rest at the softness of her breasts.

They lingered. She, thinking the tightness of her sleeves constrained him, undid the buttons at her wrist; his hand reached out and pulled her against him. Cool dabs of his pearl waistcoat buttons on her spine.

His kiss brushed the nape of her neck. "Your skin is so perfect."

She raised her arms behind her head, to hold him where his warm breath sent tingles through her body. Her fingers entwined with his hair. He shivered. In that position her breasts were lifted clear. Slowly, lightly, his fingernails raked forward to the very edge of her swollen nipples. She gave a little cry and tried to shrink herself into him to force him on.

His lips on her ear; tongue curled hot on her lobe. The soft

192

pads of his fingertips, straying over her nipples, stretched threads of fire through all her limbs – a hot caress, in magical tune with her. She abandoned herself entirely to his skill.

The negligee slipped off. Cool freedom. Hands on her bare shoulders, easing off the sleeves. Naked to her waist against his clothes. Perhaps he might not undress at all? What would that be like?

Fingernails raked her elbows her arms her ribs her breasts her neck. . . he turned her face to his. . . lips opened and closed. . . tongues met. . . hands at gentle havoc all through her.

The twist of her neck hurt. She rose and faced him, lifting up her skirts to straddle him. His lips sought her nipples, suckled her tenderly. She gasped at its wet cool shock.

She occupied his lips. Her fingers, willed of their own, at his tie collar studs, button by button. . . waistcoat, shirt, open. His restless hands ran light. At her waist they found the last hook of her negligee, the ties of her petticoats; the press of cloth eased the falling petals of her clothing all around them. A Venus from the sea, she rose in a foam of white silk and pale flounces of fine cotton.

Her greatest fear, fear itself, had ebbed; his confidence was her.

Strong hands firm around her waist eased her beside him. She sensed that he would like to pause, laid her hand upon his. He looked at her uncertainly. Smiling, she reached for one of the brandy glasses, took a sip, and held it out to him, asking, "Am I a disappointment this time, too?"

He sipped and placed the glass back on the table, breathing fire. "You are stupendous."

"It doesn't feel wrong. I always thought it would feel sinful." She lay back upon the slope of the divan. "Tell me what to do, I don't mind. Tell me everything. Make it last. I want to feel everything. Tell me how I make you feel." She closed her eyes. "I love your voice."

He drew the string of her harness. Open delicious easing. Caressing hands their way to her suspenders and slip them off her stocking tops. He rolled her to him, onto her stomach, and loosened the back suspenders, too. They fell all in a soft rustle behind the divan. His trousered knee touched the backs of her thighs. She parted. From the small of her back, down, round, and up to her navel, her drawers were open to him.

A tug at the ribbon and her waist was free of the last pressure of clothing. His fingertips massaged her naked waist, her loins, the curve of her back, the two tight moons of her bottom. He stooped low over her, clasped her tight between his hands, and raised her to his lips, which now followed where his hands had pioneered. He laid her down again and knelt beside her, leaving her wide open. His nails scratched lightly upon her hips. His fingertips shivered up over her thighs. The backs of his fingers went down between them, cool into that warmth. Fear and thrill made her clamp tight.

His trapped fingers began a sinuous movement there; his free hand slipped deftly beneath her, down, around, up. Rippling fingers met – two gorgeous-mailéd snakes. Pleasure made her grip her thighs, release, grip again. He caught the rhythm. Waves of ecstasy flushed through her. His skill took her unawares; he was careful of the ultimate. It passed, leaving her invigorated. She sat upright.

"Oh, to burn always with this hard, gemlike flame!" he said. "To maintain this ecstasy!"

She leaned over him. "Why doesn't it feel sinful?"

He whispered, "You're an artist. Whatever you do is right."

She undressed him. She had not expected It to be so red so urgent-looking so large so hard so warm so fine-grained so gnarled. His fine nude body gleamed red in the firelight. He gestured at the bearskin rug and reached behind the divan for an enamelled tin box. In it, a tiny sponge. Its purpose she guessed.

She stood before him, knees touching his. The fire glowed hot on her back. Deep in the shade of her, his eyes burned. "Hold me," she said. "This time don't stop."

He stood, lodged between her thighs, not quite there yet, running his nails the length of her spine. He pushed and withdrew, withdrew and pushed, with a gentleness that maddened. Her flesh craved violence. Then magic began to reach in, with the night, the firelight, the brandy, the incense, the hard beauty of his body, and his voice: you are magnificent, you are thrilling, you are lovely. He could touch her anywhere and the sensation of it would run throughout her body

Time became a continuum of their pleasure; pleasure's swing was time's new pendulum. To its beat she came – gasping, crying at the power of it. Her legs buckled, unhousing him. She fell to

194

her knees, panting for breath, arms about him, kissing him, kissing It. One-eyed. Hot. Salt. Honey. He slid beneath her, took the sponge and pushed it home. He swiftly brought her back to that plateau. She marvelled at the endless pleasures of this simple act.

The deep, lustrous fur of the bearskin cocooned her head next to the animal's, giving brief visions of its gleaming eye and shining teeth. His voice, low and vibrant in her ear, "Oh Tess. . . oh my darling. . . oh my love. . ." as he came at last. It was so cosmic she hardly realized she had joined him, fusing them in one harmony.

Dawn woke her to a pink ceiling. A cab outside. The half-draped bedpost nudes. The fading incense. The happy disorder of their sheets. The exhausted male body at her side.

She eased herself over him and laid one breast upon his lips.

"Enough!" he said.

She laughed and hugged him. Her husky voice in his ear said, "Never!"

He pushed at her, gently, meaning go away.

She settled on him more firmly. "You don't know what you've done," she said.

"Mmmmm."

"You've slipped the panthers free."

Chapter Twenty-Seven

Dante began painting the backcloth and scenery for *Solomon and Sheba* – or, rather, for *Sheba and Solomon*, as Saunders now *insisted* it be called. Tessa decided to help him. She walked there that first day, by Smithfield and Lincoln's Inn, avoiding the direct route past Segal's house in Finsbury Close. She loved to walk now. She loved the way her body felt as it moved. Her whole perception of it had changed. She stepped out through the bearable fire of the early-morning sun, between tall cliffs of the houses, and revelled in the fact of being new-alive – feeling her life stretching out before her like these golden, sunlit streets.

And never mind what Simon tried to say. Simon was becoming a bore with his talk of "other ways". For an artist *all* ways were good.

The play was to be staged at the New National Theatre in Russell Street, between Drury Lane and Covent Garden. But when she arrived she found the place shuttered and barred. Someone told her to try the stage door in Jacob's Lane, and there, after a certain amount of hammering, she managed to rouse a grumpy caretaker who told her the scenes and flats were being painted at. . .

"It's all right, Murdoch," a familiar voice interrupted, "I'll see to the young lady." It was Sudden Death Davitt, in yet another loud check suit. He took Tessa by the arm and steered her back toward the front of the house.

"Are you aware there's a bus ticket stuck in your hatband?" she asked.

He chuckled. "That's no bus ticket, gel. That's the winner of the two-thirty today at Kingsbury. Leastways, until two-twenty-nine it's the winner. And if you've come to see Connie, love, you're about two hours early."

Tessa explained she would be helping Dante.

"In that case you want the *old* New National Theatre," he said. "It's just round the corner. I'll take you there."

He led her past Covent Garden. The early-morning fruit-and-flower market was packing up and salesmen were washing down their stalls or sluicing water over the pavements. She had to lift her skirts a dozen times, and run a gauntlet of scurrilous innuendo from every pub doorway, before they reached the relative sanctuary of Long Acre. There, facing them, stood an abandoned theatre over whose entrance Tessa could just make out the name, half-obscured by flyposters: The New National Theatre.

"Home sweet home," Davitt said. "That's where the scenery's stored – and painted. You'll be working in a house of memories, gel. Charley Dickens gave his first public readings in there. For the children's hospital. Must be all of thirty years ago."

"Who does it belong to now?" she asked.

"Me – in a manner of speaking. Me and Gloab. I closed it

196

when he opened the other National, in Russell Street. We're in that together, see. I've rented this place out to a printer, the auditorium part, anyway.''

In that case, she wondered, why had he been so desperately short of cash only a few months ago with Saunders in Brighton?

As if he followed her thoughts, he half-answered them. ''Funny old world, ain't it – one minute it's knotted sheets and the moonlight flit. Close your eyes and turn about and suddenly it's all cigars and bubbly.''

He fished out a jangling bunch of keys and selected one. As he was about to put it in the lock, a bell rang inside. ''Telephone,'' he said. ''I'd better cop that.''

From where she stood in the foyer she could hear his half of the conversation – all about ponies and each-ways and doubles and the two-thirty at Kingsbury. She pushed open the door to the auditorium and peered inside, expecting to see rows of empty seats, festooned perhaps in cobwebs and dust; but the seats had all gone and in their place were huge stacks of paper and ranks of gleaming metal cylinders. Each pile stood on a small, wedge-shaped platform to compensate for the rake of the floor; they stepped their way downhill like terraced buildings. She wandered among them until she saw the stage. That at least was uncluttered. All the overhead machinery had been removed, so that light from the skylights could fall freely onto the platform below. It made for a very un-theatrelike atmosphere; more like the inside of some great cathedral – especially at the moment, with a shaft of sunlight slanting down almost vertically to spill in a brilliant pool upon the centre of the proscenium.

A ramp led over the orchestra pit and onto the stage. She wandered up it and stood in that radiance; she closed her eyes and luxuriated in the warmth, swaying and humming a little melody.

''Blimey!'' Davitt shouted from among the paper terraces. ''You know who you're the spitting image of?'' As he spoke he walked down the centre aisle toward the ramp. ''Did you ever hear of a singer called Miss Dolby?''

''No.''

''I heard her do the *Mea tormenta* from Hasse's *Magdalena* in this very theatre, standing in that very spot where you're standing now, Miss d'Arblay. That was a night! Seeing you there, I could swear it was her ghost.''

"Are there any ghosts here?" she asked.

"There's ghosts in every theatre, love. Your real dedicated trouper, see, he wouldn't let a little thing like death put him off. He nor she."

"I've never been inside one of these places," she told him.

He found it hard to believe. "Want to see the engine room?" he asked, pointing vaguely backstage. "It's a whole rabbit warren down there."

He went ahead of her, lighting up the gas-jets over the narrow stairways. He spoke of the productions that had come and gone here in its heyday – Rumsey and Newcombe's Minstrels ("the old Twelve Stars"). . . Henry Irving and Ellen Terry in *The Taming of the Shrew* ("as perverted for the modern taste by Garrick"). . . Mrs. Rousby in *'Twixt Axe and Crown* ("you never saw the like of that, gel. She's Princess Elizabeth, see, in the Tower. And she hears them building the gallows outside her cell window, because her wicked sister, Bloody Mary, is going to hang her. And she gives out this speech ending with a great scream that tears the whole theatre in half! People came night after night just to hear that scream!"). . . and *The Last Days of Pompeii* ("poor old Labouchère lost a fortune on that!"). As they wandered from one abandoned dressing room to the next he brought them all back to life, until Tessa could almost smell the collodion and greasepaint, the gin and the beer, the sweat, the excitement, the fear.

"Oh, it's the life, Miss d'Arblay. It's the life! I won't say as it isn't going to kill me with worry and debt. But even Nellie Gwynne never went back to selling nuts and oranges, did she. Any of us could move down the street and sell fruit and flowers and have a normal life – but there's none I know as wants to."

When they reached the principal dressing room, she sat before a great rococo mirror and tried to imagine the clock eating up the seconds until not one was left to divide her from the ordeal of her début. In a way, despite Davitt's eulogy, it did not seem so different from everyday life. Time swept everyone onward to face their own inevitable moments. She looked up to see a speculative glint in his eye. She smiled and said, "I could never even think of going on the stage. Don't worry!"

After a brief silence he said, in tones so solemn they were almost portentous, "It's Connie who worries, love. Not me. She

198

worries about *you*."

Tessa was astounded. "I can't think why." The whole place suddenly seemed very quiet; all those ghosts had fled.

"What really happened that night down at Olympus?" he asked.

She shrugged and looked away.

"That Segal ought to be given in charge," he added as if he thought it might encourage her. When it failed, he sighed and sank upon a vast davenport behind him. She watched him in the mirror. He stroked its red-plush surface as if a long-forgotten memory were just returning to him. He looked up, first at her, then at her reflection; he realized her eyes were upon him and he smiled.

"Bit of history here," he said, patting the seat at his side. The smile faded. "Sad bit of history – and a tale against myself. Or myself when young." He smiled again. "That's how you'll know you're getting old, my love – you'll find you can begin to forgive the youngster who made you what you are." He looked around at the dust, the cracked plaster, the worn floorboards. "I was young when *all* this was young. First week I owned it. I was a real peacock in them days – you'd not credit it now, would you? Me dressing so modest and all." He gave a cackle. "But I was a real right-down reg'lar peacock then. I was going to open with a revival of *White Lies* and I wanted to 'launch', as they say, a brand new actress on the London stage. I didn't know who, but I put the word out and about. And this young lady came to see me – I could tell you her name, but I won't. And she was good. I mean – she was good. I was so excited, I come straight down to her dressing room here – this very dressing room – to tell her she was my new leading lady. But she got the wrong idea, see. She thought I was only after one thing. A lot of women think that way, you know."

"And aren't they right?" Tessa asked.

"No!" he said scornfully – and then added, "Not more than nine times out of ten." He continued through her laughter. "And I'll swear my bible, this was one of those tenth times, but she didn't understand that. She started peeling right there where you're sitting now. Someone must have told her I'd expect it, see. Then she come over here." Again he patted the davenport at his side. "Well, of course, I wasn't going to say no, was I! I would today, but I was too young then, see. I mean – I'm only human, aren't I.'' He vanished for a moment into the memory. His face crumpled. ''Human! It was a human bleedin' disaster. If I could go back, say to the Recording Angel, tear a page out, chum – *that'd* be the page. She'd never done it before! Nor she wasn't ready for it. I mean, she was disgusted by it – and rightly. Rightly. It *is* disgusting if it's not done willing. She just broke down crying half way. She got up. She put her clothes back on. And she walked out that door.''

After a silence Tessa asked, ''And a month later they fished her out of the river?''

He laughed sourly. ''You ought to write for the stage, Miss d'Arblay. No. This is real life. The truth is a lot worse than that. The truth is she went back to her quiet little home in Finchley – or wherever it was. She married some poor geezer she didn't much care for. What am I saying, Miss d'Arblay? I'm saying that inside three weeks she threw her life away – because of what we did here. It made her feel. . .'' He seemed unable to find the exact word.

''Worthless?'' Tessa suggested.

He nodded. ''Nothing mattered to her. So she just threw her life away. Of course, she came out of it in the end. They always do – that's the sorry part of it.'' He fixed Tessa with his eye. ''They always mend. And then they're sorry. She came to see me – was there still a part? But it was too late. Two years too late. The spark had gone.'' He looked at Tessa, a fleeting desperation in his eyes as he pleaded the shreds of a defence that must have helped him at the time. ''What did I do? Was it so wrong?'' He looked down at the couch as if he might catch himself at it still. ''It was nothing! It's going on all over London – even now, ten o'clock in the morning. A million times a day. It was nothing!'' He smiled wanly at Tessa. ''And she was sitting in that very chair!''

Tessa saw the buried point of the story, of course. She sprang up and began to pace around. ''Mr. Rosen should be here by now,'' she said.

Davitt grinned. ''That must be him as's been knocking down the stage door for the last minute. Didn't you notice?'' He stood up, too, and opened the dressing room door. She heard the hammering then.

200

As they went to let him in, she said, "Give Connie my love. Tell her she's not to worry."

"I already did, gel. That Tess d'Arblay, I says to her, she's got her head stuck on right. She's not going to do nothing daft. Not like poor old Miss Knighton – there! I told you her name now!"

"Of course I wouldn't."

"As long as you remember – most people ruin their life by living happy ever after. Up till then the fairy story's fine."

Tessa laughed. "Tell her I may pop over and see her this afternoon. Or tomorrow."

It was not only Dante waiting there but half a dozen scene-shifters, too – Dante looking wickedly elegant as usual. Davitt gave him the stage-door key and left, saying, "Don't let me interrupt the good work."

Dante changed into overalls and the two of them spent the morning measuring up the backdrop and getting the men to arrange the flats in their proper order. Whenever they took a break Dante ignored her and spent his time joking with the other men. He could be a man's man when he wanted, always ready with an aggressive little piece of banter. Men looked up to him and he enjoyed the conquest as much as he enjoyed his easy way with women. Tessa could see it happening, but didn't know how she could stop him.

After lunch he went to discuss some points with Marcus Gloab and Davitt. The scene shifters, being on full pay, snoozed or played cards. A plan then came to her; an inkling of it had crossed her mind that morning, while Davitt had been taking her around backstage.

The abandoned theatre contained enough bric-à-brac to furnish a good-sized shop. She took a turkey rug from one room, gilded chairs from another, a gas ring and some ornate lamps from a third, a tin bath from somewhere else. . . and she assembled them all in the principal dressing room, where the great rococo mirror made the place look double its actual size. The sumptuous davenport was broad enough to sleep three side by side – if sleep was what they had in mind.

Chapter Twenty-Eight

At six that evening the scene shifters left for the other theatre. She and Dante worked on until the filtered light grew too dim, just after seven. Most of the afternoon they had spent stooped over the backdrop, which had been laid out flat upon the stage for squaring-up and blocking-in. They had made a good beginning.

Dante straightened himself wearily. "I just don't feel like dressing for dinner," he said. "Do you?"

"We could have a meal sent down from the Holborn Restaurant?" she suggested. She knew this area well because her colourman, Cornelissen, had his shop in Great Queen Street, not far away.

Dante looked around the deepening gloom and pulled a face. "Here?" His eyes took on a faraway look. "Oh Tess, if only we were in Montmartre! I know exactly the little café I should take you to. Full of the weirdest people – dancers, pimps, whores, absinthe drinkers. . . artists."

"There's a little place in Kemble Street. That's probably full of whores – if it's *their* company you crave."

He shook his head. "English whores! Great, pale rustic cows with kind hearts and leather bodies! I suppose it'll have to be something from the Holborn Restaurant, then. Shall we go to a music hall or pub first?"

"No – I'm ravenous now. Aren't you?"

He looked dubiously at his watch. "But it's not yet seven thirty."

"Now," she insisted.

He shrugged. "Your word is my sentence. What's their number? Two-five-five-three, I think. I wonder if the telephone here is still connected?"

"The one in the booking office is."

While he went in search of it, she slipped down to the dressing room to light the gas-lamps and set some water to heat. She was back on stage just in time to look as if she'd never left it. "We're in luck'' he said. "They'll be with us in ten minutes. I told them I'd be waiting at the stage door."

She led him off stage-left to avoid passing the dressing-room with its tell-tale glint of light beneath the door. The out-waiters arrived in much less than ten minutes, the restaurant being only three streets away. Tessa took charge at once. "You may collect the trolley tomorrow," she told them. "We shall be dining here every evening for at least the next fortnight."

Dante looked at her in amused surprise. The waiters demurred – until she overpaid them; then they were quite agreeable to leave the collection of the trolley over until morning.

"My treat," she told Dante as she led him to the stage-right corridor and their new boudoir. She skipped ahead, leaving him to negotiate the trolley through the doorway. He didn't look around properly until the door had closed behind him. But then he was quick to take in the situation.

"I even found sheets and blankets," she told him.

He grinned. "Just in case we find some odd use for them."

"And these gorgeous silk dressing gowns. The wastefulness of theatre people!"

They washed, half-undressed, and slipped into the silk gowns before they settled to a quiet, relaxed dinner, which they washed down with an extravagant champagne and a beaujolais. "Nuits St.-Georges," Tessa read the label and laughed. "Saunders called it Naughty Saint George's."

"Talking of Saunders – she's damn good, you know," he said. "I was watching her at rehearsal this afternoon. You wouldn't believe such a silly, scatterbrained, disorganized creature could reach inside herself and find such a regal Sheba to display. My hair quite literally bristled on my neck to watch her."

"Oh, I must pop over and see her myself tomorrow. I've missed her."

"I wondered why you didn't come today. Now I know!" After a pause he added, "Poor old Saunders! I suppose there's a touch of madness in all great artists." He grinned at her. "I wonder what's yours?"

"Would you call her mad? Just because she took that job with Segal? That was your doing. Why did you make her go there?"

"Make her! She was a free agent."

She narrowed her eyes at him. "You know you had the power

then to make her do almost anything. I just want to know why that – why go into service with Segal?"

He shrugged, as if to say the topic was hardly of interest now. "I suppose I was amused to see how far she'd go." He grinned. "That's the glory of an artist's life, isn't it – this unquenchable urge to see how far we can push things. We try to make paint do the impossible. Art is magic. The same with people – how far can we magic them, even though they're perfectly free to choose a million ways?"

She laughed, not believing he was serious.

"Otherwise," he concluded, "what's the point of *King Lear* or *Moby Dick* or any of it?"

She saw he was serious.

He went on: "Women are magic. But they need men just to tell them so. Saunders is full of conceit about her acting, but in reality she has no idea how magical she is. It's the same with you and your painting. You weren't conceited about it, but before you met me you had no idea what magic is in you." He put his finger under her chin, making a specimen of her face. "Stay near," he murmured. "You'll learn everything about yourself."

In vain she looked for warmth in the promise. "Why did you ask me what my madness was?"

"We all have a madness waiting for us."

There were tears behind her eyelids, just waiting to spill. "Don't, Dante. Please stop talking like that."

"There there!" he mocked.

The tears fell silently. He did nothing to stop them. She hugged him, trying to provoke some compassion. When he withdrew his warmth the loss was as acute as any death.

She was calm again; she told him, "Saunders sent Davitt over here this morning to try and wean me away from you."

"You're a free agent."

In those same gentle tones he had also said you're wonderful.

"The kind of madness I'm prone to," she said, forcing upon herself the cheer he withheld, "is being here with you."

He laughed, almost proudly. Then he kissed her. The hurt, like Segal's brand of pain, went suddenly.

"Seriously, Tess," he said. "If you went mad, what form d'you think it'd take?"

"Sensual pleasure! This afternoon, while I was arranging all this, I kept thinking of us enjoying ourselves here – doing all those different things with each other – and I was almost going mad with longing, you know. If those scene shifters hadn't been there when you came back ...!Oh Dante – I think about us all the time. Panther-feasting. No – that sounds silly. What can we call it?''

''There's the old Anglo-Saxon word?''

''I don't like it. People swear with it, too.''

''What about *pleasuring*?''

She clapped her hands, but then looked at him suspiciously. ''Do whores use that word?''

''Not to my knowledge.''

She relaxed. ''You're clever, Dante. It's exactly what we do – pleasuring! I think of us pleasuring ourselves all the time. I long for our pleasuring. I itch with the longing. And then, when we're actually doing it, I think I'll die, it's so marvellous. But as soon as we've finished, that longing begins all over again. This afternoon! Oh – when we were stooped together over that canvas, side by side, talking about early Florentine artists! I kept thinking to myself – how can I be talking and behaving so normally – as if there were nothing going on inside me! Chatting about Giotto and Piero della Francesca when all the time there's this hurdy-gurdy of pleasuring turning round and round in my mind.''

''Why wouldn't you like it if whores also called it pleasuring?''

She shivered.

''Is that the effect they have on you?''

''I'm sorry for them. But I also hate them. They don't seem like women – not to me. They're like thieves who've stolen our outward form. I always feel they're mocking me. And men – they mock men, too. I've heard them.''

''And yet you're sorry for them?''

''In a cold, dutiful sort of way. Talking of cold, Saunders told me once – her sister Pol has . . .''

''Pol Saunders?'' he asked in astonishment. ''Is *that* Pol the sister of our own dear girl? It never even crossed my mind!''

''D'you know her?''

''Everyone does. She owns the plushest house in . . .''

''She *owns* it! The way Saunders spoke, I thought she only worked there.''

''Oh no! I don't imagine Pol has ever 'worked', not in that way. Now *she's* a panther if ever there was one! Men have literally killed themselves over her.''

"So Saunders told me.''

"Her place is only just up the road, you know. In High Holborn.'' He looked around their boudoir and smiled. "If you hadn't done this out so nicely, I could have taken you up there tonight. She lets out rooms for pleasuring, too.'' He chuckled. "Some of the highest-born ladies in the land have spread the gentleman's relish there! While your thieves-in-women's-clothing were playing the same pranks just inches away in the next room. What a world, eh?''

"I don't want to know about it.''

Her answer infuriated him. "You shut your mind to everything!'' he shouted at her. "If you go on saying no to life, it'll turn round and savage you. When I suggest something like that, you should leap at it with joy. You don't know how privileged you are! I had no one to guide me.''

He was right, of course. This dreadful no-saying impulse was fatal to her development as an artist. An artist had to understand so much *more* of life than an ordinary person.

She was about to say yes when he added, "You ought also to know that Pol's is the house where Segal wrote the rough drafts of his living thesis on pain in the female body – and pretty rough some of them were, too.''

A sudden sweat rippled over her. "Does he go there still?'' she asked.

Dante laughed as at a private joke. "No – he's planning greatness. His own bodily assumption into heaven, no less!''

"Would you like to take me there?'' she asked.

"Tonight?''

"If you like. Or what about tomorrow night? I've already planned tonight.''

"Tell me why you want to go there?''

"Because it still frightens me. Because the idea of our pleasuring once frightened me, too. Because I know I've got to overcome these fears. Because I want to learn about me. Because you can help me – *only* you can help me. Because I want to be near you for always and always and always.''

He smiled and lay still. Lovingly she undressed his beautiful hard body. Lovingly she whispered all her desires into his ear.

Chapter Twenty-Nine

"Sin is a feeling," Tessa argued. "It's not something you can simply look up in a book or copy out of some ancient old list of Thou-shalt-nots. Sin is what you can feel – *here!*" She tapped her breast. "And if you don't feel it . . ."

"That's one of the places, all right," Saunders agreed. "But you can't get away from it: Sin is sin – and two wrongs don't make it white."

"If you haven't got that feeling about it in your heart, in your mind, then it's not sinful."

Saunders shook her head sadly. "That Demon must go down on his knees every day and bless the Devil for sending you. He's only *using* you, Tess love. Like he did with me. Like he does with everyone. It's all just a game with him. He wants to see how far he can drive you away from where he found you. He'll drive you out into the wilderness and then . . ."

"But it isn't the wilderness. Maybe to you, but not to me. For an artist there's no such place as a wilderness, no such time as a leaden minute. Art knows the alchemist's secret. Art turns lead into gold."

"What about your Rev. Liddington, then?"

"He's not *my* Rev. Liddington."

Saunders looked steadily at her.

"Anyway, what can he say?" Tessa asked. "Only what they've been saying for two thousand years. It's failed." When Saunders remained silent, she added, "At least Simon Liddington knows better than to try and talk me out of what I've decided to do – what I've *freely* decided to do. I wish there were more like him."

Saunders shook her head sadly. "How is it that everyone else can see it and you can't? He's got you absolutely in his . . . you've got about as much consistence as putty . . . Ask any. . ."

"What d'you mean everyone else?"

"All the scene shifters . . . the cast . . ." Saunders shrugged uncomfortably.

"Have you been going around talking about us?"

"There's no need, pet. Try and stop them! They've all noticed it. The Demon says jump and you jump. They're not blind."

"But they are – and so are you, Saunders. You're all blind if you think it's. . ."

"I suppose you imagine it's love. . .!"

"But that's just what I *don't* imagine! Love is so commonplace. Love enslaves people. It makes them. . ."

"Hah! And you're not enslaved? You really think you're not enslaved?"

"I know very well I'm not. I'm a free agent. So is Dante. We're free to discover everything that lovers discover – but without the slavery of love, without that awful addiction. Probably no one else except only two artists could do it. That's why I say you're all blind. We're the first woman and the first man to reach in perfect freedom for a new kind of human inter. . . of human. . . oh what's the word?"

"Human interest?" Saunders suggested. When Tessa didn't respond she tried: "Human race. . . human failing? Human sacrifice?"

"Oh shut up!" Tessa laughed.

"Human cry?"

"Human relationship! We're creating a new kind of human relationship, Dante and I. Naturally ordinary people wouldn't be able to see it. Artists are the unacknowledged legislators of the world. Even I wouldn't know what to call it."

"I call it unacknowledged slavery. Legislators can pass bad laws as well as good, you know. There's no law against it."

Tessa smiled forgivingly. "Anyway dear, I came here to talk about you, not me. Dante told me yesterday you were simply marvellous as the Queen of Sheba and – though I know how you hate it when I agree with him – I'm afraid, now I've seen you, I do! I can't help it. I think you're going to be absolutely stunning. You are sheer genius! I know Davitt was half-teasing that night at Olympus when he said the part was made for you, but I think you've surprised even him . . ."

Tessa went on in that vein and, of course, Saunders was too much of an actress to want to stop her or to go back to their former rather disagreeable conversation. Tessa did not mention, even in passing, that Dante might take her to meet Pol one of these evenings.

In fact, "one of these evenings" proved to be that very evening. She thought Dante had spent the afternoon discussing the costumes with the wardrobe people, but he must have been at least part of the time at Pol's because when he returned, just as she was packing up, he told her to put on her best clothes and prepare for an evening such as she had never known before. It filled her with a hollow excitement.

In the old caretaker's apartment was a huge tiled bath with a thundering gas geyser. She loved to take baths-by-the-hour up there. The inlet was at one end, the overflow at the other, so she set the geyser to its slowest rate, to give a continuous trickle of piping-hot water into a bath already full to the overflow. That evening she lay there, a languid pink lily, weightless in the water, dreamily passing into and out of a shallow, steamy slumber; and while her back, aching from her toil, revelled in the warmth and luxury, she considered how fortunate she was to have met Dante, and to have seen through the hollowness of ordinary life; she dreamed of the new, better, more honest way of life to come. Sometimes it was hard to understand how it was all going to happen, but "out of dung sweet flowers do grow," as he often said.

Her luxuriations came to an end only when an impatient Dante threatened to break down the door.

Her skin was strawberry blotched waterlog wrinkled. Though she bathed often she was still able to rub crumbs of soft skin away as she dried herself. It left her peeled to her nerve ends. The touch of her dressing gown, though silken, was so exquisitely ticklish as to be painful; she shrank from its contact. But later the tight clutch of her corset and the cooler air of the dressing room ended her sensitivity. She put on a new evening gown of pale cream silk. Its flimsy sleeves and bodice were of spotted net, gathered at her neck and half way down her forearm with small bands and bows of jet-black taffeta. Her flesh showed through like a colour shot in satin. Over her bosoms a few widely spaced pleats of ruched gauze tipped a further slight wink in the direction of modesty. She used some of Saunders' leftover stage makeup to darken her eyes and redden her lips, just a little, and was astonished at the transformation.

Dante stood behind her for these finishing touches, looking down at her in the great rococo mirror. The glint of the gaslight in his eyes was mellow and reassuring. "Will I do?" she asked.

"You're a swan," he told her. "You're my own beautiful, stately, precious swan."

He was in his faultless evening dress, with blue mother-of-pearl buttons down his waistcoat and a peacock-blue satin cummerbund. He had a new silk cape lined with the same gorgeous material.

"I'd like to show you off to all the world," she told him. "I'd love to start at one end of Piccadilly and walk right along it on your arm, and go into all the clubs and theatres and restaurants, and down Regent Street, the same, and through Trafalgar Square, and right up the Strand, showing you off to everyone."

He laughed at her fancy. "Those dainty little silk shoes would be a sorry sight at the end of such a progress! The next best thing would be to sit at Oscar's table at the Café Royal – in the public restaurant."

She bit her lip in excitement. "Would we be allowed?"

"Let you be imperious enough and who would dare say us no?"

"Oh Dante – let's try!"

And so they went to the Café Royal, where, sure enough, she was able to sweep grandly past the major domo and take her place at that most coveted table. "Drink sparingly as yet," Dante advised her. "Leave your senses sharp."

Oscar had not yet arrived but it was the custom in his circle to drop in for something light around this time – an omelette and some fruit, say, or a cold collation and cheese – and then return for a full dinner after the theatre. She chose cold smoked trout and a French salad; he toyed with some caviare; they drank a glass each of a Bollinger '82, intending to leave the rest for the host of the table.

They were on the point of rising when Wilde himself and Bosie Douglas arrived. "We've had such an amusing day, my dears," Wilde said at once; he was delighted to see Tessa again. "We went to Hampton Court and lost ourselves in the maze."

". . . which is not as easy as it might appear," Bosie added. "The ground plan is such that a child might solve the puzzle, so it took our combined genius to lose ourselves utterly. We were quite *distraits.*"

"Hedges can be so terrifying," Wilde put in. "One's imagination populates the unseen landscape beyond with minotaurs and maenads and bacchantes."

"Yes, I can't see you as a countryman," Dante told him. "Neither in Arcady nor in Nether Wallop."

Bosie smiled. "Well now – I don't know so much about Nether Wallop . . ."

But Wilde interrupted, "Oh the countryside has been greatly overrated. Besides, there's so little of it left these days; it's all become so busy and industrial. Sheep may still graze there for all I know, but – safely? I hardly think so. No – the only true countryside today lies at the heart of our great cities. I am inordinately fond of Regents Park, you know – where if not sheep then certainly carriages may safely graze. Why, only yesterday Bosie's pater's brougham took half the paint off my best phaeton – yet look at me: not a scratch! I wonder where *he* was going in such hurry, by the way! I'm reliably informed there's nothing to the north of the park but a place called 'St. Johns Wood'. I don't somehow associate him with sylvan saintliness." He gave a theatrical shudder.

They beguiled twenty minutes or so with this sort of banter and then went on to The Royalty in Dean Street to see the new production of *The Scarlet Letter* with Forbes-Robertson in the lead. Then they went slumming in Soho and ate oysters at a stall. Then Dante invented a supper engagement and they parted company, Wilde and Bosie to return to the Café Royal, Dante and Tessa to go on to Pol's.

Tessa already had a mental picture of the place, helped by Saunders' image of wasps around a honeypot. She imagined the house with all its windows lighted as for a grand ball, and strains of music on the air. Every other minute cabs pulled up and disgorged more and yet more gentlemen in evening dress to join those who thronged the pavement outside in excited, buzzing groups.

As their cab rattled on over the oak-cobbled streets she kept her eyes peeled for the first sight of such a place – which was how she came to miss the somewhat drab façade with its unlighted windows and air of silent desertion. She was astonished when the cab turned off High Holborn and into a little covered alley that

211

curved around to emerge in South Square. At the inner end of that curve was a short flight of steps flanked on each side by a pierced iron screen. It was thus possible for a lady to step down from a cab and trip up the steps to the door at the top, which was never barred, and even her own husband could not have recognized her.

The inner doors to the lobby were controlled by a "kaffir," who knew Dante; he bowed solemnly to them both, summoned a maid, and said, "Show Mr. Rosen to the Chinese Room."

The maid took them down to the souterrain (it was too gorgeous to be called a basement) and showed them into a low-ceilinged room, all black and gold and red. They took off their shoes at the entrance. The air was faintly tinged with a perfume that might have been incense, though it had a tangy edge to it, like eucalyptus. There were no furnishings save for two screens and a low table; but the floor was one continuous, firm mattress, liberally sprinkled with silk cushions of all sizes. The maid, who was standing at one of the screens, beckoned to Tessa.

"We'll get into the right costume straight away," Dante said. "The spirit of the thing."

The maid helped her undress completely and slip into a thin oriental gown of fine cotton, milk-white in colour and printed with peacocks and dragons in the subtlest tints, all tied in at the small of her back with a huge silk bow. "It's a nice warm night, madam," she said – as if their business needed some such innocent excuse.

Tessa nodded in amused agreement. "Are we going to eat?" she called out to Dante, who was undressing behind the other screen. "I'm ravenous."

"You'll see," he said.

"Chinese food," the maid whispered. "Doesn't make you feel heavy, see." She patted her own stomach.

The meal was a bewildering succession of little bowls. She saw it all rather dimly because their only light came from two candles floating in dishes of scented water on the little table. There were red Chinese lanterns here and there about the room but their light was more suggestive than revealing. The floating candles were of beeswax and laid a heavy, musky sweetness on the air.

Dante showed her how to use the chopsticks. He looked so firm and ravishing in his oriental gown, which was dark blue with small abstract motifs in black and gold all over it. They lay among the cushions and fed each other or themselves as the mood took them, washing it down with sip-sized glasses of an extremely dry white wine. Then there was jasmine tea, which made flushes of light sweat pass over her. Then fingerbowls of water with an astringent, citron aroma. She loved the ritual delicacy of it all – everything so neat and perfect.

When the last little bowl had been cleared away she wriggled nearer to him and began to caress his arm. The candlelight shining upward into his face, gave him a satanic look, especially with the red lanterns all around them – but it was satanic-thrilling, not satanic-frightening.

"Now," she said, and closed her eyes.

"Now," he agreed and, pushing aside the table, opened a small trapdoor, cunningly concealed in the design of the rug. She sat up again and watched him. From a small well in the floor he drew forth a number of vaguely oriental-looking objects – a polished-brass spirit lamp, a jar full of smoke-blackened silver spoons, a lacquered cabinet with several tiny drawers, and a handful of lacquered bamboo tubes, something like decorated penny whistles except that they were twice as long and had only one hole.

He lit the spirit lamp with a wooden spill from one of the floating candles and placed it in the well in the floor. He searched in several of the drawers and from one of them took a spoonful of a pale crystalline powder.

"What is it?" she asked.

"Surely you know."

"Opium?"

He smiled, half to himself, and put the spoon in a small bronze cradle that held it over the flame.

"I thought you scoffed at it?" she went on. "Didn't you call it a short cut?"

"Think of it as skimming a page before you go back and read it properly."

"I never read like that."

"Every day something new." He handed her one of the long tubes and took one himself. "Do it like this." He settled himself among the cushions on the opposite side of the little well from her, and rested the tube in one of several half-moon nicks in a collar

213

running right around the bronze cradle. The open end of the tube was a mere inch or so above the spoon, where the melting resin was just beginning to give off its fumes. He lay on his back and rested the other end of the tube on his moustache; the actual end was plugged off but just a quarter of an inch from it was a single hole in the side, like a finger-hole in a penny whistle. This he now applied to his nostril, penning it there with a curl of his upper lip.

He inhaled deeply. She saw the pale fumes sucked into the pipe. "Aaaaaah!" he gave out a long sigh. "You try it," he told her, already half-lost to the dreams.

She copied him, settling herself as comfortably as possible before she laid her tube to rest above the smouldering powder. The urge to pray entered her mind but no actual prayer followed it. She inhaled.

For a moment nothing happened. Then she felt the cushions melting beneath her and her body began to float. More – she herself began to dissolve into air. She inhaled again and then the ecstasy hit her. It was not sexual – not visceral, not of the blood and tissues; it was purely in her mind. She was overwhelmed by a marvellous mind-liberation, like the first dizziness of wine – but here was no dizziness; she was open and cool. She was in that room, she was Tessa, and these things were all happening.

There were new dimensions of peace and joy. Cosmic. Not *her* joy, but everyone's. It had been there all the time, like air and just as free. It always would be there. The defect was in her that she could not freely reach up with her soul and breathe it – except like this. Dante was right, as Dante was always right. What power lay untapped within the soul, housed in its silent reaches; if we could but slip it free, command it as easily as we say "move!" to our muscles or "breathe!" to our lungs . . . oh the might of it then!

She floated in the seraph calm of that Elysium, how long she did not care. When her body began to know again its weight, when solid cushions nudged beneath her, she saw Dante preparing a second miracle spoonful.

"Well?" he asked.

She shook her head, too lost to speak.

"Come over here. Lie beside me. You've hardly begun."

While she crawled around and rearranged the cushions he fished in another of the lacquered drawers and brought out a box of small white tablets.

214

"What is it?" she asked.

"Put one on your tongue and let it dissolve slowly."

"Is it opium, too?"

He nodded. "The effect of the smoke wears off quickly. That'll preserve the elation. Have you ever known anything like it?"

She snuggled against him. "Never!"

"You just wait!"

This time they soared up together. The tube grew a mile long. She saw it from inside herself and from outside, too. She was both watching herself and *being* herself. She watched Dante as he gently loosened the bow of her costume; she felt its pressure slacken and the silk fall away from her. She saw him caress her thigh; she felt his hands make the same gentle, repetitive caress from her hip to her knee, from her knee to her hip, again and again and again and again . . .

It was a new kind of eroticism. It did not pile up that old, monstrous imperative to climax and die. Each action, every action, *any* action was its own climax. If he caressed her thigh, which did for a century, his action held its own fulfilment; within the myriad small movements that made up each stroke she felt nuances of a pleasure unheralded. It was so when he kissed her, which filled her second century; and so, too, when he took her breast into his lips; and when he feasted on her opened body – which bore her into the millennia.

She was now so centuries-old in these new pleasures that he and she and space and time began to coalesce in novel partnerships. The Tessa-who-felt and the Tessa-who-observed began to experience each other as separate selves. Each woman could assume some aspect of Dante and caress the other's body as a man might caress – and feel. She could turn this way and feast upon becoming male – or that way and gorge on her own femininity, but as an outside party, conniving at her own pleasure. Two Dantes there were, who could occupy her in different ways, even while she was discovering her second womanhood. One could lie behind her, the other in front, while above her lay that second self, drowning her in breasts of melon.

Or was that second woman really a third man? Or a fourth woman? Incarnations of their aspects were filling the room whichever way she turned. They smiled at her. She smiled back. They were all at such peace with one another.

215

Now there was no world but this; no people in it but themselves – in all these different aspects. And all they did was full of meaning. Whether they lay together, lodged in fire that wrote the limits to the universe – or apart, staring into all those each-other's eyes – blue eyes, brown eyes, grey eyes, green eyes, protean eyes – their acts were a wonder and profound.

Surely, she thought, if there were truths and beauties beyond these, they must also lie beyond the endurance of the human frame? Yet what did she know of endurance? Who was she to set a scope to wonder?

The floating candles had gone out. Now only the dim paper lanterns cast their scarlet light. She turned in that new, infernal darkness to find Dante.

And saw instead . . .

Doctor Segal!

Trapped in that gluelike panic which belongs so curiously to dreams, she tried to unremember him, for only memory could have summoned him here hot to Olympus.

No! Not Olympus. To Elysium.

Oh please let it still be Elysium!

Oh Dante, Dante – be my god again.

Come as a raging bull, come as a shower of gold.

Come in my caverns measureless to man, here where time is infinite at last.

There, where time was infinite at last, Dante stood before her and turned himself into Dr. Segal. And Dr. Segal turned back into Dante. A two-headed god, beckoning her, repelling her, and smiling at each other.

The Segal-head loomed over her, paper-faced as on that night. A voice told her clearly – or was it her own voice? – or was it Dante talking to Segal? – that opium dulls all pain. She smiled to hear it – or was it Segal who smiled? If pain were pleasure, what would opium do?

The opiate pains began. She watched herself scream. She heard herself writhe. *Look! See*! she told herself – or perhaps it was Segal who gave those cries of triumph. His fingers were mountain-huge. Her well-trained body remembered correct responses to each pressure. Her conniving flesh reinvented all her torments at his hands.

But this time there was something – other. At the height of her

216

torment, when she thought her screams would cut her mind in two, she found herself locked in Dante's arms and ecstatic to the sinuous movements of his body as, like some gorgeous mailéd snake, he. . . but then Segal's torturing fingers would be at her again.

And so until the end of time; until she was backed against the far palisades of the universe, upon whose rampart fingers ranged the dark spirits, staring dispassionately down upon her where she lay locked in immortal love and mortal combat with the twin-headed god of love and pain. While they stared on, unmoved, she cried out at the torture of her endless orgasm and laughed in joy at the ecstasies of unending pain. And it went on and on and on. . .

Chapter Thirty

They did not often take opium – certainly not often enough to affect herhealth or appearance. That astonished her. The "dope fiends" of popular belief were depraved creatures with hollow eyes and sunken cheeks, their hair and teeth falling out, and themselves given to uttering random, maniac cries, as devoid of meaning as they were pitiable. It showed how wrong all popular beliefs were. Dante was right. People are sheep.

On the other hand, she had heard whispers of men, the pillars of local society, who, after their deaths, proved to have been addicts – all unsuspected by those around them, even by the closest. So that showed what little harm it did. She owned a looking-glass image that proved it, too.

But their work at the theatre did not prosper. Dante, for whom it had only ever been a commercial project, grew bored with it and left the details increasingly to her while he vanished, no one knew where. "You're an artist, Tess," he would say, giving her that devilish smile. "You'll cope."

Soon he was leaving just about everything to her. Whole scenes for which he had done finished-looking sketches proved impossible to transfer to the full-scale flats and drops, either because they revealed parts of the stage machinery or because bits of business devised during the rehearsals required a change. Increasingly Dante was not there to make those changes and Tessa had to improvise for him. Finally she had to do what any good designer would have done from the beginning – go back to the sources.

She remembered there was a book in her father's locked Freemasonry cabinet all about the building of Solomon's temple. She went back home to consult it.

It was Thursday, the first day of September. The leaves clanked drily on the trees, hinting at the autumn that was now only weeks away; but the city still sweltered. Every building threw back the heat. Behind those façades she could sense an anger at the baking air and a longing for the releasing cool of the evening.

"'Orrible bloody murder," a newsboy shouted gleefully. "Woman stabbed in Whitechapel!"

She remembered Sergeant Keene's comment, on that unseasonably hot day of the inquest, little over three months (and yet three lifetimes) ago: "There'll be murders done today."

She had thought she understood the remark then, but now that she was sexually awakened she knew so much better. She knew how the heat could lay that imperative urge upon the body. What of all those thousands who, unlike her, could not so easily find release?

She began to understand the sexual force as a kind of fleshly energy and she wondered if anybody else had ever considered it in that way. Did they think of it as energy at all? Surely they must. It was difficult when nobody ever spoke about it. Or did they just not speak about it to young, unmarried females? She knew all about that sort of silence.

Her walk through north London, from Holborn to Islington, was a journey across her days of innocence. Here was the street where, aged nine, she had helped an urchin bowl his hoop – and had been *roundly* punished for it (as her father had later joked). Here was the corner where, aged fifteen, she had passed what she now knew to have been a group of prostitutes. Then all she had noticed was their eyes, which were not like the eyes of other women but more like those of the caged carnivores at the zoo, saying, "I'm so different when I'm not here!" Thinking they lacked a refuge for the night she had gone back to speak to them; she had been punished for that too, this time more obscurely – by a bewildering withdrawal of part of her mother's affection. She knew that in some vague way she had trespassed into areas that were of vast importance to everyone and yet too dreadful to particularize. Instead a dispiriting fog hung over all that part of the landscape, obscuring its beauty (as she now knew it) along with its undeniable ugliness, its pathos, and its humour.

How unnecessary! And how painful the discovery had been. It made her angry to think of it. The heart-in-mouth steps through treacherous mires of ignorance, goaded onward by her love of light, colour, form, stimulation . . . the whole beautiful world of the senses. If she ever had a child, she'd let the fires of this anger blast away those fogs; she'd help the child see life honestly.

Simon might be made to understand. There was that morning by the chalkstream when . . . well, she couldn't exactly remember what they'd talked about but it had promised that sort of honesty. She wished she could go back to that midsummer morning, lying beside him in the meadow with her feet in the cool of the water. So many things were now clear to her which then had been been obscure. Would men and women ever be able to talk about such things without implying promises they did not mean or would not keep? Someone had to make a start somewhere. She and Simon could try.

She wondered where Dante kept disappearing to. Not that she had any right to demand his time, of course. He was a free agent. . .

There was a long silence in her mind after that thought. She had pondered the business of being a free agent so often lately it was beginning to bore. Very well – Dante was a free agent. Enough said.

Think of Simon again. What wonderful, mature conversations they'd be able to enjoy. Even better than with Dante in some ways, because there was less emotion – on her part, anyway. She went on thinking about Simon the rest of the way home. She reinvented him in such a convenient image that, when she took the corner into Shepherdess Walk and almost bumped into him, and all he said was, "Hello, Tess – my word but you *are* looking well!" she hardly knew what to answer.

"What d'you mean – I'm looking well?"

"Sorry. Would you rather you didn't? The bohemian life must suit you though."

She pressed her lips together. "I see!"

"What d'you see?"

"You're going to be all jolly and cool and light with me. Simon! That's behaviour from page two."

He stepped in front of her, to make her stop. There was a firmness about him she had not seen before. "You've made a choice, Tess. I think it's wrong. I believe in your heart of hearts you do too. Whether that's so or not, it can't be too long before you discover . . ."

She flared up. "What d'you know about it?"

He stood out of her path and fell in beside her as she strode out toward the vicarage. "I'm not going to brawl in the street with you, my dear – certainly not in my own parish. What I know about it is what I've heard from Miss Saunders. She . . ."

"She's an interfering busybody."

"All friends are. What I was about to say, if you'll let me finish, is that when you do make the discovery for yourself, you'll need someone like me. I shall be here."

She sighed. "I don't want to fall out with you, Simon. In fact, I've been thinking about you all the way here. I've missed our conversations. There's so much we could talk about, you know. Is Bo at home? And father?"

"You say my behaviour is juvenile – I assume that's what you mean by 'page two'? Just so there's no misunderstanding, let me break you the news that you're not the first woman I've loved – I'm twenty-six after all." He smiled wanly. "It seems to be my fate to lose my heart to young ladies who, no sooner than I am safely ensnared, vanish from me on quixotic quests for impossible accomplishments. I assure you – the rules for behaving calmly and cheerfully in such circumstances are to be found on page one-thousand-and-two in my particular manual of behaviour. And – no, both Bo and your father are out. She has taken to fishing. She trawls the Lee Navigation, where the last salmon was recorded in sixteen-oh-four. Your father reads sermons to her, so he says – though I've noticed they're bound in covers whose spine reads *Jorrocks's Jaunts and Jollities*. Why have you come home?"

She laughed. "Oh . . . damn you! I'd forgotten how *nice* you

220

are. I came home to see you."

"No – seriously."

She hardly wanted to tell him her real reason; he'd only construe Dante's behaviour as some kind of desertion. "I . . . I thought I'd done no Good Works with the nuns for some time. Conscience, I suppose."

Just as they reached the gate, she added, "Also I thought, while I was here, I could have a peep in one of father's Masonic books, about Solomon's temple. See if there're any drawings I could steal ideas from."

"You're the designer now?" he asked, impressed.

How much had Saunders been telling him? She thought it best not to answer. "So, though in one way I'm sorry to have missed Bo and father, in another way I'm glad. Father'd never let me root through his Masonic bookshelves."

Simon frowned. "Don't you think his going away is a kind of trust – and you'd be violating it?"

"Oh he doesn't *trust* me." She laughed. "He keeps the bookcase double locked. But it's all right. I know where he hides both keys."

Simon laughed too. "Oh yes, Tess – you're exactly the sort of wife every priggish clergyman needs!"

As soon as they were indoors she found the keys and opened the Freemasonry bookshelf. With growing dismay she leafed through the book on the building of Solomon's temple.

"Not what you hoped for?" Simon asked.

"Far too learned to be of any practical use. Just like my dear father! But there are one or two little drawings." She made rapid copies of them into her notebook. She was about to reshelve the tome when her eye was caught by one of the many footnotes – or, rather, by three names she saw there: Jubelo, Jubela, and Jubelum. She read on: In Masonic lore the Grand Master Hiram Abiff never completed his greatest work, the building of Solomon's temple, for he was murdered by the three Masons, Jubelo, Jubela, and Jubelum. These Three Juwes (as they are traditionally called) . . .

"What is it?" Simon asked.

"Just an old legend. The names caught my eye."

He read with her, over her shoulder: These Three Juwes . . . were part of a group of fifteen Masons of the Second Degree who, seeing the Temple nearing completion, and realizing they were unlikely to be admitted to the Third and Final Degree during the short time that then remained, therefore resolved to waylay H.A. and extract the secrets of the Third Degree from him by torture and threat of death. Twelve of these fifteen repented, however, leaving only the Three. Jubelum surprised H.A. before the High Altar, at prayer to The Most High, and threatened to kill him if he did not reveal the Mysteries. But H.A. replied that he would sooner die than yield, whereupon Jubelum smote him mortally on the right temple with the Plumb Rule, blinding him.

Staggering from the sanctum toward the N. entrance, H.A. encountered next Jubela, who likewise demanded the revelation of the Mysteries upon pain of death, whereat H.A. again affirmed his choice of death before dishonour. Upon the hearing of which Jubela smote him a mortal blow with his Level to the left temple.

Crawling now toward the E. entrance H.A., his brow wet with the perspiration of his agony, made the Sign of Grief and Distress to relieve his sufferings. He was stopped by Jubelo, who, claiming to have had congress with JaBaalOs and to have the power of restoring to H.A. his life, demanded in return to be told the Mysteries. For the third and final time the dying Master declined to yield, whereupon Jubelo took the Heavy Maul and dealt the third and final mortal blow, to the face.

They disembowelled The Master, seeking an augury of. . .

"Pretty gruesome," Simon said.

She seemed not to hear him.

. . . Then, "growing fearful of what dread thing they had done," the Three Juwes fled. But the remainder, having divided themselves into three Fellow-Craft Lodges, set out in pursuit. The first found nothing. The second found the mutilated body of H.A. The third apprehended the Juwes at Joppa and there suffered them execution by the flaying of their feet, the lancing of their eyes, and a drawing and quartering of their bowels, to remind them of the three mortal blows and other mutilations they had dealt their Master.

The fortitude of H.A. and his willingness to embrace *three* deaths rather than reveal the Mysteries has been held forth as an example to Freemasons ever since; the symbolic re-enactment of his murder is the central initiation rite of all three Degrees.

As to stories that the Juwes cooked and ate parts of his vital organs, Wilkinson and Day are of the opinion that this legend confuses several better-known mythical themes in which gods and demigods devour their enemies and even their own children. (see also my *The Saturnine Feast*, p522.)

Similar stories that brazen rings were placed at the feet of the executed Juwes to establish to power of H.A. (whose particular Mystery was the Just Working of Brass) are later embroideries.

The Masons have also used this exact form of execution as their most solemn punishment, both within their ranks and without. Today, it need hardly be said, the ritual is observed in symbolic form only; but the expelled Mason is thereafter treated as dead by all his former Brethren.

The power this legend has exercised on the minds of Freemasons down the centuries may be attested by the fact that the site of the Mitre Tavern (in what is now Mitre Square in the City of London), the most important meeting place for London's Freemasons since the Eighteenth Century, was chosen because of its associations with a Sixteenth Century murder that bore many curious resemblances to the murder of H.A.

It is said that one Katherine, a holy woman who had the power to multiply bread and wine, was praying at the high altar of the Priory of the Holy Trinity (which then stood on that site). A crazed and jealous monk, begging her to reveal her Mysteries, and being refused the same, cried out that she ought not to pray among the religious but should instead be at the nearby lay church, St. Katherine Cree (which still stands today). He swore to martyr her even by that method once used so barbarously on St. Katherine herself. He accordingly fashioned a crude "Katherine wheel" of knives and stabbed her so many times she was effectively flayed and disembowelled. He then did himself to death in the same manner and with the same knives.

As a further curious footnote it may be pointed out that the Mitre Tavern is presently the meeting place of Hiram's Lodge and the Lodge of Joppa as well as being . . .

She lost interest in the rest of the tomfoolery, but the footnote had explained a lot of things. No wonder Segal was so angry with her, especially if he had been drummed out of the Freemasons in accordance with the prescribed rituals.

Simon was still reading – or rather, rereading the words.

"Thinking of joining?" Tessa asked.

Normally he would have laughed. His frown deepened.

"What's the matter?" she prompted.

"Hang on a mo." He left the room and returned almost at once with a copy of the *Pall Mall Gazette*. Its main news story was an account of the stabbing of a woman, Mary-Ann Nichols.

"It's all over London," Tessa said. "The newsboys were shouting it as I walked over here."

His finger singled out one paragraph: A curious feature of this crime is the murderer had pulled off some brass rings which the victim had been wearing and these, together with some trumpery articles which had been taken from her pockets, were placed carefully at the victim's feet.

"What a grisly coincidence," she said.

"I shouldn't read it all," he told her. "It's pretty awful. But elsewhere it says she was disembowelled, too."

She went on reading. He saw the blood drain from her face. Thinking she might faint, he held out his arms to her. She dropped the paper and fell into his embrace. "I'm sorry," he soothed. "How thoughtless of me, darling. I shouldn't have. . ."

"It's not that. It's not that."

"What then?"

"It says she was also called Polly Nichols."

"Yes?"

"I met her once – in fact, the same day I first met you. She was looking after a little girl. . ."

He cleared his throat. "I'm afraid I was unintentionally eavesdropping at that point. I heard Miss Saunders telling you the story. The royal baby? You sent her back to warn them – there were two of them, weren't there?"

"Four altogether. Two of them were there that day but I don't remember the name of the other one. Saunders'll know. Oh, I wonder if it *is* the same woman? Perhaps it isn't. They all have the same names – endless Anns and Pollys and Marys and Annies and Lizzies – and they all call themselves by the name of their current paramoors, like badges of pride. It's probably not the same one."

"If it is. . ." he said.

"It isn't," she told him firmly. "It can't be. Anyway, I don't want to think about it any more. Kiss me."

Chapter Thirty-One

The murder was the talk of London. It ought not to have been.

In April some man with a knife had done unspeakable things to a woman in Osborn Street, nearby. And in August, also in Whitechapel, a woman had been stabbed more than forty times. Neither murder had caused any unusual stir; stabbings were not uncommon in that part of London, especially in the small hours, when drunken men and desperate old whores started brawling. But no one thought this latest murder was in that category; the sacrificial arrangement of the corpse and the ritual disembowelling set it apart. A thrill of terror ran through the city.

"It's brilliant!" Dante told Tessa.

"Brilliant? How can . . ."

"Oh, I should love to meet this man – he's a true artist. With half a dozen strokes of his knife he seizes the imagination of millions. What wouldn't I give to . . ."

"Stop it! I know you're only being deliberately provocative."

He gave her arm a pitying squeeze. "Poor Tess! You'll end up like the ox that runs with the bull – you'll know the *what* of it, the *how* of it, the *why* of it, but to no avail. You're finally doomed never to throw off the shackles of your bourgeois philistine origins. The *doing* of it just won't be in you, poor thing!"

"But . . . this brutality. There's no redeeming . . ."

"Don't you see – the real genius of this man is to have done it there, in Whitechapel of all places."

"No, I don't see. Why of all places?"

"Haven't you thought about it at all? Stabbings are ten-a-penny down there, and yet he's made his work the talk of the nation. You could stab a woman any-old-how in Park Lane and you'd win headlines. But to do it in Whitechapel! It's like throwing half a dozen strokes onto a canvas, but strokes of such genius that you could hang it in an exhibition of thousands and you'd still win the accolade. Believe me, this man is a prince among murderers. I'd give this hand to meet him."

"But the woman had a right to live," Tessa protested, knowing well that Dante would demolish her.

One of the scene shifters snorted. "Poxy old tart like that!"

Tessa flared up at him. "I suppose you knew her?"

The others laughed. He answered, "I suppose you did!"

"As a matter of fact – yes!" Tessa said, embarrassing them all.

"I say! Did you?" Dante asked.

"I don't want to go into it now. I think she might be one of those women I told you about – with the little girl who gave a *right royal curtsey*. Remember?"

"Good heavens! It grows more interesting by the minute. But to get back to your point, my pet – the right to life. If you don't yet understand that art is all, then your apprenticeship hasn't even begun, and all your skill and seeming genius is mere trickery. Art is supreme. To preserve the highlight on the fifth rib of Rembrandt's *Flayed Ox* I'd sacrifice the whole population of London."

"Including yourself?"

"No point in that. Someone's got to survive so as to appreciate the majesty of the sacrifice. This woman's utterly meaningless life and rather commonplace death has been enobled by art. But oh – if I had been there to record it! I should make him immortal, this genius and his knife!"

She went on painting the scenery. His panegyric was growing stale. Several times over the next hour or so he tried to revive the subject but her silence gave him no foothold.

He must have had ears like a cat. He heard the approaching voices almost before the outer door to the theatre closed again.

"That's Marcus Gloab," he said to Tessa. "Best foot forward now. He likes us to treat him as royalty. Run out and greet him, there's a good girl – no need to actually bow backwards all the way here. I'll just slip below for a quick wash."

The scene shifters had gone over to the other theatre half an hour earlier.

Gloab, looking quite different in his sober morning coat, gave no sign that he recognized her. Davitt, who was with him, had already warned her this would likely be the case; he backed it now with a wink and a reassuring little smile.

"Where's Rosen?" Gloab asked. Saunders had been right to say that the foppish "Mars" whom they met that night on

226

Olympus bore no relationship to the real man. Marcus Gloab in London, in one of his own theatres, was a figure of authority and awe.

"He had an accident with some colour, Mr. Gloab," Tessa explained. "He's gone below to wash it off."

They walked in silence down through the terraces of paper and printing cylinders until they reached the point where all the scenery and the backdrop came into view at once. Tessa stood and gazed at it proudly. Its inspiration was far more *her* than Dante; it was her style and her range of colour. And thanks to Dante's absences over these last weeks, the actual design was more than half hers, too. She glanced across to see how Marcus Gloab was taking it.

"What in fuck's name is *that*!" he yelled. His face was bloodless. His nostrils trembled. He turned his fury on Davitt.

Little indiarubber Davitt fished jauntily in his briefcase and drew forth the sketches Dante had made. "Same as these," he said.

"Except," Tessa added, "we've had to make one or two small changes to allow for business or to complete the masking."

Gloab ignored her; he hardly glanced at the sketches. "Any fool can see they're the same," he thundered. "But what the hell are they?"

Davitt gave a sticky little laugh. "They're Rosen's. He told me he'd shown them you and got your say-so."

"I've never seen them in my life. They're fucking awful. How could you possibly believe I'd give them my say-so?"

"Well, I did wonder. . . But he was so. . ."

"What he showed me were perfectly respectable designs for. . ."

"What's wrong with these?" Tessa cut in, feeling she ought to stick up for Dante until he was here to defend himself.

Marcus Gloab appeared to have difficulty locating her. "*Wrong* with them, little girl?" he echoed. "You said it yourself – they're 'an accident with some colour'!" He looked again at the scenery and drove himself into a new fury. "Of all the dog's dinners I've ever been asked to look at, that's the f. . ."

"Don't you dare use that word again, Mr. Gloab," Tessa flared up at him. What on earth was keeping Dante?

Her bold contradiction was all the excuse Gloab needed. He

227

rounded on her and thrust his face forward until it loomed only inches away. She did not flinch, even when he began to shout. "This is my theatre, little worm! Those are my backdrops, little worm! I paid for that colour, little worm! It's my production, little worm! And if I'm paying your wormy little wages, I own you, too, little worm. So I'll say any . . ."

"You aren't and you don't!" Tessa, though seething with fury, was outwardly calm.

"What did you say?" The edge was off Gloab's anger.

Davitt skated breezily out where the ice was thinnest. "No, Gloab old chap – er, you don't actually pay Miss d'Arblay's . . ."

Tessa could see Gloab gathering himself up like a mighty wave to annihilate his "partner." To save Davitt she turned on him in pretended anger, shouting, "You stay out of this, Davitt! Your opinion isn't wanted, thank you very much." To keep her momentum she turned back upon Gloab. "And I asked you a question, Mr. Gloab. I'll overlook your insults. You own so many lives it must be hard to keep tally of them all. Now you've discovered that I don't belong somewhere down there among the gaslamps and powderpaint, perhaps you'll try to keep a civil tongue about you and tell me what you think is wrong with these backdrops?"

"Wrong!" he roared, but he was now fighting to regain the whiphand, and in the flicker of his eyes there were the hurt intimations of a rare defeat. "I'll tell you what's . . ."

"Before you go on," she interrupted, "someone ought to inform you that Dante Rosen is one of the finest painters in Europe. And in case you think I'm just the little worm who mixes the colours, I'll tell you that I was a pupil of Sir Frederic Leighton."

"Leighton? Who's he?" Gloab's primed aggression steered him into this stupidly unthinking response. "Oh – Leighton! Ah!" For a moment then he was nonplussed. He said, "I apologize if I was a touch salty, Miss Doubleday. Perhaps we'll wait for Mr. Rosen?"

"Perhaps you'll try and remember your manners while you do so. I'll go and see what's delaying him."

In the dressing room a message was scrawled across the great gilded mirror. In Dante's hand (and Saunders's leftover make-up) it read: *Blame the Juwes! Catch me when you can!* Still praying it was

228

a joke, she wandered around the maze of backstage passages, calling his name softly enough, she hoped, for him alone to hear – if he was anywhere there.

But he was not. Seething again she returned alone to the auditorium. As she walked up the final passageway, before she came into view, she heard Gloab saying to Davitt, "We've only got ten fucking days – seven to the dress rehearsal – so what the fuck are we going to do, eh?" He saw her then. "Well?" he asked.

"He's been taken ill," she said.

Gloab frowned and started to move toward her. "I must go and see him."

"No!" she said, walking directly at him and speaking with all firmness. "*You* go, Davitt. I want to talk to Mr. Gloab. I have a plan to rescue the production from this present crisis."

It worked. Gloab was, of course, far more worried about his play than about his painter.

"You have Rosen's sketches?" she asked. "The ones he showed you – not these other things?"

His eyes narrowed with a blend of hope and caution. "Yes?"

"Can you bring them here?"

"I'll send them . . ."

"Bring them, send them, never mind. You just get them here by lunchtime and I'll guarantee you'll have your scenery a week today – in time for your dress rehearsal."

His relief was undisguised. She gave it scope before she slipped the blade in. "And I want twenty pounds from you, Mr. Gloab."

He grew angry again. "Twenty quid! For one week's work! That's daylight robbery."

"It's not for me. I want no fee. I consider it a matter of honour to help the production. I need the money for the people I'm going to have to hire. Five of them, one week, two pounds apiece. I'd hardly call that robbery, but you can take it or leave it."

He grunted. "I'd still call it robbery." He looked toward the back of the stage. "Davitt!"

"Never mind him," she said. She'd noticed how readily he responded to a firm command. "You go and look out those original sketches. And get them round here at once. I'm going to organize some help. I'll want that twenty pounds now if you please."

"I never carry money."

"Don't lie to me, Mr. Gloab. If I don't get it now, you don't get your production next week. You balance those two."

Gloab peered at her. "Who are you?" he asked.

"As far as you're concerned, I'm the little worm who's going to save your bacon."

He counted out the money – four crisp, new fivers. His whole manner suddenly changed, as if the thought of handing over money to her – actual money – had switched on a different Marcus Gloab. He counted the notes yet again, this time peeling each one with a lingering, sensuous motion. He held them high so that he was staring over them, among them, into her eyes. "You've got a really good line in anger," he said. "Miss . . . Doubleday, is it?"

She shrugged, not caring whether Gloab ever got her name right.

He went on, "It's a long time . . . in fact, I can't remember the last time anybody spoke to me so . . . ebulliently."

"Whose fault is that?" she asked.

He giggled. She saw traces of Mars Gloab breaking through. "You could earn money by it," he told her. "I'd pay you. And damn . . ."

"You want everyone in your pay! You just can't bear having to deal with someone who's not another little worm . . ."

"Oh no! Oh no!" He suddenly thrust the money into her hand and held it there, as if he had made an electrical contact. "Surely you understand – I *want* you to insult me. Tell me how stupid and incompetent I am. Sneer at me." He saw the bafflement growing in her face and became almost incoherent in his desire to make her see. "Slap me if you like . . . even take a rod to me – ooooh!" He shivered at the delicious thought. His hand, still in hers, still cool and soft, trembled.

If this was a trick to switch off her anger, it was certainly effective. The whole business was so absurd she was more intrigued than repelled. "You *want* me to humiliate you?" she asked.

"Yes!" He was radiant. "You could do it so unutterably well. And I'd pay you, too. Pay you equally well. Oh say yes!"

She plucked her hand from his. "I'm afraid I don't understand. You want me to walk up to you and start shouting abuse and . . .''

"No no no! Not in public. I have an apartment in St. Martin's Lane. We could go there?"

She began to laugh. "And I'd just stand there and hurl insults at you?"

"Well . . ." He wrinkled the bridge of his nose encouragingly. "And tie me up, perhaps. And whip me – take down my trousers. . ."

Understanding dawned. "I see!" she said. "And then you, I suppose, would take down my . . ."

The shock in his face was genuine. "Never!" he cried. "I would be far too much in awe of you ever to . . . why, I worship you already. I would never dream . . . oh, you would be my goddess, my Goddess of Discipline, Miss Double. . ." He smiled. "Miss Discipline? I shall call you that from now. Miss Discipline! Yes! I would not dare to touch the hem of your raiment. I should be your slave, your abject slave. You'd be sacred to me. Your body, your soul, your will – sacred."

It was just too absurd. She was sure now that he was planning some elaborate revenge on her for humiliating him in front of Davitt. She smiled indulgently. "You're saying you'll pay me to go to a room with you and shout abuse and tie you up and whip you – is that it, Mr. Gloab? Shackles for you, shekels for me!"

"Yes!" He was bright-eyed with anticipation. He pointed at the money in her hand. "That many shekels!"

She turned on her heel and began to walk away.

"Double!" he shouted.

She turned. "We're just wasting time," she told him. "You get me Rosen's original sketches."

A crafty look crept into his eyes. He ran to her, put his face uncomfortably close, and whispered, "Fuck!"

She recoiled. "You're disgusting! You nauseate me!"

It produced a paroxysm of delight in him. He scampered off happily among the printer's stock.

She found Davitt staring disconsolately at the message on the mirror; he had been too frightened to re-emerge while Gloab was still there. "Who's old Rosen got it in for?" he asked, nodding at the scrawl. "I'm not a Jew. Gloab's not a Jew. What's he on about? You don't look Jewish to me either."

"It's nothing to do with Jews," she said. "It's Jubelo, Jubela,

231

and Jubelum – remember them? That's why it's spelled like that.''

"Blimey. I thought that was over till the next time. I still don't see his game, though."

"I do. It's called cowardice. He wanted to spring these designs on Gloab when it was too late to change them. Your visit here this morning came just three days too soon. So he's run off in a funk. Mind you, I think Gloab's wrong to call them bad. They're marvellous.''

Davitt sniffed dubiously. "I must say I always had my doubts. They may be art but they're not commercial. Definitely not commercial.''

"Well – it's a pointless argument now. Anyway, listen . . .'' And she went on to tell him what she had arranged with Gloab as far as saving the production went.

He chuckled. "Clever – very! Yes, not bad! But you're in a fool's paradise if you think you'll ever see that money, love. Twenty quid? Off of Marcus Gloab? Hah!''

She showed him the four crisp notes. His jaw dropped. "You're in the wrong trade, gel,'' he said.

She laughed. "What trade should I be in?''

"The one you just invented – you've got the field to yourself, my darling, 'cos no one else can do it.''

"Do what?''

"Take your actual folding geld off of Marcus Gloab!''

She told him then the extraordinary conversation she had just had with the man. "I think it's some sort of trick,'' she added. "He didn't like it when I stood up to him, when he discovered I'm not one of his little worms. Especially as it happened in front of you. So now, next time, if there is a next time, he can just giggle and pretend it gives him some kind of perverted pleasure.''

"Well now . . .'' Davitt cleared his throat and with much circumlocution and begging with his eyebrows and "you know?'' and letting his fingers finish the ends of his sentences . . . he managed to explain it to her.

"No, no,'' she said airily. "You've got it the wrong way round. It's men who do it to women. It's called flagellation. It goes on all over London.''

He explained that, too.

"Dear God!'' she said. "I can just about accept Segal's . . .

affliction, or whatever you might call it. After all, he seems to have been wounded-in-love by some woman called Cynthia. But this . . .'' Then she grinned. ''Here! Why not put Gloab and Segal in touch with each other! Just take a commission!''

Davitt joined her laughter. ''You got the right spirit, gel, but it won't work. It must be with women, see. There's no pleasure in it else.''

''Pleasure! D'you understand it, Davitt?''

''Understand, love? Well, there's understanding and understanding. I mean, I understand it like I understand the public taste in music hall acts. I can book an act that would send me to sleep – but I know the public likes them. Same with this. I could coach you (for a fee of course, hem hem!) to take that forty-quid-a-go off of old Gloab. I'd know exactly what to tell you. But as for understanding, no, I wouldn't rightly understand it.''

''It's amazing! No one ever talks about it. One never sees it referred to anywhere. Yet every time the subject arises, like when I talked about it to Sergeant Keene, and now with you, everyone goes on as if it's as common as cobbles.''

Davitt nodded. ''Still – forty quid, eh? Don't it tempt you? Not even a little bit? It's like the key to the bank. And I'd only want the usual fifteen percent.'' He wrinkled his nose the way Gloab had done. Which of them had caught it off the other, she wondered?

She became businesslike again. ''Not at the moment. And talking of keys, what I want from you is the key to this place. Dante must have gone off with the one we used. So you'd better arrange for the locks to be changed and for me to have the new key. I wouldn't put it past him to come back and tip paint over everything, even if we do, by some miracle, get it finished in time.''

''Dante Rosen?'' he asked tendentiously. ''You can't mean Dante Rosen!''

''I know, I know – you warned me. Saunders warned me. Etcetera etcetera. Consider it said. Let's waste no more time.''

When Davitt had gone, she went to the Academy Schools and then to the Slade. There she rounded up five women students who – some for a lark, some for the two pounds – were willing to pitch in with her and work every daylight hour and many gaslight hours beside to repaint the scenery after Dante's original designs.

233

Her feelings as they spread a pale grey wash over all the work she and Dante had done were complex. There was a great deal of herself in those designs, so part of her hated doing it. But that part of her had been tied up with Dante; so there was also a savage sort of pleasure to be had in hurting herself – as a punishment for getting so caught up with him. So the more it hurt in one way, the more it satisfied her in the other.

Between rehearsals Saunders came and helped, too. Seven women together. Tessa thought it marvellous. Because Grandpa d'Arblay had been such a splendid tutor, she had never attended a school. And she had not been much in the company of girls her own age at other times, except for the occasional party or dance – certainly never for a sustained period like this. She remembered Dante's sneer, that women could live happily together without men; now she welcomed the thought and wished it true. The seven of them were certainly happy together. She loved to listen to their gossip, which was so delightfully innocent. Even when they talked about the men at their colleges it was all at a distance – a matter of sighs and looks-full-of-meaning. For Tessa, after her experiences with Dante and Segal, her reading of Huysmans and so on, it was all so charming and lovely.

They finished the work early on the Friday evening; the dress rehearsal was on Saturday. Marcus Gloab was so delighted he lashed out several pounds more on a grand dinner, sent out from the trusty Holborn Restaurant and consumed in high glee upon the stage. They parted with vows to keep in touch and protestations of lifelong friendship. Tessa almost slept the clock around.

She was awakened the following afternoon not by any sound but by an awareness that someone was in the dressing room with her. It was Saunders – but Saunders looking solemn as never before. As soon as she saw Tessa was awake she thrust a newspaper before her.

Tessa blinked as she struggled to sit upright. "Why aren't you at the dress rehearsal?" she asked.

"We've taken a two-hour break. They want to redo some of the costumes. Read that."

"Isn't it going well? You look so worried."

"Read!"

She read. It was another "'orrible bloody murder" in

Whitechapel. Again the victim was a part-time prostitute in her forties. The newspaper had come out in a special edition, full of the most appalling details.

"Awful," Tessa said as she passed it back.

"Doesn't the name mean anything to you?" Saunders asked.

She looked at the report again. "Annie Siffey?" she said. Her stomach seemed to fall away inside her. "She's not. . .?"

Saunders nodded. "And look how the body was found – throat cut from ear to ear – abdolmen opened and part of her innards carried up over her left shoulder. . . what's it sound like?"

Tessa felt the hair bristling on her neck.

Chapter Thirty-Two

"It's not much to go on," Davitt said doubtfully. "All right – some mad pork butcher's going round cutting up old blowsabellas in Whitechapel. That's a long way from Segal, love. And even further from Olympus."

"Yes but you can see Connie's point," Tessa answered. "The *way* they were butchered was exactly. . ."

"Not the first one – not that one in Bucks Row. They didn't even know she'd had a knife anywhere near her stomach until they got her to the mortuary. The second one I grant you." He shivered.

"And what about the connection between them?" Tessa added. "The royal-baby story. That. . ."

"Royal-fairy story's more like it!" Davitt sneered. "What? D'you think Segal and Prince Eddy go swanning off down Whitechapel once a week, carving up boozy old tarts!"

"No! Of course not. All right – maybe it is a fairy story, but it *does* link both the victims. You can't deny that – nor the fact that they told Connie. And Connie told me. . ." She didn't complete the sequence but from the way he nodded she saw that Saunders must have told him how the tale had gone on to Dante – and thus, probably, to Segal, too.

"I wish Dante'd turn up again," she said. "I'm sure he's at Segal's. I'm not going up there."

"If you do spot him," Davitt sniffed, "there's a little matter of two hundred pounds for work not done. But as to these murders, I don't care who's going round knifing old carrion, as long as Connie stops thinking she might be partly to blame. She opens tomorrow – I mean, tomorrow evening's the biggest thing in her *life*." Davitt gripped her arm to stress the importance of it all. "What's a few drunken old belters compared to that? I don't care what the truth of it is, gel. I wouldn't care if you had photos of Segal, knife in hand. All I want is Connie – *free* of it. Tell her any lie. Tell her you've seen Rosen – tell her Segal's been back in hospital with another horse kick for the last ten days." He cackled richly and shook his head. "That was a good one!" But he was serious again when he added, "Tell her any lie you like – but make it a good'un."

Tessa made it a very good'un.

The opening night of *The Queen of Sheba* was a resounding success. There were fifteen curtain calls and even the severest notice the following morning could find nothing worse to carp about than "evidence of haste in some of the scenery." Tessa was surprised at how the cast and backstage people took this comment to heart – and how they all rallied round to reassure her. With knowing nods and winks, they said the critic must have been relying on inside information – because, of course, the scenery had been immaculate, darling, no sign of haste at all. This comforting was so prolonged and vehement she began to think the critic must have been right after all.

She realized she'd never be a theatre person. They seemed so confident and so much larger than life, and yet they all had a desperate need of the kind of reassurance they were now dishing out so liberally (and so needlessly) to her. Their lives, their friendships, their obsessions . . . all were so fleeting. Left to herself she would have stood their arguments on end. "It's only a play," she would have said. "Just a bit of make-believe. It'll only exist a few weeks, and then we'll all be worrying and sweating over something else with just as much intensity and just as many tears. So what's it matter if there are one or two signs of haste? The scenery does its job."

She'd never be *theatre*.

But it didn't stop her from accepting an open commission from Marcus Gloab to design another of his productions and to supervise the painting of it. He'd been rightly impressed at the way she'd organized and managed the rescue. "And what about that other 'commission' you offered me?" she asked.

He winked jovially and shook his head. "Not while you're one of my little worms, precious," he answered. But at the door he paused and added, "Mind you, next time I'm in a blue funk – do try again. My refusal may not be quite so. . . insouciant!"

Tessa lived a week in that hermetically sealed world where performance was king, where the simple cry of "Beginners please!" could pack away a score of private lives – with all their tragedies, jealousies, loves. . . disasters – and unite them in a piece of grand nonsense that ought not to occupy the mind of any serious person for more than a minute. When the very air she breathed was so laden with make-believe, how easy it became even for her to imagine that Segal really was back in hospital – or, to the contrary, that her fears about his role in these murders were themselves part of the airy-fairy all around. The papers were full of the story. The East End was in uproar. The police were arresting suspects by the dozen and letting them all go again when they furnished a good alibi, or even a good address. It was easy to see it all as part of some larger theatre "out there".

But back at home in the Old Vicarage, less than a mile from the scene of the second atrocity, it became harder for her to shut out the doubts. In the end she told Simon the story – with minor modifications, of course. She hadn't herself been in the grotto; Davitt had told her about that. And it was a maid who had been tortured by Segal – one of the talkative kind.

"No wonder you were a bit odd that morning," he told her.

"Was I?"

"Blunt."

"I loved that walk with you. I wish we could go back and have that conversation all over again."

Their eyes dwelled in each other's. He nodded enigmatically.

They were touring the churchyard, ostensibly looking for loose slates on the roof; but they had already made two circuits and he had not once raised the binoculars to his eyes. It was past the middle of September and the air was now quite autumnal, ripe with mists, imprisoning the sun in a red-gold pallor and filching its power to burn and goad.

"So what it adds up to," he said, "is that there were these two women who claimed they were looking after a love-child of one of the royal princes. And now they've both been murdered by the same method and within ten days. And the method resembles, in the second case certainly, and possibly in the first, that ritual Masonic killing we read about. Next: in Dr. Segal's house are a number of prints by Rembrandt, Hogarth and others showing a more elaborate form of the same ritual. It was re-enacted on Midsummer Eve, again by Dr. Segal, in some kind of childish but unpleasant pantomime at Olympus. The same Dr. Segal has a deep-seated hatred of women, bordering on the insane. And the thing that links all these instances is the fact that these two women told their story (or fairy story) to Miss Saunders. She told you. You told Rosen. And Rosen *may* have told Segal. Have I left out anything?"

"Yes, I forgot to mention that Dr. Segal is – or was – a Freemason."

"When did he leave?"

"I don't think he left. I think he was expelled – and we both know what ritual they must have used!" She went on to explain about Peter Laird's inquest, Sergeant Keene, and the visit to Sir William Gull.

"It's all terribly circumstantial, Tess," he said at last. "I mean, all these little facts *seem* to add up to a damning case, but just consider this: If it turns out that Rosen *didn't* tell Segal, then everything else is sheer coincidence, meaning nothing."

"I know." She nodded unhappily.

"There must be dozens of ex-Masons – hundreds perhaps. Anyway, who says it's an ex-Mason? And there are literally thousands of women haters – it's almost an epidemic these days."

"I know – I know!"

After a short silence he said, "Then why don't we just forget it?"

"Because there were *four* women taking it in turns to look after the little girl."

"I'd forgotten that. Who are the other two, d'you know?"

She shook her head. "We could probably find out from the others at the Refuge – if they aren't all too scared out of their wits to talk about it."

"D'you think we ought to go to the police as well?"

"I think we ought to do something – find the other pair of women – get them to safety. I mean, that would be the most practical thing. I don't suppose the police would even believe me. Segal's a police surgeon after all."

"Being a police surgeon doesn't mean much – only that he's on a list of local doctors they can call in when they want to get a drunk to walk the chalk or say, 'The Leith police dismisseth us.'"

"Oh, I thought he was practically part of the force."

"No!"

"In that case" – she brightened – "I might even risk a lecture on intuition from Sergeant Keene."

They noted two broken slates and then, duty done, telephoned Scotland Yard to make sure Keene would be there. They took a cab to Whitehall. She got the driver to go about through Russell Street so that she could show Simon the New National Theatre with Saunders's name largest of all on the awning.

Scotland Yard smelled like a boys' school, Simon said – one that was heavy on mud and light on chalk. The great stone corridors and tall gloomy windows were in the same "abandon hope" style of architecture, too.

Sergeant Keene sat at an orderly desk with orderly piles of paper awaiting orderly disposal; she and Simon felt, as they were probably intended to feel, like intruders. He had mugs of hot chocolate fetched for them, but it was the last of warmth and sweetness they got out of him that day. He heard Tessa's story through in silence; he noted it down carefully; and then he fell asleep for a good minute.

When he woke up, he said, "So what we have here is we have a doctor with prints by Hogarth and Rembrandt, eh? Have you any idea how many Rembrandt prints and reproductions there must be knocking around the world, Miss d'Arblay? Never mind. We've also got two old street cruisers telling a tale straight out of *Alice in Wonderland*. I'd like a farthing for every time I've heard a tale like that – I'd've retired rich twenty years ago. And we've got a theatrical gentleman (whose name is not unknown in this building, I may say) who alleges that Dr. Segal got up to high jinks with an actress and a sheep's tripes on Midsummer Eve. Then we've got a housemaid, anonymous, who alleges that Dr. Segal pinched her in the dark one night. Tut tut! And him a gentleman and all! We also have reason to believe that Dr. Segal was booted out of the Freemasons. As if this evidence wasn't already damning enough, we've had a supreme stroke of good luck – the sort of thing every detective dreams about. We've actually run down a footnote in a book about the building of Solomon's temple which says the architect was murdered, three thousand years ago, in a manner similar to that employed on Annie Siffey in Whitechapel just over a week ago. And from this we infallibly deduce that the same Dr. Segal is – have I got it right? – the Whitechapel Murderer?" He sniffed. "All over London, Miss d'Arblay, people are looking out their windows, seeing neighbours they've never liked, and saying to themselves, 'I'll bet he's the bloke what's killing all these poor women!'"

On their dispirited way home Tessa said, "I knew it would be absolutely pointless going to him." She laughed ironically. "In fact, you could call it an intuition."

Simon comforted her. "If we hadn't, my dear, you'd never have slept easy. All we can do now is to track down the other two women and warn them . . . help them, if they need it."

"You're being so good to me, Simon. I know you don't believe it any more than Keene does, but at least you're humouring me."

"But I do believe you. My own first thoughts were even more far-fetched, I'm afraid."

She was puzzled.

"When I read your father's book, remembering the details in the paper – and what Saunders told you about the royal baby – I thought it might actually *be* Freemasons. Officially, I mean. But, of course, that's what he wants people to think – Segal, or whoever it is."

She wondered if one could fall in love slowly. Or did it always have to come with a crash, as it had with Dante?

Chapter Thirty-Three

There had indeed been four women; but the nuns could remember only the name of Elizabeth Stride – "Long Liz". And Long Liz seemed to have vanished. In the usual East End fashion no one could say for certain whether she had gone away or whether she was still around. . . somewhere. Every inquiry brought a helpful response – yes, she was seen only yesterday (or was it the day before?). . . in the Weaver's Arms. . . in the Black Swan. . . in The Ringer's. . . it was always a pub. Or someone thought they saw her touting for trade in Commercial Street. . . in Dorset Street. . . in Fashion Street. . . yesterday afternoon. . . the night before last. Their questions never drew blank; their actual searches drew nothing but.

"One begins to understand the problems of the police," Simon said wearily.

After a few days of it they were ready to give up with a good conscience. Then one of the more articulate young women from the Cole Place refuge came to them, early one evening, with word that Lizzie Stride had definitely been seen not an hour since in The Britannia in Dorset Street.

They went at once. Long Liz was drunk almost past coherence. As her name implied, she was a tall woman; her fair frizzy hair was dirty and unkempt, and her face was lopsided because most of her lower teeth were missing on the left side. One of the others told them she had said she only wanted to get fourpence – for the lodging house – but she'd earned it and spent it four times already that day. All the Whitechapel whores were drinking more than usual, staying off the streets; the terror of the murders was almost palpable.

They took Liz outside and walked her up and down for a good quarter of an hour, until her speech began to grow intelligible. At first she was all bravado; she swore she wasn't drunk but was merely subject to fits. Beneath it all they could see how terrified she was. When she became a little more coherent she managed to tell them that the child was with the fourth woman, a Marie Kelly.

"Where?"

"Marie's young. Marie's pretty."

"Yes, but where is she? And where's the child?"

"Marie can take care of herself."

"Are you saying you don't know where she is? D'you know where the child is, then?"

"Marie took her to the artist."

Tessa's heart fell like a stone. "The artist?" She and Simon exchanged glances. "I hope you mean an artist called Sickert," she said. "Not one called Rosen?"

"Sickert," the woman answered. At least, that was what they thought she said, for at that moment, perhaps in part-association with the name, she was herself sick. She laid a real Persian carpet in the gutter. Or mostly in the gutter; part of it went over Tessa's dress and a further part over Simon's trousers.

They had to go home at once for a change of clothing, leaving the poor creature in the care of one of her less drunken companions. They got the address of her lodgings, a dossing house in Fashion Street, and left fourpence with her to pay for the one doss at least, saying they'd return tomorrow and make more permanent arrangements for her safety. The landlord agreed not to serve her any more liquor that night – but, of course, there were other pubs. There were pubs in every street.

Late next morning they returned to the dossing house but the keeper there said Long Liz had already gone out for the day. The pubs were just opening. They went back to The Britannia, where the landlord said try The Bricklayers' or else a lodging house, farther along Fashion Street, where she lived on and off with a docker called Kidney. . . and so the hunt became a dispiriting repeat of last week's searches. They gave up and took a cab to the West End, to Sickert's studio in northern Soho. There, too, they drew blank until, just as they were leaving, a friend of the painter's called to a neighbouring studio and told them Sickert had gone away for a week or so.

Tessa asked where; he became evasive and asked why they wished to know.

"We're really interested in the whereabouts of a Marie Kelly," Tessa told him. "And a little girl who's with her – Alice Crook or

Cook?''

The man grew even more wary. He asked what their interest might be.

''We think she may be in danger,'' Tessa explained. ''Someone told us the little girl's mother used to work near here and that Mr. Sickert knew her.''

The other looked about them and then, drawing closer, said almost beneath his breath, ''You may be assured she is safe. They are both safe. Sickert's taken them over to France with him – to Dieppe. He'll lodge them there with friends.''

They tried to learn more but he said he knew nothing beyond what he had told them – and he had only done that because they were obviously respectable and were plainly worried. All he knew was that it was a matter of great secrecy and he'd be obliged if they said no more about it to anyone, now that they were assured of the safety of the two females.

Tessa almost twisted her ankle in her jubilant descent of the staircase. Back in the street she skipped like a twelve-year-old. ''Oh Simon,'' she said. ''Until we heard that just now, I had no idea what a *burden* the worry has been. Isn't it marvellous? It's like a great fog lifting. What shall we do now? Let's go to the zoo. Let's do a matinée. Let's go up the river to Hampton Court.'' She frowned. ''No – anywhere but Hampton Court.''

He laughed at her sudden good humour. ''What's wrong with Hampton Court?''

''Never mind. We can go anywhere else. You say.''

''Let's just go for a stroll in Regent's Park? It's only up the road.''

An hour later they were sitting on the terrace of the restaurant in the Regent's Park Zoo, with the caged wild beasts on either side and the placid green acres stretching southward before them. Only the occasional church spire projecting above the treetops, and, to be sure, the endless, distant rumble of iron wheels, gave any hint of the mighty city beyond.

''Oh I do hope it's all over,'' she said.

''Don't start that again! Of course it's over. We'll find Lizzie Stride. Don't worry. It can't be too hard the second time. Then we'll have done everything we can.''

They sat awhile in silence, enjoying the tranquillity of the scene; and then Tessa said, ''Perhaps I ought to go and have a

243

word with Sir William Gull?''

''Tess!''

''Well then I really could say I'd done everything.''

''What d'you think Sir William could do?''

''Don't you think he might be more inclined to believe me? I mean, Sergeant Keene starts out with so many prejudices – against me, against the very idea that any member of the public, let alone a stupid woman with her head in a paintbox all day, could have anything useful to say. And he's very prejudiced in favour of Segal. At least Sir William already knows what sort of a liar Segal is.''

Simon reached across the table and touched her hand. ''No, Tess. Drop it, eh? You really have done everything humanly possible.''

She smiled gratefully. ''Just repeat the dose every five minutes, please.''

''You know what I think?''

''What?''

''I think you don't *want* to start painting again.''

She pulled a face.

''Well, you don't deny it. I'll tell you what else I think – I think you ought to go back this very afternoon and pick up your brushes. The longer you leave it, the harder it'll be.''

She bent down the brim of her floppy straw hat to shade her eyes from the lowering sun. ''Perhaps I ought to give up painting altogether – now, while I can. Maybe it was just a phase in my life. Bo says I'll never get a husband while I paint so intensely.''

''Oh *she* decides? Shall I talk to her about that?'' His hand, still near hers, crept alongside. ''Or to you?''

''Not . . . not just yet, Simon.''

His hand remained, warm beside hers on the cool marble. ''What did you do in the theatre?'' he asked. ''Apart from scene-painting and telling dear Connie Saunders how wonderful she was?''

She gave a little shrug.

''You must have done something else,'' he pressed.

''I went to hell and back.'' She meant it humorously but it didn't come out quite like that. When he didn't reply she added, ''Not really.''

His hand curled into a fist; he thumped the table gently. ''I

244

love you, Tess. You know that. But when I say I'm worried about you, I'm not trying to publicize my own feelings." He pulled his final punch on her hand itself. "Something happened, didn't it?"

"Did it?"

"You tell me."

She shook her head.

"Or tell someone. You oughtn't to bottle it up."

She forced a smile. "It's just these murders, Simon. Honestly. It'll be all right now."

"That's what I thought – until about half an hour ago. But now I think your concern for the other two women, obvious and very proper though it is, I think it's actually . . . it's almost as if you're diverting your own attention from something much deeper. Something you're unwilling to admit even to yourself. Is that possible, Tess? Is there anything like that?"

"What happened half an hour ago?"

"Why don't you answer me?"

"What changed your mind half an hour ago?"

"The fact that we'd solved your ostensible problem – the other two women – but had obviously in no way solved your real one. You're as tense and nervous as ever you were. So, at the risk of repeating myself, Tess, what *is* our real problem?"

She bit her lip, fighting an impulse to cry. When she could trust herself to speak she said, "My real problem, Simon, is that I once believed – no, not 'once' – two short weeks ago! I believed Dante Rosen was the finest man in the world. I thought he and I were going to pioneer a new kind of relationship between men and women. My problem is – how can I ever trust my own judgement again?"

Chapter Thirty-Four

They never saw Liz Stride again. She was murdered that same night in a yard in Berner Street, off the Commercial Road in Whitechapel. Her throat was cut from left to right but, according to the papers, there were no other visible mutilations. Her name was not given out until the following day, Monday, October 1st, but Tessa already knew it could only be Long Liz – for within an hour of her death her killer claimed a second victim. Her name, the site chosen for her discovery, and the pattern of mutilations on her body – all left no room for doubt.

The name of this other victim was first given as Kelly – Kate Kelly – but that was soon contradicted. Kelly was the name of the man she lived with and she had given his name when she was picked up as drunk and disorderly earlier on that final evening of her life; she had been released around 1 a.m. and was murdered during the next hour. Her true name was Catherine Eddowes, or, some said, Conway – but never mind, for a time everybody had thought she was called Kelly. In Tessa's mind there was no doubt but that the killer had fallen into the identical error.

Kate's body was found in Mitre Square.

Her throat had been cut from left to right.

Her abdomen had been opened and part of her entrails were thrown up over her shoulder.

Triangular nicks had been made in her cheeks with a sharp knife. She had then been laid out formally.

A portion of her apron had been cut off and then deliberately placed at the foot of a nearby wall – a gruesome link between the body and the message on that wall, which ran: The Jews are not the men to blame for nothing. . . or: The Juwes are to blame for nothing. . . or: The Juwes are the Men That will not be Blamed for Nothing. . . or, as Saunders might have said, ''something like that, anyway.'' The confusion in the various reports arose because Sir Charles Warren, Commissioner of the Metropolitan Police, had personally visited the site and ordered the message to be rubbed out – for fear, he said, of disturbances among the large Jewish population in that area.

These details emerged piecemeal over the following week or so; but from the start, as soon as she had seen the name Mitre Square, Tessa had known Segal was in it.

Simon, regretting that they had not made more strenuous efforts to trace Long Liz, tried for Tessa's sake to pooh-pooh the idea.

But she insisted. "It's just as you yourself said, Simon. He *wants* the Freemasons to be blamed. That message he left on the wall – that's Segal saying to Sir William Gull and all the others who threw him out so ignominiously, 'You've turned me into one of the Juwes! You're not going to blame me for nothing, my friends!' So he's doing everything he can to pin the name *Mason* on the murders: the way he mentions the Juwes, the disembowelling ritual, the wounds on the face, and, loudest of all, his choice of Mitre Square for what he *thought* was going to be his final killing. He thought he had Marie Kelly. I hope to God Sickert manages to work that out, too, in Dieppe or wherever he is."

"But it still doesn't prove it's Segal, Tess."

She snorted. "You weren't tortured by him!"

He breathed in sharply.

She hesitated a fatal half-second too long before she added, "Nor was I, of course. But I saw that maid. You didn't." She could hear how false it rang.

"Tess!" he exclaimed. "Oh, woman!"

"It doesn't matter now," she said crossly.

"By God it matters to me! I don't care whether or not he's the Whitechapel Murderer – but if he laid a finger on you, I want to know."

She smiled at his earnestness. "Why? What'll you do?"

"Take a horsewhip to him. I'd have him grovelling on his knees outside your room for a week, day and night, begging your forgiveness."

She gave his arm a squeeze. "That's very. . . it's most. . . oh dear – what can I say that won't sound patronizing? I'm deeply touched by it, Simon, my dear. Honestly. But you needn't worry. In the end I managed to get the upper hand – by a pure fluke. Or upper knee to be precise. In fact, I was so angry I hurt him rather more than I intended. He was in hospital several weeks, you know.''

''Hospital!'' He looked at her in a new light. ''Good God! D'you mean he didn't hurt you at all?''

''Oh he hurt all right. Like billy-oh. It was the worst pain I've ever . . . but it didn't last. I mean, as soon as he stopped, it stopped.''

''And there was nothing lasting?''

''You be the judge of that. You met me about an hour after it all happened – at Stonehenge.''

For a while he could only stare at her. Then he remembered. ''When Rosen went away so suddenly – he said, 'I'd better see how Segal is.' That's what he meant.''

''And you said, 'Naught shall go ill – Jack shall have his Jill.'''

''From *Midsummer Night's Dream*.'' He smiled at the memory. Then the actual words caught up with him and he closed his eyes tight. ''Lord – did I really say that? I meant . . .''

''It doesn't matter, Simon. It's of no consequence now. Just one more ghastly coincidence.''

''What are you going to do?'' he asked.

''I'll go and see Saunders first of all. I must. But what can I say? Three of the four are dead and the fourth called herself Kelly. There's no point in lying now. What can I say?''

''We'll have to keep her occupied. I mean, she must be made to feel she's doing something useful about it. Why don't you and Davitt and she all go and see Sergeant Keene? If the three of you swear to what happened in the grotto – I assume you were also part of that?''

Tessa shook her head. ''They wouldn't do it, my dear. It would mean dragging Marcus Gloab into it, and he's their bread and butter for the rest of the century.''

Simon was shocked. ''Surely they wouldn't be so lacking in public spirit!''

''You don't know theatre people. They want to do personal, warm, individual things. Saunders'll want to find Marie Kelly and stay with her and comfort her and talk ten-to-the-dozen and be frightfully heroic. I'm sorry if I sound a little censorious, I don't mean it like that. It's just the way they are.''

''What about taking her with you to see Sir William Gull? If you can convince *him*, then I'm sure he's the sort of person who could go and talk directly to Sir Charles Warren.''

Her eyes lit up. ''You've got it, Simon – that's absolutely it!''

As their cab passed the New National Theatre they saw a notice on the awning which read, ''Miss Saunders is indisposed. Miss Kitty Nash will play the part of Sheba.''

The doorman told them Saunders was resting in Davitt's apartments in the West End – in, of all places, Berners Street.

''Yet another grisly coincidence,'' Simon said as they drove up to the entrance. ''Give or take an *s*.''

''Oh, if only it would all prove to be coincidence! If the killer really turned out to be this elusive 'Leather Apron' fellow the papers keep talking about!'' They were admitted to the apartments by the porter. As they climbed the stairs, Tessa added, ''Actually, there's yet another coincidence. Did you know that a leather apron is part of the uniform of every Freemason!''

Saunders must have heard her voice echoing in the stairwell; her own muffled cry came from behind the stout oak of the apartment door: ''Tess? Is it you?''

''Of course it's me. Aren't you going to open?''

''Who's with you? You're not. . . are you alone? Who's that with you? I can hear. . .''

''It's Simon Liddington, darling. What's the matter with you?''

''Are you sure it's him?''

''Stop being silly, Saunders. Open up or I'll get quite cross!''

''We're both sure it's me, Miss Saunders,'' Simon called.

A bolt was shot. Then another. Then a chain. Then a lock. Then a second lock. The door swung a tentative inch open on a captive chain. Saunders's eye appeared in the crack. The one-inch strip of her face expressed enough relief to share out among half a dozen lesser actresses and still leave too much for a common mortal.

It took them almost an hour, with occasional help from Davitt, to get her back to normal, or as normal as Saunders ever got: an hour of tediously going over the same ground, first to make her understand that Marie Kelly and the little girl were safe – indeed, that they weren't even in the country – and then (a far harder task) to convince her that she had nothing to reproach herself for; if anything, Tessa was ten times as much to blame. They were so successful at this latter point that Tessa almost ended up in the miseries from which they had rescued Saunders – though, lacking Saunders' sense of drama, she didn't show it so proudly.

The turning point came when Saunders asked, "Well, what are we going to *do*?" Until then the idea that she would do anything except cling to Davitt and make him add a new lock or bolt to the door every few hours had not entered her mind.

"You remember Old Sir William?" Tessa asked.

"Old *Father* William." Saunders corrected her with a prim smile. "It's years since I did that one. 'You are old Father William, the young man said, and your hair is excessively white. . .' Or something like that."

"No! Old Sir William – Sir William Gull."

"Oh – Sir Wily!"

"Yes! Sir Wily!"

"Why didn't you say? What about him?"

"We thought you could exercise your charms on him and. . ."

"I don't need him now." She nodded a grin in Davitt's direction.

"My goodness, Saunders," Tessa said angrily. "Don't you heal quickly! We're not talking – just for these next few minutes now – we're not talking about plans to further the career of one Connie Saunders – if you can possibly bear to contemplate that thought?"

Saunders's laugh was a rich gurgle as she hugged Tessa, told her she was quite right, that herself ought to be whipped, and to go on, please – what about Sir Wily?

"We thought that if we went to see him, he knows already that Segal's a rogue and if he's any judge of character, he'll suspect a great deal worse than that. He must also have the honour of the Masons at heart. So if we tell him about that ritual in the grotto. . ."

"Here, leave Gloab out of it!" Davitt chimed in quickly.

Tessa smiled an I-told-you-so at Simon and went on: "We needn't say anything about Olympus and Marcus Gloab – we can lie and say it all happened at Finsbury Close – and if I tell him about what Segal did to me that night, and. . ."

"What did Segal do to you that night?"

"Never mind, now. It was exactly what you warned me about. So crow all you want."

But Saunders did not crow; instead a slow grin split her face.

250

"Were you the 'horse' that kicked him in the antipodes then? Hey!" She turned to Davitt. "SD – here's that strong-arm act you wanted!"

Simon laughed. "Nothing becomes real, does it Miss Saunders, until you can pull a curtain up and down on it!"

"And bask in the applause," Tessa added.

They both laughed. Saunders only dimly grasped the point. She turned again to Tessa, eager to hear more of the plan, especially as it looked like making some demands on her greatest talent.

"Well that's it," Tessa said. "Once he understands that he didn't solve the problem of Segal just by expelling him from the Masons – in fact, that Segal is now threatening the entire brotherhood by making it seem as if they're the ones who are killing off these women – then Sir William's bound to go straight to Sir Charles Warren. I'll bet he's a Mason, too. But oh, Connie love! – wouldn't it be grand to get the whole problem off our minds? You could return to the theatre and I could go back to my easel. . . think of it!"

Saunders thought of it and squared herself to the decision. "I'll do it!" she said, as if they had just negotiated a particularly difficult contract in her favour. "But only you and me, Tess. I think we'll get more out of the old darling than if the Rev. Dr. Liddington comes along, too."

After more discussion Simon reluctantly agreed, but he said he'd follow in a second cab and wait outside; they couldn't stop him doing that.

The evenings were drawing in. The lamplighters were already on their rounds as the women's cab pulled into Brook Street. There was no wind. The air was chill. Smoke from the city's myriad chimneys rose just so far before it levelled off and wove its familiar autumnal pall. A classic London fog was brewing.

This time they were admitted only as far as the hallway. There was an oppressive atmosphere in the house, more so than could be accounted for by the change from bright May to sad October. A youngish man of not more than thirty years came from the room where they had sat and talked with Sir William last time; he introduced himself as William Gull, the son of the house. Tessa mentioned their previous visit and explained that they had further information to pass on. He replied that his father was unwell;

could they perhaps entrust this new information to him?

Tessa did not get far; as soon as she mentioned the Whitechapel murders he burst out angrily: "Are you more of these wretched spiritualists?" Without waiting for an answer he added, "You may as well know you've made my father's life a positive misery. It's entirely your fault he's so low in health. You go back and tell your Mr. Leigh or whatever he calls himself . . ."

"Mr. Gull – we have not the faintest notion what you're talking about," Saunders interrupted. She then tried to explain the connection between Segal and Sir William – that this was a medical matter, a professional matter, a Freemason matter . . .

In the end he believed them and apologized for his outburst. But it made no difference. It seemed that a spiritualist group had received messages from "the other side" about the identity of the murderer and their "spirit guide" had directed them to inform Sir William Gull. This had been some two weeks ago, after the second murder, and ever since then they had made life at Number 74 a misery. So, he concluded, even if what they wished to tell Sir William about Segal was every bit as important as they seemed to think, he was still going to prevent them from seeing him. They only wanted him because he was a senior Freemason; they would just have to find someone else in that category and tell their tale to him. He was very sorry – but there it was. His father was an old, frail man who'd already suffered a number of strokes; his health was more important than anything they might have to say about this Dr. Segal.

They argued for several minutes more but he remained adamant. They had no choice but to return to Berners Street and try to think of someone else whom they might alert.

When they emerged from the house, Simon's cab pulled forward and stopped right by them. "You take this one," he said. "I'll walk back to Grosvenor Square and get another."

On the spur of the moment Tessa said, "No! I have one last bow to draw at this venture. You take Connie back to Berners Street, Simon dear. I'll go and have a final crack at Sergeant Keene."

"But why should he listen to you now any more than he . . ."

"Because – I've just remembered – I mentioned Mitre Square to him last time. That must count for something. He's a funny man, old Keene. When I first suggested 'borrowing' the photo

252

from Peter Laird's post-mortem, he just laughed and walked away. Yet a few days later he turned up with the thing and said, 'Good idea!' He's the sort of man you hit on Monday and he says 'Ouch!' on Wednesday.''

Simon laughed. ''I'll come with you then.''

''No. I think I'll get further on my own. He's known me since so-high. But in front of you he has to act the proper policeman and laugh at female intuition and all that sort of nonsense – you saw him.''

In the end Simon agreed – once again, reluctantly.

''I'll be an hour at most,'' she promised.

The cabby, having overheard it all, had meanwhile hailed down a passing colleague, so there was now a second cab to hand. Tessa leaped in, before Simon could suggest a compromise, and said, ''Scotland Yard, please driver.''

But as soon as the two cabs were out of sight of each other she said, ''I've changed my mind. Please take me to Tite Street in Chelsea.''

For too long she had put off her confrontation with Dante Rosen.

Chapter Thirty-Five

No theatre could have staged that moment of reunion better. A dank autumn mist had come rolling down the Thames from Putney. In the Chelsea reach it united with the smoke and now cocooned the world in soupy darkness.

Dante must have been expecting someone, for as soon as she paid off her driver she heard the opening click of his studio door. Her heartbeat hammered in her throat as she slipped through the gate and began the short walk up the curved garden path to the brief flight of steps before the front porch. He flung the door wide and stood, legs braced apart, a dark silhouette against the brilliance behind him – so bright it threw giant projections of him outward onto the rolling banks of fog. The curve of the path plunged her into the heart of that outcast darkness. "You won't get home tonight," he said.

She walked straight in, past him. There was no one else in the studio. "Who were you expecting?" she asked.

"You, of course." He closed the door.

"Hardly!" she told him.

She saw then that this was merely a place for preparing and storing his canvases; the studio proper must be upstairs.

"You did well, I hear," he said. There was, of course, not the slightest trace of apology or awkwardness.

"No thanks to you!"

He laughed in an injured tone. "How can you say that? It's *all* thanks to me, surely?" After a pause he said, "Are you afraid to look at me?"

She saw a reflection of him, darkly, in one of the windowpanes and she was afraid. The sight of him, even half-obscured like that, the sound of his voice, his nearness, like a vibrance upon the air – she had forgotten the power of these things when she had so blithely changed her destination. But she forced herself to say, "Afraid?" and to turn and face him.

She drew a sudden breath. "You've been hurt!"

Delicately he fingered a scab on his left cheek. "It's nothing. Have you come to thank me?"

"You've got no shame!"

"An artist with a sense of shame? It's like a whore with a heart of gold. Nice people lose races. Well if you haven't come to thank me. . .?"

"I'd like a glass of wine."

"Of course." He went upstairs to get it. She poked around for a while, looking at his canvases. He was the sort of painter who worked on eight or ten at a time; they were all in various stages of incompletion. Quite a few were in "her" new style – so his admiration for her work had been genuine. It made her feel absurdly pleased. After ten minutes, when he still had not come back with the wine, she hesitantly went up after him.

There was a sharp turn at the top, presumably into his studio. The door was slightly ajar. She pushed it – and found him standing just inside, holding a glass of white burgundy ready for her – and a smile, also ready. "I know you so well," he said.

It forced her to smile back. Then she saw they were not in his studio but his bedroom. "No, Dante," she said.

He shrugged. "You're a free agent. You'd like to see my studio? Let me go ahead and light the lamps."

She followed him out and across the landing. He carried the wine bottle loosely slung, corking it with one finger. It struck her as an erotic gesture, intended as such. She tried not to look at it. The smell of him, that old familiar smell, was erotic, too; there was no way she could escape that.

Most of the work up here was also in the "new" style – quick gouache sketches of the Thames, landscapes, a bit of Kew Gardens. He was beginning to develop it away from her immediate influence. The colours were getting flatter. He was playing more with the sheer decorative power of shapes, so that the first impression – out of the corner of the eye, so to speak – was of samples of wallpaper. The impact of them began to excite her; it was as if they unlocked another door for her, showing a ten-second vision of a year's potential work. She felt an itch to begin at once.

"I'm trying to get that. . . there's no English word for it – that *coup d'oeil*. The strike-of-the-eye!" He put the bottle and his glass down for a moment to allow him to punch his fist violently into his open palm. "That first flash of vision before you sort out the distances – when everything's still flat. Like a Japanese print. That gorgeous flatness of everything."

"But Japanese prints are much too stylized, surely."

"Or not stylized enough? The only thing I want to steal from them is their sense of flat-solidity and their appreciation of the sheer decorative quality of the shapes." He surveyed his work. "It's exciting, don't you think?"

She nodded.

"You started it, now I've taken it further." He waited for her reaction to that before he asked – seriously: "Why don't you move in here?" Then he laughed. "Get your revenge! Steal my tricks, as Saunders would say."

To her amazement she almost heard herself agreeing. His way of putting things could make the outrageous sound normal. She had to take a conscious grip and force herself to say, "Actually Dante, I came here to talk about something quite different."

"You came here to talk about Segal. I know." He picked up his glass and the bottle and began to walk back to the door.

255

"You know?"

He nodded. "Are you going to stay the night?"

"How do you know?"

He put his head on one side and grinned at her, as if to say, 'Really! What a question!'

"It *is* Segal, isn't it – he's the one who's doing these appalling murders?"

"Of course." He held out the wine bottle. Too astonished to notice, she allowed him to refill her glass.

"Do you *know*?" she asked. "Absolutely know? Or have you simply reasoned it out like me?"

"Who else could it be?"

"So you were lying that day at the theatre when you said you'd give your. . ."

"I'm very likely to tell the truth in front of those morons of scene shifters! I'd forgotten how beautiful you are, Tess – how much your beauty stirs me! What about you? Did you forget me? I mean the exact effect I have on you? Why have you come here? Be honest now. Is it *merely* to talk about Segal?"

His manner of posing the question – begging it with his eyes and tone – made her doubt her answer. She tried to think. The decision had been made in the context of. . . what? Reassuring Saunders. . . getting to the bottom of things. . . doing something positive – how hollow the reasons rang now. It had all seemed so certain and simple out there; but in here, in this exciting moral twilight where Dante lived, things became more complex. What had her real motives been? Her conscious mind was like Saunders – it would say anything, and keep changing the story, until it heard the applause.

Just when these doubts were at their height he dipped the spoon back for one more stir: "And why choose such a night as this? Even before you set out you must have known the fog would close down and make your return impossible."

Not wanting to believe it, she went to the window and shaded its glass with her arms. The mantle of the street light, only four or five yards distant, was a dim red button on a field of darkness. It illuminated nothing, not even its own cradle.

He came and stood right behind her. He slipped a hand around her waist. "No, Dante," she whispered.

"I heeded that word once before and was wrong," he

murmured in the rich tingling dark of her ear. "Cook us a pair of omelettes, there's a good girl. I'll cut some bread and cheese. I've got a stilton that'll lift your scalp!"

"That pub on the corner of Tedworth Street," she asked, "does it have the telephone?"

"The one on the Embankment does. Why?"

"D'you think we might find some blind person to lead us there? I could get a message home, telling them not to worry."

He broke into a slow grin. "Where did you tell them you were going?"

"Scotland Yard."

He roared with laughter. But when they were in the pub and he heard her say into the apparatus, "Please connect me with the Metropolitan Police Station, number three-five-three-six," he frowned.

She left a message for Sergeant Keene, to relay onward to Simon if he telephoned – just to say that she was staying at the Temperence Hotel in the Strand for the night. She chose it because it was not in the telephone book.

"Your favourite tipple," he said, handing her a glass of rich black stout. "You really were going to Scotland Yard."

"Of course I was. Thanks. Someone's got to stop Segal before he finds Marie Kelly and the child. Will you come with me tomorrow? You must know things about Segal – things you've never told me."

"We'll talk about it," he said. "Cheers dears."

"Cheers. You mean you will?" The bitter malt scoured clean her mouth.

"We're not ordinary people, Tess. Ordinary people can muddle through their lives without much need for thinking. When they get into difficulties, they can reach down an easy answer off the shelf. Dear me, I seem to have discovered a murderer. Sixth Commandment. Good. Got that straight. Offences Against The Person Act, 1861. Getting warmer. Please can you connect me to number three-five-three-six. And then it's kiss my overburdened conscience! All too easy, Tess. Drink up and we'll go back and you can make us those omelettes, eh?"

"Only on condition you'll promise to come to the police tomorrow."

Ponderously he formed the word *no* and then whispered it.

"I'll go home then."

"You won't get a cab."

"I'll walk."

He waved her goodnight, swiped an abandoned evening paper off the neighbouring table, and settled to read it as if she had already gone.

She went to the door and stared out at fog so thick she wondered if she could even manage the hundred yards to Tite Street, let alone the miles between here and Westminster.

She returned to him. "I'll plague you all night until you agree," she warned.

He smiled. "If that's sauce for the gander, I'm your goose."

They finished their stout and went back to his studio; she made the omelettes, he cut the bread and cheese; they finished the white burgundy, too.

"I'm sure Oscar'll be at home tonight. You know he lives only a few doors away? Shall we call on him?"

"I don't think so."

"He's greatly taken with you."

"With a female? I thought he was the other way."

Dante rolled his head in his hands. "Oh, woman, woman! You're a holy terror with your categories. The 'other' way! That's got poor old Oscar neatly trussed, what? He's one of the 'others'! Little Segal, too – what's he? A 'murderer'! Like any backstreet ruffian with a knife. Never mind that he's probably one of the great artists of all time – the world will never forget these 'crimes' of his, you know. You might as well call me an 'illustrator'."

Already her head was swimming with his arguments. She could see all the errors in them, but each one slipped away as she tried to grasp it. "How can you not call him a murderer?" she asked.

"Because he's an artist of murder – and the artist is the important part. Not his medium. In the end, his medium is of no significance at all. One can be an artist at *anything*. The whole purpose of art is to banish these fearful conceptual nets you keep throwing over human activities. This goes in that box, this goes in that one. . . You're at it all the time, woman. You kill the human spirit. How has your own genius survived at all? I'm sure I can't explain. It must be some mighty force, that's all I can say. Just think how great it would be if you didn't spend all your days

258

digging in your heels and saying no and trying to get the panthers back on their golden chains! You'd roar through this age, Tess. You'd roar through history!''

All certainties dissolved. She saw his truths ranged beside hers and could no longer choose between them. All possible statements were equally and simultaneously true.

"If you don't want to call on Oscar – and he could tell you these things so much more clearly than I can – will you strip off and let me paint you?''

"No."

"There you go again." He sighed. "What then? You promised me no peace until I saw your point of view. What I forgot to tell you was that I already understand your point of view. I saw it in my gilded youth when all the world was one last rose of summer. I'm a hundred years beyond it now. I've come back to fetch you – one of the few other spirits of this age who can possibly make that journey in" – he pulled out his watch and looked at it – "the next eight hours." He put the watch back and smiled at her, his most engaging smile. "What d'you say, Tess? Don't you *want* to understand? A window in your life is slipping past a window in mine. Tomorrow the opening won't be there any longer – just a blank wall. This is the first and last chance in your life to make that century-leap in understanding. What about it? Surely the prospect entices you?''

She nodded.

"You're a free agent, of course," he reminded her. "That means you're equally free to retreat. That would be the *comfortable* thing to do.''

She lowered her eyes.

"Come to bed." He held out his hand.

Its touch was an ancient magic.

The fog had banished the world; they were its first, last, and only children, naked, reinventing Eden.

"What about some opium?" she asked.

"Tonight we have the greatest narcotic, the greatest stimulant, the greatest aphrodisiac of all – the naked truth!''

He went out to his studio and returned with two lamps. Their light shone warmly, softly, on his nakedness, making his body seem more gemlike to her than ever. There was a sketchbook under his arm; on the cover of the sketchbook there was blood.

He put it down in front of her and then climbed over the bed and lay down behind her, behind and a little below. As soon as he was against her she felt his excitement grow. She made to open the book but his hand came round and stopped her. "I'll show you," he said.

With his thumb he furled the lower corner of the cover, as if he were going to open it; but he paused and said, "Tell me what you think of Dr. Segal."

"I hate him."

"Tell me everything, Tess."

"I'm afraid of him."

"Is it only him you're afraid of, or does he make you afraid of something in yourself, too?"

Thickly she said, "Something in myself."

"Tell me about that. What are you afraid of in yourself?"

She began to sweat. He was now completely stiff; she lifted her thigh to let him in. As he expanded her he said, "It's the night for truth, remember."

"You know how when you take opium you can feel you're two people at the same time?"

"Can you?"

"That's how I feel anyway. Well, that night down at Olympus – it wasn't so clear – not as clear as with opium – but I felt I sort of divided into two people, and one of me was maddened by the pain and desperate to find somewhere to hide from it. But the other half . . ." She couldn't find the exact words.

"Enjoyed it?" he suggested.

"Not really. She connived at it. She took part. She almost saw it all from his point of view."

"Why d'you say 'she'?"

"I daren't think it was me." She wriggled her hips. "Move in me. Pleasure me."

He put a hand to still her. "Tess! Did you hear yourself? You 'didn't dare think it was you'! What a confession! All your failure lies there, enshrined in that one statement. You didn't dare! You discover there's part of you that can make a leap of the imagination far beyond the ordinary. In the midst of being tortured you can *become* your torturer. You have the power to leap from soul to soul, from woman to man, from victim to master – and how do you treat this stupendous power? You

260

didn't dare think it was you! In the same way you painted over some of the masterpieces of this century – because you believed you could 'paint a lot better than that'! Lie still, damn you.''

"Don't you want to pleasure?"

"Not the old way. Tonight we eat of the tree of knowledge, not sensation. It'll give us an orgasm to rock the gods in their heaven. Did you hear what I was saying just now?"

"Yes."

"And?"

"Everything you say can sound like the truth. I can't judge the truth any more.''

"What's happened is that the old half-truths by which you've guided your life up until now can no longer match that primal power in you. They've brought you so far and now you begin to rise above them. You've just set foot upon that magic level where all you do is right. All you say is true. Two and two makes five – that's true up here. Two and two makes nothing – that's also true. Simultaneously! In eternity everything is simultaneous. The birth and death of the universe occupy the same moment, and all that goes between. Everything coexists – you and your tormentor. You coalesce. You become the same. Oh Tess – you actually made that transition! And then you threw it away because, like any stupid little schoolgirl, you were frightened by a bit of pain!''

"You make me sound so . . ."

He calmly opened the sketchbook.

The first page showed Mary-Ann Nichols with all her mutilations. "D'you think *she* made that transition?" Dante asked. "Was Segal artist enough to achieve with that common clay the miracle he wrought on you that night at Olympus?"

She noted every detail of the drawing – even to the fact that Polly Nichols was wearing the same dress as she had worn that afternoon in the refuge. Nothing had any meaning now. She hardly even felt her own body.

Segal cutting out her uterus.

"Did you draw all these at the time?"

He laughed. "How could I? I was holding the lantern."

"They're **very** good drawings."

Dante's own hands arranging the brass rings at her feet.

He chuckled. "We've got them scared witless. The people are

261

in terror. Their governors in fear. They think it's Masons, of course. Segal's a genius – he thought it all out. They'll never be able to act against us.''

''They're like Rembrandt's flayed ox,'' she said. ''Or his anatomy lectures.''

Annie Siffey, guts over her shoulder. Legs up and a little apart. She could almost feel what it would be like.

Dante began to shiver. ''Genius! Pure genius! Did you see how poor Sir Charles Warren came tumbling down east, like a shot off a shovel, to wipe out the writing on the wall!'' He was trembling now. ''Genius!''

Sir Frederic Leighton leaned over them. She was not surprised to see him. Everything coexisted now. ''I like the way you've handled the tone and local colour in this one,'' he said genially. ''You've got darks within darks within darks. They're very rich.''

Dante didn't even thank him.

''He's an artist,'' Tessa felt she had to explain. ''He takes no part in the actual murders. He merely observes.''

''I observe!'' Dante laughed. ''I observe that Sickert thinks Dieppe's the whole of France!'' He was tortured with lying still in her. ''You turn the next page,'' he told her.

The double murders. The wrong Kelly, flesh and all out.

''Aaaaaaaah!'' Dante pumped and pumped himself into her. She felt it happening. Nothing more.

She found her way back to the Embankment, more easily this second time. Why hadn't she realized before how easy it would be? She hadn't wanted to! She giggled. All you had to do was go along the Embankment, keep the Thames at your right, and you'd arrive in Westminster sooner or later.

''You all right, miss?''

''Yes, thank you, officer. She knows this part of the Embankment very well. She'll soon be home.''

''Er . . . she?''

''Yes,'' Tessa laughed. ''Who d'you imagine you're talking to?''

''I see. Of course, miss. D'you mind if I accompany you?''

''There's really no need, you know. But why not? She's fond of a bit of company.''

Her fifteenth policeman sat beside her in the Black Maria, with the sixteenth walking on the kerb outside, holding a lantern, all the way up Shepherdess Walk to the Old Vicarage.

There was a muted conversation at the door. Then Bo came running out. "Oh Tessa, my dear. Such a night! Where were you?"

"She couldn't get a cab. She had to walk."

"Oh, my dear! Mr. Liddington went out looking for you – to Scotland Yard."

"She telephoned there. It's all right."

"Come away inside. We'll soon have you nice and warm and snug in bed. Poor child!"

Our Father which art in heav'n . . .

And Gobless Mummy and Gobless daddy and Gobless little Sukey . . .

You're rushing it again, child. Start at the beginning and say it properly.

G o d   b l e s s . . .

And there's no need to say it so slowly now!

Her room heaved. The ancient spars and timbers cracked in the gale. The old galleon rode out the river storm. There was old Magwitch in chains. Blood dripped on her – she closed the pages of the sketchbook and blood squeezed out from between the pages. She had to swim to the safety of Bo's room, across the shark-infested floor. She giggled. She knew it was a game, really, but the most real game she'd ever played. Bo would explain things to her.

A bright tranquil moon shone through the great stained-glass window. Where was the gale? Where the fog? This was her home. Here she was born. Here she had survived the unforgettable, forgotten terrors of childhood. Here she was safe.

Bo's door was an inch or two ajar. It opened with a sigh on oiled hinges. Tessa's shadow slipped across the uncreaking floor. The hand in her mind was already lifting the sheets. The body in her mind was already creeping in as she used to when this was her mother's bed.

There was a break in her vision. Her real hand and body could not follow. Another body was already there. Two Bos? Her mother and Bo? What year was this? Her *father* and Bo! Side by wrinkled side, smelling of soap and peppermints and eucalyptus oil and bay rum.

263

She remembered a child, herself, as remote as history. She and that child chattered desperately – of anything . . . anything – as they climbed back between her cold, deserted sheets. She clutched the child to her, a pillow. She stuck her thumb into her mouth and rocked her child and wept soft cool unimportant tears until she was fast asleep.

She awoke next morning, herself again, cold and stiff. She was sore behind her eyes, sore in the muscles of her throat, stiff in her back, and . . . and her legs had gone to sleep.

She rolled over to ease the ache in her back. Her legs didn't follow. They must be wound up in her sheets. The sheets must have cut off the blood supply. She reached down to unravel them. She touched where her thighs were – or ought to be – but all she could find was the pillow. What was the pillow doing *there*? Also it felt too hard – like someone else.

It *was* someone else!

But how could someone else be where her own thighs ought to be? And where had her thighs gone? Heart in mouth, she raised the sheet, ready to slam it down again if she saw something dreadful.

What?

Anything. It could be anything. She didn't want to think about what it could be.

She looked. She did not slam down the sheet. It slipped from her grasp and settled silently on . . .

On mystery.

There was nothing in the bed that shouldn't be there. Her own two thighs in her own cambric nightgown lay on her own goosedown mattress – exactly where they ought to be.

She had wet the bed during the night.

She had no sensation whatever below the level of her navel. Instinctively her hand went back between her thighs. It was all quite dead.

When Bo came to see how Tessa was this fine morning, she found her niece lying frantic on the floor, trying to pull herself back up by the mattress cover; all the rest of the bedding lay in havoc around her.

"Why Tess, whatever is the matter?" she cried.

The little girl looked up at her. "Oh Aunty Bo – she's lost half of herself!" she howled.

Chapter Thirty-Six

"You forgot – I'm a doctor too," Simon argued.

"But a doctor of archaeology," the Rev. d'Arblay began, "is hardly . . ."

"For the love of God!" Simon exploded. "Forgive me, sir, but I am in fact a medical doctor – a qualified medical doctor."

"As well? What a . . ."

"You can't have practised much," Bo pointed out.

He nodded unhappily. "That's true. And yet in my training I did come across just such a case as this. A girl whose hand became paralysed when she was about to marry a much . . ."

"But Tessa wasn't about to marry," her father pointed out. "And anyway, it's her legs, isn't it?"

"That isn't the point, sir. The point is she, too, faced an intolerable . . ."

"I'm sorry to hear you think marriage is beside the point, Simon," Bo told him. "I assure you that for a young, unmarried woman, it's very much . . ."

"It's beside *this* point, Mrs. Fletcher. I'm trying to tell you about the hysterical response to an intolerable . . ."

"Hysterical you call it? I see nothing hysterical in that young madam. She's as calm as alabaster. If anyone's entitled to feel hysterical, I am. I'm the one who . . ."

"I'm not talking about hysterics, Mrs. Fletcher. That's an entirely different – oh look, forget I said the word. The point I'm trying to make is that there is a certain *mental* response – the mind responds in a certain way to intolerable pressure. There's a breaking point that . . ."

"Did you try a good smack?" the Rev. d'Arblay asked. "That always used to have a most salutary effect. I remember once when she went bowling hoops with . . ."

"She wouldn't feel it, Gordon dear. She's got no feeling below her waist – or so she *says*."

" . . . she was *roundly* smacked for it!" He chuckled. "Bowling

265

hoops, you see.''

''Very amusing!'' Bo turned to Simon with a let-us-two-grownups-sort-this-out grimace. ''What is your suggestion, Doctor Simon? What did you do with this other young lady?''

''Well they tried all the usual treatments – cold water. . . incarceration among strangers. . . hearty meals and massage. . .''

Bo's eyebrows shot up at that. ''Massage?''

''Nothing worked.''

''Therefore?''

Simon scratched his head diffidently. ''I don't want to claim I cured her or anything like that. All I did was sit beside her and talk and let her talk, and talk, and talk. . .. And in the end she woke up one morning and the paralysis had gone. All the doctors said it would have cleared up anyway – as, of course, these things usually do. But they don't always. And with a strong-willed young woman like Miss d'Arblay. . . Anyway, what I'd like to propose is I'd like to sit and talk to her, and let her talk for as many. . .''

Bo glanced uncertainly at her brother-in-law. ''What d'you think, Gordon dear?''

''I'm for any course of action that works. She lies up there, happy as a sandgirl, eating her head off, and it's disrupting the whole household. Do whatever you think best. Why don't you marry her, Liddington? That might cure her. At least she'd be your problem then and you could do whatever you liked about her.''

''Thank you, sir. I'll go to her at once.''

When he reached the half-landing the Rev. d'Arblay called after him, ''And tell her it has my blessing, my boy! Whatever you decide to do. Carte blanche.''

Simon paused at the door and said a brief prayer. He put on a smile and gave a gentle knock.

''Come in,'' she called.

As he came to her bedside he asked, ''And how old are you today, Tess?''

She pulled a face. ''Twenty-four – and the joke's wearing thin.''

''I'm glad it's a joke now. It seemed quite serious at the time.'' He drew up a chair and sat astride it, the wrong way round,

266

leaning on the back of it, staring intently at her. "Perhaps all of this will seem a joke soon."

"Did she really behave like a little child?"

He nodded.

"It's hard to understand. But then" – she waved a hand at her legs – "she doesn't understand this, either."

"Could it be all part of the same thing, Tess?"

She appeared not to hear him. She looked around the room. "Oh – did you get her those roses, my dear? They're heavenly."

His nod was tighter. "D'you think your childish behaviour and your paralysis are part of the same thing?" he repeated.

She gave a trapped little shrug. "She told you. She doesn't understand it."

"D'you know why you're talking about yourself as a third person? She does this. . . she does that. . ."

"There was a reason. Someone told her it." She scratched her head in vexation. "It's so vague. There's a whole foggy part there. It was fog. . . and windows passing each other in the night – a window in her life. She explained it then." Tessa laughed at her own stupidity. "A silly dream. It must have been."

"D'you understand why you're taking it so calmly? You aren't nearly so upset by what has happened as one might expect. Indeed, at times you're quite cheerful."

"Of course she's upset." She tried to look upset but then burst into laughter. "Except you're so solemn. Your face is very funny when you go all solemn, you know."

"Flowers. . . my face. . . what are you going to do when you run out of distractions, Tess? Is it possible you might even answer my question? It's a very simple question, after all."

"You're wasting your time. She hasn't the faintest idea what you're talking about."

He didn't respond. She looked at him. She looked away. She straightened her coverlet. "You shouldn't be alone with her," she said. "Men and women together. She was repeatedly chaste."

"Are you saying 'chaste' or 'chased'?"

"*C'est défendu*. Do what thou wilt."

She pulled the sheet up tightly and smoothed that, too. She tried to hum a tune. "She knows you're only trying to make her speak." She hummed some more. "What d'you want her to

267

say?''

"The truth. Talk to me about being paralysed. Try and get me to feel what it's like.''

"What d'you *think* it's like! Use your imagination.''

"Can you remember the moment when you first realized it had happened to you? Tell me what that was like.''

She stared out of the window a long time. He hardly dared to breathe. "There's her studio!'' she said with an air of great discovery. "She'd forgotten all about being a painter. Good heavens! How could she forget that? There are all sorts of things . . . flat colours, for instance. Tricks to steal from the Japanese.''

"Had you forgotten about working in the theatre? Or Saunders – d'you remember Saunders.''

She nodded. "She knows you think she's going off her head, Simon. She can remember all that. Dante Rosen . . . Segal . . . the murders . . . all that! She'd just forgotten about painting. That's all. It's nothing to make a great song and . . .''

"What d'you remember about Dante Rosen?''

"If you really want to help – *do* you really want to help?''

"Of course.''

"Then d'you think you might slip over there and bring back some of her sketching things? Like an angel?''

"Later. Tell me what you remember about . . .''

"No, now! The light will go. She could sit and sketch you while you ask her all these stupid . . .''

"Tell me what you remember about Dante Rosen.''

A crafty look flitted across her face. "His voice,'' she said. "His w o n d e r f u l voice. His b e a u t i f u l eyes. His m a r v e l l o u s hands!''

"What makes his hands so marvellous, Tess?''

She giggled, then, remembering herself, became serious again. "He paints with them, Simon. One of his paintings can earn as much as your stipends would bring you in five years. What d'you say to that? Don't you think it's m a r v e l l o u s?''

"What else do you remember about him?''

And so he went on, relentlessly pressing her to talk, winkling her out of her silences, enduring her sheathed insults, hauling her back from her detours. Sheepdoglike he circled her and lay in wait where she could see him, and cut her off, and feigned attack . . . until he had her at the open mouth of the fold.

Then his whole manner changed. He appeared to lose interest in their conversation. He took her pulse, noted the hammering of her heart, and asked, "Which of your drawing materials did you want me to fetch?"

Her relief was so great he wondered she could not see it herself – and draw the appropriate conclusions. He had no idea whether or not he had done right in breaking off his inquisition there. It was simply an intuitive feeling that she might be more cooperative next time if she felt it was always going to be safe and he was never going to drive her into a trap.

The following day he thought he must have been wrong. All he had done was train her to be far more adroit at evading the thrust of his questions.

And so it went for several days. Trying to reach into her mind and grasp her problem was like fishing for a cake of soap in near-boiling water. It struck him that he might have more success if she weren't here, in her childhood home. Too many ghosts. *Thou oh God seest all* – the invisible frieze on every wall.

He expected an argument about moving her, from Bo at least. Her agreement surprised him. The resistance came from Tessa herself. She behaved as if he were threatening her life. He hoped it was a good sign.

Late one afternoon he carried her down to a cab and drove her over to the Davitt-Saunders apartment in Berners Street. Saunders was at a matinée. As Tessa had said, she healed quickly. But there were still half a dozen locks on the door.

Tessa lay sullenly in her new bed, glowering up at him. He wondered if he had, after all, done the right thing.

"For days now," he said, "you've resisted telling me anything about Dante Rosen. Today, I hope. . ."

"You want to hear about Dante Rosen?" It was almost a snarl. "Very well – I'll tell you. Dante Rosen is an artist. Dante Rosen is a free agent. Dante Rosen is one of the unacknowledged legislators of the world. You're not fit to touch the hem of his raiment."

Simon hid his delight. "Welcome back, Tess," he said.

She appeared not to understand. "I know what you really want to find out, Dr. Liddington! You don't deceive me."

"What's that?"

"You want to know did Dante Rosen ever fuck me! There!"

He watched her breathing defiantly. The pupils of her eyes were huge; he thought she had never looked so lovely. He mastered himself and asked, "And did he?"

"He did," she snapped. But his outward calm had robbed her fire.

"How many times?"

"Every night. Ten times a night."

"Ten?"

His scepticism stung. "I lost count," she taunted. "We fucked standing, we fucked kneeling, we fucked lying down, we fucked on top and underneath and sideways. From the back and the front. And . . ." His impassive face infuriated her. "There's more. D'you want to hear more."

"I want to hear everything – if you want to tell me."

"Oh don't worry about what I want! Don't worry about me. I'll bet you don't know that Saunders has a sister called Pol. I'll bet you don't know about Pol's house in High Holborn. You've carried your compassion like a begging bowl into every low *casa* in Whitechapel, but Pol's kaffir would take one look at you and throw you out on your ear. Pol's house is only for fine gentlemen. But I'm allowed in! There now! Me and Dante. We smoked opium and I don't know what else. I whored there for him. I spread the gentlemen's relish. Miss Discipline, they called me. I whipped gentlemen to fletters while . . . and I lay with a goat – I mean a bear. And wild, hairy men . . ." She gave up for lack of breath, and because her voice was breaking up, and because her imagination was drying.

"When you and Dante . . . fuck . . ."

"Don't say that word. I hate it! We don't call it that."

"What then?"

"We call it . . ." Her voice was now all over the place. Her face was bloodless. Her whole body was shuddering – including, he noticed, her legs.

"You call it what?" he pressed.

"Pleasuring." That was the word in her mind, but it came out as a series of bitter sobs. She went on trying to say the word, and the sobs went on tripping it up and burying it. In the end she yielded and the tears overwhelmed her. He sat beside her and let her cry, and cry, and cry . . . until it petered out in reflex little sobs. Soon their sharpness dwindled to mere sighs. And then the

calm rise and fall of her breathing reasserted itself. "Oh Simon."
There was a rough saltiness to the words. "I deserve everything,
don't I. This paralysis is God's righteous punishment on me."

"That's what I really want to talk about." He smiled.
"Tomorrow? May I come back and talk with you again
tomorrow?"

"Don't lie to me! You just want to get away and never come
back. I've disgusted you."

He put a finger under her chin. She looked up at him, a child
expecting a slap. He leaned over and kissed her so gently she
hardly felt the touch of their lips.

"You still love me?" she breathed.

There were tears in *his* eyes now. "It overwhelms me, my
darling. I couldn't live without you."

"After what I said?"

He tried to gulp down the lump in his throat. He touched the
tip of her nose. "You think you're the only one to have such
fantasies?"

Saunders returned soon after. "Some people have all the
luck," she said. "You ought to get out and about a bit, d'Arblay
me old duck. Blow away the spiders."

"It may have escaped your notice. . .," Tessa began.

"I know what – come to the theatre! You can have the royal
box. You and Mr. Liddington. He hasn't seen me in *Sheba* yet has
he? Be a bit of a treat for him, too."

Tessa laughed. "Suddenly all is clear! Very well, Saunders.
What about tomorrow night? If he's free, which I imagine he will
be."

And so it was arranged.

When he came, rather late the following day, she tried to
reassert her control. "Sit!" she said, smiling sweetly. Then:
"You may kiss me." And, when he had done so: "First question
please!"

"No questions today, Tess. They'll have to keep. Oh what a
time I've had of it!"

"Before you start – we're going to the theatre tonight.
We're. . ."

"I know. I met Miss Saunders. That's one of the things. . .
but I'll have to meet you at the theatre. I've neglected my parish
duties so. . . Anyway. . ."

271

"Take a breath. Sit down. Take another. And begin at the beginning."

"What a day!" He took off his jacket, reversed the chair, and straddled it. "I went to see Dante Rosen.

She froze.

"I went to his place in Chelsea. But his cleaning lady told me he's gone away for a couple of weeks. To France, she thought. So I left him a note, which he'll read when he comes back – telling him all our fears concerning Segal – I probably exposed myself to a dozen actions for libel! And then I thought, hang it all – in for a lamb, in for a sheep . . ." He gave a puzzled frown. "Something not quite right there . . ."

"You've caught the Saunders habit!" Her laugh was nervous.

"Quite right! I was with her this afternoon. But I'm coming to that. Anyway, I thought to myself – why not go and see this Segal fellow in person! What harm can he do me? Only throw me out."

"Simon! You didn't!"

He nodded. "And as you'll observe – I'm unscathed. Anyway, I went to see Miss Saunders, remembering you once told me she'd worked in the Segal household. And she took me to meet his cook, a Mrs. Hamble, a widow, very pleasant, who has a couple of hours off each afternoon and usually goes up and sits in one of the quadrangles in Bart's – which is where we found her. Most interesting!"

"I wish you hadn't, Simon. I don't want to have any more to do with all that."

"D'you want me to go on?"

She shrugged.

"I thought it would set your mind at rest. We can't make the police understand it was Segal – but at least we can frighten him so much he'll stop. Marie Kelly has to come back some time."

There was something in the back of her mind about Marie Kelly. She couldn't remember.

"But listen," he went on, "we're not the only ones to suspect Dr. Segal. One of the maids noticed he was out on both the nights of the first two murders. So then they took turns to watch his comings and goings. Nothing unusual until the night of the double murder, when, once again, he was late! He came back at a quarter to three that morning, in a carriage none of them had ever seen before. Or since. This strange carriage went directly to the mews, where he got out and ran upstairs to his surgery in great haste. The carriage went on at once. He spent half an hour up there, with the blinds drawn, before he came over to the house and went to bed – where he slept until late the following afternoon.''

"Has any of them gone to the police?''

Simon pulled a face. "Of course. I suppose Segal's name is now in a list of about ten thousand others. Ever since the City Force put up that reward, the names have been coming in like flies. But that wasn't all. Listen to this! One of the maids said she'd noticed a disgusting smell – she thought it was a dead rat – in that Masonic room of his. You know the one? Miss Saunders told me she'd showed you around in there.''

Tessa nodded.

"Well, when she told her master about it he flew into a towering rage and threatened to dismiss her and I don't know what else. Then he kept some incense constantly burning there until late that night. The following morning the smell had gone. That was the day before yesterday. I suppose you've not seen today's papers?''

She shook her head. He took out the latest *Gazette*. One of the news items stated that a Mr. Lusk, Chairman of the Whitechapel Vigilance Committee, had received a parcel containing part of a human kidney in an advanced state of putrefaction; the accompanying letter, sent "from hell,'' claimed to be from the Whitechapel Murderer, who said he had cut it from one of his victims.

"Catch me when you can, Mr. Lusk!'' the note concluded.

"That was about forty coincidences too many for my stomach,'' Simon told her.

"What did you do?''

"I had to lie, I'm afraid – by implication, anyway. I waited for Segal to return home – that's why I'm late – and . . .''

"You didn't talk to him!''

"Talk and more. I told him I'd received confession – implying I'm R.C. may God and Canterbury forgive me! – which pointed strongly at his involvement in certain recent murders . . .''

"Simon! He might have killed you! He still might!''

"Well, I expected him to fly off the handle again, but not a bit of it. A milder-mannered little fellow you never saw. He said he'd

273

been a doctor for a long time and he knew precisely the sort of unfortunate, hysterical woman who lives under a compulsion to invent stories like that about men – always about men who attract them strongly. It's their way of bottling up emotions they otherwise have no means of handling . . . and so on. I must say, he made a most plausible case. He even told me that when I'd been a priest for as long as he'd been a doctor, I'd recognize the ailment at once and treat it with the outward sympathy and inward contempt it merits."

"You shouldn't have exposed yourself to such danger."

"I think I took care of that. I told him I'd left a sealed letter with the diocesan solicitor, to be opened in case of my unnatural death. It's been a day of lies, I fear – but all in a good cause. Above all, I wanted to set your mind at rest, darling."

She held out her hand for his. The touch of him was comforting.

"Don't you want to draw?" he asked. "I sent your things over."

She shook her head.

"D'you know you moved your legs yesterday?"

Her eyes went wide.

"When you got in such a lather. There was a decided twitch or two. How often do you try to move them?"

She stared at her legs beneath the counterpane. Her neck shivered with her concentration.

He squeezed her hand. "It'll come."

"D'you mean it's not real? There's nothing really wrong with them?"

His eyes held her. "There's no physical reason why you shouldn't walk."

"I'm not inventing it, you know."

"Not you. Something inside you is. *She* is. It's not rare – this kind of paralysis. I'd say you're one of several dozen in London at this moment."

"Did you ever come across it before?"

"Once. A young girl who was about to marry a man she didn't particularly care for. Her hand became paralyzed. I often wondered about that – her *hand*, you see."

Tessa didn't see.

"Well, her father was about to give her *hand* in marriage. So

274

some secret part of her said, 'Give it for all I care. It's useless, anyway!' She sort of cut it off, made it not-part of her.''

Tessa pulled a face. ''That's a bit farfetched.''

''Probably.'' He took the newspaper back. ''But interesting, don't you think?''

''Anyway, it's nothing like that with me.''

''You'd know best about that.''

''No one's forcing me to do anything.''

He nodded.

''And one doesn't talk of giving *legs* in marriage.''

''No. You're right. Different case entirely.''

''Anyway, why would I want to make my legs not-part of me?''

He looked interested. ''Oh, it's only your legs now? Feeling's returned to the other parts has it?''

She withdrew her hand sharply. ''I thought you said you had parish duties?'' When he failed to respond she added, ''And you can wipe that smug smile off your face. I know you think you're being terribly clever. You and father are two of a kind with all your pat ideas. You ought to try living in the real world, where it's mostly twilight all the time.''

He rose and shrugged on his jacket. ''You're right! Too much idle chatter. I'll see you at the theatre.''

Chapter Thirty-Seven

''I have to go and open the inner door,'' Simon explained to the cabbie.

''Take your time, sir,'' he answered.

''I won't be two shakes,'' he told Tessa.

''Simon?''

He came back and poked his head inside the awning. ''Yes?''

''Thank you for a wonderful evening.''

''The pleasure was all mine.''

''Kiss me?''

275

"I'll only be gone . . . mmm."

Their lips met. She trembled.

"Won't be long," he said again.

She watched him crossing the broad foot-pavement and she knew the answer to her earlier question – one could indeed fall in love slowly.

No sooner was he out of sight than there were sounds of a struggle somewhere behind her. The cab swayed. People were fighting – either on the cab or hard against it.

"Oi!" she called out.

No one answered. The struggle quickly reached a climax.

"Simon!" she shouted.

There was a shout "Tjaaaaaah!" behind and above. Then the crack of a whip made the horse bolt in the direction of Oxford Street.

"Simon!"

In her last glimpse of Berners Street she saw him come dashing out of the apartment house. He spotted the runaway cab and set off in hot pursuit.

Taking the turn east into Oxford Street they almost ran down several pedestrians. The frightened horse began to slow up though the driver seemed to be making no effort to control him. One brave man dashed out to grasp the reins.

"Damn you, sir!" the driver cried and cut at him with his whip.

The driver was Dante Rosen. Tessa began to scream at passers-by for help.

At the corner of Perry's Place, a mere hundred yards from Berners Street, Dante reined down to a trot. A figure stole from the shadows and leaped up into the cab. Segal. She knew him by his smell – quite apart from the knife he now held against her, dangerously close in the swaying vehicle. "Stop that screaming," he shouted.

The cab had gathered speed again. Simon must still be in pursuit. They galloped on over St. Giles's, along the new extension of Oxford Street, where the busy shops gave way suddenly to a teeming rookery of slums on the south and, on the north, to the quiet, respectable, tree-lined squares and avenues of Bloomsbury. Traffic here was thinner. They went even faster.

"Where are you taking me?" she asked.

"To a feast."

"Dante!" she shouted.

He did not answer.

"I hope we don't lose that clever young man of yours behind us," Segal added. "I'd like to invite him too."

But somewhere around High Holborn, Simon must have lost them. That would have been about the limit of a running man's endurance. Unless, unseen by Dante, he had taken another cab.

She thought they might be going to stop at Pol's, but they swept on past, now at a fast trot. On over the viaduct they went and down into Newgate, to the City.

"Where's this feast being held?" she asked.

"Indoors." He had put the knife away.

She tried with all her might to move her legs. If only Simon were right! But there was not a flicker of a response there.

Once in the City they let the exhausted horse slow to a walk. She knew where they were going now – north to Finsbury Close.

"You've wasted your time," she told him. "I'm paralysed."

"What are you talking about?"

"From the waist down. I'm useless."

He took off his tiepin and jabbed her in the thigh. She felt nothing, of course. He burst into laughter.

He was still laughing when they arrived at the mews behind his house. Dante leaped down from the driver's dickey. He handed the whip to some unseen man, saying, "Lose it. Don't be long. Take it the other side of the artillery ground." He came around to the front, where he could see her. "Sorry if I frightened you, pet. Quite a thrill, what? Hop down." He held out his hands.

"The fates do conspire," Segal told him. "She's paralysed from the waist down. It rather changes things."

Dante's face came into the dark, near her. He gripped her thigh. She felt only the tug of the cloth at her waist. "Are you serious?"

"Try her with your tiepin," Segal said. "Not a spark."

"My my my! It *does* change things. Come on then, I'll have to lift you across. We're going in that other coach."

"Where did you vanish to?" she asked.

"What are you talking about?"

"When you ran away from the theatre that day."

He laid a hand upon her cheek. "Tess! We've gone about a

million miles beyond that – don't you remember? Tonight you join us in Elysium, the three great artists of our age. . . you remember. Anyway, it's for me to ask where *you* vanished to!''

"I? I didn't run away. I had to stay and finish the scenery."

"No! A fortnight ago – in Chelsea."

"I'm talking about four or five weeks ago. The day you ran away – when Gloab came into the theatre. I went to Chelsea that night and. . ."

"No! *Last* time you came. The night of the big fog."

She was silent.

"Have you forgotten?" he asked.

"I've never been to Chelsea when you've been there."

"Tess!"

"Never."

"So it's all wasted! You don't remember anything? All the planning. . . Tonight we're going to observe Segal at his most unkindest cut of all. And we'll be indoors. No need to hold the lantern. We can both draw it as it happens. We shall lift ourselves to immortality." He raised his hand and turned her face into a sliver of reflected gas-light. "Does none of this mean anything to you?"

"It sounds like the ravings of a madman. Take me back to. . ."

"You know that Segal is the Whitechapel Murderer? You haven't forgotten that, surely?"

"I don't want to think about all that any more."

He shook her useless legs. "Poor old thing. Well, we shall have to find some other part for you. If you aren't to be my greatest triumph, perhaps you can be Segal's. He still thinks of you as unfinished business, you know. One way or the other we'll have to get you there. Hup!" He hoisted her in his arms.

She drew breath to scream again. He dropped her back in the seat and put his hand over her mouth. "Please, Tess," he begged. "Please don't. Don't force us to stop you, eh? Segal has a scissors in there for snipping the vocal cords. It's horrible."

He hoisted her again and carried her across the cobbled yard to an as-yet unhorsed carriage beside the coach-house door. The third man set off to lose the stolen cab somewhere beyond the artillery ground.

She sat there a long time, alone and in silence. She knew she ought to be thinking about her predicament but her mind remained an almost wilful blank.

Segal opened the door, climbed in, and lit the lamp. Ignoring her, he upended a large black bag over the seat; there was a clatter of surgical implements. He began checking them – an amputating saw, scalpels, bistouries, catheters, eye probes, retractors, and catlings. One by one he wrapped them and returned them to the capacious black bag. Before he had quite finished, someone – the third man presumably – backed a horse between the shafts.

Dante helped him with the harness and then climbed in, seating himself opposite her. Her arms ached from keeping herself upright. He turned down the lamp and gave a knock with his cane against the roof. The cab set off into the dark of the unlighted mews. They crossed a main thoroughfare, almost deserted at that hour, and plunged into a maze of cramped streets between low cliffs of tenements and courts. The meanness of the lighting, the drab sides of the buildings, the rough, cartworn paving – all told her they were heading into the East End, downhill into Whitechapel; the strong, sour smell of the poor was all around.

After about fifteen minutes they pulled to a halt. Dante held his arms out to her. "Can you edge yourself nearer the door?"

He lifted her out. Segal took a last look around inside the carriage and then told the driver to come back at five. The man clucked at his horse and pulled off into the darkness. Dante held her securely; she felt absurdly safe – insofar as she felt anything at all.

He surveyed the grimy façade of the tenement and gave a dour chuckle. "She's up there waiting for me. I'm the finest gentleman she's ever favoured. I won't be sorry!"

"Who?" she asked.

"You know who."

"Come on!" Segal said impatiently.

They stepped out across a broken foot-pavement and up a narrow alley, or it might have been a courtyard. Segal was hard behind, breathing like a badger.

Halfway along the alley she heard a change in the echo of their footfall. Dante turned left. By the sound of things they were now in a passage or hallway; dim slits of lamplight under doorways.

279

They went upstairs. "Is this the direct way?" Segal asked.

"No. There's another way. Also we can escape by the window in the last resort."

At the head of the stairs they came to a short passage with a door at the end. The light beneath the door was bright. Dante knocked gently. "'Tis I, my dove," he cooed.

There was a giggle from within.

He pushed open the door. The woman's smile turned to a frown when she saw Tessa in his arms and Segal behind. "'Ere, what's all this then?"

"We're *all* going to have fun, my angel. This is how the toffs do it, you know."

"All four? Together?" She was still dubious.

"As snug as bugs."

She laughed then and said after all she was only young once.

"In the midst of life . . ." Dante sighed. He kicked a drab wooden armchair close by the bed and set Tessa down in it.

All the while he spoke to the other woman, "You lie down on the bed, my dove. My friend here will arrange you to his satisfaction."

"Isn't it going to be with you?" She was full of disappointment.

"Impatient, impetuous, ardent creature! It's going to be with *all* of us!"

Giggling, the woman lay on the bed as Dante told her.

Segal put down his medical bag. The wrapped implements made no sound. "'Ere – what's in that?" the woman asked. She was beginning to grow suspicious.

"Things," Segal told her.

"What things?"

"Things to help increase our fun. You'll see." He took off his jacket and began to force loose his collar stud.

"What are you doing?" Dante asked.

"I must be naked. She must see she has no power over . . ."

"Too risky."

"But she must see."

"Just undo your fly. Expose yourself."

Reluctant to obey – or rather, to see the wisdom of Dante's suggestion – Segal struggled briefly with his stud before abandoning the effort; then he angrily undid his fly and exposed himself.

"'Ere, you're a man aren't you!" the woman said unconvincingly. She made a lacklustre grab at him and began to stroke and pull. Segal turned inquiringly to Dante. "For Christ's sake do something about it now," he said. "You promised me we'd do this one my way. You promised you'd help."

Dante sighed and went over to the woman. "Listen Marie," he said. He touched her brow. "You hear me?"

She stopped playing with Segal. "Of course I hear you, sir."

"Good. Lie down. Close your eyes now and listen. Hands at your sides. Now from this moment on, you will not be able to talk. You'll . . ."

"But whisper," Segal prompted him. "Make her able to whisper."

"Yes. You'll be able to whisper. You understand that?"

She whispered: "Of course I understand it, sir."

"Good. You're doing very well, my dove. Also, when I touch your forehead again, you won't be able to move. Not a . . ."

"Her face," Segal said angrily. "She must be able to move her face."

"You'll be able to move the muscles of your face, but that's all. You understand that, too?"

"Of course I understand that, too, sir," she whispered.

"Tell her she'll be able to feel everything," Segal insisted.

"You'll be able to feel everything, but not to move – except your face." Dante touched her brow. She stopped breathing. Segal was too busy testing her pain reflexes to notice. But Tessa, watching the whole thing in a dreamlike horror, saw it. "She's stopped breathing," she told them.

Dante laughed. "Listen Marie. You can breathe, too. You can breathe and move your face muscles – but that's all you can move."

The woman gulped huge draughts of air. "Well done, Tess," Dante said. "Nearly spoiled poor Segal's fun before it even started!"

Segal began to undo Marie Kelly's clothing, but he was over eager and his hands fumbled it. Angrily he got off the bed and took up his bag, tipping its contents over the threadbare carpet. He selected the curved bistoury and ripped her red linsey dress from navel to neck. The curve on the blade saved her flesh, as yet.

"Oh please, sir," she whispered hoarsely. "Please, please don't do no more. Stop this joking now, sir."

Segal laughed. "That whispering's very good, Rosen. I must thank you." He turned again to the woman. "Go on! Go on!"

Dante shook his head in a kind of contemptuous pity. He took out a small sketching block and began to draw. Then he seemed to remember Tessa. He looked over at her and said, "I'm so sorry, Tess, I forgot to introduce you. This is Marie Kelly."

At the top of her voice Tessa screamed, "Help! Murder! Police!"

Chapter Thirty-Eight

Quick as a cat, Dante seized up some of the bedlinen and threw it over her head, pulling it tight. It was the unwashed linen of an unwashed whore and her unwashed drunken guests. Tessa vomited. Dante made a wad of it and tore a strip to gag her. "That was stupid, Tess," he told her.

"Stupid Tess may get us hanged," Segal said. He was listening intently at the door. Marie Kelly's frightened eyes followed every move. Now she understood.

Dante was scornful. "I'd like a guinea for every cry of murder I've heard in these streets. Go back to your work you stupid old hen."

"Her arms aren't paralysed, you know. She'll pull that gag out, the first chance she gets."

"No, she knows much worse things could happen to her."

Segal listened at the door for a while longer before he returned to Marie Kelly. He leaned over her, looked deep into those rabbit eyes, and whispered, "My bride!"

"Please sir," she whispered, "if you must kill me, kill me quick. Don't do those things to me you done to poor Annie." Great tears rolled down her cheeks.

Segal furled her dress halfway up her thighs, which he then parted widely. He looked at the result critically. "Now," he asked the air. "Flay the feet first? Or resect the pubic arch? Or a little experimental laparotomy?" He looked at her head. "Or the eyes?"

"Turn up the lamp," Dante said, "and move it nearer her head."

Marie Kelly began to whisper Hail-Marys.

Tessa sat there, with the filth in her mouth, thinking horror could not run wider or deeper, knowing it had hardly begun. How could that blockade in her mind be lifted!

She prayed as never before. "Our Father . . ."

"Oh please . . . please . . . aaaaaah!" Marie Kelly whispered. There was blood now; Tessa could no longer look. She made a noise behind her mask.

"Oh dammit!" Dante said. "This is no use. I want to *talk* to you. Listen, Tess – you've seen there's no use in screaming. In these streets every drunken lout who comes home and starts to maul his wife about raises a cry of murder. I'm going to take the gag off you. But if you do try that screaming again, Segal will do the easy thing."

He loosened off the gag.

"I brought a sketchbook for you."

Tessa breathed free again. It occurred to her that a sketchbook might be her only way to leave a message.

The pleading whispers from Marie Kelly determined her. "Oh sir, it hurts so, it hurts me so."

"Very well," she said, feeling all the guilt of Judas.

"Can you see from there?" Dante asked. "Live skin appears to flay rather more easily than cadaveric."

She made a deliberate mess of her first drawing, tore it out angrily, rolled it into a ball, and threw it to the floor.

Dante retrieved it. "Mustn't leave evidence. We can't be sure the first man here will be a Mason." He unfurled it, looked at it critically, and gave it back to her. "It'll come," he said. "You'll do better."

She put the crumpled paper against the bottom of her sketchbook, not inside its cover. She made a little drawing of Segal's head. A good one. Dante came over and looked at it. "Didn't I tell you." He turned to Segal. "And didn't I tell you, too? We needed the feminine insight. We've concentrated too much on the physical. She's got your soul here."

Blood and Segal came near her while he looked and she tried not to cringe. He chuckled with pride.

Dante laughed. "You've got him, love! He's *my* masterpiece, too, though. What was this Segal before he met me? A Rough Ashlar – a little tuppenny-ha'penny medico. Hardly more than an Entered Apprentice. And now he ranks beside Caligula and he outshines the great Marquis! I've made him my Perfect Ashlar."

While he was so wrapped up in his achievements she wrote on a corner of the discarded drawing, "The murderers are Dante Rosen and Dr. Gwyllam Segal."

"And it's the same with you," Dante continued. "What were you? An unknown, unloved, unawakened, unaware little vicar's daughter – and yet you were also one of the great, undiscovered talents of our age! What would this night be without either of you?"

In the background Marie Kelly's whispered sobs and fragments of prayer were growing fainter.

Tessa added the time and date.

"Oscar and Poe and Dostoyevsky can only write about it. But I *do* it! My Segal will take his place in history tonight."

She signed it.

Marie Kelly's last words were, "Holy Mary. . ." After that she made only sighs and whimpers. Segal murmured endearments as he cut and hacked and slashed and sawed her dying body.

Dante drew intently, asking Segal to move aside every so often while he captured this or that small detail.

She sketched Dante. Buried within her was a past-Tessa who would always love him, who would remember only the lake in Victoria park. . . the bedroom in Golden Square. . . their little lover's home of a dressing room. That alternative, childlike Tessa would never understand this scene. There were other Tessas, too, buried within her and past the power of explanation. Curled-up children, the walking wounded of her still-young life, slumbering yet, but forever threatening to awaken and turn upon the one who had to live "up there," exposed to the real world, enduring its explanations, making sense of its lunacies.

What surgeon's knife, what chemist's balm could reach them now?

"How apt," Dante said, "that it was your story of the royal

marriage and the baby girl which began it all. It satisfies each of us. Segal achieves a revenge on the Masons that will leave them in disarray for generations. And you and I will establish forever the grandeur of artistic freedom. We set ourselves beyond the last prohibition.''

"But that story wasn't true," she pointed out. "It was nothing but tarts' gossip."

He laughed. "What is truth? It was *artistically* true. Nothing else matters. You should have seen Sickert's face when I told him the women were looking for a cool thou' from His Royal Highness! True or not, there was *something* in the story. And you may be sure the news went straight to Marlborough House and to Sir Charles Warren. So . . ."

"Rosen!" Segal interrupted him. "Make this stupid whore talk to me!"

"Don't interrupt me."

"She's stopped breathing. Make her breathe and talk again."

"She's stopped breathing because she's dead, you fool. You've killed her. Now get on with the rest of it."

But an angry Segal turned on him menacingly. "Then bring her back to life!"

"Don't be absurd."

Segal raised his bloodstained knife. Bits of flesh clung to his hands and sleeves. "Do it!"

"Listen Segal." Dante touched him on the shoulder. "You know what you have to do, don't you."

Segal was calm at once. "Of course I know what I have to do, Rosen."

"Then get on and do it as quick as you can, there's a good fellow." He smiled at Tessa. "My creation!"

Segal bent again over his victim. The corpse was now barely recognizable as human.

"The masterstroke was when we left those brass rings at the feet of that first woman, Polly Nichols. We wrote on the map of Darkest Whitechapel, 'Here be Freemasons!' Can you imagine the flutter in all the Masonic dovecotes? All the grand Masters in England, with His Royal Highness at their head – every time they open a Grand Royal Arch Chapter they prance around like schoolboys, ritually disembowelling the three Juwes. And now here it is in real life! And who's the victim? Someone who's threatening blackmail against the Great I-Am of the whole brotherhood. And the same with the second murder . . . and the third! Lordy lordy lordy!'' He giggled. ''Is this a Masonic killing, they must have asked themselves? Are some members of the Mystery taking the law into their own hands – as, indeed, the Teaching entitles them to once they have passed beyond the Third Degree? And, listen angel, shall I tell you the beauty of it?''

''Tell me.''

''*They still don't know!* And what's more, they never will. They'd much rather see these murders go unsolved than run Slippery Jack to ground, in case he proves to be a Brother. After all – who's getting hurt? Four tarts who deserve every cut. Your little story, darling, purchased our immunity.''

''You're ill, Dante my dear. You must . . .''

''You're the one who's ill, angel. You can't even walk. But I'm a free spirit. I'm an artist – a pure working.''

''You're going to kill me, aren't you. Or Segal is. I know.''

''I promise you I'm not. You're my creation. I have too much confidence in you. No – you'll take up your bed and walk out of here as free as me.''

''I'll tell the police.''

He laughed. ''Again?''

Anger and frustration pricked behind her eyelids.

''No, angel,'' he said. ''The Masons will deal with this in their own way.'' He turned to Segal. ''Listen Segal – until I say 'have you finished?' you won't hear anything I say or anything Miss d'Arblay may say. D'you understand?''

''Of course I understand, Rosen.''

Dante turned back to Tessa. ''Alone at last!'' He grinned. ''What happened when you first went to see Sir William Gull, eh? When you took him the photo that friend Segal here had so injudiciously used for his post-mortem on Peter Laird? (Laird died of an opium-induced heart attack, by the way – not that it matters now). When you showed Sir William that photograph, did he go to the police – which was the only proper course? Not a bit of it! That isn't a Mason's instinct, you see. Close ranks! Deal with the villain ourselves! That's their way. That's what they'll do now.'' He nodded at Segal's busy back. ''They'll deal with the poor old fellow.''

''How?''

"In their civilized way, of course. This ritual-murder stuff is just a comic pantomime to them nowadays. They'll get him locked away quietly in some private asylum for the rest of his life. He's quite obviously insane. Have you ever seen a clearer case?"

"Yes. As a matter of fact."

He laughed. "Oh Tess! You've got courage. We're going on to greatness, you and I. . ."

A saw going through live bone buried in flesh makes a ghoulish noise. There was a crack as some final shard splintered. Segal was out of breath. "There!" he said.

"Have you finished?" Dante asked.

"All but. Just put the brass rings at her feet."

Dante dug them out of his pocket and winked at Tessa. "I'm best man tonight."

They put the two brass rings at the feet of the corpse. "My Master Piece!" Dante said.

Segal began to collect the implements, several of which had fallen to the floor. Dante went on looking at the corpse. "The horror. . ." he whispered to himself. "The horror. . ."

While he was distracted, Tessa slipped her message beneath the moth-eaten cushion on which she sat. She made one supreme effort to shock her limbs into life. She put her hands firmly on the armrests of her chair and then, leaning forward, hurled herself into an upright stance.

The horrified faces of the two men.

For a moment she thought she had found the trick. She swayed. But then her knees sagged under her and she collapsed once again, a helpless mound on the floor. There was a bloodstained knife right before her face. She grasped it and lashed out, catching Segal in his calf. He cursed. His blood welled darkly. She made another stab, this time at Dante. But he stamped on her arm. The knife cut a light nick in the glossy patent leather of his shoe and then bounced away somewhere behind her.

She waited for them to murder her and go.

Dante stepped over her, picked up the knife, and dropped it into the bag. Segal was twisting a tourniquet below his knee, made from the gag Tessa had been forced to wear.

"I'll kill her," Segal said.

"No you will not. Hurry up at that. Jubelum will be back with

287

our carriage in three minutes.''

He bent over her. ''Listen, Tess – you're a free agent. You're an artist. You're free of the world. Free of its morality. Free of *me*, even! You're free, Tess, my angel.''

She lay like a stone. The last sounds of their departure dwindled and died.

Free!

The coach halted outside. Its door opened and slammed. It moved away up the street.

She lay on the floor, out of sight of the corpse, knowing she was free. She did not want to be free. She did not want to face freedom.

Test your legs!

NO!

You can move them now.

NO!

You're free of him.

NO!

Free.

She stirred. Pain was first to return. Her feet moved painfully beneath her. They took a little of her weight. The pain grew. Up on one elbow. Pressure on a knee . . . it was like learning from a textbook how to stand.

More pain. Onto the knee, onto both knees. Pain took away her breath.

When she stood she mustn't be able to see the corpse.

Still more pain as she swivelled around. On all fours, like the beasts of the field. Less pain – or all life a pain. Dulled to it. On one ankle. Tolerable. Foot under her. Push. Is this how it's done?

Pins and needles! Lemonade in the veins – laughter-pain. Stop me! Stop! Starbursts in my toes. Roman candles along my calves. Push!

Push!

She had her hand on the doorhandle when she knew she'd have to turn and look. Nothing would be worse than the vision her imagination would serve up hereafter. She closed her eyes and turned.

And opened them. It was appalling.

Innate sympathy impelled her forward. She had a vague notion she might put the pieces back together, but in the end she could not bring herself to touch them. One of the corpse's eyes was still open. She closed it. Then she stooped and kissed the woman's brow, which was unmarked. No words occurred to Tessa but there was a promise made.

Her final act was to remove the two brass rings. She put them in her sketchbook. The message remained below the cushion.

The room was chill. The landing outside, cold. The passageway below, freezing. When she reached the street she thought it looked vaguely familiar. She ran to the nearest streetlamp. Dorset Street, not too far from Long Liz's former lodgings.

What chance had they – any of those women? With all of London's hundred-square-miles to hide in, their poverty and ignorance had kept them pinioned here in these few mean streets, fish in a rain butt.

Long she stood beneath that lamp. A man approached her. "'Ello ducks. Cold morning. Come down the Britannia for a nip of grog?"

He was covered in blood. He laughed. "It's from the abattoir, love. I work in the abattoir. I know who you thought I was!"

There were no words.

"No?" the man asked.

She shook her head. A cab entered the street from the Spitalfields end.

He shrugged. "Suit yourself, of course. But I'd not hang about."

His footfall dwindled. The cab passed her. The door was flung wide suddenly and Simon leaped out. "Tess!"

All her life she had stood there waiting for this moment. He threw his arms around her. She clung to him with every shred of her strength. "Simon . . . Simon . . ." She repeated his name over and over.

"Thank God you're safe. Oh thank God! I've been out of my mind . . ."

A second man poked his head from the cab. "Is she all right?" he asked.

"Yes! Yes! Yes!" Simon cried exultantly.

"They did it," she managed to say. "It was beyond . . . awful."

Simon hugged her tighter yet. "Don't," he said. "It's all right now. You're going to be all right, Tess."

The other man got out. Young and handsome, too. "You take her away now," he said. "I'll go up and see . . . I'll . . . I'll get another cab."

The dream was closing in all around her. "Who was that?" she asked. They were already in the cab and bowling along at a smart pace.

"Sickert. I couldn't think of anyone else who knew where the Kelly woman lived."

Chapter Thirty-Nine

"Simon was right then," Bo said grudgingly. She paced around Tessa's room straightening things that didn't need it, and turning her paintings and sketches to the wall. She knew nothing of what had happened during the night. She was simply glad her niece could walk again.

"Nonetheless, I'm going to get up," she told Bo. "I don't care what he says. I've spent enough time lying around uselessly this week." When Bo made no reply, she added, "And why are you so fidgety? You make me dizzy."

"Do you actually remember much of last week, Tessa dear?" Bo asked.

"Whenever you say 'Tessa dear' in that tone, it means. . ."

"But do you remember much?"

"I remember everything. Why?"

"Everything."

"Why?"

"Oh nothing. It's just. . . Simon. . . I mean, the way he explained things to your father and me was that you had faced some shock, some burden of discovery. . . something that proved too much for your frailty to bear. And I. . ."

"Frailty!" Tessa exploded.

"Well, perhaps not frailty, dear. What I mean. . . oh, I didn't think it was going to be quite so difficult!"

Simon *was* right, though. The fraught self-absorption that followed Bo around like a fussy cloud was exactly the tonic she needed. Saunders's heroic, self-sacrificial tenderness was not. He had been right to bring her home.

She said, "You might look out that dark brown costume of mine – my 'most sober Sunday' as mother used to call it. Be an angel? No – not an angel! I'll never again call. . ."

Bo was stung. "Why not? Why wouldn't you call me an angel?"

"Never again!"

"Ah! Now we come to it. Is this the thing you mean?" She held out a sober suit in brown worsted.

"Yes. Now we come to what? Is there a white cotton blouse in there? With broderie anglaise down. . . yes, that's the one. You're going to make a jolly good ladies maid, Bo."

"You see, Simon said your paralysis was the effect, or rather it was your way of coping with something that placed an intolerable burden on your loyalty or sympathy. . . something of that sort."

"It's all nonsense, of course. You know how men love to elaborate on anything that's essentially simple. I'm quite sure I simply fell and bruised a nerve or something."

"Y e s."

"Why so doubtful? Don't say you believe Simon."

"Well – I can't help remembering that night. The night before it happened. I wonder – did you by any chance – I mean, I'm not accusing you of anything so childish as sleep-walking – much less of prying around – good heavens, no! But what I mean is. . ."

"What you mean is did I come into your room during the wee small hours?" She watched her aunt's face crumple – and envied her simplicity. "Yes I did. It was unforgivable of me. I'm very sorry – but I'm also very happy for father and you."

"Tessa!" Bo was scandalized.

"What d'you mean – *Tessa*!"

"What a wicked thing to say!"

Tessa roared with laughter. "Who's talking? Anyway, what's wicked about it? The saying or the doing?"

"It's all wicked," Bo said crossly.

"Well stop it if that's how you feel."

"I can't. And nor can your father. He's worse, but I can't put all the blame on him."

Tessa shrugged herself into a woollen vest and then the blouse. "How cold is it outside? Shall I need another woollie? Poor Bo – you get the worst of both worlds."

Bo stared at her, open-mouthed. "You just *want* to shock me. Perhaps when you're a bit older you'll understand."

"I understand already." She turned and looked her aunt in the face. "Did you honestly think that the sight of you and father sleeping peacefully side by side, like a pair of good kippers" – Bo looked fearfully around – "Did you suppose that was the 'unbearable stress' which left me paralysed for the best part of a week?" She laughed. "Oh Bo! If you but knew!"

"If I but knew what?"

"Never mind. It was something in my private life. It's all over now. It's all settled. It won't happen again. And etcetera and etcetera. I'm going out today to tie up one or two loose ends. A slight promise I made to. . . someone. Is Simon around?"

"When you say you understand already. . . do you mean. . .?"

"I mean exactly what you think I mean."

"Oh!" Bo sat down heavily, looked around for something to fan herself with, and ended up using her hand.

Tessa said calmly. "Paralysis coming on?"

"Oh!" The fanning grew more frantic. Then it stopped altogether. "You don't mean. . . not with. . . not Simon?"

Tessa bit her lip uncertainly. "I don't *think* so." She looked around. "Pass my diary. I'll just make sure."

At last it dawned on Bo that her niece was joking. Her annoyance changed shade but not intensity. "Oh you're wicked, Tessa. You're a wicked girl. It's no joking matter."

"In the end, Bo," Tessa said quite seriously, "in the really really last resort, that's *all* it is: a joking matter. The Creator's last laugh. And God help those who can't take a joke!"

Bo shook her head in bewilderment. "I just don't know what's come over you. I think you need a good cold bath and go straight back to bed. You're not well, my girl."

"You find me – what? A little out of touch with reality?"

"A *little*!"

Tessa stared out of the window. Simon was walking up from Bleeding Heart Lane, through the vegetable garden. "Just for today, Bo, it's the best place for me."

Simon glanced up and saw her. With her finger she mimed, *you stay there!*

He pointed inward at his own chest.

She nodded.

He saluted.

"Who's out there?" Bo asked.

"Simon. He's going to take me to Dante Rosen's studio in Chelsea. I hope."

"Oh dear! I never liked that man. I know I never met him either. But I still never liked him."

"Don't worry. I'm not expecting to find Dante himself at home. That's the whole point of going."

Since they might have several calls to make that day she decided to take the dogcart, with Tyker at the reins.

"I knew it was hopeless to order you to stay in bed," Simon commented as soon as they were off.

"I don't understand it myself," she told him. "What happened last night was like its own cleansing. Like lancing a boil. What's that line in Wordsworth's Preludes? A monstrous reservoir of something and guilt, built up from age to age, that could no longer hold its loathsome charge? Something like that, anyway – to coin a phrase! It was like bursting a reservoir."

"What can I say? The newspaper accounts are . . ."

"I actually feel quite flat, today." They passed a newsboy who was shouting, "East End Fiend kills again! Worst ever murder!" She said, "It doesn't seem to refer to me at all. Maybe it's lack of sleep. I could face Dante Rosen – I could even face Segal – without a qualm. That's why, if there's anything left to be done, it's best done today."

"Like what?" he asked.

"You said Sickert was sure he could cope with it all. I must see for myself."

"Talking of Sickert – I forgot to tell you – the little girl is safe. She's still in France."

It was a bright day, almost noon. They drove through Westminster, past Parliament and the Abbey, and out along the Embankment. The sun at its zenith was still chasing away the wraiths of overnight mist off the Thames. The sky above was a pale blue, shading to grey toward the horizon.

"This city created Whistler," Tessa said, looking at the

colours.

"It created Segal, too," he told her. "What are you going to do if Rosen is there?"

"I don't know. Prove to myself it really is over. I think – in a way – Dante almost wanted to be caught. I'll be very surprised if he's still in Tite Street."

A little later she said, "I suppose I ought to try and forget it as soon as possible."

"No, you ought to talk about it," he told her. "I'll listen. Even the hundredth time."

She took his arm. The riverside air on her cheeks, the golden autumn sun, the smart clip-clop of the horse's hooves . . . the gift of life was sweet.

"You'll never exhaust my capacity for loving you, Tess," he said.

"I'd have gone quietly insane under that street lamp if you hadn't come along."

At the studio they were greeted by an affable middle-aged man wearing a velvet smoking jacket, a tassled fez, and baggy Parisian trousers. Name of Dilke. He was so obviously a painter – so screamingly obviously a painter – that Tessa could not believe in him for a moment. Just in case they should doubt him, he had brought his palette and brushes in his hand to the door. He hardly knew how to hold it; his pipe kept getting in the way.

Simon made the introductions and said: "We're looking for Mr. Dante Rosen."

Dilke nodded knowingly. "I never had the honour of meeting the gentleman," he said. "He gave up his lease here about a month ago and has gone . . ."

"But I visited him here only last week," Tessa lied – to test him.

"Ah, perhaps I mean a week or so," Dilke answered vaguely. "What's time to an artist, after all!"

"Money," Tessa said. "The same as it is to anyone else. Be he milkman, policeman, or Freemason."

A fleeting dent in Dilke's assurance.

"You've moved astonishingly quickly, Mr. Dilke," she went on.

"My brother-in-law is the landlord, Miss d'Arblay. I'm just keeping the place warm for him. Mr. Rosen, if you're interested, has gone to the South of France for the winter, lucky chap. Poste-Restante, Marseilles main post office, if you want to write." He looked up at the watery sun. "Now if you'll excuse me? November days are short. One likes to make the best of what little daylight there is."

"Yes," Tessa said. "Almost a shame to spoil those nice new brushes!"

When they were back in the dogcart Simon said, "You were a bit sharp."

"They're covering all the traces, Simon."

"Who?"

"I don't know. The police? The government? The Freemasons? Someone with a lot of power. If I'd been feeling just a little more lightheaded, I'd have shouted 'Stand to attention!' at him, just to see the effect."

Simon laughed. "Segal next?"

"I think we'd better."

At Finsbury Close he popped down to the kitchen for a word with Mrs. Hamble, the cook he had befriended. Almost at once he came racing back and beckoned her to join him. She sprang down the steps two at a time.

He had caught his excitement from the rest of the servants, who were all sitting around the huge, scrubbed table, chattering like teeth. They stood up as Tessa entered. The butler yielded his chair; the manservant gave up his to the butler . . . the displacements ran until the scullerymaid had to go out and fetch herself a stool. By then they were all jabbering away again. From a confusion of accounts Tessa managed to piece together something of the story.

They had watched the master last night and realized he was up to his usual games, the way he'd behaved on the nights of the other murders. About midnight a young woman had called to the surgery in the mews. She had been the victim, they were sure. Drugged. Rosen had to carry her. A short while later the two men and the woman had all gone off in the same unknown coach as those previous times.

This time they persuaded a constable to wait for the coach to return, hoping to catch them red-handed. But then around five o'clock some detectives had come to the house . . .

"Sickert must have called them," Simon said. "On our way

from Soho to Whitechapel he stopped and used the telephone.''

. . . and they'd sent the uniformed man away. But these weren't your usual detectives. Not rough-spoken ex-army types. These were all men of education. All very senior officers. And not a uniformed man in sight. The butler was sure that some of these supposed detectives were, in fact, doctors. One of them most certainly was – Sir William Gull. He'd called on Dr. Segal once before, back in the spring.

Around dawn Segal and Rosen returned. The police made no attempt to arrest or detain the coachman. They just sat indoors, 'like patients in a waiting room,' one of the maids said. And they didn't really arrest them, either, another pointed out; it was more as if they were holding a court then and there, on the spot. Yes, twelve of them, including Sir William, sat around the big table in the dining room and Mr. Rosen and the master were invited in and then they talked for half an hour or so. And then they all went away together in the coach. And before he left, the master told the butler he was selling up the practice and moving abroad, and they'd all get tiptop characters and three months wages and they weren't to gossip to anyone about anything.

And then an hour later some of the men came back and they took away everything in the 666-room, as they called it. Everything! They stripped it. And the wicked statues in the garden; they took them, too. And they gave orders that all the master's things were to be packed and they'd call again this afternoon for them. . .

As Tessa and Simon were leaving, one of the younger housemaids came up to her and asked if she knew Saunders's address as she wanted 'particular' to get in touch with her. Tessa, unwilling to give the address of Davitt's apartment, told her there was a matinée that very afternoon; why didn't she go down to Covent Garden and see her after the show?

Back in the dogcart they faced a crucial decision.

"It's a regular hornet's nest, Tess," Simon said. "Do we drop it now, or. . ."

"I don't know," she sighed. "It certainly looks as if the law – or justice of some kind – is taking its course. Shall we drop it?"

He grinned with relief. "Whither away?"

"Home for lunch!"

But as the dogcart rattled along she felt the two brass rings in her pocket, and conscience said, "On the other hand. . ."

When they reached home they found Bo in high excitement. "Oh Tessa!" she said. "Please don't scold me now. I do hope I've done the right thing. Only he was so insistent. And such a nice man, too. Do say you're not cross?"

"About what? How can I be cross or not be cross if. . ."

"Well I'll tell you if only you'll stop talking, dear. I can't get a word in. He's offered you three hundred guineas! Look!" She handed Tess a piece of writing paper. A very Civil Service hand, proud of its penmanship, had written:

Dear Miss d'Arblay,

I have the honour to be Principal Private Secretary to Lord Verschoyle. While on a visit this morning to the Whitechapel Foundries, to inspect the progress of some bronzes commissioned by Her Majesty's Government, my eye chanced to alight on a noble and delightful bust, which, I am told, is one of your works. Believe me, Miss d'Arblay, it is one of the finest pieces of sculpture I have seen and if you should ever consider parting with it (and if you will not consider it indelicate of me to offer money to a lady with such exquisite sensibilities as you so patently possess) then may I hereby offer a paltry three hundred guineas for this piece?

I am aware that this is probably only a fraction of its true worth, but it is all and more than I can afford.

Should you wish to discuss the matter further, I may be found at his Lordship's Offices in Whitehall. . .

Tessa had read enough. Her eye dropped to the signature. . . T. Knox-Riddell. She passed it without a word to Simon.

"Three hundred guineas, Tessa dear!" Bo said. "I had no idea your work was so good. Why did you never tell me?"

"It was on the tip of my tongue half a dozen times," Tessa explained. "Something more important always intervened – like how to snare a husband. You know?"

"I showed him all your other things. Over in your studio, and upstairs. He was most impressed, he said. But he's. . ."

"But he didn't want to buy any of it!"

"No, he's really set his heart on that bronze."

Tessa nodded grimly. Then a thought struck her. She raced upstairs and looked for her sketchbook – the one Dante had given her last night. It was there, all right. Empty. Every drawing she had made in Marie Kelly's had been taken. She went back downstairs.

Simon handed her back the letter. "Fairly blatant," he said.

"What are you going to do about this offer?" Bo asked.

"I'm going to Scotland Yard," she said. "This afternoon. What do they call theft when it's by daylight – is it burglary or robbery? I can never remember."

Chapter Forty

A different sergeant was sitting at Keene's desk; a most polished man – and surprisingly young-middle-aged in a force where three stripes were won only after long service. His name was Dysart. He told them he thought Sergeant Keene had mentioned he might call in for some brief refreshment in the Northumberland Arms.

"Forgive me, Sergeant Dysart," Tessa asked, "but has something happened?"

"It's better he should tell you that himself, Miss d'Arblay." Then he frowned, as if her name had just rung a bell – though he had clearly been on the edge of his seat ever since he'd heard it announced. He opened his drawer and pulled out a list, which he pretended to consult carefully. He looked up at her again. "Miss *Tessa* d'Arblay? Of Shoreditch?"

"Islington, actually."

"Ah yes, quite. Ah, Miss d'Arblay, may I ask you to be so good as to return here in an hour's time? Shall we say an hour? Would that be quite convenient?"

"The Rev. Liddington will accompany me."

"Oh, I don't think that will be . . ."

"The Rev. Liddington will accompany me. Meanwhile, will you give me some idea what it's all about?"

Dysart's eyes narrowed uncertainly. He looked Simon up and down.

She added. "You may tell your superiors that the Rev. Liddington is fully conversant with the . . . with the topics we are likely to discuss."

Dysart nodded. As he escorted them to the door he said, "Rev. Liddington, sir – you would be Church of England, I take it?"

They found Keene sitting alone at a table tucked away in the corner of the almost deserted saloon bar of the Northumberland Arms. He was too experienced a drinker to be drunk, but, by his colour, he had at least one sheet to the wind.

"Sergeant Keene!" Tessa called out.

He turned ponderously and looked at her. "*Mister* Keene," he said, rising to his feet.

She led the way to him among the empty tables. "Have you left the Force?"

"In a manner of speaking, Miss d'Arblay. What may I offer you both?" He held her chair for her.

"A small brandy, please," she said. "The day is turning raw."

"The same, thank you," Simon added. He sat opposite Tessa and pulled a dubious face.

"Raw or boiled, this day needs no excuse," Keene answered. He shouted the order to the barman and then sat again. "This day of all days. I should've listened to you last time. Might have prevented three deaths."

"How d'you think I feel?" she asked him. "When I first heard the women's story, I thought it was such a hoot I told Dante Rosen. We all had a laugh about it!" She put her hand to her mouth to hide the tremor of her lips. Tiredness was making her vulnerable.

Simon caught her arm and squeezed. "If self-recrimination becomes the order of the day, we'll all drive ourselves insane."

"What have you to reproach yourself for!" she said.

"Don't ask! Why didn't I go back and make *sure* Long Liz got to safety? And after that, especially after that, why didn't I go to Sickert and make *sure* he understood the mistake over Kelly? Why did I leave both matters to chance? As I say – don't ask." He turned to Keene. "Can you tell us what's been happening?"

"They've got the pair of them – Segal and Rosen. Locked away for life in some loonie bin in France. They're on the Dover road now. All neatly arranged." His tone was disgusted.

"And the coachman?" Tessa asked.

299

He shook his head. "They won't touch him. He's widely known in Islington. If he disappears as well, there'll be too much explaining to do."

They sipped their brandies as they absorbed this news.

"It smells worse and worse each minute," Simon reflected.

Keene nodded. "I've known some shocking things in my time on the Force. . ."

"Have they actually dismissed you?" Tessa asked.

"In the most gentlemanly possible way. You've heard of Lord Verschoyle? It seems his lordship has a large country house out beyond Kew. He's recently installed a valuable art collection and now he wants a permanent watchman. It's a pensioned job, with all my years of police service counted in. . . nice little cottage in the grounds. . ."

"But you must have been coming up for retirement soon anyway?" Tessa said.

He laughed sourly. "So I can't refuse it, can I? They even brought Mrs. Keene into the office – lunchtime, this was – because 'of course, the decision affected her, too!' Horse-apples! What it meant was I couldn't open my mouth with her there except to say how extremely grateful we both were."

"Which you did?"

"Which I did – d'you blame me?"

"Of course not," they both told him.

"Your replacement," Tessa said, "that new sergeant, has he. . ."

Keene snorted. "Dysart? He's no sergeant. Supposed to be on secondment from the naval bulldogs. He's a military man, I grant you. But an officer if ever I saw one."

Simon shook his head. "Such organization! I assume Sickert's a Mason, too? I assume his telephone call this morning was what started things moving? Well, that was around half past four. . . five o'clock, this morning. And virtually within the next six hours they'd spirited away Dante and Segal, put a new so-called painter in the Tite Street studios. . ."

"Found something to bribe me with," Tessa said.

"And moved Dysart into my desk by eight o'clock this morning," Keene added.

"It hardly bears thinking about," Simon said.

"They've been prepared for weeks," Keene agreed. "Have

another."

"My shout," Simon told him.

When they returned to the Yard, Dysart was waiting for them at the main door. "The meeting's been set up elsewhere," he explained as he ushered them into a government carriage; they drove a short distance down Whitehall. He looked anxiously out of the window. "Getting thicker," he said. "There'll be another pea-souper tonight."

"It may delay the Channel ferries," Tessa told him. "Europe could be completely cut off."

The sergeant glanced at her, uncertain whether or not she was joking or telling him she knew about Segal and Rosen. She smiled at a small victory.

They pulled up outside an impressive classical building; a cut stone inscription identified it as the Home Office. The doorkeeper came forward, saw Dysart, saluted, and stepped smartly back into his booth. The sergeant led them up a huge stone staircase. At the top he turned to Simon and, pointing to a tall mahogany door, said, "You, Rev. Liddington, will find someone in there who wishes to have a particular word with you."

"He's not leaving my side," Tessa said. "I made that a condition."

Without even looking at her Dysart answered, "You are not making any conditions, Miss d'Arblay." He waited for Simon to move.

"Either we both go on or we both go back," Simon told him.

"I'm afraid it isn't going to be like that, sir," Dysart said.

The big mahogany door opened. Framed against the dimming window stood a bishop in full purple front and gaiters – an absurdly rural figure amidst the imperial pomp of carved stone and gilded plaster.

Simon turned at the sound. "My lord?" he asked.

The bishop crooked a finger at him. Simon turned back to Tessa and shrugged. She nodded his release.

After the door had closed again Dysart said, "And if you'll be so good as to come this . . ."

"I'm staying here," Tessa said.

"I'll have you carried."

"I'll scream. I'll make such a fuss I'll bring people out into all these corridors – too many for you to conveniently . . ."

"It's Saturday afternoon. There's hardly anyone here. Anyway, what are you so afraid of?"

"What d'you think I'm afraid of!"

"We're all gentlemen, you know. No one's going to compromise you."

"That's the least of it. I'm worried because no one knows we're here. No one knows we've met you again. The last witness who saw you with us, the police constable at . . ."

He began to laugh. "Is that it! You think we'll spirit you away, too!" He was suddenly serious again, almost tender. "My goodness – I had no idea – what a time you must have had of it!" He tapped the bridge of his nose while he thought. "Do you know anybody who is connected to the telephone? Would it ease your mind if you telephoned someone now and told them where you are? Arrange to meet them later this evening, perhaps?"

She agreed. He took her to the apparatus and she telephoned Davitt at the theatre. "'Ello gel!" he chuckled. "Here listen – don't never telephone me from the Inland Revenue will you! I had a heart attack when they said the Home Office. How's the runaway horse business?"

"I'll tell you about that someday."

"What you doing down the Home Office, anyway?"

"You've seen the newspapers? Last night? Marie Kelly?"

"Oh Christ! Not that!"

"Don't worry, SD. It's over. It really is over. They've got them. I'm making a statement. I just wanted to catch you before you left the theatre. Can we all have supper tonight – after the show? Can I bring Simon Liddington?"

"Course you can, gel. You know that. Anytime. Put you up again, too. It's going to be another corker tonight."

She was about to thank him and ring off when he said, "'Ere, I must tell you Connie's latest. I must tell someone – she's a scream!"

"What? Go on – I could do with a laugh, as she says."

"I'm standing by the window, see, looking at the fog and feeling a bit down. And she says – listen, this'll kill you – she says, 'I'll spend a penny on your thoughts'! How's that, eh? Spend a penny on your thoughts!"

Tessa laughed with him. "So, SD – she's turning into a critic, too!"

"Here!" he cried. "Not so sharp! Oh and another thing – what's between you and this Cissie Rogers you sent down to see Connie?"

"I don't know any Cissie . . . oh, you mean the maid from Segal's house."

"She only wants to work at Pol's! Are you turning procurer or something?"

"Good God! I had no idea!"

"She's the one Segal used to flog. She's going to miss the extra income. She's got the sniff of real geld now, see. Funny old world, eh?"

"Hilarious!"

She rang off and turned to see Dysart looking at her strangely. "What's up with you?" she asked.

"You have a natural talent for clandestine work, Miss d'Arblay. D'you know that?"

"I'm trying to shed talents, Mr. Dysart. Not acquire them. Now where d'you want to take me?"

"You're also an extremely disrespectful young woman. You'd better not talk to Lord Verschoyle like that."

Her eyes gleamed. "Am I to meet him? Why didn't you say!"

Dysart sighed and led her to a room a mere two doors down from the one where Simon and the bishop were. He gave a minion's knock. Tessa caught him off balance – in an underling's frame of mind – just as he was opening the door. She asked: "Are you the one who offered for my bronze?"

"No," he said where he might otherwise have ignored her question. Then he was annoyed to have let slip the admission. "Miss d'Arblay," he snapped, "I have the honour to present the Right Honourable, the Lord Verschoyle."

Tessa gave him rather a jerky handshake and said at once, "I hope you're going to explain to me why you and your men are doing such absurd things, Lord Verschoyle."

He frowned. "Young lady . . ."

"That policeman pretending to be a painter out in Tite Street! In that ridiculous costume and carrying those beautifully clean brushes!"

Verschoyle looked to Dysart for protection. He was a tall, florid man, not unlike Oscar Wilde at first glance. A second glance, however, revealed qualities of hardness that Oscar lacked – or at

303

least failed to radiate.

"Miss d'Arblay," Dysart began. "I tried to tell you . . ."

"And sending a man down to bribe me to silence."

Verschoyle smiled. "You put it too modestly, Miss d'Arblay. The bronze is a masterpiece. It may actually be worth three hundred guineas."

It was the grossest flattery, and yet she was absurdly flattered by it – enough to break the flow of her anger. Verschoyle saw his chance and leaped in. "Not yet, to be sure. You've built no reputation as yet. All it needs, though – and of this I am as sure as one may be sure of anything in this life – all it needs is a few years of steady application both as paintress and sculptress – and then Rosa Bonheur must look to her laurels! Please be seated."

The chairs, deeply upholstered in polished tan leather, were arranged around a fire that did little to dispel the chill, bright though it burned. The room was vast. Art-by-the-yard and gilded plasterwork struck all the right visual notes in the deepening twilight. She smiled up at Verschoyle. "I see it now – the big but palatable half-truth will enlarge the gullet sufficiently to enable it to swallow the even larger quarter-truths that are to follow. Is that the principle?"

His lordship massaged his brow as he took his seat. "You're not making it any easier, Miss d'Arblay."

"Well I didn't intend to, Lord Verschoyle. None of this is my idea."

"But why so angry? Surely you understand why . . . certain things . . . had to be done?"

"I understand that murders were done. I understand that the authorities, in some form or other, have apprehended the murderers. I gather – though I protest I do *not* understand – that those authorities have already held court, found the murderers insane, and have arranged their incarceration for life on foreign soil – all quite contrary to the most elementary justice. Not only that, I discover those same authorities are now behaving in a hole-and-corner manner that would brand any other party as criminal. Further, I surmise that the press and people will be told not a word of all this . . ."

"Not quite true," Verschoyle said sharply.

Again it halted her flow.

He went on. "You ask, and quite properly, about the public's rights in this whole sorry affair. Let us talk about the public's rights. The public has a right to sound government. The public has a right to solid institutions in which it may place every confidence. The public has a right to look up to its leaders – among whom I naturally include the aristocracy and the monarchy.'' His eyes narrowed. ''Are you among those who claim some spurious right to assassinate the sovereign – not the person, you understand, but the institution and thus, accidentally as it were, the person?''

''Don't be absurd.''

''I'm glad to hear it. What, then, of the *reputation* of the sovereign and her family? May that be assassinated with impunity?''

''Or?'' Tessa prompted.

He frowned. ''Or what?''

''Or is it above criticism?''

''We're not talking about criticism, Miss d'Arblay. We're talking about calumny. Four foul-mouthed, deluded unfortunates were roaming London and calumniating our beloved royal family. Two or three equally deluded and probably insane defenders of the royal honour decided to deal with them. And you. . .''

''But it wasn't like that at all! Is that what people have been telling you?'' She waved at Dysart. ''In that case, you're as deluded as everyone else.''

Verschoyle shot Dysart a glance. Then, to Tessa, ''Perhaps you'd care to enlighten me?''

Tessa related all she knew – even her own unwitting part in telling Dante about the four women. She could see that much of it was news to him. But she also saw that, as she neared the end of her recitation, he had somehow performed an act of mental digestion and had fitted all the new intelligence to all the old preconceptions. The opening words of his response confirmed it: ''I must thank you for being so frank, Miss d'Arblay. I can imagine what some parts of your narrative must have cost your honour to reveal. But everything you say only doubles my conviction that we have been right in all we've done. The partial truth, as relayed to me, was bad enough – but the full truth! What? Are you seriously telling me you believe that the tale as you have told it should come out in open court? Have you not even considered the hissing and spitting that would follow *you* to the end of your life! Had you thought of that?''

She hadn't, of course – and now it showed in her face.

Verschoyle was quick to seize upon it. ''So now you have every reason to understand why we, for our part, have been so eager to protect the reputation of our dear sovereign and her family – who, both by tradition and by their own innate nobility, are unable to answer their calumniators. You at least would be able to speak up on your own behalf. In time, who knows, you might even persuade some small proportion of the populace to credit your tale of devilish influence and. . . ah. . . hysterical paralysis. It would be your right to speak up. But Her Majesty has no such right. Their Royal Highnesses have no such right. We live under a constitutional monarchy, which means that four harlots may traduce the crown all they wish – spread whatever drunken, foul-mouthed lies their perverted imaginations can devise – and yet the royalties involved must hold their tongues!''

Tessa felt all her solid ground crumbling. ''Aren't we straying from the point?'' she asked. ''Surely it's very simple – by acting in this illegal way *you* pin the appearance of guilt on the monarchy. *You* make it seem that there is, after all, something to hide.''

He nodded, as if he accepted the point. ''We must balance one set of risks against the other, young lady. That's what government means, you know.'' The strengthening firelight was helping to mellow his expression – and, she felt, his mood.

This perception made her moderate her own tone with him. In a calmly reasonable voice she asked, ''Where's the risk in announcing their arrest, giving out the charge, rehearsing the evidence at the magistrate's court, and then finding them unfit to plead on grounds of insanity? Surely they *would* be found unfit to plead? Don't you see – your actions give credence to. . .''

He was already shaking his head. ''D'you really suppose we haven't given thought to it?'' His eyes twinkled. ''D'you think that Lord Salisbury, and the Lord Chief Justice, the Lord Chancellor. . . the Archbishop of Canterbury. . . all those honourable people whom we have naturally consulted on an issue so grave – d'you honestly suppose that they do not have the interests of British justice at heart? D'you suppose we have not all of us struggled our utmost to pursue the strict letter of the law?

But stronger and quite exceptional arguments to the contrary have prevailed – namely that the risks involved are far too grave."

"Risks?"

He nodded sadly. "Risks, Miss d'Arblay. I believe that, notwithstanding your narrative to us, you have led a somewhat sheltered life, have you not? I don't think you can possibly imagine how the newspapers would behave after a finding of 'unfit to plead.' The bribery they would attempt – of court officials, of the medical witnesses, of the gaolers, of the warders at the lunatic asylum, of recently released inmates who might have been in contact with the two unfortunate men. . . oh! – the possibilities for a betrayal of confidence are endless. Don't you see? It would only take one little crack – one little snippet – and then they'd be on to it like ferrets! They'd be down at your nun's refuge. . . they'd winkle out those people who took part in that childish Midsummer ritual you described. . . they'd swarm all over your house, your father, your aunt, your loyal and trusted servants. . . And not just British papers, either, but Continental ones. . . even American ones." He shuddered. "They'd print every bit of stray gossip, every lying tittle-tattle from disgruntled servants – and it would all be magnified up as revealed truth! They'd cite each other as the foundations of yet more grandiose lies. . . there would be no end to it." He stared with kindly eyes into her dumbfounded face and said, in tones that were now as smooth as velvet, "So you see – we really have given it a great deal of thought. We know that our way is best. Or, rather, it is the least-worst. There can be no 'best' in these wretched circumstances."

As she was leaving she said, "But Rosen and Segal – they'll talk to their French warders. Dante speaks perfect French, you know. It will still leak out."

Verschoyle smiled. "We haven't sent them over there alone, my dear. Several dozen lunatics have given themselves up to the police over these last months, all claiming to be the Whitechapel Fiend. Some of them very plausibly, too. We've included the best of them in the party. The French understand. . . lunatics sent abroad for their own safety. . . lunatics who risk death at the hands of the mob if they are kept here. We all oblige each other in such matters."

307

If anyone at the height of the Marie Kelly murder had predicted to Tessa that before the next day's light had quite fled she would feel a twinge of pity for Dante Rosen, she would have staked her life against it. Yet now, in her weakened and exhausted state, she did. She thought of Dante, locked away forever among babbling fools, all laying claim to what he had called his Master Piece, and tears of compassion pricked her eyelids. He would be sixty years a-dying. Even the death of Marie Kelly had surely been more merciful than that.

Seeing the change in her, Lord Verschoyle became quite worried. He took her elbow and guided her out into the great corridor. "I'm placing my own carriage at your disposal, my dear," he told her. At the same time he snapped his fingers and Dysart ran ahead to make the arrangements.

Tessa could have accepted his opposition, his anger, his contempt – even his pity if it had been scornful enough. What she could not take now was his tenderness with her. She could not believe that she deserved it. Sobs racked her body.

He was wise enough to ignore her – or at least to make no special allowance. He went on speaking calmly, his voice resonant and soothing, as he walked her up and down the corridor; and at last the emotion drained out of her and she was ready to go.

"Our country," he told her, "owes you a debt it can never acknowledge – much less repay. But you may be assured that whatever it is in our power to do in unseen ways will be done. And you of all people will know those powers are not small! I speak not just for the government, you understand, but for that more permanent, unseen, substratum of governance which persists despite elections and the passing fashions of mere democracy. I don't know of your circumstances, but from this day forth you will never want. If you live to be a hundred you will never want.

"But all this is for the future, my dear. We must also think of now. And for now I want you to promise me you'll go straight home, or to the home of some dear and trusted friend, and there place yourself in the hands of a physician. Will you promise me that?"

She smiled at the peculiar aptness of his words and gave him her promise.

"And now," he said, "let us see if my lord has finished his talk with your friend." He gave a light knock to the door.

In a short while the bishop appeared, downcast of countenance. Verschoyle frowned. "Trouble?" he asked.

"I fear so."

Verschoyle turned to Tessa. "Is he a close friend of yours?"

Tessa was astonished to hear herself say, "We mean to marry" – half-astonished, anyway.

Verschoyle smiled broadly to hear it. He turned to the bishop and said, "All's well. This young lady, my lord, has a more sensible head on her shoulders than half the present government." He gave Tessa's arm an avuncular squeeze and added, "Let us go downstairs in search of your impetuous young fiancé, eh?"

The bishop remained.

Simon was waiting by the doorkeeper's lodge. His face was ashen white and his clerical collar was missing.

"Darling!" she called out.

He saw she had been crying and his face darkened.

"Where's your collar?" she asked. "You look a sight."

"I'll never wear it again," he said. "What did they do to you?" He looked pugnaciously at Lord Verschoyle.

"Nothing," she told him. "Lord Verschoyle here has been kindness itself to me. Allow me to present you to him. The Reverend and Doctor Simon Liddington."

"No longer Reverend," Simon added as they bowed to each other.

"Young man," Verschoyle answered, "I gather you have a second string to your bow – which, if what you say is true, is probably just as well. Are you, in fact, a doctor of medicine?"

Simon nodded warily.

"Then I confidently hand this brave young lady into your care. Treat her. . . well. And after you are married – why, treat her well!"

Simon stared in bewilderment at Tessa. She shrugged. "I didn't mean to tell anyone."

His mood turned to joy. "Not even me?"

She tried to smile and instead slipped back into tears. He put his arms around her.

The bishop began to descend the stairs. Verschoyle put on a public-speaking voice and declared, "Remember, young lady, the province of your sex, though subordinate, is one of peculiar privilege. A woman's life is sheltered from temptation. A woman's life is in league with those silent yet sleepless charities which bless without seeking applause. That duty of submission, which is imposed upon you both by the nature of your station and the ordinance of God, disposes you to that humility which is the very essence of womanly piety. Your physical weakness, your feminine trials, your inability to protect yourselves in this cruel world – these all prompt that trust in heaven, that implicit willingness to lean upon the Divine Arm, which is a woman's most enduring strength and her chiefest jewel.''

With a movement of his arm as smooth as his speech he wafted the bishop onward and out, leaving Tessa and Simon alone.

Tessa let out her pent-up breath. "He knows," she said. "He knows exactly what happened to me – and yet he can say that!''

"His mind was on other things," Simon told her.

"A plague on them all!'' she said. Her lips went up in search of his. They met and she was overwhelmed with her love for him.

"Take me home," she whispered. "Take me anywhere you like. Oh Simon – just *take* me!''